Smiling Through Tears

by

SOPHIE LANGSTONE

Libra Publishing

A CIP catalogue record for this book is available from the British Library.

ISBN: 978-1-5272-5279-0

Typeset by Avon DataSet, Bidford on Avon
Front cover by Saintbury View Design
Cover painting © Pen-y-ghent and River Ribble by Keith Melling
Printed and bound in Great Britain by Clays Ltd, Elcograf S.p.A

MIX
Paper from
responsible sources
FSC
www.fsc.org   FSC® C018072

LIBRA PUBLISHING
www.Libra-publishing.com

Part One
Soma Sema

1

ARRIVAL

For in that sleep of death what dreams may come,
When we have shuffled off this mortal coil,
Must give pause.

Hamlet, Act III by **William Shakespeare**

He is woken by a nurse entering the room and opening the curtains. A warm golden hue of light fills the room. She is dressed in a crisp white uniform with navy piping around the collar and sleeves and her blonde hair is swept up into a curl and secured above the nape of her neck. She has come to alleviate Alasdair's pain and has interrupted his thoughts.

They are all that is left or soon will be if the physicians are right. They are his thoughts, his canzonets as Ezra Pound called them. In the silence of the small hours last night he thought about it. 'Don't try to be clever or philosophical. What do I feel? What are my emotional reactions? I have lived in this body, soon to return to the dust from whence it came, for nigh on eighty years. I have suffered and pondered and taken life seriously. I have tried to make sense of it. I have tried not to make a fool of myself. So what about it, will this be the end of everything for me?'

The pretty young nurse has sparkling blue eyes which together with her smile light up her face and he immediately relaxes, as she sets about removing the expired morphine patch and applying a fresh dressing. She then replenishes his water jug and looks at Alasdair.

'Shall I help to make you comfortable?'

As she asked the question, she approached his bed, already knowing the answer, and helped him sit up and then puffed up his pillows. She waited for Alasdair to say something.

'That's much better, nurse. Thank you.' He looked up. 'The pain is like an old bothersome acquaintance, sidling around, and yet knowing that in some inexplicable fashion he has a right to be there.' He waited for her response.

There was none, as she wasn't sure if she was supposed to laugh. She wasn't surprised by his eloquence, as she had been nursing him since his arrival and looked forward to the time she spent with him, listening to him. She knew he was an academic and a popular man by the number of visitors, who came and stayed longer than was usual. She broke the silence.

'It will soon ease and you will feel much better once you are showered and dressed after breakfast.'

Later in the morning and feeling tired after the exertions of showering and dressing the very Reverend Alasdair Sommersby relaxed into the sofa and closing his eyes, sighed with relief. He was pleasantly surprised when Rose popped into his mind.

Rose had astonished him. He never considered himself as attractive and certainly not to a beautiful girl full of vitality and disarmingly unaware of her sexuality beyond flirting. Rose was in her last year reading History, when they met. Alasdair was a Senior Lecturer in Theology. He remembered the incident with the car keys. What a wicked joke that was!

He knew he was popular. A good storyteller. After all he had twenty years of writing sermons and almost ten years at a grammar school keeping pupils on their seats during Religious Education. Driving a red MG Midget sports car was probably an additional attraction and stood Alasdair apart from his peers, as did the longer hair sometimes tied in a pony tail. He was and remains a rather plain looking man of slight stature with poor eyesight, hence his thick lensed glasses just like Michael Caine when he played Harry Palmer in *The Ipcress File*.

Perhaps it had been a mistake to play tennis with Rose and her friends? Afterwards, he couldn't find his car keys and when he caught up with Rose, she giggled. 'It will cost you!'

All day he worried about what that could mean, until he met up with the girls at the end of the day. They kept him dangling as they huddled together, stifling their giggles as they agreed the conditions for the return of the keys. They burst out laughing and then Rose declared, 'You can have your keys if we each have a spin in the MG.'

Life has a way of throwing up coincidences. Even so, he was surprised and nervous to receive her telephone call a few years later, hear her sparkling voice flirting with him.

She said, 'I've been posted to the York office for six months, I should love to meet you again.'

Always polite and interested in others, Alasdair didn't hesitate and asked, 'When?'

Once the arrangements were made, he reflected that perhaps he should have resisted. His intentions were honourable, after all he was fifty-two years of age and very happily married to Ruth, but his emotions were carrying him every which way.

He had never known a woman like Rose neither before nor since and was grateful for experiences that, while not unique, were nevertheless rare for most people, and indeed, many people go through life without having them at all. In a petite frame, Rose was as bubbly in character as her curly dark hair; she was a natural beauty and didn't see the need to wear make-up. Her only extravagance was expensive perfume, something Alasdair couldn't possibly afford to buy her and saw no reason to as she was just as happy with the small tokens of affection generously given in the form of poems and prose.

It wasn't long before Rose sweetly allowed Alasdair to discover her naked beauty. The pure pleasure in a curve. The beauty and fullness of the aureoles of her nipples. The nipples themselves swelled up in a majestic splendour from dark, thick, red brown stippled circles that demanded the gentle stroking of a fingernail.

Rose wrote admirable poetry with more than a hint of Lovelace in it, romantic cultured, refined and fastidious. She herself was like that. She was as soft and fragile and feather-light as the gossamer underwear she adored. Her mouth was like the silk she wore. They snatched moments in a soft haze of gauzy passion that did not make too many demands on either of them. The whole episode correlates round the edges of his memory. She was the embodiment of woman, exhaling a kind of ethereal eroticism in silk camiknickers. Indeed, she wore silk underwear, very brief and expensive with diminutive legs to the knickers. There was a classical, structured side to her character, which chimed beautifully with her sensual wistfulness, a kind of charming wantonness. He once admitted to Rose, who could never ever have enough sex, 'Thank goodness we're not married, darling as I could never keep up with you.'

To which she responded delightfully, 'You have your clever hands, darling. We would manage very well.'

Once when they were together, she was reading a poem of John Donne's and handed it to Alasdair. 'Read it aloud. We shall make it come true as we read?'

What a difference a little imagination makes to love. It was a ridiculous suggestion, as if they could bear to avert their eyes away from each other. They both knew the essence of the poem and the haunting power of a few words . . .

> *Licence my roaving hands, and let them go,*
> *Before, behind, between, above, below.*
> *O my America! my new-found-land.*

While living in York, Rose rented a small studio flat in Goodramgate just a short stroll from Betty's Café Tea Rooms, where they often met. To provide a reason for his absence from home, Alasdair arranged with the manager that he would play the piano at six o'clock in the evening for an hour once a week to fill in when their regular pianist had a free evening.

A long time after Rose returned to London, Alasdair arrived home to find Ruth Sommersby sitting upright on the sofa with her hands clasped tightly together in her lap holding a letter from Rose and a packed suitcase by her side. Rose had sent several letters, none of which he believed were embarrassing and he had just put them in the top drawer of his desk.

Ruth handed the letter to him, looking him straight in the eye. Her eyes were red and her skin was puffy. She had been crying, a lot.

She snuffled, 'I found this today.'

He took the letter and sat down. He took his time. Alasdair knew full well its contents, but he needed time to focus on some logical and innocent explanation and was relieved to notice that it wasn't dated.

'I can see why you might be upset. This is a young student from college, who appeared to have a crush on me a while back. Not sure why it is in my drawer as I would certainly have meant to throw it away at the time.'

The silence between them, although a few moments, seemed an age, so much so that Alasdair got to his feet and sat beside Ruth, who allowed him to put his arm around her and then yielded into his arms as he embraced her while stroking her hair and kissing her forehead.

A little while later, when he was waiting for the kettle to boil, Alasdair thought to himself, 'Was I that naïve? It seems so.'

The next day he called Rose at her office in London asking her to be more discreet and not to write. Over the years, they kept in touch. After all they had shared a lot of zany, amusing and erotic moments, but she had the world to discover and she soon met lots of wonderful young men eager to love her. Many years later Alasdair met her husband, who he instantly liked and Rose saw that, and it pleased her. If work brought her northwards they would meet briefly even after his retirement. The Boars Head, Ripley was the perfect meeting place for a quiet chat and coffee. He enjoyed hearing about her husband, their two girls and was in awe of how she managed her career and family life. How Rose with a degree in history had achieved a successful career in accountancy and eventually consultancy was a source of amusement to him. Not so much in touch as the years have passed by, but always in his heart. He thought, 'I must call her soon and tell her.'

Alasdair had settled in well at St Dunstan's, happy to fall in with their routine. Although he had been ill for nearly five years, it was still a shock. After a recent routine blood transfusion, he had been violently sick, throwing up blood and bleeding profusely from his nose. The following day his doctor decided to call for an ambulance. He was in hospital for several days while his Haematology Consultant did tests and finally told him that they could do no more. The blood transfusions over several years had caused a dangerous iron overload. Alasdair's platelets weren't working and he was getting progressively weaker.

St Dunstan's Hospice is a large and imposing stone built house, set in several acres of parkland just a few miles north of Harlow Carr Gardens. His room is small, not dissimilar in size to his college room at Peterhouse, Cambridge. There the similarity ends as this tiny room oozes cosiness and prettiness. It has large full length windows filling one end of the room, so that he can look out at the garden and valley beyond while in bed. It has a small two-seater sofa and coffee table to one side and a wing chair to the other. The wallpaper and curtains are a matching pretty pale blue Toile de Jouy. One of the scenes shows a small boy with a fishing-net over his shoulders, another depicts two lovers having a picnic. The bed linen is pure white cotton, cool to the touch and the pillow has the fragrance of lavender. Someone has understood how important such things are to someone feeling so poorly.

There is a tall heavy glass vase on the small oak chest of drawers bursting with autumnal colours of gold and red chrysanthemums. Lady Rossiter has already been to see Alasdair, the flowers are from her garden. This tenderness affected him deeply, because she could so easily have ordered them from a florist.

Every other surface in the room is covered with greeting cards. In the top drawer of the bedside table is a large battered brown envelope bulging with assorted papers, some typewritten, some penned on scraps of paper and card containing poems, musings and favourite stories.

It is September 1999 and each day the sun rises a little later through a fine mist and floods the room with a warm golden yellow light. It is still warm enough to sit on the terrace and read the paper. The abundance of summer is over. The acers are turning red and the many dahlias in strong vibrant colours are a delight. Later a nurse or one of his friends will take him around the garden.

'What a taste life has.' Alasdair thought. 'I can feel it on my tongue, fragrant and spicy, slightly harsh, just enough to avoid blandness, sometimes very far indeed from blandness, but never merely sweet, and never cloying. A sweet taste that is not only sweet and not only fragrant, but has a strong, refreshing, piquancy.'

He once read somewhere that one touch is worth a thousand pictures. It is true. A good deal of thought revolves round the recollections of sense perceptions, touch, smell, taste. And there is really no substituting one sense for another. That is why erotica in the form of books or pictures can never fully satisfy. Love needs all the senses.

The previous night his thoughts had turned to the 'immortal soul locked in a perishable body' idea and he couldn't accept this dichotomy, this sundering of what is essentially a unity. Everything he is, everything he has become is through the body. And as his mind and spirit have helped to shape it, so has it helped to shape his mind and spirit. Had he possessed a different body, his personality would have been different.

It is all superstition and invention, this soul-body combination; a combination to be dissolved, like an unholy wedlock at death. At death, when the body, that flesh which has surrounded him with love and given him so much inexpressible joy, will be thrown away like rubbish, a disposable envelope, so that the real thing the soul can make its journey into the infinite, pure and undefiled, leaving the now redundant body.

How ungenerous. How ungrateful. It is all ancient superstition, from God knows how many millennia ago, and fostered by the desire that something should live on. So it is the body that must die, and the soul that must live on, to survive immortally. What matters, if what survives is only a poor bodiless spectre, squeaking and gibbering like a bat in the gloomy halls of the House of Hades? For that is the fate of the poor soul. Greeks and Babylonians alike know only of gloom, and the absence of the bright gods. The gods of the underworld are, like their kingdom of the dead, gloomy and morose. Shaul of the Babylonians the Sheol of the Hebrews, the Pit, is all darkness. The brightness of Yahweh never shines there.

The later Hebrews were much nearer to actual human experience, when they talked about simply seeing the totality of a person, without dividing that person up. You are aware of someone approaching as an object in space–time, in our terms; they make an impact upon you; they remind you that you do not alone occupy the space we call life. And then you meet them; you speak together; you become aware of their personal dynamics, and of the interplay of your freedom and theirs, of your will and theirs, of your willingness to accommodate and theirs, and so on.

Specialists in Hebrew thought-forms might well take a different view from this, but the idea is still a perfectly valid one. It gets rid of a confusion that has haunted Western and Eastern thought for centuries. And it is a confusion, which has resulted because men have seldom come to terms with the idea of the body. Religion tends to be a nature cult in which the cyclical physical processes are divinised or a body-denying premise in which the body is a disposable container for what really matters, the soul. And this soul is indeed, nothing but an invented abstraction to hang what we call ourselves upon. Some Greeks used to say *Soma Sema*, which means *the body, the tomb*.

Alasdair, his thoughts interrupted and without hesitating, remembered and recited out loud a verse narrated by Rabbi Ben Ezra in Robert Browning's poem.

"Grow old along with me!
The best is yet to be,
The last of life, for which the first was made;
Our times are in His hand
Who saith "A whole I planned,
Youth shows but half; trust God. See all, nor be afraid."

2
NIDDERDALE

What is uttered from the heart alone, will win the hearts
of others to your own.

Johann Wolfgang von Goethe

Frances Campbell met the nurse coming down the corridor and asked, 'How is Reverend Sommersby?'

'Comfortable.' She smiled reassuringly. 'I have just settled him and replaced the morphine patch.'

'Tea sounds like a good idea, then?' She turned around, heading back along the corridor to the kitchenette to prepare it.

Shortly afterwards, she tapped on the door before entering, tray in her hands and her face lighting up as their eyes met.

'Hello darling.' She said, placing the tray down before embracing Alasdair. 'How are you today?' She held him close for a few moments.

He looked at her, took her hand and smiled. He breathed in her fragrance, always L'air du Temps, and watched her settle down. Frances shone. She was tall with fair skin and her hair, which she wore in a bob-cut, was highlighted and glistened in the sunlight. Impeccably dressed and elegant in Jaeger, although not particularly pretty, she was comfortable in her looks. What she lacked in beauty she made up for with her naïve charm and her abundantly good nature resulting in the most warm and generous smile.

She sat down beside him on the little sofa having already placed the tray on the coffee table and produced two foil-wrapped chocolate hearts from her bag. Frances had been to the library and produced a book of short stories by Raymond Carver, which she considered would be light enough reading for him together with *This Week*, which she knew he took regularly in addition to *The Daily Telegraph* in order to get a different view of the news. However, it was *The Times* Frances opened and finding the crossword folded it neatly and handed it to Alasdair saying, 'There we are, shall we start?'

Alasdair took the paper and found his pen while she looked on. He could do the crossword in thirty minutes and in recent years had shared with her the mysteries of the cryptic clue. They worked the clues out aloud until the answer was formed with Alasdair leading the way and just once he waited patiently, in order to keep her interest, and allowed her to get the answer first.

'Alasdair, do you remember when we used to drive along the side of the River Nidd to the Yorke Arms for lunch?'

'Yes, darling. Yes I do.'

'I have asked Sister if I could take you for a drive. Would you like to?'

'Very much so.'

'Lovely, let's get ready.'

Both wrapped up in warm coats, they left arm in arm with Alasdair using his walking cane in his right hand for extra support. It had rather an attractive art nouveau styled silver top and he felt rather dapper using it. Frances loved driving her silver 740 Volvo Estate. Bought second hand, it now had approximately 150,000 miles on the clock. An approximation, because years ago, her youngest son had smashed the clock when he was being particularly naughty and arguing with his brother. Frances had no plans to get it fixed, but it made gauging when to stop for petrol rather difficult. Today, she had filled up on her way to St Dunstan's.

They set off in the direction of Ripley, where they would take the road to Pateley Bridge and beyond to Ramsgill. Of all the villages in the Upper Nidderdale, Ramsgill is the jewel. The river ran to their right rippling down fast over the shallow stony bed and they looked beyond to the splendour of the fells with fields divided by grey dry stone walls and barns built as if they are coming out of a stony out-crop. The only living creatures were sheep grazing on the slopes. Frances drove slowly and let the sun streaming through the window, warm her skin. They passed Gouthwaite Reservoir and motored on towards Ramsgill. On another day they might have continued to Lofthouse and How Steam Gorge, a favourite destination when her children were younger. Ramsgill is a grouping of comfortably proportioned stone cottages centred around a large immaculately kept green and harmonious church. The Virginia Creeper which engulfs the Yorke Arms looked magnificent, its leaves having already turned to a fiery red. The Yorke Arms was an old shooting lodge and is now a very comfortably furnished inn with rooms.

Albeit sunny, there was a distinct chill in the air and on arrival they were pleased to find a fire blazing in one of the rooms and comfortable chairs where they decided to settle. Alasdair ordered a Whisky Mac for himself and Sauvignon Blanc for Frances. They were given menus and they sat back and enjoyed their drinks, whilst browsing and discussing options before ordering. Neither felt like eating a big meal and so they chose from the starters with an eye on the *Warm Almond Tart* afterwards.

Once seated in the dining room, a young and smartly dressed waiter brought a basket of warm bread together with a jug of water and glasses, before returning with two plates of *Marinated Smoke Duck with Hazelnut Raisin* decorated with delicate salad leaves in a light lemon dressing. It tasted just as good as it looked and they enjoyed the silence of eating.

The warm fire and the gourmet food were having a good effect on Alasdair and he both looked and felt happy. They decided to share one portion of the warm tart. It was served with crème Anglaise. Coffee at St Dunstan's may be of a good quality instant, but nothing compares with real coffee and Alasdair relished the opportunity to choose from a list of exotic blends. He chose a Brasilia coffee described as having a rich intense flavour with a hint of praline.

They arrived back at St Dunstan's just after three o'clock and Alasdair immediately slumped into the armchair and put his head back, closing his eyes. He said. 'That was lovely, darling. Thank you.'

'Yes, it was,' she replied. 'I'll be just a few minutes making tea.'

Alasdair sipped the steaming rich brown liquid and smiled at her. 'This must be Yorkshire Tea.'

'It certainly is. It's the best.'

Soon after, when Alasdair was feeling revived, he mused, 'The longer I live, Frances the more I love stories. I seldom argue with people these days, not only because ones' approaching death makes arguments otiose, but because people don't seem to be persuaded very much by arguments anyway, at least as far as change of behaviour is concerned. And victory in argument, I have always felt, is a sterile thing. Far better it is to get under the skin of whatever we are talking about by means of a story. And much of the wisdom of the world is contained in stories, fascinating stories often with a surprise ending, a sting in the tail, a twist that blows your mind. I love stories like that, I collect them.'

Frances started to tidy up the papers and put the cups back on the tray and he sensed she needed to leave soon.

He pointed encouragingly at the top drawer of the little chest by his bed.

'Darling, be so kind, open the drawer. You'll find an envelope with jottings and stories.'

Frances opened it and pulled out a large dog-eared brown envelope and handed it to him.

'It would please me so much if you would look through and find a story to read to me.'

She smiled as she looked at the contents, some were hand written, some had been typed on an old manual typewriter with an ink ribbon. There were pieces of paper, some just scraps. She looked through and started to make sense of what was in her lap and scan the contents. The first one which looked as though it might be a story was removed and she gave it to Alasdair to see.

'Yes, that will do very well.'

Frances read the story of Diodoros.

Diodoros

There was once a Greek philosopher who lived in
Chios, off the Asia Minor mainland. His name was
Diodoros, not to be confused with the historian
Diodoros of Sicily. He was born about the time of
Democritus, whose theory of atoms was all the rage.

Diodoros, while still a young man discovered what he
believed to be the secret of history. This is not
unusual, nor as fantastic as it might sound. You may
know that Dialectical Materialism makes the same
claim as does Oswald Spengler in his admirable
'Decline of the West'.

If what he had discovered was true, it meant that the
course of human history could be plotted, and
therefore, to some extent, predicted and in spite of
this being alien to the Greek view of things, it was
a very exciting prospect for Diodoros.

The discovery took the form of a theory, carefully
and slowly built up on the ethereal but imperishable
framework of pure logic. Unfortunately, the logical
process was not complete. Imagine a program for a
computer which is loaded into the system and nothing
happens because there is a single, tiny formula
missing from the program. Such is an illustration
of the situation in which Diodoros found himself.
His theory was complete except for a single logical
step which it was essential to make but which eluded
him completely.

In his distress, he confided his problem to a dear
friend who could be trusted not to reveal his
researches and to his delight, his friend replied,
'Diodoros, your difficulty is surmounted. In the city
of Thebes there lives a wise woman, a prophetess. To
her, Apollo, in gratitude for the receipt of a

13

favour, has granted an extraordinary gift. She has the power to give the true answer to one question and one question only which shall be asked of her by one person in that one person's lifetime.

It is only a handful of people who are admitted to her company, and I am one of them. I am sure that, on my recommendation, she will allow you to visit her and that she will grant your request and give you the information you require to make your wonderful program complete.'

Diodoros was overjoyed. Thanking his friend profusely and receiving at his hands a letter of recommendation, he made all the arrangements for the voyage to the mainland and after some months, found himself at the house of the Wise Woman of Thebes.

Attendant maidens led him through sweet groves of blossoming trees, along winding paths bordered with scented flowers, until he came to a pool in the midst of which the delicate spray of a fountain refreshed the air. And, lying on silken cushions on a couch of carved marble lay the Wise Woman.

She was beautiful. She was the most beautiful thing of all creation that his eyes had ever lighted upon. And when she spoke, her voice held the mystery and rippling secrets of many waters.

'Philosopher', she said. 'Welcome to my house. My husband is away hunting so I have a little leisure. I know why you have come to me. And I can satisfy your desire. You have a question to put, a question that means everything to you. Ask it, and I shall give you a true answer. But remember, you may only ask one single question, one only. And you will never have the opportunity to ask another as long as you live. Do you understand?'

'I do, Lady,' Diodoros replied. 'Then what is your question?' said the Wise Woman. And Diodoros replied, 'What time is your husband coming back from the hunt?'

She laughed, 'Alasdair, that was delightful.' As she rose, getting ready to leave Frances asked, 'Do you need me to do anything?'

He smiled up at her. 'No darling, just a kiss.' She bent over him and kissed his soft lips, brushing her lips gently against his neatly trimmed moustache. She squeezed his hand and left quietly. He cared for Frances and was reminded of her unselfish devotion.

It wasn't long before Alasdair was aware of pain. This time it was so acute he called out 'Aaargh . . . .', and reached across to the hand-held device to activate and alert someone that he needed help.

His thoughts returned to the cause of his pain. 'My old friend again, who knows me so well, who searches me out in my down-sitting and in my uprising, who comes calmly and patiently to give me a daily lesson in submissiveness and humility. No fake humility this. No religion-engineered spiritual exercise for the good of the soul. No contorting his natural buoyancy and optimism into the semblance of self-abasement! No. This is the real thing. This is the genuine, dyed-in-the-wool article. That deep, profound humility that cries out and bears its own echoes resounding, calling, calling, shivering into a thousand fragments of acceptance of absolute acknowledgement of mortality, of vulnerability, of helplessness, of utter impotence.'

The same pretty nurse entered his room after gently knocking, but not waiting. She was sure of a welcome.

'Bless you,' gasped Alasdair. Relieved she was here, he gathered together his strength and determination and putting on a deep theatrical voice, exclaimed, 'Bless you. You bear like Hebe, the divine opiate of my personal Olympus.' His pain was lost in their laughter.

After she left, he looked through his collection of CD's and chose *Only Trust Your Heart*. He closed his eyes listening to the sultry jazz voice of Diana Krall and reflected. 'Oh Rose!'

So rare a gift . . . this rose . . . this lovely rose . . .
  But are there not a thousand roses sighing
With perfumed breath within a thousand gardens?
And see this grass with the tinctured blood . . .
  So many hues of blood . . . of dying roses.
Look at this pool . . . it holds within its heart
    The true, eternal, once-begotten rose
    Of which all other roses but reflect
  A pale impermanence, a shadow's shade.
And yet this rose . . . this lovely rose is like
    No other rose that ever kissed the air.
For this, this very one that now I hold,
Her eyes admired, her fingers plucked, her soul
  Delighted in. It was her own sweet hand
  That took this rose and put it into mine.
      It was her lips, open to give
Her breathless kisses, touched this clustered bud,
And, like those lips, it blushed, and blushing broke
    Into a petalled mouth of golden flame.
  This rose, so rare, is like no other flower;
  No flower that is or was or e'er shall be.
Death cannot claim it, nor can time devour
    This one, red rose my lover gave to me.
    Behold, how like the ivy or the vine
    Do these fair laces amorously entwine
    To press this urgent foot into its shoe
  And make them into one instead of two.
But, Madame, let they thoughts reflect on this,
  That sweet unlacing task at last is done,
  Love conjugates the two, to make us one.

On Tying His Mistress's Shoelace by **John Donne**

3

RETIREMENT

*'. . . . . . . what the soul knows is often unknown to
the man who has a soul.
We are infinitely more than we think.'*

Kahlil Gibran

It was just after one o'clock and Alasdair had finished what he could of his lunch, when he heard Anthony's familiar tap, tap on the door. Without waiting he came in to greet Alasdair.

'Hello Father. How was lunch?'

He put the large bag he had brought with him on the floor. Contained in it were fresh pyjamas, underwear and the usual things Alasdair needed. Anthony and Susan live nearest to St Dunstan's in Upper Heaton and had undertaken to do this for Alasdair. He put his arm around Alasdair's shoulders and bent over and kissed him. Alasdair sensed the smoothness of his skin and the pleasant fragrance of his aftershave.

'Good to see you, son. Lunch was fine. I just wasn't very hungry.'

Alasdair loves all of his children, but Anthony just a little bit more. He was the first born, the thrill of seeing him for the first time and lifting him into his arms remains. In that moment, his heart was so full it felt like bursting and such joy can only be a once in a lifetime moment. They smiled at each other and Anthony busied himself with putting away the fresh clothes and collecting a bag of soiled linen to take home.

He looked at his son admiringly. He was a few inches taller than Alasdair, very good looking, his chestnut hair cut short to compensate

17

for a receding hair line and he moved with elegant comportment.

'The sun's shining, shall we try a little walk in the garden? What do you think, Father?'

'Why not? We can have a cup of tea afterwards.'

He began to slowly raise himself from his chair. Anthony helped him on with his coat and then took his arm and they ventured out into the warmth of the afternoon sunshine, Alasdair holding his walking stick in the other hand.

It was tough for Anthony to see how frail his Father was. Only a few weeks ago he had been as energetic as ever. This decline in his health had happened very quickly and he valued their time spent together. They walked very slowly along the terrace and down the steps leading to the sunken garden with stone paving surrounding a low pond with large lilies floating effortlessly on the surface. The September sun flooded down, warming the grey stones of the wall behind them. They found a bench to sit on and breathed in the fresh air. Alasdair looked up at the sky. North Yorkshire has lots of sky. He missed the moors already and hadn't been up Sutton Bank and across the moor to Whitby to see the glorious landscape that awaits discovery, a landscape of sky and swathes of purple heather. He and Ruth had never regretted moving from Sunderland. They had always felt North Yorkshire was their natural home. In the early days Alasdair rode his motorbike with Anthony riding pillion and Ruth and the little ones in the side-car. They would head out towards the high grassy hills and wide valleys where rivers twisted among the trees and solid grey stone farmhouses lay among cultivated land enclosed by dry stone walls.

Anthony likes order. He has co-ordinated a rota of friends and family to ensure his father has company every day. Alasdair had given him a list of books to bring from home. There they sit, piled up on the low table waiting, past pleasures to be re-visited. Reading passages from books, magazines or his old sermons, poems and stories has enabled visitors the chance to stay a little longer if they wish, when conversation dries up and is replaced with the inevitable awkwardness of silence. What to say, how long to stay. It is so much easier to share an activity than trying to think of something interesting to say and thus avoid clichés.

Sitting beside each other in the garden, Alasdair lifted his face to the warm sunshine, closed his eyes and half listened to Anthony telling him all about everything and nothing. It was just the best feeling to be beside his son and hold his hand. All too soon the autumnal chill of late afternoon ushered them back inside.

While Alasdair settled himself, Anthony went to the kitchenette along the corridor to make tea. It was always Taylor's Yorkshire Tea.

'Do you remember when we used to ride the motorbike together. Sometimes with Mum and your brothers in the sidecar? Looking back the days seem full of happiness and I have to think hard to remember our poverty. I don't think we ever wore crash helmets in those days? Did we?'

'I certainly didn't. My friends were so jealous at the time. I must have been twelve, when you bought it.'

'It was actually a second-hand Triumph TR6 Trophy model and I felt like Marlon Brando when I let the throttle out.'

'I know you did Pa. You used to drop me off at St Cuthbert's wearing black leathers. Crickey! Even then you had an individual look. Look at you today wearing one of Mother's earrings and your hair tumbling onto your collar. I have always loved that about you, a chameleon approach to wearing clothes for each occasion. Whether wearing a tweed jacket and breeches to visit Lord Rossiter or riding around Moreton on Milo sitting on your American saddle wearing leather gaucho pants. You are the only male member of our family to own a pair of tight black leather trousers. You never ceased to surprise your parishioners. No wonder they loved you so much.'

Alasdair smiled, 'In earlier times, when we lived in Ashington, we were happy. I never think of us as poor looking back. I remember us visiting The Ashington Group, pitmen painters in their hut. I met Oliver Kilbourn and remember him talking about his plans for the paintings to be put in trust. He told me that when they started painting, it had been to appreciate art, but that painting had become a passion. We had moved away by the time they closed the pit in 1988. That year was awful knowing that people you had known were suffering. The men returned to work not because they had stopped believing in what they were fighting for but because houses were being re-possessed, marriages were breaking up and the kids were going without. There was no end in sight. It was certainly one of the darkest times in our history.'

Picking up *The Daily Telegraph*, Anthony sat down and in silence started to browse the newspaper until it was time to go and as if to introduce his departure, he looked up as he folded his newspaper and shrugged, 'Another bomb, this time in Moscow and an Islamic group in the Caucasus is being blamed. Some are suggesting that the bombings are a *false flag* in order to legitimise military activity in Chechnya.'

'Putin seems to be manoeuvring for the presidency again.' Alasdair responded, as he looked up and saw his son was already folding the newspaper and tidying away the cups and saucers. 'Give my love to Susan and thank her for my goodies.'

As Anthony was leaving and Alasdair was resting with his eyes closed, drifting into sleep, he heard voices just outside his room in the corridor. His door was ajar and he just made out Anthony's voice talking to Alasdair's Haematology Consultant from Harrogate. She had known Alasdair for five years as she fought to keep the cancer in check and had seen him more often recently as the time between blood transfusions shortened. He distinctly heard her say, 'Your father's condition is worsening rapidly.'

Alasdair felt a physical pain as the words sank in and he found himself experiencing a panic attack and for what seemed an age, he couldn't breathe. The fight was coming to a close; the cancer had won! A death sentence! When she entered the room, Alasdair couldn't hold back his tears. She took his hand and kissed it and brushed her own tears away with his hand.

Anthony seemed to Alasdair to be one of life's plodders with no particular talent other than a common sense ability to work hard at his job for British Telecom, which he had done until he took early retirement last year. He now enjoys doing part time jobs, the latest delivering huge water bottles to offices. Susan still works for British Telecom as an IT Consultant and has no plan to retire just yet as her hours are flexible. They never fully explained to him why they had a civil wedding ceremony. Did Anthony's early years attending church services sometimes twice on Sundays put him off? Why did they never talk about it? He rather hoped that it was Susan who made the decision. He is too tired now to broach the subject. It really doesn't matter now, but it did then.

'He will be back in a couple of days,' Alasdair tells the nurse who has just popped her head around the door. 'Upper Heaton isn't too far away and it is easy for him to drop-in, even for twenty minutes.'

Alasdair pondered aloud to himself, something he had been doing more and more since Ruth's death and he had been amused when he found himself doing it in public and having to apologise. Twenty minutes. He had spent his working life with a built-in clock for twenty minutes. He had a dozen or so well chosen phrases ready, when he needed to leave a parishioner's home, his favourite being, 'No, I am so very sorry, I cannot stay for another cup of tea. I must get home to save my marriage'. He used that one a lot. Not far from the truth as Ruth was very possessive and Alasdair never forgot his close encounter with her rage over Rose. He was very careful never to give her any reason to doubt him after that. He did insist that a mobile phone was out of the question. This he considered to be an electronic tag and that was a step too far.

Retiring from Clifton College hadn't been the heartache he thought it would be. In recent years there had been so many changes and the focus of the college had moved away from training teachers. The latest move to combine with another local college, under one Principal and management team had meant a lot of change. Theology as a subject had become less popular and when it came to it, Alasdair was relieved to go.

His meeting with the Bishop had gone well. Alasdair was complimented on his contribution as Chaplain to the College and he was kind enough to acknowledge Alasdair's achievements before asking him, 'What would you like to do now, Alasdair? Any thoughts?'

Alasdair had not thought beyond the end of term, so had little to offer in the way of plans. Fortunately for Alasdair, the Bishop had thought about it and asked him, 'How would you like the idea of being Priest in Charge at St Lawrence's in Moreton just over a hundred on the electoral register?'

As it was a fair way from Alasdair's home, he was unsure until the Bishop explained, 'The living includes a vicarage. A small stone built cottage nestling below the church.'

'I'll think about it.' Alasdair hesitated, 'I'll discuss it with Ruth and let you know.'

The way forward was to rent out their home as income. Alasdair wasn't sure how Ruth would like the idea. So later in the week, they drove out to Moreton and had a look and met Harry Bainbridge, Church Warden, who showed them around St Lawrence's and the vicarage. Two months later Ruth and Alasdair settled into the vicarage at Moreton and soon after that, their house was let. And so began their life in the North Yorkshire parish of Moreton. The village had no pub or shop. Lord and Lady Rossiter lived at Moreton Park, set back a distance from the main road and reached by a gravel drive lined each side with poplar trees and pastureland. Sheep grazed in one of the pastures, separated by a ha-ha running the length of the drive. On approach to the main house were kennels and large garages above which was a large attic space used for shooting parties. There was an expectation that village events were held there and Lord Rossiter was always willing to oblige. Proceeds were given to the Parish Council to be used for the good of the community.

Jacqueline was Geoffrey's second wife. The first Lady Rossiter lives in London and both their daughters live abroad. Jacqueline had moved to Moreton with her daughter into a rented house on the estate after her divorce to one of Lord Rossiter's business associates. It wasn't long before their affair started. It wasn't the first time and it wasn't going to be the last time that Geoffrey would have affairs with women living on the estate.

Over the years he had sold off several of the larger houses including The Dower House, where his mother had lived. The farms and more modest cottages were still owned by him and the whole estate covered a vast acreage. Lord Rossiter also owned shooting rights on moorland past Stonebeck Up and beyond.

At the age of sixty four Alasdair learned to ride a horse. There were so many people living in the vicinity who had horses. Many rode with the York & Ainsty North Hunt. The Arkright family lived at South View, a large farm house with stables and paddocks. Vicky, their eldest daughter was happy to spend time riding out with Alasdair and teach him the basics. It wasn't long after she went to university that he took on the exercise and management of her horse. Milo was a black Dales Pony with a silky mane and abundant leg feathers. It was then that Alasdair started visiting his parishioners on horseback. Milo was only fourteen hands high and his calm and kind temperament suited Alasdair very well. Fortunately for Alasdair, Vicky had four siblings of whom two were old enough and keen enough to help if Alasdair was unable to muck out. So it suited everyone, including Ruth who needed Alasdair to have an interest.

4

HARVEST FESTIVAL

Go sit upon the lofty hill,
And turn your eyes around,
Where waving woods and waters wild
Do hymn an autumn sound.
The summer sun is faint on them;
The summer flowers depart.
Sit still, as all transferred to stone,
Except your musing heart.

from *The Autumn* by **Elizabeth Barrett Browning**

The Harvest Supper is a firm favourite in the Moreton parish calendar. Alasdair only had to fall in with the routine which had taken place for as long as people could remember. As he was the editor, publisher and sole contributor to Moreton News he put the notice in the September issue and the community got on with it. The church would be beautifully decorated by mothers and their children. Those involved in the tradition produced bucket loads of chicken casserole which was served with rice, kept warm in the small kitchen above the garages at Moreton Park. This would then be followed by apple crumble and piping hot custard. All anyone had to do was take their plate and cutlery with them. After the Harvest Festival service, the congregation made their way to Moreton Park; there waiting for them on arrival was a warm room with a glowing fire at the far end and two rows of tables decorated by Lady Rossiter and her team of volunteers. Lord Rossiter as host served everyone with wine, beer or lemon squash.

When appetites were sated, the evening turned to entertainment. The tables were moved to allow for dancing. Alasdair with Harry Bainbridge, the organist at St Lawrence's, took it in turn to play the piano and to get things going. Those who wanted to perform came prepared to sing a song, recite a poem or do a party trick. Both Alasdair and Lord Rossiter came prepared with at least one recitation. On these occasions Lord Rossiter was very jovial, so different from how he could be over any difficult issue to do with St Lawrence's or anything else for that matter. The warmth from the fire and the effect of alcohol loosened inhibitions and the party swept along. The little ones were happy to sit with their grandfathers listening to their stories. Alasdair as master of ceremonies started the games with *Fetch the Apple*. He placed two chairs at one end of the room and lined up two teams of six players at the other end of the room. He then gave the teams two teaspoons and told them how to play the game without using hands. It doesn't really matter what happens next as everyone starts shouting instructions and eventually one team claims to be the winner. Everyone playing receives an apple. Another favourite, *Pass the Orange*, had to be done from chin to chin; it was such a funny sight as tall fathers tried to pass the orange to their small children and then back up to their Mummies. After *Musical Chairs*, Harry Bainbridge would strike up the piano and Alasdair would lead the singing of favourites like *Don't sit under the apple tree with anyone else but me*, *Sentimental Journey* and then the finale. Everyone, who could, formed a circle and off they went.

Oh! Oh! The Oki Koki
Oh! Oh! The Oki Koki
You put your left leg in. You put your left leg out
In, out. In out
Shake it all about
You do the Oki Koki and you turn around
That's what it's all about . . . . . .

Some new acquaintances were made and old ones refreshed. All in all, a very happy evening. And that was it for another year.

Next on the calendar would be the forthcoming Moreton Christmas Party.

Alasdair was woken by a tap on the door followed by Frances coming in with a tray. 'Hello,' she said. 'Time for tea?'

Alasdair turned to Frances. 'Do you remember when I kissed you? We'd been spending quite a lot of time together after your divorce?'

'I remember. We had just returned from a walk around Studley Royal and Fountains Abbey. We were saying goodbye in the hall. You took me by surprise, Alasdair. I never imagined for one moment you would swoop me into your arms and kiss me firmly on the lips.' She took his hand. 'It was of the moment.'

After pouring the tea and offering Alasdair his choice of cake from a selection bought from Betty's earlier in the day, she continued,

'It was a difficult time for me, it had been dreadful going through the divorce. I was naïve to suppose that divorce would free me from Edward's financial meanness and spiteful behaviour.'

'That doesn't surprise me at all Frances. When Ruth and I came to your dinner parties, I was rather taken aback how Edward never even picked up a plate to help clear away. It was noticeable, how he seemed to be always putting you down. I did my best to avert attention and lift the mood with a story, but Ruth and I often came away feeling anxious.'

There was a long pause, Frances looked out beyond the window to the garden and then she turned to Alasdair. She smiled,

'Tell me about Anthony's visit?'

'Oh, it went very well. He has been so good to me over the last few weeks.'

Frances got up and turning towards the chest of drawers and seeing the two bronzes enquired, 'These look interesting.'

'I asked Anthony to bring them from home last week.'

'How did you acquire them?'

'The greyhound and puppy is by Pierre-Jules Mêne. As a regular collector I was on Tennant's mailing list and liked the look of the running greyhound, so I went to the auction in Leyburn with Ruth making it a pleasant day out. First stop was Masham for coffee and thick buttered cinnamon toast at The Mad Hatter's Café, then onto the auction in Leyburn. I was lucky that day, only one other bidder who couldn't have been serious as he dropped out far below its' real value. The Frederic Remington was given to me by Lord Rossiter on my retirement. It is *Arizona Cowboy* and is my favourite, not because of its' value but because it is a surprisingly thoughtful gift from Geoffrey, who keeps this side of his nature rather under wraps.'

Smiling at this revelation regarding Lord Rossiter, Frances looked through a selection of CD's asking Alasdair, 'Shall we listen to some music?' She handed a few for him to choose from.

Alasdair selected Pascale Roge playing Debussy's piano works.

'I prefer Preludes Premier Livre, please Frances.'

They listened in contented silence to the wafts and wisps of tone and delicacy of touch, which conveyed the music's mood. Frances left quietly, when she noticed he had dozed off. She didn't want to be late meeting up with Philip.

Frances and Alasdair have been good friends for several years and enjoyed many jaunts into the Yorkshire countryside often stopping for coffee in Masham. It is only a short drive. There is no supermarket, instead tucked between the old stone houses that line the market square, is a bakery, a butchers and a greengrocers, one after the other. He used to enjoy taking Frances to The Mad Hatter's Tea Room in Church Street, something he had done so often with Ruth. There are two rooms with bow windows either side of a central door and hall way. Alasdair's favourite was the room on the left with the cricket caricatures and memorabilia. He liked to see across the market square and gaze out at life passing by.

Once he took Frances together with Philip and Oliver. After they had enjoyed tea and crumpets, he drove them to the Druid's Temple near Ilton, a folly of all follies looking like a scaled down version of Stonehenge. The boys enjoyed playing amongst the stones and amid the trees finding old campfires and shelters made of branches covered in ferns. Frances had prepared a picnic lunch. Afterwards, he was pleased he had shared this special place with them.

Alasdair first became acquainted with Frances after she and Edward moved into The Dower House. He made a polite call to the house soon after the family had moved in and met Edward's parents, who were busy in the garden. Frances and Edward were at work. The boys and their nanny had gone swimming in Harrogate. Alasdair decided to call another time.

On meeting Frances that warm summers' day, she had seen him before he dismounted and came out to greet Alasdair. The instant his eyes rested on her, he was struck by the rare beauty of her form and the unaffected grace of her attitude. Tall, yet not too tall. Her shoulder length hair framed her thin almost angular face. It was the briefest of encounters because unfortunately Milo was a little restless and trod on her foot, which was probably quite painful. He took his leave graciously and rode down the road to the neighbouring village store and purchased a heart shaped chocolate covered in red foil. This he later presented to Frances as an apology from Milo.

'You caused quite a stir the other day,' she told him. 'Edward's mother was quite taken aback by your appearance in an open neck shirt, cowboy hat and leather chaps.'

Before he could reply, Edward came to the door behind Frances and saw the red heart in Frances' hand and noticed her blushes. He said what he believed would be amusing.

'Hello Vicar, I would be worried if you weren't so old.'

'What a bloody idiot,' thought Alasdair.

Alasdair became a frequent visitor as there was always their nanny at home to talk to. Sometimes his parents were there too as they often seemed to be helping out doing various chores, which seemed to please them. Once when he called, Frances was alone and he saw her bruised face. When they sat down for tea, he also noticed bruises to her legs. Alasdair felt sad. Such a waste! It made him so cross, that this abrasively charming and successful man should cause her pain.

It was just after eight thirty the following day, when Frances arrived on her way to work at Harrison Wallis Solicitors in Harrogate.

'Good morning, Alasdair. Nurse told me you are up and about. Can't stay too long as I have to be at the office for nine thirty.'

'No matter, it is lovely to see you. It is a comfort knowing you will come to see me.'

Frances was already getting *The Times* out of her bag, so he could get stuck into the crossword. 'Is it today Alex is coming?'

'Yes, he is driving from Aldeburgh and should arrive after lunch. He is staying with a friend tonight and will pop in again tomorrow morning before he drives back to Suffolk.'

'I see South View is up for sale. I thought you might like to look at the estate agent's brochure.'

'What happy times we had mucking out the stables, pottering about together.'

'I looked forward to the routine after Edward left. It was something practical to do and kept my mind uncluttered for a couple of hours. You were so kind to me during that year, when it seemed everything was falling away from me. I'm still not sure what to do and what I actually want out of life.'

'Frances, I think a lot of people pray for things they don't really want. They've been told they ought to pray for things . . . maybe love, humility, peace and they do, but their heart really isn't in it. Honestly, I think it's better to wait until you really want something very bad. Then ask for it and go on asking. It may not be something very good, but I don't think it matters very much. If it's bad God won't give it to you and at least your asking comes from the heart. If I were God, I'd rather have a man ask me for a yacht he really wants than for love and purity because his Vicar told him to. If he wants a yacht badly, he can learn to want love badly. But if he doesn't really want anything, there's not much I can do. To pray from the heart, that's it.'

'That's profound. I like it. To pray from the heart.' She moved to collect her bag. 'I will remember.' As she left, she turned around, 'Have a lovely time with Alex. I will be here tomorrow just after four o'clock.'

One of Alasdair's favourite stories is a tale by a great Russian, the man who wrote '*War and Peace*', Count Leo Tolstoy. He wrote many powerful short stories and one of the finest is the tale of two friends. It springs from a question that we can ask, what really makes God happy. What do you think? What makes God sit up and say to the angels, 'Look at that!' The answer is simple: the thing that makes God really happy is to see a man loving his neighbour in a way that costs him something, giving love that isn't cheap, love that takes effort and self-sacrifice. You may think that this is pretty obvious. But it isn't. A great many religious people of all faiths would strongly disagree. They would tell you that what really pleases God is when people say their prayers, or tell God they love him, or go to worship in a church or temple, or meditate, or deny themselves pleasure. All these are very important. But what a father wants, well what Alasdair wants is to see his sons affectionate, loving to each other, standing by each other, helping each other out. That's what cheers him, far more than writing letters or telling him what a great father he is.

Jesus of Nazareth put this very strongly. He painted a picture of the whole world of people spread out like a living sea before him, and being divided to the right hand or the left. And he says to those on the right, 'You are blessed and happy because you fed me and clothed me and helped me and sheltered me'. And they say 'But we've never seen you before in our lives.' And He says, 'No. But because you have done what you have to help your brother man, you have done it for me.'

THE TWO FRIENDS

Two friends once lived in the south of Russia in the
old days before the revolution. They were both,
believing, god-fearing men and they determined to
save their money and make a pilgrimage to Palestine.
It was to be the crowning achievement of their
lives.

Nicolai said to Ivan, 'Imagine Ivan, we will see
where the Christ Child was born, we will walk by the
Sea of Galilee where he taught, we will tread the
sorrowful way where he carried his cross. And Ivan,
if we pray, oh if we pray hard, we might be granted a
vision of the Christ, the Master himself. Just think!
If we should! If we should see him!' So they set off.
And after a few days they came to a farmhouse where
they stopped to ask for food. The place was poor and
run-down, the wood-work unpainted, the furrows full
of weeds and the farmer in despair. 'My son has gone
for a soldier', he said. 'My wife is ill, there has
been blight on the crops and I can go on no longer'.
The poor man wept.

'Look Nicolai' said Ivan, 'Tomorrow you go on to
Palestine. I'll stay here for a couple of days to
tide this old chap over; I can easily catch you up'.
So Nicolai went off next day, but although he didn't
travel very quickly, no Ivan caught him up. So he
went on to Bethlehem. And he stood in the Church of
the Stable and knelt where the Christ Child was born
and where the Blessed Virgin cradled the Saviour of
Men in the circle of her arms. And his devotion
welled up like a river in his heart. Then he went to
the Sea of Galilee where the Lord of Love healed the
sick and cleansed the lepers and where he told the
stories of his Father and His love of men, where he
called Peter and where he forgave Wendy of Magdala.
And he went on to Jerusalem. And it seemed to him

that he could hear the cruel shouts, 'Crucify him!'
And the sound of the nails being hammered home and
the long last cry from the cross. And he wept. And he
prayed to see the King of Glory who had suffered for
him. But he saw no vision. Not even when he stood in
the Church of the Sepulchre from whence goes out the
Easter fire of new life, not even then, though his
heart was alive with fire, did he see his Lord.

So at last he turned his feet towards home. And as he
journeyed he remembered the wonder of his travel. So
the days passed. Until, of a sudden, he saw it, the
vision, not in Palestine but in Russia. There by the
roadside, with the glory of the setting sun making a
halo of glory behind him, there was the Christ! He
had granted him sight of Him at last. At last he saw
the Christ. Trembling with joy he fell to his knees
and the vision spoke, 'Did you enjoy your pilgrimage,
Nicolai?' It said. 'I couldn't really leave the old
man on his own?'

Leo Tolstoy's story *The Two Friends*
adapted by Alasdair Sommersby

5

BORDERS OF THE KNOWN WORLD

'And in the end, it's not the years in your life that count,
it's the life in your years.'

Abraham Lincoln

'Hello Dad. It's me Alex.'

Alasdair opened his eyes and beamed up at his son. 'Alex, how wonderful.' He shuffled himself upright in the chair and held out his arms. Alex moved towards his father smiling and embraced him. 'How are you, how's Rachel?'

'Fine Dad, we're both fine. Rachel is in Los Angeles with Emily. I've been in Aldeburgh. I'll go back to London in time to collect Rachel from Heathrow next Friday.'

The tallest of his sons, Alex is well over six feet tall. He was endowed with artistic genes and absorbed himself in classical studies. He recently retired as a lecturer in Art History at the University of London. He still looks like a student, dressed in a shabby royal blue corduroy jacket and jeans with his greying hair combed back and curling slightly over his collar.

'Alex, do you remember Adam's wedding? The first time I saw Emily in her punk pink and that tiny short mini-skirt in black. I savour that image. It is a very happy memory.'

'Dad, we have a lot of happy times to remember. All of us. We were happy.'

'I am spending most of my days thinking and remembering. I

know I have to let go, but I also want to recapture my life in my head. When I close my eyes it is like watching a video of my life. I have to slow the speed down so I don't miss the best bits. When I fall asleep I am clutching onto the images and stories which have been part of my day.'

'Look, Dad I have brought *The Daily Telegraph* and *The Field* for you to browse when you want to. How about I make us a nice cup of tea? I popped into Betty's on my way here and bought us a fat rascal to share. I just need to find some butter when I make the tea. I won't be long; I'll just be in the kitchen along the corridor.'

Alasdair made himself more comfortable. He was sad for Alex that he had to retire early a few years ago when Chronic Fatigue Syndrome was diagnosed. He seems happy enough and he often accompanies Rachel on her trips abroad with the British Council and gets involved in the occasional research project in art history. He has recently been to Frankfurt to give a lecture on the Bauhaus Movement.

It's a long journey from Aldeburgh and so Alex has arranged to stay with an old school friend overnight in Thirsk. A pattern has evolved during these past few weeks and he and his brothers have sorted out a rota to see their father. Anthony is the closest and he visits more regularly and keeps Alex and Adam informed of their fathers' well-being. For now, Alasdair's appetite remains healthy and he appears to be eating well and a small portion of a fat rascal is a nice treat. Alex settled himself into the large armchair near the window opposite his father and began to relax.

He can do the journey in just under four hours including a comfort break. The two of them spent a little time being quiet, while they read and looked out onto the garden as Alex relaxed after his journey.

After they had finished their tea, Alex felt better and was anxious to engage his father in conversation.

'I am just reading the review on *American Beauty?* It is directed by Sam Mendes with Kevin Spacey as a lacklustre suburban everyman whose life is coming apart. It begins with him jerking off in the shower.'

Immediately, Alasdair looked up. He had meant to look astonished,

34

even offended at such language, but he saw Alex was looking for such a response and just couldn't help himself laughing out loud.

'Definitely one to take Rachel to see on her return.'

It was Alasdair who changed the topic.

'Alex, I remember when Ruth and I came down and stayed with you and Rachel in Aldeburgh. What a charming place it is. You are so lucky to live so close to the sea.'

Rachel had inherited Wimborne Cottage from a wealthy aunt years ago when she was struggling to bring up Emily. It is a very pretty double fronted white cottage with the garden backing onto the beach. Alex and Rachel also have a large mansion flat in Westbourne Terrace in London, but Alex prefers to live in Aldeburgh, when Rachel is travelling.

Ruth and Alasdair stayed with them the summer before Ruth's death. They had driven down in the MG, which added much pleasure to the trip for Alasdair. He had been in his element and they stopped often to browse in antique shops or take a turning off the road to see where it led, a packed lunch and a flask with them at the ready should they find a nice view.

On one day Alex took them to Southwold, where he had a beach hut. Southwold has a few good junk shops which occupied them in the morning and then they parked closer to the beach and unloaded their picnic basket, making their way down towards the beach, walking along the promenade towards the pier. They saw the row of white wooden beach huts neatly spaced out along the grey concrete of the sea wall. The blue doors stand like columns of sapphire against the white paintwork. They walked along the pier to make the most of the sea air in their faces and then on further down the beach to where more beach huts where nestling amongst the sand dunes and mounds of coarse grass. Here the owners of the beach huts are unrestricted in their use of colour and they are painted in red, yellow and blue. One stood out; it was painted pale blue with a yellow window shutter. Alexander's was painted in blue horizontal stripes on white. He bought it when he retired with the lump sum portion of his pension. Opening the shutters revealed an interior of pale blue with book shelves taking up one side and a number of stacking chairs on the other. To the rear was a pine worktop with a pretty blue gingham gathered skirt to hide a storage area and on the floor a rather faded sea-grass mat.

They immediately started to sort things out and put chairs onto the wooden decking and then make the most of a lovely sunny day taking in the sea air. Once Ruth and Alasdair were settled, reading their papers, Alex got the prima stove going and put the kettle on. Ruth drew their attention to the vastness of the sea beyond and as she often did, recited from memory.

'*We are tied to the ocean. And when we go back to the sea, whether it is to sail or to watch — we are going back from whence we came. John F Kennedy.*'

Alex bent down and kissed his mother. 'Well done, Mum. Well done.'

It was warm enough to venture into the water, but no-one really wanted to swim. They were happy to look for shells along the beach and let the gentle swell of the sea cover their bare feet.

Alasdair realised he had drifted off and was interrupted by Alex, kissing his hair.

'Cheerio Dad,' and he left.

Alasdair smiled but didn't open his eyes. He would return tomorrow.

That night like every other night at St Dunstan's, Alasdair woke up at around two o'clock in the morning. He didn't try to go back to sleep, instead he allowed his thoughts to drift into his consciousness. He wanted to savour and re-live his memories. His retirement with Ruth at Moreton seemed like yesterday. He was often unfaithful in his affection towards other women, but his love for Ruth remained constant. He judged himself as a man and a husband rather than a clergyman. He prayed for himself as he did for other sinners.

St Lawrence's Church is only a short distance from The Four Seasons Hotel, a glamorous and romantic manor house surrounded by beautiful landscaped gardens. As Priest in Charge, it wasn't long before Alasdair received requests from couples to be married at

St Lawrence's. This was something frowned upon by the previous incumbent. Alasdair saw things differently and so with Evelyn Bainbridge's help, who happily gave her address for one of the parties, weddings at Moreton became very popular and the financial contribution to the Diocese grew in no small measure. After all on a good Sunday, the congregation for Morning Service would only be about thirty and on a cold winter's morning as few as ten.

It was on such an occasion that Alasdair met Octavia at the wedding of her daughter, an up and coming actress in Emmerdale. Octavia was a Barrister working in Leeds and being a widow with grown up children now lived for her work. That didn't stop her loving Alasdair entertaining her. Although a beautiful woman can excite him, if he does not feel some kind of love, he is impotent. He liked Octavia a lot.

In an intimate moment, he invented a piece of verse. She cried, 'You're a fucking poet!' Followed a moment later by, 'And you're a poetic fucker!'

How sweet it is to receive a compliment when one knows from the circumstances that it is sincerely meant. She was slender and beautifully formed, sweetly proportioned and easy to persuade into changing attitudes.

She had a strong voice when she liked, and would groan in a low gravelly whisper, 'Make it last, make it last . . .' while she touched his back from neck to buttocks, so his body began to shiver with pleasure. Like a woman he liked to be caressed. He would feel the strong fullness of her hips as they relaxed and her flesh opened like a flower to the heat and light of those delicious moments prior to orgasm. When it came she would cry out, half sob and half laugh from the joy through her body. He relished occupying the space she'd just vacated and covering himself with a sheet still scented with their happiness.

Octavia taught Alasdair not to be afraid of women. She told him, 'If you look at the old myths and fairy tales you will find a very ambivalent attitude about women. Take the goddess of three forms for a start, Selene the moon-goddess in the heavens, Artemis the huntress on earth, and Hecate the goddess of the underworld. The mere existence of the idea of the vagina dentate demonstrates the unease, which underlies men's attitude towards women. Most men do not really like women. They like other men. They prefer the company and their topics of conversation, their attitudes to life and their preferences in almost every aspect of life. They will marry women. They will desire to copulate with them. They will display them like trophies. But they do not really like them. You must be different, Alasdair, you must like women. You must in a word, befriend women. I promise you that your efforts will not go unrewarded.'

Octavia loved wine, especially the wine of France. They were drinking a 1975 Pomerol from the Gironde region, when she quoted Oscar Wilde.

'This wine is like God slipping down your throat in velvet knee-breeches.'

Alasdair capped it by saying, 'It's like a girl angel crying in your mouth.'

She had the last word.

'And this is an old French description which I heard from a very aged man near Frejus, 'C'est aussi comme la Sainte Vierge Marie faire pipi dans votre bouche.'

A few weeks after they started seeing each other and were at ease, she asked him,

'Have you done this often?'

'No Octavia, this is not at all my usual practice, but I simply could not resist you.'

'Oh, I thought perhaps that you were a practiced seducer.'

The precision of this utterance was delicious. Alasdair repeated the words to himself delicately and scrupulously to savour that moment for always.

> *What is this light that radiant shines*
> *Upon the plateaux of my mind*
> *As though the gleam of humankind*
> *Combine with fire of source divine?*
> *How cam'st thou gently to unseal*
> *The casket wherein lay concealed*

Such thoughts as love has since revealed
Of how to give and how to feel?
Oh let me feast on they discourse
And slake my thirst at they dear source
Till, gorged on words we seek the balms
And sweetness of each other's arms,
And there is a different knowledge find
That feeds the senses, not the mind.

What have we here? A dying man thinking about death, is it a nonsense? He is cheered by a recollection of a woman. He deprecates the soul-body idea. He consoles himself by thinking of another woman. He speaks of stories and of authority and remembers words of a woman about not being afraid of women.

Feeling uncomfortable, both mentally and physically tired, Alasdair located the console and pressed the large red button in order to alert a nurse, who promptly responded and came in to help him. After helping him back to bed, she decided to give him a mild sedative. Seeing the glass of whisky, which Alex had poured, she decided to ignore it, looked straight at him and smiled.

'You will feel much better after a good sleep.'

'Thank you so very much for your kindness.'

Closing his eyes and breathing deeply, he began to think about the question of how the possibility of living after death and the non-existence of the soul be resolved?

It was the old Rabbis of the Pharisees, who first thought out a plausible answer. Wise old chaps, they were and some brisk young theological students among them. Long-chinned lads with a wary eye on what the other fellow was dreaming up from his study of Torah. The longest-chinned ones among them made the prophets their special study, and the wisest theologian of all, was the man who edited the Genesis parables.

They began by saying that there are three things, which are beyond man's control and always will be – history, the neighbour and death.

That history is impervious to man's manipulation needs no argument. The slightest acquaintance with the deeds of men convinces

39

one that only a fool would dare to predict what will happen next, particularly in the wider world of international affairs. Whenever men have confidently affirmed that they knew what makes the wheels of history go round, their theories have been rendered worthless by the next revolution or the next world war. No philosopher of history would dare to predict what the future holds.

Similarly with one's neighbour. Who is he, this strange man who stands so close to me, a footstep away or an ocean's breadth away? Whoever he is, he is my other self. If I want to make him predictable, I can do so by bending him to my will so that his future is determined by my control of him. But then, see what happens. He becomes simply an extension of my own personality. And I am myself diminished. Imagine a man born and brought up on a deserted island, fed by mysterious messengers whom he never sees. How little of himself he would know. How meagre would be his sense of personhood. But now, imagine another person beside him, and another and another, how his vision of himself and his capabilities would expand, wider and wider. In controlling my neighbour, I am limiting my own self-disclosure. Only by allowing my neighbour to be as unpredictable, as free, as I wish myself to be, can he truly be my neighbour, and I truly am myself.

And death. If death is a simple, natural phenomenon, to be experienced by all living things, why do we make such a fuss about it? Why do we, yes even the atheists and humanists, have our ceremonies and memorial services and our talk of loss and sorrow and memories? Why do we enter the deaths of people in the calendar of our lives and erect our stone monuments with their hopeful symbols? Men have sought to convince themselves that death does not really exist. True, the body dies, but the body is merely a shell. The real you, the soul that can never die, death does not exist for it, for it is immortal.

But those wise old birds, the Pharisaic Rabbis would have none of this. Death is the end. The terminus. *Ad quen*. Death is the ultima Thule, a far away region of each man, the ultima period of philosophical cosmography. Death means exactly *finis*. And pope and prostitute, warlord and wimp, philosopher and fool, saint and sinner

40

within his bending sickle's compass come. And there is no reprieve. Death may be postponed in the years to come, it will never go away. When it comes; when that last prick of the needle which haunts you searches out the last physical sensation at another's hands that you will experience, how will you behave?

You could exit the stage with a light laugh and a witty epigram. You could lie in solemn state with your family around you and priests consoling your last moments with their prayers. You could rail at the cruel test of a universe which destroys a life so long in years and so short in fulfilment of desires. Or you could simply say, 'What the hell,' and just let the whole bloody thing go.

But whatever you do, you can do nothing; you can only make grimaces of one sort or another, to please yourself or to comfort those about you. Death takes away any possibility of using your freedom, except to use it in acceptance.

6

THE SHOOT

Whatever it's like out there, he thought,
It won't be like this.
All I want really is
To lie in warm obstruction and to grow
Always.

The day came for him
As come it must for all
To be thrust out shrieking.

But when the bitterness of birth was past
He stretched at ease, held safely,
Staring at sunshine in astonished joy,
Soothed by a voice
Which he had known in his dreams.

His thoughts as throughout his life are never far from searching truths. His sermons were always searching rather than giving the congregation answers. At Clifton, Alasdair along with other lecturers spent happy hours debating and mostly arguing their philosophical ideas.

Where can we go now? If those gentle scholars with their knife-sharp minds could be with us now, how they would agree with Sartre. He abused the humanists and liberals for kidnapping the thoughts of religious teachers and philosophers, and then after making abstractions from any activity which could be called divine, claiming that they were their own natural born children.

Not so, wrote Sartre. They are merely abstractions, symbols of your own wish fulfilment. If you get rid of the divine, you get rid of any meaning at all, not merely when you are talking about values, but when you are talking about anything.

The brave philosopher Bertrand Russell echoed this view in *The Perplexeties of John Forstice*. Without the existence of the divine, we have no grounds whatsoever for any kind of activity or belief except what we choose to make our own. If there is no ultimate reality, we can invent any sort of reality we want, but of course, it will not be the real one, because there isn't a real one. Life is irrevocably absurd. There is literally no meaning in it. We have to invent our own meaning but we cannot claim any absolute authority for it.

Alasdair had breakfasted in his room. He had enjoyed a small bowl of porridge sprinkled with demerara sugar and a swirl of cream. He was showered and dressed well before Alex arrived just after nine.

Without getting up, he raised his arms to embrace his son and looked at the book in his hand.

'Thanks, Alex for bringing *Naska*, I want to give it to Frances later today. It's her birthday.'

'I spent a while looking through your bookshelves, Dad. As well as *The reign of Princess Naska*, you have collected several in similar decorative bindings, all published by Blackie.'

'That's right. Your grandfather owned a book of poems by Shelley one of a series of books published as The Red Letter library and the elegant art nouveau style of the book cover attracted me to read it. Years later when browsing in second hand book shops, I kept seeing more of the same. The stylised book covers stood out. So I started to collect them and learned about the artists who designed them, particularly Talwin Morris and his collaboration with Charles Rennie Mackintosh. My collection soon grew and now I have at least twenty.'

'Dad, I think they are quite valuable.'

'Good, take them. Enjoy them and hopefully one day you can sell them for a lot of money. I mean it Alex, it would give me a lot of pleasure.'

'Thanks, Dad.'

'If you decide to pop in before you drive back, there are other books I should like you to have. Just let me think about it and we can write down a list.'

Alex went to the window.

'A rather bleak day today, the clouds are hovering and rain is expected later. It is too cold to take you out into the garden. Shall we go downstairs and have coffee in the drawing room?'

Alasdair nodded as he raised himself with Alex's help and they spent the next hour enjoying each other's company in conversation and drinking coffee.

All too soon Alex had to leave for the drive to Aldeburgh. Alasdair remained in the drawing room and thoughts tumbled into his mind and he embraced them allowing his memories to circulate before concentrating on something or someone in his past. He closed his eyes.

From the middle of October the sound of guns is heard all around Moreton. As Alasdair saw himself as part of the community rather than apart, it wasn't a surprise when he announced to Ruth that he had asked Martin, Lord Rossiter's gamekeeper if he could join him on the occasional shoot on the estate and also up on the moors during the grouse season. He chose fine days to beat. It can be a bitter experience standing still in a wet field of stubble surrounded by a cold wind waiting for the guns to be in position, if the sun isn't shining.

Arriving early, Alasdair stood in the stable courtyard and looked out on a landscape of untroubled peace. The long moist furrows of the newly turned soil glistened under the golden autumn sun, contrasting with the pale yellow of the stubble fields and the grassy pastures where sheep clustered around their feeding troughs. There was no wind and the smoke rose straight from the farm chimney beyond the house.

The stable yard began to fill with an odd assortment of vehicles. Several had integrated dog crates and looking out were excited dogs. Most were English Springer Spaniels, but there was one black Labrador and he would accompany the men who would retrieve the birds. Everyone awaited instructions from Martin. They had all been doing this for years with the exception of one or two young boys who were with their Dads for a good day out and to earn pocket money. Those with dogs discussed their progress in recent field trials. Martin assembled everyone and described the areas to be covered during the day's shoot. An estate worker, arrived, driving a tractor towing a covered trailer to pick up the beaters. He was a tall muscular man in his late fifties wearing heavy boots and country coloured camouflage clothes with waterproof gaiters from waist to ankle buttoned at the sides. There were variations on this dress code. Alasdair had dressed carefully in order to fit in. While everyone waited, the driver sat on the low stone wall; he lit a cigarette and amused them with a tale about searching for truffles and how squirrels can search them out.

'I watched a squirrel on my lawn this morning, chased him off and then dug very carefully.'

He then gave an opinion on which truffles were best, but attention to what he was saying dwindled as Martin rallied the group into action.

Martin handed out radio handsets to those who needed to be in contact with him. Dennis handed out the flags made from plastic feed sacks stapled on to hollow plastic rods. The first drive of the day was Snowdrop Copse. The tractor led the trailer along the winding drive, over speed bumps and out onto the main road and towards the copse. Working groups were agreed with precise and clear instructions. Tom, a prepubescent youth, paired up with Jo and his father Rob, who used to be a gamekeeper and had two English Springer Spaniels with him. Ruby would work in the morning and Duke would remain in his Land Rover ready to work in the afternoon. Top dog was a black labrador called Ben whose grand-father, father and littler brother had been All England Field Trial Champions. Three drives were planned for the morning and two in the afternoon. It was a beautiful autumnal day towards the end of November.

The tractor turned left down a single track road and stopped. Rob and the young lads were dropped off at the top of the hill in a field of tall dried and decaying maize foliage. They would work down the field towards the copse working with Ruby to drive any birds feeding in the field. While driving in the field, they used their flags, which made loud whooshing noises when waved in swift and strong downward or sideways strokes. Ruby ran in and out of the maize never far from Rob's side.

The remainder were dropped further down. Once over the wire fence they spaced out every five yards and waited. Before they could start beating, the guns had to be in position. Then they started, working slowly through the wood beating the trees and fallen logs calling out and making as much noise as possible. The branches overhead created deep shadows as they walked among the dead leaves. Some imitated the sound of the pheasant call, some barked. The ground was covered in brambles and leaves, which had fallen downhill into mounds. The beaters made their way through an undergrowth of smaller trees under the canopy of larger beech trees. The drive included one of the feeding stations on the right flank which was surrounded by a low electric fence and beyond that a tall wire fence. This is where the birds were raised and some continue to return to feed and roost. All the time the beaters were working their way inwards, reducing the space between them, towards one area in the copse where the birds would have little choice than to fly. At this point a line of rope with long strips of plastic bunting was laid on the ground and for some obscure reason the birds won't cross it and so take flight. When the birds take flight they are still very high on the hill and the guns are a long way off far below. The guns never shoot at low flying birds, as it has to be a fair challenge and safe for the beaters.

About eight thousand had been reared and by the end of the season three thousand will have been shot. All are carefully picked up and later sold to a game merchant. At the end of each shoot, one of the estate workers collects the birds from the guns and retrievers; he loads them into crates on his quad bike and takes them straight to the cold store. The guns get to take home two brace of pheasant and four brace of partridge. On this day, the guns were all family and Lord Rossiter was looking forward to an enjoyable day. He only allows two lets during the season for paying guns and it is on these days that the estate recoups the cost of running the shoot together with the money made selling the game.

When the last birds flew out of the copse, Martin blew the horn to indicate to the guns to stop. The beaters were now altogether halfway down a steep hill and the tractor was waiting a good way off below. The descent wasn't easy for Alasdair, but he took advice and went for a longer but less steep descent. Both banks either side of the stream at the bottom were steep and muddy and already had huge, deep foot prints left by men ahead of him. Jo came to his rescue, a rather handsome young man with a thick mane of longish bright yellow hair and a freckled, rosy face. He climbed back down and jumped over the stream and took Alasdair's hand to lead him first down the bank, then to jump across. With the momentum of the jump he pulled Alasdair up the other side. He couldn't thank Jo enough. It would have damaged his pride not to have made it. Martin shouted from a short distance away.

'Well done, Alasdair! Ready for the next drive?'

'Hot coffee first!'

Then they all climbed into the trailer and sat very closely together on a hard u-shaped wooden seat; the dogs were lifted in by their scruffs. Rob drew out the grid for noughts and crosses in the mud on the floor of the trailer with his stick and drew a cross; Ben joined in. Dennis informed everyone, 'I am going down to Somerset next month to help on the Lydford Estate near Castle Cary. There is a wild boar causing problems locally. We are going to cull him. They say he is forty stone!'

He had everyone's attention.

A burly man called Arnold chipped in, 'My old friend Tom, years ago had an encounter with a boar. Their tusks are lethal. He has a scar from his ankle to his thigh!'

As he grimaced he spread his arms to indicate the size of the tusks. Arnold's hands were those of a man who worked in all weathers: they were bluish red in colour, thick skinned and very swollen. Alasdair looked around him and noticed that he was the only beater wearing gloves.

Dennis continued, 'The problem is they want us to stalk the boar, not drive him. What do you think of that?'

Tom frowned, 'Rather you than me, Rob.'

This led to an exchange of descriptions of past encounters with boar, elk and bear. Rob, it appeared had spent a season in Norway.

Two more drives and then lunch. Hot soup awaited them in the mess-room. The guns had lunch in the long room upstairs together with Lady Rossiter and her entourage, who had spent the morning at Harlow Carr Garden.

In the long room above the garages, there is a huge stone fireplace at one end from which a large deep orange flame rose from the logs burning. Martin joined the guns. Alasdair stayed with the men.

When Alasdair left for home, it was dusk and he passed the guns near the house, they were still picking up birds with their dogs. He waved to Lady Rossiter, who isn't really a country lady by nature, but there she was with Geoffrey helping. Alasdair left with warm feelings in his heart and elated with the pleasures he had experienced during this day in the life of a country estate. This was a day like any other during the past centuries of country pursuits by the gentry. Some things have changed like the quad bike making life easier for Martin and an electric fire in the mess-room. Alasdair changed his thoughts to home.

'The perfect end to this day will be a cup of strong tea together with hot toast oozing with butter and sitting by the fire with Ruth.'

He wondered how her day had been, she planned to spend the morning painting and then join the girls for lunch at The Mad Hatter in Masham. She had kept up with her friends from their days at Clifton College. Ruth retired from teaching ahead of Alasdair and spent long hours painting for her own pleasure, rarely selling her paintings. They adorned every space on the walls of their sitting room, up the stairs and beyond. Each year several would be hung at the Arts Society exhibition. She would take lots of photos in France and Scotland, where they spent their holidays and on their days out in the Dales. She had been working on a portrait of Susan from a photo taken last summer in their garden. She was sitting in a deckchair, bathed in pink sunshine wearing a large white sun hat. Even when

Ruth painted she dressed to a code learned during fifty years of being married to a Vicar. Her hair was tied back in a bun. She chose from a selection of dangly silver earrings, which reminded her of their bohemian days when art, philosophy and literature embraced their lives. Underneath her heavy dark green painting apron she would wear what people expected, a twin set and straight skirt with a kick pleat. Once she had applied mascara, blusher and lipstick, she would be ready to meet *her public*, whoever they were and whenever they rang the bell. Yes she would have time to paint before lunch.

He smiled as he thought about greeting her and looking into her smiling eyes and touching her. Their nights together were still something he looked forward to and afterwards he would curl up behind her stroking her long white hair until she slept and then he too would drift off to sleep. Going home felt good; it felt as good as it did, when they fell in love before he left for Cambridge.

He noticed that the bare branches of the trees were still as they stretched across the cold dark night sky pierced with stars. He couldn't wait to get home.

7

A BIRTHDAY

What? Happy?
Happy on your birthday . . .
When the slender tendrils of time's web
Dipped in fatal acids
Etch their tiny imprint on your cheek?

Happy?
Happy when each succeeding birthday
Dries but by a fraction . . . yet by a fraction . . .
The once immeasurable reservoir of youth
And the long green summer afternoons
Melt imperceptibly to dusk?

Happy?
When the serenity of your brow
Is stitched and pleated by sorrow's busy needle
And your mind is tired
But by a little . . . tired of revolving old questions
To which is found no answer?

Happy?
And now at last it is spoken . . .
When the heart can find only an instant less . . .
But an instant less . . . of passion?
Happy? Happy Birthday?

Yes. Happy.
Happy because you are a flame of life
And you are in my arms.

Through overcast skies, the golden sun tinged with pink cast a mellow light through the window where he was sitting downstairs reading the papers and browsing through magazines, which until now he would never ever have dreamed of reading and certainly not buying. He surprised himself by enjoying reading *Hello* and he was amused by the superficial layer of their lives that celebrities allowed readers to know about. It also shocked him that celebrities were paid by the magazine to intrude into their lives, mainly their wedding days.

He dozed rather than slept and thought about Frances, whom he had first met in the late eighties, when she and Edward moved into The Dower House. It wasn't long after Ruth's death that Edward moved to London and within a year they were divorced. Alasdair began to call around more often, knowing that Frances might like to see a friendly face. As time went on they often went for drives into the countryside where they could walk and he hoped she could relax. When she and the children moved to Ripon, it was much closer and easier for him to see Frances, especially to talk over her problems. He had tried to comfort her and advise when he could. There wasn't a time when Frances didn't have to face and cope with emotionally worrying issues, whether the sale of The Dower House, Edward moving to America and most upsetting of all, the escalating behaviour of the boys.

It was Philip who suffered most after the divorce. He just kept losing his temper and the older he got, the more physically aggressive he became. This affected Oliver because he often got the brunt of it with bruises, bumps and cuts. The boys spent several holidays in Florida with Edward and his new wife, which they both seemed to enjoy and therefore it wasn't surprising when Oliver announced that he would prefer to live in America. Philip wasn't asked whether he would like to do the same. There was obviously history between Philip and his father.

All the time, he had known Frances, he wished he could have just put his arms around her and held her. Did he love her? Yes he did. Just once he let his guard down. Just once he couldn't control his ardour. Was he disappointed when she rejected him. Yes, but in the long run he actually preferred their easy friendship. It wasn't at all complicated. It was honest and he was very fortunate to have her friendship now.

Now. Alasdair has to be brave. Knowing he is going to die. Adjusting to the certainty of death. Soon. He has to find the strength to put up his guard again in order to protect his family and friends. Doing so, helps him face his own fear.

One of his treatments since arriving at St Dunstan's that Alasdair looks forward to is a body massage. He had never experienced this before and was delighted how his body reacted to the gentle kneading hands of another human being working on the muscles of his shoulders, back, legs and arms. So, he was expecting a knock on the door and at the appointed time he was helped downstairs to the treatment room, gently lit with sweet smelling candles. After-wards, he was wrapped in a warm dressing gown and left to enjoy a cup of tea before returning to his room for a nap. He didn't want to be too tired when Frances arrived. Today is her birthday.

When Frances arrived just after four o'clock, he rose slowly from his chair and held out his arms to embrace her.

'Happy, happy birthday, darling,' before kissing her on both cheeks. Collecting his walking stick, he asked, 'Shall we have tea downstairs?'

Frances took his arm and they went down in the lift to the drawing room, where a table in the bay window was already laid out for tea. As they sat down, Alasdair asked, 'Afternoon tea or Champagne?'

A waitress was at hand to take their order and suggested, 'Champagne fits the occasion.' They smiled at her and nodded in agreement, before she turned away to bring a bottle of champagne together with a selection of sandwiches. Once the champagne was poured Alasdair offered a toast, 'I am honoured to be your friend and wish you happiness today and always.'

They clinked their glasses together and sipped Champagne.

'Thank you for the beautiful flowers you sent. I love the white roses and lilies with the blue eryngiums; they look extremely impressive on my mahogany side table.'

After tea, they returned to Alasdair's room, where he picked up a

52

wrapped item and handed it to Frances. 'I asked Alex to collect this from home. This is for you.'

Frances took the parcel and undid the tied ribbon and carefully removed the wrapping paper to reveal a book *The reign of Princess Naska.*'

'Thank you Alasdair.' She exclaimed, then she smiled and kissed him saying, 'It is a wonderful gift and I will treasure it.'

'It is a first edition. The binding was designed by Talwin Morris. Look closely and you can see his elongated monogram in the bottom right corner.'

Later, he took the familiar brown envelope from the drawer of the bedside table.

'Frances, I think it is time for a story. This time I shall read to you.'

He looked through his papers and smiled.

'Thelma will do nicely.' And he began to read aloud.

THELMA

One day Thelma was sitting dejectedly in the middle
of her cage; to a casual observer she might have
looked all right because she seemed to be munching
as usual, but really she was muttering to herself.
'I am a creature that moves, in predestinate
grooves, not a bus, but a tram.' She muttered
fretfully. 'Bred and born in a cage, nothing to
do, no means of self-fulfilment, no freedom...why
bother to do anything?'

Just then the lab technician, Arthur, opened her
cage, thrust in a large handsome male rat, and
quickly shut the cage again. Thelma's mood changed
abruptly. But this happy episode in Thelma's life was
not to last long; the male rat only wanted one thing
and once he had obtained it Arthur took him away
again. 'Damn!' said Thelma, 'I thought I was making a
bid for freedom, but now I see I was just being made
use of. The Rat!'

'But then come to think of it', she reflected 'he
didn't look much in command of the situation when
Arthur took him away again. More like a struggling
bean-bag actually.'

But in an incredibly short time Thelma began to have
an inward conviction that she was soon to have
company and already had a purpose. So she fussed
round her cage, which was in fact a pleasant and
commodious vivarium with all mod cons, and chose the
best corner of it, out of draughts and as far as
possible from enormous prying eyes, to build a
comfortable nest with the hay thoughtfully provided
by Arthur. And there she produced a healthy litter
of squirming blind pink babies and she loved them
and was happy.

For some days a Student had been coming to look at
Thelma from time to time and making notes. Thelma
thought the student was well-disposed but one day
she committed an outrageous act. She put her
enormous hand, as big as a small cat and yet oddly
like Thelma's own in its fragile boniness, into the
cage and deliberately lifted all the babies out of
their warm nest, placing them at the opposite corner
of the cage.

For a moment Thelma panicked. She rushed up and
down the cage, she stood on her hind legs and waved
her tiny hands impotently in the air, and she
screamed and cursed. Then she recollected herself.
She remembered her mother telling her that in
circumstances like this every true female rat
immediately carries all her babies back to the
nest. The Professor had said so in the Dreamtime.
So she did that. And the student made notes.

During the next few days the same thing happened
several times. Thelma couldn't count, but on the
fifth occasion something snapped. 'Right, that does
it', she said. 'Word of Professor or no Word of
Professor I am not carrying these children back
to the nest one more time.' So she set to work and
made a new nest round her offspring where they lay
at the wrong corner of the vivarium. 'That'll confuse
'em', she panted. 'They never guessed I'd think of
this. Now I <u>have</u> done something free and
unpredictable.'

Tired out with emotion and hard work, she curled
herself round her family in the new nest. The
student made more notes, grinning like a rat from
ear to ear. 'What a lovely smile' thought Thelma, 'I
believe she's pleased? I believe she's on my side...
or did she plan for me to do it? No, it's only
Professor who plans. I wonder if he did plan it
though...oh blast it all, can't I do <u>anything</u> of my
own free will?' She sighed, and curled up tighter.
'Oh what the hell,' she said. 'What does it matter? I
love my babies. Actually I quite love good old
reliable Arthur and that student. I suppose in a way
I even love Professor, without whose prevenient
grace I should never have been bred. Oh well.' She

fell asleep. A little later the Professor walked
into the lab and went over to Thelma. He looked at
her new arrangements with a baffled expression for a
few minutes and went away again. Thelma did not
notice him.

He paused, 'Frances, there is only one meaning to be extracted from this tale. Meanwhile many people see no meaning in it at all. But there is. That is what stories are for. To see, if you can see what they mean.

There is really no substitute for this. You either see what it means or you do not. And if you do not, you will not be changed by being told what it means. For example, imagine a curtain; when it is drawn Botticelli's Prima Vera is revealed. Now what do you say to someone who asks in all honesty, and it is the first time he has seen the picture, "Tell me why it is a masterpiece?". What can you say? Or imagine a man seeing *Hamlet* for the first time and asking the same question.

Picture a woman, side-saddle, on a black horse. Horse and rider are immaculately groomed, and without visible incitation the horse is performing a beautifully controlled passage. One either catches the breath or one doesn't. The picture bears its own authority over one, one freely admits one's captivation by it, or one doesn't.

I remember once hearing the trumpet virtuoso, Louis Armstrong play. He stood, with a group of ageing black men in what looked like a large aircraft hanger. It was full to capacity. He walked to the front of the stage, raised his trumpet to his lips, and blew eight notes. That was all he needed. Whatever meaning can be attached to the words *the blues*, that was its meaning. And, as he replied to a woman, who asked him, "Mister Armstrong, what is jazz?" "Ma'am if ya gotta ask ya'll never know."

Knowing and knowing that one knows and knowing that what one knows is significant, that is the basis of authority. And either one recognises this or one doesn't.'

'Alasdair, thank you for making my birthday special.' She rose and kissed his cheek.

'Time for me to go. I hope you have a comfortable night. Sweet dreams.'

'God bless you Frances.' He took her hand in his squeezing it gently. He then closed his eyes.

8

FALLING IN LOVE

Season of mists and mellow fruitfulness,
Close bosom-friend of the maturing sun;
Conspiring with him how to load and bless
With fruit the vines that round the thatch-eves run;
To bend with apples the moss'd cottage trees,
And fill all fruit with ripeness to the core;
To swell the gourd, and plump the hazel shells
With a sweet kernel; to set budding more,
And still more, later flower for the bees,
Until they think warm days will never cease,
For summer has o'er-brimm'd their clammy cells.

from *To Autumn* by **John Keats**

Alasdair had been reading a book by an eminent American psychiatrist in which he deprecates *falling in love*. He talked of *desire to cross ego-boundaries*, and so forth. Falling in love never lasts, he wrote as if that was a disadvantage.

Of course it doesn't, but then neither does a roller-coaster ride or a good dinner or writing a poem. Who on earth expects it to last! That's the last thing it does.

The trick is, of course, to make use of the momentum that falling in love gives. As the man says, the boundaries are down, so keep them down. You want to please the girl, so go on pleasing her. She will love it. It isn't a question of replacing the passion, it's reinforcement, an addition, an active working, not just at *learning to have things in common, doing things together, working at it*, as if a relationship was some sort of moral achievement. That really is dismal, just like the books that make love a moral achievement. They even make sex subservient to a *fulfilling relationship*, for God's sake!

Love isn't like that, but then, love isn't like anything. He believed that this author, like so many others was on the good old reductionism tramline; love is *translated* into religious terms or psychological terms or biological terms or whatever takes the man's fancy.

But then, this is typical of Western man in these days. Everything must be reduced so that it can be compassed by the human mind. There must be nothing beyond the reach of its' tentacles. For then it can all be controlled, ordered, synthesised, divided and reconstructed into whatever shape he pleases.

There must be nothing anarchic, nothing uncontrolled, nothing outside comprehension. And hence there must be no absolutes. For absolutes, and there can only be one Absolute, in the end, the Absolute prevents man from running every bloody thing and therefore screwing things up.

And this is the best thing in the world for us. Life, which is fully at our disposal, completely plastic in our hands, is a nightmare. It is the stuff of totalitarianism. We need to be possessed by what we know not. We need freedom to say 'I couldn't help it'.

Our age is possessed by a kind of pragmatic, positivistic puritanism. You can't really enjoy something, you can't really progress at something unless you are working at it, making it happen, making your ego–ideals come true. And you must never admit failure. Failure, properly interpreted by the reductionism method, simply means that your research is not as complete as you believed.

From all this we are delivered by falling in love. For perhaps a few brief, but wonderful hours, we are delivered from the depressing need to justify ourselves and released into a magical world in which poor men become rich and plain girls become beautiful and swineherds become desirable and cottages become palaces and beat up old Ford Escorts become chariots of the gods. We experience grace. We experience the given. It is the *giveness* that lies behind all life.

Alasdair was woken by a tap on the door followed by Adam entering, his arms full with a large bunch of Chrysanthemums from the darkest red to the palest pink.

'How are you Dad?' asked Adam as he approached the chair where Alasdair was resting and hugged him before he could stir and rise.

'Not too bad, Adam. It is lovely to see you, son.'

'I have ordered coffee for us, which will be waiting for us in the drawing room. Pity it is raining, far too cold to walk around the garden.'

'Right you are then. I'll just freshen up and we can go downstairs.'

When they were settled enjoying coffee, Alasdair asked, 'How is Trudy?'

'Very well. She sends her love together with the Chrysanthemums.'

'That's very kind of her. I will ask someone to put them in a vase. Has she finished her nurses training?'

'Her final exams are next year. I am very proud of her for changing career and doing something she really believes in.'

'What is Sarah up to?'

'I think I told you that she hated sixth form college right from the start of term. She had a long hard look at what she wanted to do and decided to apply as an apprentice in a precision engineering company in Ongar. She starts after Christmas.'

'Sounds like both the women in your life are doing just fine. What about you? How is business?'

'It's good. It took awhile to build up a client list after leaving the BBC, but winning the set design contract for a new drama series in the New Year will keep me very busy.

'Shall we move into the dining room. I am pretty sure they will be serving lunch soon?'

Adam nodded and they slowly re-traced their steps along the corridor and chose a vacant table in the dining room. Once they had ordered lunch from the menu, Alasdair remarked, 'June seems a distant memory, so much has happened recently. I did enjoy coming to stay and spending time with you all. We were lucky to get tickets for Matthew Bourne's *Swan Lake*. It was Sarah's reaction that surprised me. She couldn't stop talking about it afterwards and how beautiful the male swans were. I agreed.'

'She still talks about it. A very special memory for all of us, don't you think?'

'I certainly do Adam. Look here's lunch. Let's tuck in.'

They had both chosen steak and mushroom pie with broccoli and carrots served with a rich gravy. The crust was golden brown atop succulent braised beef, shallots and dark gilled mushrooms. It was piping hot. After they had cleared their plates, Alasdair leaned back into his chair and smiled at Adam.

'My goodness, that was delicious.'

'Agreed. Comfort food like this reminds me of my school days.'

'Yes, your Mother somehow managed to put wonderful mounds of good food on the table for us, despite having so little money. Do you remember helping in the kitchen garden when we lived near Ashington?'

'One year we had so much rhubarb that Mother was overwhelmed making jam and you ended up taking armfuls of the stuff to give to parishioners.'

They waited until the waitress had cleared their plates before Alasdair handed Adam the menu. He asked, 'Would you like dessert, Adam?'

'I'm too full. Couldn't eat another thing.'

They decided to move to the more comfortable chairs in the drawing room and ordered more coffee.

'Do you remember Walter, one of my oldest friends?'

'Not that I can remember, Dad.'

'He telephoned today and plans to visit next week. We were at Peterhouse College together.'

'Walter graduated a year ahead of me and was great fun. He was an eccentric, even then. He adopted his own style, while most of us were trying to fit in. He was tall and athletic in stature with a mop of light blonde hair and wore colourful waistcoats and matching bow ties. We often spent lazy afternoons punting on the River Cam discussing Russell and Satre. He was conscripted into the army and after the war, he was ordained and moved back to the South West.

He remains unmarried and a fine example of the contented bachelor, which today's conformists cannot fit into their pigeon-holes. To be at all respectable these days one must either be married, divorced, living with someone or be a homosexual of one kind or another. We kept in touch and then quite suddenly, he became deeply disillusioned with the Church around the time the Synod was debating the ordination of women and when the first women were ordained at Ely Cathedral, he took early retirement and became a Chaplain at an independent school. Anyway, he phoned today and is coming to see me next week.'

'Does Anthony know?'

'Yes, it's in the diary. Walter taught me a great deal about love. He would say, "Keep the momentum going, always remember, love is not something that you possess, that you dole out like a miser a bit at a time from your moth-eaten purse. Love is something that you must allow to possess you. Then you are never *working at it*, you are only letting it work through you. Believe me my friend, believe me, you will find that the passion, the madness, the possession of that first falling in love will be transmuted, the bubbles of champagne will still be there, I promise you, but the richness of the liqueur will mingle subtly with it." I have found his words to be true. Love is not something we have at our disposal. It is something we are at the disposal of. And this is not a moral or religious matter, it is the basis of all reality, of everything that exists and that makes sense. And it operates majestically in love between man and woman. It brings its own future. It shows what games to play. It tells what words to utter. It is uncontrived and unconditional. There is no learning without pleasure. And pain. But life will bring enough pain. You must bring the pleasure. There is no learning without desire. Desire is holy.'

'He sounds a rather interesting friend. Did he marry?'

'No, a confirmed bachelor and very happy. I am looking forward to seeing him.'

Once the coffee cups were cleared away, Adam suggested they put the television on to catch the latest news. They agreed and sat silently and contentedly.

The next day Adam arrived shortly after ten o'clock. He was pleased to see that his father was already dressed and sitting contently in the armchair listening to the radio and reading the Sunday Telegraph, which had been separated into topics of interest and the majority leisurely discarded.

Adam looked out at the garden beyond and bent over his father kissing him lightly on the cheek.

'Good morning, Father. I love this time of year, the sun filtering through the morning mist.' Adam picked up one of the discarded sections of the paper and sat down on the sofa.

'Thanks for popping in. Don't stay long. I know you will want to get off and avoid the weekend traffic back into London. Would you like coffee?'

'No thanks, Dad, I've already had plenty of coffee this morning over breakfast.'

A nurse came in to enquire whether Adam would be staying for lunch with his father and Alasdair replied, 'Not today, he has a long journey home to Chiswick, but thank you for suggesting it.'

After she left, Alasdair turned to Adam and asked, 'Most of us look back to earlier days and remember long summers, do you think it is a trick of the mind, willing ourselves to pick out the best bits. One summer, I remember so well when we first moved to York and for the first time we could afford a proper holiday. We went to Buttermere in The Lakes. Do you remember?'

'Of course I do. That was the year Alex, Anthony and I went out onto Crummock Water on our own in the sailing dinghy; the water got choppy and we all ended up in the water and if I remember, Mother was furious because she had to wash all our clothes.'

Alasdair smiled and reflected on the contrast of images during their journey across the Pennines as they left the grey stone outcrops of the Yorkshire Dales driving passed Kirkby Stephen towards the gentle landscapes of The Lakes.

His thoughts were interrupted by Adam.

'Time for me to go, Dad. I need to get onto the A1 before the weekenders head south.' Adam got up and put on his coat and then gave his father a good long hug.

'Thank you, son. Give my love to your gorgeous girls.'

'Yes, Dad. I will be up again next weekend.'

Whenever he sees the boys, Alasdair in the quietness of solitude reflects on the past. He wants to remember, to cherish the memory and re-live it in glorious technicolour. It wasn't long after Adam left that his thoughts drifted back to Ruth.

Even now, he chuckled to himself about the secret he and Ruth had kept all these years from family. It was the day he and Ruth had a civil wedding long before their church wedding when he reached the age of twenty-five, a stipulation of the Church of England and the age at which a newly ordained priest could marry.

That morning, he and Ruth together with her friend Peggy and Walter met outside the registrar's office in Hartlepool Borough Hall. Ruth looked like a summer morning, with her golden hair and blue eyes and fresh bloom on her cheeks. Her hair was coiled into a French pleat and for all of her five feet she looked elegant in a fitted light wool suit, the shade of pale lavender. She and Peggy both wore corsages made by Ruth from roses collected from her landlady's garden. When they had all greeted each other, Ruth gave Alasdair and Walter matching button holes. It was all over so very quickly that they decided on brunch together before heading off in their separate ways. Alasdair and Ruth caught the train to Seaham where they stayed for two nights at a small guest house on the harbour.

They managed to see each other at least once a week, depending on petrol rationing. It didn't seem a hardship as so many others were suffering in much harsher ways. They were happy and Alasdair had done the right thing by Ruth and in spite of his chosen vocation. With the energy of youth and enthusiasm for fun they made love anywhere they could laughing and playing. He chasing her, catching her, leaping on the bed and very often falling off the bed.

Yet all this while their happiness was compartmentalised and separate from the anguish and worry they both experienced in those years when the country was suffering and the war dragged on.

Hartlepool had suffered during the 1930's, but now the country needed ships and it brought prosperity to the town. It also became a target for German raids, something that was always on Alasdair's mind back in Thornley.

It was at this time that the United States made a dominant material contribution to the war effort by supplying aid to Russia and Britain and creating great air and naval armadas. Alasdair's brother Richard was serving in the Royal Navy protecting the convoys. His occasional letters home gave some news but mainly they relied on the radio broadcasts. The Italians yearned to escape from the war and Fascism. In July 1943 the Allies began to disembark from an armada of war-ships on the coast of Sicily and the Italians offered little resistance on the beaches. The Germans fought on holding the Allied soldiers at bay for five weeks before retreating. Mussolini was arrested later that month.

9

THE DEEPEST LOSS

Death is nothing at all,
I have only slipped away into the next room.
I am I, and you are you,
Whatever we were to each other, that we are still.

from *All is Well* by **Canon Henry Scott Holland**

It was a few weeks after the service at the Crematorium that Alasdair collected Ruth's ashes. They had decided a while ago that they would both be cremated. It was Alasdair's wish to be laid to rest by the West door of St Lawrence's, but there wasn't room for a burial plot, just enough space for a small plaque and room beneath for their ashes. He had chosen a slab of Yorkshire stone and the stonemason at Ripon Cathedral had carved a reeded border with scrolls in each corner and below a simple cross were the words 'Beloved wife and mother' with her name and dates. There was space underneath for his details when the time came.

On that dreadful evening, Ruth and Alasdair had enjoyed a really good *Toad in the Hole* for supper and like a good'un he went to make a pot of tea and wash the dishes while she settled down to watch the BBC News. He had been gone barely ten minutes, when he returned to the sitting room. He placed the tray on the small low table in front of the fire and picking up a cup for Ruth, he turned towards her thinking she was dozing and said,

'Ruth, darling.'

But she looked so still and didn't look up, so he put the cup of tea back on the table and knelt down beside her, putting his hand on hers.

'Ruth? Darling?' There was no response and so Alasdair put his face even closer and repeated,

'Ruth?'

He then checked her breathing and when finding none, checked her pulse by placing a finger firmly to the side of her throat under her chin and waited a few seconds. He then knew she was dead. Alasdair took Ruth's' hand, put his lips to her ear and spoke firmly, purposely and without shouting,

'Darling, darling. My darling, I love you so much.'

At first panic swept through him followed by a shudder reaching the pit of his stomach. He kissed her. Then he stretched his body taught raising his head backwards before letting out a silent howl. Crumbling into an embrace on her lap, he sobbed.

He didn't rush to call Dr Muir. He just wanted to remain still with Ruth, a few minutes respite before the inevitable. When Alasdair finally called Dr Muir, he suggested he call the Ambulance Service as he was sure that a sudden death would require investigation. What he meant was a post-mortem.

He phoned each of the boys. The next few days were a blur. Friends rallied round and all the arrangements for the funeral went well, but after all the activity there was left this empty, painful space. Adam and Alexander stayed as long as they could before making their tracks homeward. Anthony stayed another night with his father.

Parishioners helped him during the next months. One of the Church Wardens phoned around and soon diary dates were agreed to make sure that Alasdair had little time to worry about such mundane things as shopping and cooking. A rota was adopted for *dropping in* to see him. It seemed to him, that they also had internal twenty minute alarm clocks. Their company was welcomed as was their understanding for the need for privacy and time to mourn.

Alasdair stayed on at Moreton just long enough for his tenants in York to move out and make arrangements to move back home. Without Ruth he realised that he didn't have the energy to engage with Lord Rossiter, whenever he lost his temper. It was time to let someone else take the reins. He had received the diagnosis just days before Ruth's death, Chronic Myeloid Metaplasia. He wasn't sure what it really meant, was it cancer, would it develop into cancer? He needed to call Dr Muir and ask more questions, but things got in the way and the days passed and he hadn't told Ruth. Now he would telephone Dr Muir.

It was gone twelve, when he roused himself from his thoughts. Anthony and Susan would be here at six o'clock and that left a large gap to fill. He decided to have lunch in his room and settle down and read *Three Men in a Boat*. He knew the story well and enjoyed Jerome K Jerome's prose. A good decision because he passed the time in good humour and with the help of the nursing staff was comfortable and experienced no pain. For a time he was oblivious to his fate.

On the dot of six, there was a knock on his door as Anthony followed by Susan came in to see him. There was much embracing and smiling. Susan busied herself with arranging the flowers she had brought for Alasdair.

'They look lovely Susan. Thank you.'

'I've ordered tea to be served in the dining room Dad, after *Songs of Praise*, hope that's OK?'

'Of course. I could do with getting out of this chair. I have been reading all afternoon. Good to have a change of scene.'

Alasdair felt stiff and awkward as he rose from the armchair with the help of Anthony. He needed his support. He was looking forward to watching *Songs of Praise*, he never used watch it, but since coming to St Dunstan's it had become a a regular highlight of his week. He enjoyed watching it with Anthony and Susan rather than on his own too.

Supper was always a cold buffet. The main hot meal of the day was at lunchtime. Later in the evening Alasdair would have hot chocolate. He rarely had the biscuits offered as he had so many lovely treats to choose from given to him by visitors.

They chose a table by a window, and Susan fetched a selection of sandwiches cut into delicate triangles to share. Later she returned with small bowls filled with a selection of blueberries and raspberries topped with a generous dollop of Greek yoghurt.

A pattern had emerged for Anthony and Susan to visit on Sundays and join him for supper and Alasdair looked forward to this certainty in his routine. His daily routine was planned by the staff at St Dunstan's and with each day came new surprises as his friends visited and talked about the past. They were careful not to talk about their futures. He spent long periods thinking and listening to music. The days were passing far too quickly.

After supper, a nurse helped Alasdair to his room to monitor his pain and attend to his personal hygiene and help him change ready for bed. Once done, she returned to see Anthony and Susan.

'You can go up now. Reverend Sommersby is comfortable.'

They went upstairs to say goodbye to Alasdair. He looked refreshed.

'Susan,' he said, 'before you go, come and sit closer.' He beckoned her to join him on the sofa.

'You will enjoy this story.' Alasdair handed her the sheets. 'Would you like to read it?'

She looked over the pages and relaxing into the sofa, smiled at him.

'Yes, of course I will.' She read *The Wolves* aloud.

THE WOLVES

In the winter of 1870, I was visited by an old
friend, a carefree young bachelor named, Vasili
Lermontov. We had been students together before he
left St Petersburg to manage the family estates
after the sudden death of his father.

After greeting one another, I could not help but
notice his agitation which, coupled with an air of
suppressed excitement, made me sure that something
and something of an amatory nature was in the air.

And indeed, as soon as supper was over, he poured out
his story. It seemed that he had become infatuated
with the charming wife of a neighbouring Count
Sergei Czernovsky. I was not in the least surprised
at this, as he was notorious for his amours in our
student days. But I was afraid that he had bitten off
more than he could chew, for the Count was a huge
man, wildly devoted to the hunt, who possessed a fine
collection of rifles and a pack of huge Russian
wolfhounds, and who was moreover, insanely jealous
of his pretty wife.

The particular madness that had seized Vasili was
this; he had long wished to present his beloved
with a beautiful diamond necklace, which he had
inherited from his late grandmother. It was a
magnificent piece of jewellery, and moreover, very
large, wreathing rather the shoulders than the neck
of its happy wearer.

The problem was, of course, how to deliver this
necklace to his inamoratas in such a way that the
Count would have no suspicion as to its origin. So
the two idiots had hatched themselves a plot. She
was to tell her husband that an old aunt at Vlaminsk,
some seventy or eighty miles away, had left her this

necklace. She was to do this while her lover was
present, and he would suggest that, as he had
business near Vlaminsk, he could pick up the
jewellery and deliver it to her. Thus, they fondly
believed, suspicion would be allayed and she would
possess a gift which would always remind her of the
man she loved.

I at once saw a thousand objections to this plan and
indeed, begged Vasili to abandon it. To no avail, he
was convinced that nothing could possibly go wrong
and took his departure the next day with a happy
smile on his lips.

And so the days passed. Until, one morning, I was
awakened by my manservant who said that he had sad
news for me It appeared that Vasili was being driven
in his sleigh by his groom at night through the
forest when they were attacked by a pack of wolves
maddened by hunger during the hard winter. Both men
were torn to pieces.

After I had recovered a little, my mind went back
to our last meeting and I said to my man, 'Did you
hear that anything was found on or near the sleigh?'
To which he replied that he had heard nothing of
that.

A fortnight later, business took me near the estate
of Count Sergei and I determined to visit him on the
strength of a meeting some months before, to see
what I could learn. For, I must admit I was curious
to see his wife, whom I had not met so far.

The Count welcomed me affably enough and invited me
to supper. At that meal, his wife was present. How
pale she looked, how drawn. 'You must excuse my wife,'
said the Count, 'We have lost a very dear friend in a
tragic way and naturally, she is most upset.' Supper
passed in an atmosphere of some restraint, quite
understandable. And after it, the Count turned to his
wife and said, 'My dear, a very strange thing has
happened. I have not told you so far, but I want to
prepare you for some sad, but at the same time,
amazing news. This morning, my chief huntsman called
upon me to ask me to follow him. I did so and he led

71

me to the courtyard. 'Master', he said. 'Last night
we killed a huge white wolf and I would like you to
see it.'

'I walked over to where the beast lay on the cobbles
and there, my dear, lay the largest wolf I have ever
seen, limp in death. But there was something stranger
still, much stranger. But you must both come and see
for yourselves.'

Clothing ourselves in our fur cloaks, we followed
him into the courtyard. There, holding a torch was
his chief huntsman. And before him on the ground was
the form of a huge white wolf.

It was at that moment that I stepped back in amazed
horror. Fastened round the neck of the great beast
was a string of fire that danced in the torchlight
and glowed with an inner depth of splendour. It was
the great diamond necklace. The Count's wife fainted.

I am still a comparatively young man, but there are
some things I know. I know that it is extremely rare
for wolves, even hungry wolves, to attack human
beings. I know that the Count was a very astute and
cunning man. And I know that wolves do not fasten
necklaces round their own throats.

10

CAMBRIDGE DAYS

Companionships,
Friendships, acquaintances, were welcome all;
We sauntered, played, we rioted, we talked
Unprofitable talk at morning hours,
Drifted about along the streets and walks,
Read lazily in lazy books, went forth
To gallop through the country in blind zeal
Of senseless horsemanship, or on the breast
Of Cam sailed boisterously, and let the stars
Come out, perhaps without one quiet thought.

Cambridge Days by **William Wordsworth**

Alasdair was groomed and dressed early today as he expected Walter to arrive sometime around eleven o'clock. He had plenty of time to read *The Daily Telegraph*. He wasn't tired but didn't want to start reading a book and become engrossed when Walter arrived, so he amused himself by looking through his personal papers to find something amusing and short to read. He had several poems written by Rose and he pulled out one written in her large rather childish hand in green ink. He smiled as he remembered their time together. She had ambivalent feelings about their love affair. She knew it was wrong. She properly called it *sinful*, and yet she enjoyed it so much she felt that somehow, on another sort of plane in another dimension of judgement, it really wasn't all that bad. It was naughty, very, very naughty, but not absolutely culpable.

Many educated women would share her feelings. The poem has a
nice Tudor ambience about it.

> When treason willed that you and I should love
> Then did the Saints in airy realms above
> Avert their eyes and say, 'No harm is there
> For reason reigns and they'll from sin forbear!'
> And when they saw with Love we'd made a pact
> To arm ourselves against the lure of th'act,
> Not to submit, but only in the mind,
> Thus thwarting sin that hovers close behind,
> They cried, ''Tis well, we need not supervise.'
> But when we crept with stealth and reaching arms,
> To dally there awhile with love's sweet charms,
> Whispering, ''Tis but a moment's thing, we'll not stay long,
> For we are mindful of the Sirens' song.'
> The Saints in discontent cast down their gaze
> And saw we'd tricked them with our artful ways,
> In wrath did they then shake their fists and cry
> 'This wayward pair shall with our law comply!
> Let's make them by their conscience be beset
> Lest like those other lovers they forget,
> Who played until the serpent brought them shame
> And gorgon-headed guilt turned sour their game!'

Walter and Alasdair were at Peterhouse together and he was the
most accomplished student with a punt that Alasdair had known. He
handled it like the gondoliers handle their boats, with a long drive
leaning on the pole corresponding to the beautiful sweep of the oar,
followed by a graceful adjustment of the long pole lying on the surface
of the water to set the boat's head in the right direction.

He loved to punt, and the boathouse men would trust him to take
out a boat in the worst of weathers. He liked, of course, to show off,
but he also wanted the challenge of having an unwieldy craft like a
punt at his command.

Alasdair rather envied him. Mind you, he would not have been anyone but himself. He was perfectly happy with his own inhibitions and doubts and self-deprecation, for in those days at university at eighteen, many took life with immense seriousness. They discoursed on imponderables into the small hours finding poetry and philosophy in their relationships.

He was happy to have gone through the angst of the old-fashioned bohemian student days. He never mixed with the moneyed set, or with the sporting set, apart from a little desultory pistol shooting. Nor did he find rowing attractive. But he did love to argue. He did love to read. He and his friends imagined themselves, in youthful pride and naivety, almost as if they were thinkers and artists of Montmatre, oscillating between carefree love of life and the drama of searching for *The Meaning of It All.*

The sense of those days never left him. He remains that romantic youth who asked impossible questions about life and about behaviour, the boy who refused to conform and the lad who wanted the world to echo his own dreams and to shape itself after his own imaginings.

No, he did not at all wish to be Walter, but he did want to be like him. He envied him his physical presence, his fine physique and his effortless charm, which was the nicest thing about him. It was utterly unselfconscious, and he never knowingly manipulated people. He was simply naturally loveable. And he had a confidence in himself which contained no hint of cockiness or contempt for others.

He had a fine mind, not scholarly or academic, but highly intelligent and influenced by a kind of secret intuition which prevented him from making the kind of mistakes that intelligent people make, mistakes resulting from relying too much on the deliberations of the conscious mind.

They have seen each other regularly over the years, more so since Ruth died, taking it in turns to travel the distance between York and Crowthorne in Berkshire. Alasdair hopes he won't be too tired so he can enjoy the day with his good friend. As Alasdair counts down the last days of the winter of his life, some mornings he finds it difficult to raise his spirits. The nurses have been wonderful with pain relief and the odd cuddle when he cannot hold back his tears. Sometimes, he doesn't want to stop the tears and in privacy sobs until he feels better. A good cry is a very good thing.

Alasdair expected Walter's visit to be his first and last since moving into St Dunstan's. Nothing he could do, but accept the inevitable.

A nursing assistant popped her head around the door and informed Alasdair, 'Reverend Walter Hardy has arrived. He is in the drawing room.'

She waited for Alasdair to raise himself and then helped him to the lift and then into the drawing room.

Walter was standing, looking out of the window. He turned and strode towards Alasdair, arms open wide grinning.

'Hello, hello my dear friend. How are you Alasdair?'

At once realising this wasn't the best of questions, he didn't wait for a reply and hurriedly changed the subject. 'What a lovely autumnal day.'

They embraced warmly and Walter held onto Alasdair's arms as they drew away slightly to observe each other. Walter then took Alasdair's arm and led him to an alcove furnished with two armchairs and they sat down.

'How was your journey?'

'It would have been tedious by train, so at the last minute I decided to drive up yesterday and stay at The Crown Hotel in Harrogate. I arrived in time to have a good look around before supper and then got a good night's sleep.'

From his briefcase, he produced two copies of *The Times* and handed one to Alasdair.

'For later, I thought we could have fun seeing who finishes first.'

Alasdair laughed out loud, it was something they had been doing for years and it felt good to be with Walter again.

'Walter, what would you like, tea or coffee?'

'Perhaps later. I did wonder if you wrap up warmly we might go for a drive. What do you think?'

'You don't need to ask me twice. I'll just ask one of the nurses to help me get ready. You stay here, it won't take too long.'

It took just under fifteen minutes before Alasdair returned helped by a nurse with his silver topped walking stick in his hand. Walter took his other arm and they walked slowly out of St Dunstan's to Walter's car, which he had moved from the car park to the entrance.

'Where would you like to go, Alasdair?'

'Not too far, how about Ripley? We could have coffee at The Boar's Head, they are bound to have a fire blazing.'

'Right you are. Lets go cross country and come in via the Pateley Bridge Road.'

'Fine.'

Once they were underway, it was Alasdair who interrupted the silence by asking him,

'How are things, old man? Is retirement in view?'

'No plans, it keeps me active being with the students. I am only at college two days a week and they are not full days. I don't feel stretched at all. For me it is a good balance as I have plenty of time for other interests.'

Alasdair sighed and fell silent, looking out at the landscape and feeling the sun on his face through the window. He was pleased to see Walter.

They were back at St Dunstan's in good time for lunch and soon enjoying a glass of Shiraz while they waited to be served.

It was Walter who began to talk about their days at Cambridge, their camaraderie during late nights studying for exams. Sometimes Walter came home with him to Ryhope and stayed a few days during the summer vacation. Most poignantly, he was a witness at Alasdair's civil wedding ceremony when he and Ruth married in secret after he left Peterhouse and was a Curate in Thornley. The secret had bonded their friendship for life.

'I'm sorry you have had to cope with your illness without Ruth. You have done remarkably well to fight on.'

'Yes, it's no use pretending. I miss her with a passion. She has always been at my side. She still is. I am taking my last journey with her and towards her.'

Walter looked away leaving Alasdair to his thoughts about Ruth.

As younger men, they mostly talked about love and so it wasn't too long before Alasdair broke the silence.

'We would all probably agree that it's love that makes life worth living. But how do you get love? Can you buy it? Well, like the Beatles told us, *Money can't buy me love*. Nor can anything else buy me love. You can't buy it with loyalty. It's no use going to the general manager or the headmaster or the bishop or whoever and saying, "But look, I've given you all these years of service and loyalty . . . I've done unpleasant things for you and the firm . . . stood by you . . . backed the company up." Don't think it will cut any ice when the crunch comes and you are expendable. And the hardest thing to learn is that you can't buy love with self-sacrifice. A lot of mothers and fathers say, "Jennifer . . . after all we've done for you . . . the sacrifices we've made . . . denied ourselves . . . and THIS is your response!" It's no good. You can't buy love with anything . . . not even with love. We are free . . . really free . . . and love can only be given freely or it's not love.'

'Well said. I have nothing to add, Alasdair.'

Alasdair saw that the waitress was on her way over to their table with two steaming plates.

'Look, lunch has arrived.'

Walter raised his glass.

'To us both. To Ruth. To Peterhouse. To friendship.'

'Not forgetting, love.' Added Alasdair.

'Of course, now let's tuck in.'

They looked at the sausages, mash and steaming hot onion gravy on their plates. Alasdair passed the apple chutney to Walter and they ate in silence. When they had finished Walter took a sip of the Shiraz, sat back in his chair.

'That was yummy. Much appreciated Alasdair. I won't have pudding or I will fall asleep driving home. Please don't let me stop you.'

'I won't either. Let's just have coffee and stay here a while.'

Coffee was served with a small saucer of chocolate truffles. The time had flown by and it was already passed two o'clock. Walter wanted to be on the road soon to miss the southward bound traffic on the M18 and beyond back to the genteel Berkshire country-side and home. He was on his way home by three o'clock and happy that he had made an effort to see his old friend. He was content, although saddened in the knowledge that he would not see Alasdair alive again.

'Damme it!' he thought as he started to drive away. 'We forgot to do the crossword.'

After Walter left, a nurse brought Alasdair a cup of sweet tea in his room and made him comfortable. Seeing Walter brought his memories of Cambridge to mind and they were clearer now than for many years.

One day with Jacob Aaronson, he had sat in his study, under the calm gaze of Maimonides, one of the most prolific and influential Torah scholars of the middle ages. They had been talking about the Exile and the effect it had had on Jewish consciousness. That when disaster strikes there are three possibilities open to the believer, if he is truly and absolutely concerned with making sense of life with respect to the meaning of God. He can admit that he was wrong about his expectations of God, that the kind of God he trusted in was not consonant with the reality of the experience he finds himself undergoing. And so he can go after the gods of the people who have conquered him, or perhaps give up all belief in any kind of god at all.

Or he can decide that the appalling disaster that has befallen him has happened because he has, in some way or other, offended the true God of his belief. He has not obeyed the voice of the Lord his God. Israel had not fulfilled the Torah of God and the Exile was the consequence. To make things right, Israel must set up a system of obedience which would reflect the love that God had for Israel and the love which Israel in turn owed God.

Or he can decide that the suffering is undeserved, that there is nothing in Israel's history or behaviour commensurate with the horror that has materialised. It has occurred because of the unscriptural will of God. But the Day of Reckoning will come. One Day. God will act. The heavens will be folded up like a scroll, the Messiah will appear, the enemies of Israel will bite the dust, and the Chosen People will live for ever in the New Promised Land.

Alasdair remembered calling these attitudes the *What a fool I've been* attitude; the *Well I screwed it that time* attitude, and the *Just you wait* attitude. They reflect the three responses to disaster that are common to all periods of human history, negativism, picking up the bits and trying again, and wish–fulfilment fantasy to give you strength to bear the unbearable presence.

Jacob added the possibility of a fourth attitude which might be adopted when disaster strikes, which was to see a redemptive purpose in facing suffering with love. To see a means whereby a situation can be transformed if suffering can somehow be associated with loving. It does not mean mere acceptance, or fatalism. It is an attitude, a response, which contains the irrational hope . . . as irrational as the evil which brought the disaster . . . the hope that good can come out of evil, evil itself can be transformed, if love can be injected into the dynamics of the situation.

Now, if this is so, if this is the lesson to be learned from disaster, there are some far–reaching results. The Jews, whatever their faults always took history seriously, because history in space and time is the sphere in which man uses his freedom in irreversible decision. Their history began with the giving of freedom in the Exodus and the journey into the future was concretised by the promise to inherit and inhabit a land of their own.

At the Exile it seemed that that promise was revoked. The Land, and everything that went with it, simply passed from their possession. They lost the physical possession of vineyards and olive–yards. They lost their holy Temple, the earthly guarantee of God's presence. They lost their royal line of Kings, the Anointed of the Lord. And, most importantly of all they lost the sense of their particularity, of their uniqueness, of their being specifically under the protection and guidance of their God.

Alasdair was surprised that his memory was so good. Although resting for long periods, he was finding it easy to recall the past and somehow it was more important than the present. He was busy dying.

He noticed his tea was now too cold to drink. He looked out at the garden beyond and thought to himself, 'I am tired and feel an overwhelming heaviness. There is a longing for rest, even if it be the rest of the grave.'

11

THE HOLY LAND

Jerusalem is built of gold
Of crystal, pearl and gem;
Oh fair thy lustre manifold,
Thou fair Jerusalem.

from *The Holy City, New Jerusalem*
by **Christina Georgina Rossetti**

Alasdair and Frances were enjoying drinking hot chocolate together and listening to the news on Radio 4.

'Frances, shall we liven up and listen to Lars Edegram and his New Orleans All Stars. I am sure you bought me a CD when we saw them in July at the Harrogate Music Festival.

Frances got up. 'We really did well this summer getting to see his concert, *Take me back to New Orleans*. It was energetic and good fun.'

'Before you sit down, Frances, would you kindly get the dictionary and look up *coruscate*? How I hate to look for a word, it is an admission of abject failure.'

'Here it is. Sparkle? Flash? Glitter? It seems to allude to wit. Any help?'

'Nicely, thanks. Look.' Alasdair penciled in *sparkling* and read out the next clue.

This lifted his spirits.

'The word I struggled with, I remember the Latin 'coruscus silvis' and I remember the long, lazy afternoons and the buzzing of a coming poem in my head and the Latin master holding his Virgil and the sweet thought of the bell going soon and then out onto the playing field and the feel of the running spikes and the effortless lap after lap and the exhilaration of being sixteen and fit and in love with the Classics and in love with Sybil Cartwright. Alas, she never really loved me. I came home from holiday with my parents and brought with me my first love-gift, a small silver necklace with a cultured pearl attached. When we met and before I had a chance to offer it to her, she began to talk about a Swedish boy, visiting England whom she had met. She seemed to go on for ever about his good looks and charm. It was my first taste of rejected love. I behaved well, bowed out of her life, cut my losses and gave the necklace to my mother. Many, many years later, I met her again. She was middle-aged, a teacher and married. We never spoke of the Swede whose name is branded in my memory, it was Bengt. She had, I am sure quite forgotten. But the memory was as alive to me as was this morning's breakfast.'

Frances laughed. 'Definitely, Sybil's loss. More tea?'

'All the time I have been fighting cancer, you and I have been good friends. We could have been more than good friends. Do you regret our not being lovers, Frances?'

'In some ways, of course. It would have been fun. No doubt about it. But it would have tied me down. You would have been a pleasant distraction, but I would have wanted more of you than you could have given me.'

'Well, that's that then. I thought I would ask.'

'Come on we have had lots of good times. Do you remember that conference in Oxford for school chaplains?'

'Yes, you were planning a garden tour business and when I told you I was going down, you suggested we could go together. You were going to research the itinerary for an Oxford based trip.'

'That's right, I stayed in a rented cottage in Minster Lovell and visited the gardens in and around Oxford, while you stayed in college rooms. We had supper one evening at The Old Swan Hotel in Minster Lovell. Then we had lunch together at The Radcliffe before driving back to Yorkshire.'

'Such a shame it didn't take off. Was marketing the problem?'

'Not sure putting an advertisement in the Yorkshire Post warrants a marketing campaign. I just didn't have enough money to spend on getting it off the ground. The idea was good and now there are lots of small companies specialising in garden tours. Another idea was organic dog food. Trust me, one day someone will start a business selling tins of organic dog food.'

'I'll pass on that one.'

'Sorry, Alasdair, that was unkind of me. It's very hard to get used to the idea that you are facing the end of your struggle with cancer.'

She moved closer and snuggled into his arms and laid her head on his shoulder. Neither tried to stop their tears.

Thou art a gift to me to enhance my creativity
and strengthen my apprehension of the Truth;
Be not miserly with your intellect for it enriches mine.

My love is as a waterfall fed by the mountain
torrent of your heart and mind. Or like the flowers
of the desert awaiting the inundation of your desire.

Give me my mind
and I'll give you my body and heart,
and both shall overflow.

A knock on the door. A nurse entered and informed Alasdair that Lady Rossiter had arrived and was waiting in the drawing room.

'Wonderful. Please tell Lady Rossiter I will come downstairs directly.'

Alasdair had dressed with care. He had shaved and trimmed his moustache and beard to a rather stylish shape similar to how Sir Roy Strong presents himself. He liked the finished result. He put a warm yellow polo necked sweater under his tweed jacket which had flecks of yellow in the weave and chose a pair of light grey trousers with brown brogues. With his silver topped walking cane for balance, he set off slowly with the nurse towards the lift and down to the drawing room.

Jacqueline was sitting on a sofa in one of the bay windows of the oak panelled room looking ravishing in a Coco Channel styled woollen bright pink jacket. She immediately got up and walked towards Alasdair to greet him.

'Darling Alasdair.' She very lightly embraced him and he wasn't sure who was the more fragile of the two of them. She took his arm and led him towards the place where she had been sitting.

'I have requested coffee. Is that alright?'

'Perfect. It is so nice to see you. Let's sit down and you can tell me everything.'

Jacqueline pointed to the table where a tall rigid white designer carrier bag was overflowing with white dahlias and Japanese anemones and pale blue clouds of ceanothus. In a separate posy were floribunda white roses. She handed them to the nurse.

'Could you please arrange for someone to refresh the flowers in Reverend Sommersby's room?'

'Certainly your Ladyship.' She inhaled the sweet fragrance of the roses and then turned on her heels and left them alone.

'Jacqueline, thank you so much, they will look lovely in my room.'

'I am particularly pleased to have been able to bring you roses, the generous Iceberg came into flower again just a few days ago.'

After the coffee arrived, Jacqueline enquired of Alasdair, 'So Alasdair, who has been to see you?'

He was relieved her opening question completely ignored the state of his health. He sat well back into the chair resting his head.

'Walter Hardy came yesterday. We were at Cambridge together. He was great fun then and it did me good to reflect with him on happy times.'

He told Jacqueline about life in Cambridge during the early 1940's and how it had defined his life ever since.

When they had finished their coffee, he said, 'That's enough from me, I want to hear your news.'

She thought for a moment. She knew Alasdair knew an awful lot about her current predicament, which had been going on for months. He had been at her home with Geoffrey and his lawyer, when she had first voiced concerns about their future together and had proposed a divorce.

She sighed. 'There is certainly pressure on me to forgive Geoffrey and patch up our marriage. If I believed he would stop seeing her, it would help, but he seems besotted and they have been seen socially together on more than one occasion.'

'A leopard doesn't change his spots, Jacqueline. You must think of your own happiness. Take your time. Don't let anyone pressure you into a decision.'

'Yes, I know you're right. As you know everything is tied up in a Trust and financially it would be difficult for me.'

She noticed Alasdair tiring. 'Shall I help you back to your room?'

'Yes, please.' As he rose from the chair, she took his arm. When he entered his room his face lit up with pleasure at the sight of the abundance of flowers in several vases gracing the room. Jacqueline looked pleased.

'Perfect with the Toile de Jouy. I thought so.'

'Where to now?'

'I need to prepare for a charity fundraiser this evening for Yorkshire Cancer Research. We are having a drinks reception followed by an auction. There is lots to do. We have been very lucky with donated items as diverse as a teddy bear to a villa holiday in Greece.'

She stayed with him until he was settled and left as lightly as she had arrived.

Alasdair put on the radio to listen to the news. Radio 4 had been a regular companion during the past weeks. He closed his eyes and relaxed.

Hugo had been to see Alasdair a couple of times each week and kept his visits short, knowing Alasdair tired quickly.

A brisk knock on the door announced his arrival and without hesitation he came in and bent down to embrace his friend. He made himself comfortable.

Alasdair turned off the radio.

'How are things, Hugo? What's new?'

'Things are going well. Remember that part time facilitator job I applied for with the Open University based in York?'

Alasdair nodded.

'I went to see the Head of Humanities last week to find out more and indeed it sounds just what I am looking to do. You know, keep an interest with only a monthly tutorial commitment and a few hours of preparation and marking outside of that for each group. Currently there are four foundation courses running with an element of Humanities.'

'Sounds just what you need. When will you know?'

'Before the end of November and if successful, I will start in January.'

'Hugo I won't be here.'

They were good friends, but what could Hugo say? Picking up *The Daily Telegraph*, he looked kindly at Alasdair.

'I know.'

Hugo noticed a tray with a bottle of Harrogate sparkling mineral water and several glasses.

'Water, Alasdair?'

'Yes please. Thank you.'

They then settled into an easier conversation about the changes in education being made by New Labour. Hugo had only recently retired from Clifton and was still in touch with their colleagues and friends. Some had already sent cards to Alasdair saying they would like to visit.

'Thinking back to our days at Clifton, Alasdair, were you aware there was some gossip in the Common Room. I stayed out of it, but I did hear Ian Derbyshire say that Alasdair, although likeable is the sort of man whom men slightly distrust without knowing why.'

Alasdair smiled, 'Really?'

In his sixties, Hugo has retained his good looks. His thick wavy grey hair parted on the right with thick eyebrows set low on his forehead outlined his penetrating blue eyes. He fitted into his six foot frame neatly and today was wearing a red checked shirt tucked into his beige slacks with matching tan belt and shoes, beautifully polished.

Since his wife's death he seemed to have fledged, spending money on good quality clothes bought from Austin Reed and Jaeger. He had recently returned from a guided tour of the Holy Land and Alasdair was keen to learn more. This was the land of history, passion and the presence of Jesus and there was more than a hint of jealousy that Hugo had done something he and Ruth had dreamed of, but had not managed.

'Hugo, tell me about your holiday in The Holy Land?'

'Surely, just let me get my photo album out of my briefcase.'

He then sat down beside Alasdair on the sofa and began to describe what he had done.

'I decided to go with a tour group to The Holy Land. I flew to Ben Gurion International Airport and was met by the tour guide and later had dinner with the rest of the tour group at the Laguadia Hotel in Tel Aviv. The next morning we drove to the ancient city of Caesarea built by Herod in honour of Augustus and where Paul was imprisoned before his trial in Rome.'

Hugo turned the pages of his photo album and indicated enthusiastically towards the images he described.

'We continued on to Megiddo and Haifa where we visited the Ba'hai Gardens on Mount Carmel. We stayed at The Kibbutz Hotel in Lower Galilee. The next day we took a boat ride on the Sea of Galilee taking in the sights including visiting Capernaum and the Mount of Beatitudes where Jesus delivered the Sermon on the Mount. I was particularly pleased we visited Beit Shean National Park where they are excavating a Roman-Byzantine City. Then on along the Jordan Rift Valley to Jerusalem. It is a striking convergence of a city over 3,000 years old including twentieth century additions. Towards the end of the Great War, Field Marshal Allenby nicknamed *The Bull* led the British Empire expeditionary force during the Sinai and Palestine campaign against the Ottoman Empire in the conquest of Palestine. He commanded TE Lawrence in the campaign which ended in October 1918 and entered Jerusalem on foot as a token of respect to the Holy City. He is portrayed by Jack Hawkins in the film *Lawrence of Arabia*.'

'How interesting, Hugo. Please continue.'

'We stayed at a very nice small hotel in the centre and as we had done on previous nights we had dinner together. I mostly ate Kosher food, but avoided red meat and was surprised how many dishes had their origins in Russia, Ukraine and Poland. For dessert, I particularly enjoyed the non-dairy apple cake with cinnamon which was really delicious and very, very sweet. The next day we had a guided tour of the City and after lunch when we had a free afternoon, I paid one of the tour guides to drive me to the Mount of Olives where we had a panoramic view of the Holy City. We then drove down to Gethsemane and walked amongst the olive groves before returning for dinner at the hotel. Our final day was spent in Bethlehem before the long drive back to the airport.'

'Tell me Hugo, what did you enjoy the most?

'Without a doubt it was The Church of the Nativity in Bethlehem. I am not an emotional man but the impact and presence of being there was one of quiet religious reflection. I would have liked to stay longer. Look, here I am outside the door of the Basilica.'

Alasdair looked closely. 'Hugo, I am very pleased for you. You look carefree.'

It was time to discuss with Hugo the inevitable and make light of the arrangements for his funeral.

'Hugo, as a good friend could I ask you to interpret my wishes for the order of service at my funeral?'

'Of course Alasdair, I would be honoured to do so.'

He handed Hugo a few pages of handwriting.

'I have already started working on a sermon, which I should like you to deliver. When you visit next time could we put our heads together and come up with a service in celebration rather than in mourning?'

'If it is OK with you, I will come on Monday ready to take notes and discuss your wishes?'

'Hugo, I knew I could rely on you. Thank you. Now let's change the subject. Supper will be served very soon, shall we make our way to the dining room?'

They sat at a table by a window where they could gaze out at the garden.

'Hugo, be so kind and choose from the buffet for both of us. I will order the tea. I insist on Yorkshire Tea, hope that is OK with you?'

Hugo nodded. 'That sounds a good idea.'

Once tea was served and they were enjoying their prawn and watercress sandwiches with a hint of chilli, Alasdair asked, 'Have you seen anyone from Clifton recently?'

They reminisced about the old days until it was time for Hugo to excuse himself.

12
THE GARDEN PARTY

Echoes, flying in the Cretan labyrinth
These are the evocations of your presence
These are the diffusions of your glances
Of your movements, of your sighs
And all your inward radiance

Like the sparkling sunrays on a river
Flowing over its stony bed
Breathless softly through your body
Until it infuses it completely
Until your body is bathed and suffused . . .

When the last trumpet calls me to account
And all my past skims o'er the screens of heaven,
When reckoning fingers mark the fixed amount
Of all my sins, seven to the nth times seven;
When naught is hid and all's made manifest
By whitely shining arcs that flood the soul,
Revealing motives hitherto unguessed,
Each, singly, summing to a single whole;
What shall I say of thee . . . and of that sin
Which is most frequent, fond and fatal for mankind.

Frances arrived just after six o'clock and found Alasdair sitting on the sofa, enjoying listening to the *The Flower Duet* from Lakmè, now well known since its inclusion in the uplifting and deeply satisfying prison drama The Shawshank Redemption. He heard her enter and smiling made himself comfortable, ready to receive her. They embraced before Frances reached into her bag and produced two chocolate hearts wrapped in red foil and handed one to Alasdair.

'Is there anything I can get you?'

'I'd like a glass of whisky, please.'

Alasdair put the chocolate heart to one side for later.

'Would you like a drink, Frances?'

She went to the chest where there was a choice of drinks, from which she chose a dry Amontillado Sherry for herself and poured a Glenmorangie single malt Scotch whisky for Alasdair. She picked up the now familiar, battered envelope. Once she had re-joined Alasdair and handed him his drink, she began looking through the papers, whilst sipping her sherry, but seemed lost in her own thoughts.

'Are you alright, Frances?'

'Yes, just thinking about Oliver. I still haven't heard from him.'

She relaxed slightly sipping her sherry.

'How did Lady Rossiter's visit go?'

'It was so nice to see her. She really does care about me. It was too cold to walk around the garden, so we went and sat in the drawing room. She stayed a good hour chatting about Moreton and plans for the Harvest Supper.'

Alasdair turned away and looked out of the window, his face looking pale grey and drawn over his cheek bones, he wiped tears from his cheek.

'It isn't easy knowing I won't be there.'

Say nothing or come out with a wearisome cliche? Frances chose the former. She put on Dave Brubeck's *Time Out* and they listened in contemplative silence to *Blue Rondo*. As the music played on, they listened to the laid back mellow sounds of *Take Five*.

In the spring of 1990 Alasdair announced the date of the Summer Garden Party in *Moreton News* asking for someone to provide a venue. Someone always came forward and he would discuss who usually did what and let them get on with it until the day. One year Frances volunteered. She had done the cake stall the previous year and the

Dower House was a good venue. It was a traditional double fronted Victorian stone house. The rear garden used to be a croquet lawn, so nicely flat for putting out the tables and chairs. The house stood well back from the road with a circular drive with deep herbaceous borders and lawns on either side; this would provide additional space for stalls. The paddock was next to the house and perfect for a car park. The girl, who rented the paddock and stables, would need to move her horses for the day.

What Alasdair hadn't known was that Frances had worked in the corporate sector and was used to working towards objectives and performance targets often as part of a team using project management techniques. So Frances's approach was very different from how things had been done in the past. Edward had been keen for her to do it and had meant to help, but he was away on business in London at the time of the first meeting. Frances invited those who usually helped and Alasdair had spread the word about the village on his rounds to contact Frances should they wish to get involved.

Frances held the meeting at the Dower House and before starting she made sure everyone had a drink and put little nibbles in easy reach. She then started by agreeing an agenda she had drafted. So with a list of who had done what in the previous year they began to plan the party. The Moreton Garden Party raised money for St Lawrence's and this year Frances put forward the idea of sharing the money raised with Yorkshire Cancer Research and everyone agreed. The party included a cream tea and so an entrance fee of fifty pence would be charged. The Clapton's always did the tom bola, so once agreed they moved quickly on to decide who would be organising the books, bric-a-brac, garden plants, toys, cakes and white elephant stalls, which are the other mainstays of any English summer fete, they were then free to discuss any new ideas for the day. Frances's next door neighbour wanted to do *Splat the Rat* which was agreed, as was Henry Crampton's idea of *Find the Treasure* and he also volunteered his wife, Charlotte to do a bran-tub filled with presents and sweets for the children and their eldest daughter had suggested she do *Guess the number of Smarties in a jar*. Evelyn Bainbridge was known for her wonderful cakes but her arthritis had got worse and she didn't want to stand all afternoon selling cakes, so she suggested she would make cakes for the stall including one larger one for *Guess the Weight of the Cake* if one of the youngsters would take people's details on the day.

On the whole the person who made the suggestion was happy to organise their own idea. As it would be Frances's kitchen used to make the cream teas, she would enrol the help needed and take charge.

There was one more item on Frances's agenda, which was a new idea. She showed a local advertisement flyer representing several local restaurants and businesses. She had the idea of a programme of events surrounded by advertisements and acknowledgements. Her idea was to sell advertising space in the form of either money or a prize for the tom bola. Each programme would also have a lucky number for a draw mid-afternoon with a bottle of champagne donated by Edward.

It turned out to be a great idea as it raised two hundred pounds and in addition provided prizes for the tom-bola such as dinner for two from The Boars Head, afternoon tea for two at Betty's Café Tea Rooms and gift vouchers from the butcher in the neighbouring village. Sainsbury's in Harrogate in addition to a donation gave Frances fifty white cake boxes for the cake stall, which on a sunny day was far superior than putting cakes in old plastic bags.

Moreton doesn't have a village hall. For some reason, before Alasdair arrived it had been sold and converted into a rather strange looking house. The money raised, as it was owned by the parish, was held in trust. Frances was sure that with no public place available for the garden party, it was the perfect source of money to fund some of the expenses she needed, in particular a marquee in case of rain and the hire of tables, chairs and crockery from a neighbouring village, who were happy to loan these items for a donation to their funds. Of course she had to provide an estimate of the money required for the Church Wardens to approve.

It will be alright on the day. It was. On the day Edward mowed the paddock. Frances' sister, Vivienne Albright and her husband David arrived mid morning with their parents. David is a bank manager working for HSBC in a branch office on the outskirts of Birmingham. Vivienne is older than Frances. She is tall and Rubenesque

93

in stature with strawberry blonde hair and green eyes. Her husband, David is slightly shorter, clean shaven and was carefully dressed in casual attire. They were tasked with helping on the book stall.

After a hectic morning putting up bunting and everyone setting up their stalls, Lord Rossiter opened the garden party promptly at two o'clock.

Alasdair and Ruth always enjoyed these events, where they could meet parishioners in an informal gathering. Lord and Lady Rossiter stayed for a short time. The cream teas were going well and were a good deal for the fifty pence entrance charge. It also meant that Frances and her team never stopped. The more elderly of the ladies sat around the kitchen table buttering scones and spreading strawberry jam and cream on to an assortment of different sizes and types of scones provided by the ladies of the parish. Another team including Frances made sure that the tea urn was always filled and that tea was served throughout the afternoon. Some of the older children had been roped in and took it in turns to keep the tables cleared and wash up. It was a huge task behind the scenes and so when Lady Rossiter came in to thank everyone Frances was very grateful to her for her thoughtfulness.

Around mid-afternoon, the familiar sound of an ice-cream van was heard arriving at the front of the house, by previous arrangement, to serve ice creams and lollies.

By five o'clock it was over. The clearing up took another couple of hours and it would be the next day before all the furniture would be returned and the marquee collected.

Harry Bainbridge, one of the Church Wardens counted the money. Never had so much money been raised.

Alasdair was listening to James Galway's *Winter's Crossing* a story told through music of a group of emigrants, who sailed from Derry in the winter of 1866 headed for Pennsylvania; it was a present from Adam last Christmas. He looked at his watch and saw it was four o'clock.

'Frances will be here soon.'

She arrived a few minutes later, holding a large tray in her hands laden with a pot of tea and accoutrements together with a small plate of delicate bite size turkish delight and chocolate truffles.

'Hello, Alasdair. How are you today?'

She poured out the tea and handed Alasdair his cup.

'I am very tired and have very little energy.' Alasdair patted the sofa cushion.

'Come and sit beside me, Frances.'

She settled alongside Alasdair and put her cup of tea on the low table. He took her hand.

'When we are together you are always so happy, always smiling, but caught unaware, you look forlorn and then I catch your eye and your face lights up. I think there are tears behind your smile. Am I right?'

'Alasdair of course you are right. How much do you reveal of yourself to others? I am exhausted by the awful events I have endured, they are too awful to tell anyone else. I keep quiet and listen.'

'So I only see the tip of an iceberg.'

'You see what I feel I can share.' She smiled. 'Don't worry, optimism is in my genes.'

Frances snuggled up to him and he passed the plate for her to choose from. They both chose the rose flavoured Turkish delight and precipitating the pleasure of the sweetness they looked sideways at each other; half laughing, they popped the delights into their mouths and enjoyed the sugary sweet texture of the jelly as it melted and diffused the taste of fragrant roses on their taste buds.

They drank their tea, listening to James Galway's haunting, etherial playing of the flute, while Liam Neeson narrated *Thousands are Sailing*. They enjoyed the silence of friendship. After their second cup, Frances put the remaining petit-fours on the bedside chest. Once she had put everything back on the tray, she took it back to the kitchenette along the corridor. When she returned, Alasdair asked, 'Have you heard from Oliver?'

'Sadly, yes. I received a letter today from Oliver saying that he doesn't want me to contact him. The language was adult and must have been dictated by either Edward or Lois. Oliver is eleven years old, he wouldn't use the word *appropriate*. Would you like to see it?'

'Of course.' Alasdair read the short note and handed it back to Frances. 'Such a pity and desperate for you.'

'I have tried phoning and neither will let me speak with him. Edward alluded to the fact that after my visit, Oliver was rude to Lois.'

'I cannot imagine how you are feeling to be estranged from both your sons. Any news on Philip?

'I will catch up when I see Philip this evening. We are going to The Red Lion for supper.'

'Any progress?'

'I think so. He has being seeing Dr Powell, who is a Consultant in Child & Family Psychiatry, for a few weeks now and it is helping. I should have spent more time explaining what was happening when Edward and I divorced. It isn't easy for Philip to express the reasons why he has become so aggressive and destructive.'

'Give him time.'

'I know.'

There followed a long pause whilst she thought about her eldest son and his behaviour, which had escalated into violence towards her. Eventually, she asked, 'Shall I put another CD on before I go?'

'Something soothing, you choose.'

From the collection of CD's, she looked at one and holding it up so he could see.

'You bought this one after we saw the Berlin Philharmonic Virtuosi playing this summer in Harrogate. You particularly enjoyed the Dvorak *Serenade for Strings*. This is Dvorak's Complete String Quartets.'

She listened for a minute, aware that Alasdair had closed his eyes. Before she could say anything, he answered her unasked question.

'Darling, I just need to drift a little with my thoughts.'

She left. The music rolled over him.

13

THE CHRISTMAS PARTY

Make the most of yourself, for that is all there is of you.

Ralph Waldo Emerson

Unlike the Harvest Supper where everyone who attended the church service was welcome, the Christmas Party was by invitation to those living in Moreton. The reason for this was purely to help Father Christmas ensure every child attending had a present individually purchased and labelled. Father Christmas was fortunate to have Evelyn Bainbridge and Lady Rossiter take care of this for him.

Those attending not only brought with them plates and cutlery, they also brought food, which was placed on the long tables in a buffet style and many also brought with them beer and wine. Lord Rossiter welcomed guests offering them either mulled wine he had prepared or their choice from the selection of drinks available. It wasn't long before the lights dimmed and Alasdair stood up and asked everyone to stay silent.

'Children, I can hear Father Christmas on his sleigh. We must all sing to let him know we are here!'

Alasdair moved to the upright piano and started to play and sing the words, quietly to encourage the children to join in.

Jingle bells, jingle bells
Jingle all the way.
Oh what fun it is to ride on a one horse open sleigh!

Alasdair waved his arms.

'Everybody, please join in. The louder we sing, the more likely Father Christmas will find us.'

Meanwhile, those who knew the routine ushered the children to turn towards the entrance. They all heard the bell. Then they heard the sound of very heavy footsteps coming up the stairs. When the door opened and Father Christmas entered the room with a large sack over his shoulder, the children ran to meet him.

Lady Rossiter guided him to a seat near the fire and the little ones sat close by. Most children older than ten years were unsure as to whether to enjoy the magic or stay back nonchalantly so that the grown ups would know they were in on the secret. Lord Rossiter handed him a glass of sherry and a mince pie. Alasdair raised his voice.

'Merry Christmas!'

Once Harry Bainbridge had eaten his mince pie and wiped his beard he looked down at the children.

'Hello my dear children. I have come all the way from the North Pole to see you and give each of you a present.'

Evelyn Bainbridge came forward and after shaking Father Christmas's hand pulled out the first present from the sack and called out the name 'Jamie Clapton', handing it to Harry. In an instant a little lad aged about six years jumped up and ran towards Father Christmas. He took the parcel and shook Father Christmas's hand before running back to the arms of his mummy. Moreton is a small village with only twenty or so children and so it didn't take too long before Harry completed his task. He stood up and walked towards the exit.

'Merry Christmas Everyone!'

He waved to everyone and then he was gone, out into the night to the sound of everyone clapping as Alasdair played the Jingle Bells tune again.

This was a good time to select a pudding or cake and fill one's glass, while the children opened their presents. Soon, Alasdair started playing a few favourite tunes to get the party going. Lady Rossiter asked Alasdair if he would be so good as to play the Gay Gordon's before taking Geoffrey's hand, pulling him to the dance floor to start the dancing and the evening concluded with everyone, and indeed, everyone singing *Auld lang syne*.

On Christmas Eve they would all meet again for Midnight Mass. It was the only service in the year when St Lawrence's was full. Lord and Lady Rossiter would arrive with their guests in evening dress and proceed to the front pews, always reserved for them. Always and against current Church of England doctrine, Alasdair used the 1662 King James prayer book, in which the archaic language added melody and a sense of ritual to the occasion. Charlotte Crampton, the mother of one of the Ripon Cathedral choristers, lived in Moreton and was well known locally as a professional soprano and entertainer. If she attended the service, Charlotte would delight the congregation with a solo carol, her voice transcending high with lyrical beauty.

Alasdair's thoughts were interrupted with the arrival of his nephew, Jasper in good time for lunch. He is much taller than his own sons and has inherited from goodness knows where a mop of bright red hair and his face is sparsely covered with freckles. It is his green eyes that one first notices. They draw you in to his openly honest charm. Alasdair is very fond of Jasper.

Alasdair greeted Jasper. 'Hello, my boy! How are you?' He raised his arms to embrace his nephew.

Jasper bent down and allowed his uncle to hold him in his arms and kiss him.

'I'm very well uncle Alasdair. Good to see you.'

'Sit yourself down. We have a little time before lunch is ready.'

Once Jasper was settled in the armchair, Alasdair asked, 'How is the trip going? Tell me all.'

Jasper leaned back into the chair and smiled.

'I spent a few days relaxing in the Lake District before coming to see you and then the business starts tomorrow in London with a promotional preview evening organised by my publishers at The Courtauld Gallery in The Strand. The following day will be spent with my editor and then after that I have a couple of days to sight see and catch up with friends. Next week I will be promoting the book at The Cheltenham Literary Festival before flying back home.'

'That sounds like a busy schedule. I want to hear all about it over lunch. We will be eating in the dining room, so I will need a wheel chair. Would you pop along the corridor and ask for one?'

Jasper jumped up and after a minute or two returned with the wheelchair and helped Alasdair. They took the lift to the ground floor and headed for the dining room.

'What a delightful period room.' Jasper remarked, as he manoeuvred the wheel chair towards the bay window. 'Such high ceilings and the wooden panelling is so elegant and so very English.'

He helped Alasdair from his chair noting his frailness.

While they waited to be served Jasper said, 'I haven't been back to Northumbria since Dad died. I used to love walking along the Northumbrian coastline and visiting Grandpa Robert.'

'Richard and I had a very happy childhood growing up there, even the poverty of the 1930's didn't seem to affect us. We were lucky.'

'Please go on.'

'Well you will know your history and how tough it was for those living in the North East during The Depression. We were there. Richard was seventeen and I was fourteen when the men from Jarrow marched to London. Palmers, the Jarrow shipyard closed in October 1935 and by the following year seventy percent of men living in Jarrow were unemployed. They decided to do something about it and set about organising a protest march. The Mayor despatched letters to corporations, trade unions and similar bodies to raise money. Two hundred carefully chosen men were appointed. A second hand bus was purchased and converted into a transport wagon with sleeping kits, waterproofs and volunteers provided services such as medical attention, haircutting and cobbling. This was no hunger strike march, this was a protest that Jarrow was making to the country saying *Send us work.*'

'Did you see them?'

'Yes. Your Grandpa took us to Jarrow to cheer the men on as they left the town. He signed the petition, a huge book which was to be presented to the House of Commons. Richard and I had been saving our pocket money and we waited our turn to drop our sixpences into the kitty. Dad had already sent a personal cheque and signed a much larger one from his firm.'

They were interrupted by the arrival of lunch comprising individual ceramic dishes filled with lamb in a rich steaming gravy, topped with potato rosti and served with Savoy cabbage and carrots on the side.

Jasper finished the last mouthful and putting his cutlery neatly on the plate, waited patiently for Alasdair to finish. When Alasdair had finished, he smiled and looked up at Jasper.

'Wasn't that delicious?'

'It was just right, nearly as good as auntie Ruth's shepherds' pie.'

Alasdair was pleased Jasper remembered. 'Now getting back to my story. Would you like me to continue?'

'Yes, please do go on.'

'Fine. We first heard the music of the mouth-organ band which brought people flocking and hundreds lined the street. Then we saw the banners emboldened with *Jarrow Crusade* and everyone cheered and waved. Every day we read the newspaper to follow the marchers. The men reached Harrogate and as they marched from Ripon through Ripley and Killinghall the people flocked to see them. A meeting took place at the Winter Gardens and the townspeople of Harrogate raised a big banner saying *Harrogate workers welcome the Jarrow marchers*. When the march reached Leeds, they received a welcome donation for their return trip by train. At Barnsley the men rejoiced in the heated municipal baths. They successfully reached London. It was sad, despite considerable public sympathy the crusade made little real impact.'

'What a tremendous achievement!'

'Yes, it was a protest; it was never a hunger march as it is often believed by those who didn't see it first hand.'

They decided to retire to the drawing room for coffee.

'Alasdair, would you like to read one of my stories? I have always written short stories for my own amusement and relaxation in between each Inspector Ahearne project. I am planning to publish a collection of them next year.'

'I should be pleased to read your work.' He reached out his arm to encourage Jasper to hand him a manuscript with the title *The Shells*. 'Why don't you settle down and read *The Daily Telegraph*, while I read?'

THE SHELLS

I remember him well. I met him on the sweeping stretch of sand curving round the little bay. I had not thought to meet a living soul there, for the village beyond the headland was not a place of resort and the fishermen lived their own lives in quietness.

His head was bent as he walked, and moved from side to side as if he searched the silver sand. But as I drew closer I knew that it was not wood or coin that he sought, for his garments and his features denied it. His face was pale, pale as the creamy foam of the waves and his hands, clasped behind him, were slender and white. His fair hair swept back from his head in the wind, as the sea plants sweep in the gentle currents of the ocean.

We greeted each other as men do when they meet in a lonely place, and after some talk, walked together back to the village. 'I have lived here for many years,' he said. 'My health forbids me to work, but I possess sufficient money to live here in great happiness.'

'When I first saw you,' I replied 'you seemed to be searching for something. If you have lost a precious thing I will gladly help you to find it; if, indeed, it is not lost forever.' 'Thank you,' he said, 'but I have lost nothing. Each morning, if the weather is fine, I walk here looking for sea shells. You may think this is a trivial thing, but I am alone in the world and have never enjoyed good health. Since I came to this village I have found my thoughts drawn towards sea shells, of which, as you can see, there are many. They give me an interest in life. I read much about them and have many different kinds in my house. If it should please you, I will willingly show them to you.''

I could see that he was eager to make a friend and share his pleasure, so I thanked him and accepted. That very afternoon he showed me his treasures. They lay, not in glass cases and labelled drawers, but on tables contrived to represent the seas which were their homes.

He had accomplished this by the skilful use of coloured cloths. Of diverse textures and, arranged in subtle folds, they suggested to the imagination a variety of sea pictures. Here was the brown sand of northern coasts, rippling as the retiring waves had left their imprint upon it. Here was the deep violet of the sea as it washed into a hidden cave, warmed by a falling shaft of the southern sun. Here was the pale green of quiet seas, the rich blue of coral lagoons, the deep green of the fathomless ocean. In these settings he had arranged his shells, carefully, like jewels.

He moved among them quietly. 'Their richness and variety draw me to them,' he said. 'I like to fancy that they are alive. They are so beautiful to look upon, with their enamelled colours. And how smooth to touch, how contained they are. They live, for me, in a timeless world. They know their age. They are given to themselves in an eternal present. Their outlines separate them from the world they live in. They do not grow out of the sea as plants and seaweeds grow, rooted in their nourishment; nor are they like stones, once part of a larger existence. They are completely themselves.

The apprehension of this is sharpened for me by the contrast between their outer appearance and their inner convolutions. The smooth, simple and pleasing outline now evolves in a delightful complexity. There, in their hidden labyrinths, they live their inward life. See how the colours blend and fade on this conch shell; from a soft brown to a pink, and so, as the eye travels beneath its curling edge, to a warm, milky whiteness. Men say that shells are dead, yet, for me, in their beauty of colour, in their moulded and complex forms, in the folds which curve in upon themselves like the silken petals of a rose, they suggest life.'

As he spoke, he moved among then in an enchantment of happiness. And I, too, was happy to see him so. 'Tell me,' I said, 'in all this profusion of beauty, is there any one shell that has particularly charmed you?'

He replied with simple and open candour. 'There is, but I keep it to myself and show it to no-one. Sea shells have a mystery for me and this particular shell is the most mysterious of all. Try as I might, that mystery eludes me. And I have determined that no-one shall see it until it is plain to me. I keep it there, in a box of tortoiseshell on a fold of white silk.'

Shortly afterwards I took my leave of him. He stood in the doorway, fragile and pale as the thin, scoured bone of a shell on the clean sand. It seemed, for a moment, as I looked at him, as if he could have no life in him. But alive he was and suffused with a childlike peace.

I had a visit from the doctor the next day. He told me that my friend had died and had spoken my name before his eyes closed. Together we went to the house and I saw him. His features were composed and calm, in great tranquillity. I perceived that he had not discovered the secret of the shell and had died, happily pondering its mystery.

As I left his house, I looked at the tortoiseshell box. But I did not thread my way among the shells to open it. As I turned away, I hesitated. Had he not spoken my name before he died? He wanted me to take the box and understand the beauty contained within. I quickly retraced my steps and picked up the beautiful box with such happy thoughts of what the future would hold for me.

Jasper Sommersby, 1999

'A rather charming story of hope, Jasper. It would fit nicely into a collection. Talking of collections, Frances brought me Raymond Carver's book of short stories to read. Here it is, *Where I'm Calling From*. Would you like to take it?'

'That's a kind offer, but too much weight for travelling. I know of the book and have recently read his first book of stories, *Will You Please Be Quiet, Please.*'

Just after four o'clock, Frances joined them and they were asked by a rather demure young assistant carer whether they would like afternoon tea and some minutes later they were relaxing enjoying tea and home made Victoria sponge. Jasper appeared to be really enjoying the cake and looked at them, smiling with caster sugar all around his lips.

'Wow, this is delicious.'

Frances beamed, not sharing with them the fact that she brought it with her, having baked it herself the previous evening. Changing the subject, she spoke to Jasper.

'It is nice to see you here with Alasdair. Have you been catching up on family news?'

Jasper answered realising Alasdair was beginning to tire.

'And much more. I realise how little I know of life in the North East when Dad was growing up. I have always loved the coast there.'

'Will you have time to go there?'

'No, perhaps when I next visit. I am staying in Ripon tonight and then heading back to London tomorrow.'

Alasdair stirred and looked at them.

'Why don't you ask Frances to have supper with you tonight? Don't be on your own.'

Jasper didn't hesitate, he looked pleased with the suggestion.

'That would be fine by me. Frances, would you like to join me at The Old Deanery?'

'Thank you. Yes, I would"

'Fine, I'll book a table. Will seven thirty suit?'

'Perfectly, see you there.'

Jasper rose and before leaving shook his uncle's hand.

When he had gone, Frances tidied away the papers. She kissed Alasdair's forehead and without opening his eyes he whispered, 'Have a lovely time this evening, darling.'

14

THE OLD DEANERY

If you seek only to touch and kiss,
when love making needs the stimulation
of freely exchanged words and ideas,
you will stifle its potential.

If you take away the thing that draws me to you,
promising an inter-fecundation of minds,
the well spring of our love will dry up.

Charge me not with unhappiness
when I have stood on the edge of the precipice
and have seen Truth revealed to me
through the power of my pen.

Show me the man who thinks and feels
and yet calls himself happy and I'll show you a void.
For the blind man has more Truth in his wisdom
than he sees through scaled eyes.

The Old Deanery is a weathered stone–built, double fronted residence set back from the road behind a high wall and situated across the road from Ripon Cathedral.

Frances arrived wearing a mid calf length black linen dress and a short silk jacket of large silver circles on a black background. Around her neck was a single strand of pearls; pearl earrings completed her look. She asked at Reception for Jasper Sommersby and a minute later he came from the lounge to greet her. He had changed from his jeans into smart beige, chino's which he wore with a cherry red velvet jacket and pink open necked shirt. Frances noticed for the first time just how handsome he was. He walked over and taking hold of her arms, kissed her cheek.

'Lovely to see you. Shall we go to the Bar and have a drink?'

Without waiting for an answer he put his hand on the small of her back and guided her through the lounge into the adjacent small bar with black leather chairs and cream walls decorated with chrome art deco lamps.

Once seated and drinks having been ordered, Jasper said, 'Alasdair tells me that you have been very supportive. I am sure my cousins appreciate everything you are doing for their father.'

'Alasdair has been a very good friend to me over the last few years. I am very fond of him. Being in his company is a pleasure. Each new day could be his last. He makes the most of every minute and I want to be part of it.'

'I didn't say earlier, but I think we met at Ruth's funeral?'

'Yes, we did. Briefly.'

The waiter brought their drinks; both had chosen the house red not wanting to waste time peering through the list. After they raised their glasses to Alasdair, they became more relaxed in each other's company, and took time looking at the menus and deciding what to eat.

A short while after the waiter had taken their order to the kitchen, he returned and led them to the dining room, where they took their places at a table within a short distance of a blazing fire, close enough for Jasper to remove his jacket. The room was subtly lit together with candles on each table. Jasper took up the conversation.

'I understand your father served in the Royal Navy during the Second World War?'

'Yes, he joined the navy in October 1939 when he was just eighteen. He served on HMS Malaya when it was deployed in Atlantic convoy defence and later in the Mediterranean between Malta and Alexandria.'

'That is a coincidence because I know my Dad served on the Malaya during 1941. That's how he met my mother in New York when it was being repaired at the navy yard in Brooklyn after being torpedoed off the Cape Verde Islands.'

'That is the only part of my father's war he ever talked about, spending time in New York and seeing the sights. What did your father do?'

'He was an Artificer responsible for maintaining all the complicated and complex equipment needed in a modern battleship.'

'They may have known each other, because my father was also a TIF. He took after my grandfather and apprenticed as a toolmaker. The Tiffy was regarded as the cream of the service being more highly trained than any one else on board. They had to be expert craftsmen with skill of hand and eye and were expected to cast and argon arc weld with great precision. If you didn't carry the spare at sea you had to make it.'

She was pleased that she had participated in the conversation, added something Jasper didn't know and for the first time, Frances began to feel relaxed and comfortable in his company. Taking her glass, lifting her head, she smiled at Jasper.

'What did your father do after the war?'

'He became an engineer for a shipbuilder in Sunderland. My mother who was from a prosperous socialite family in New York joined him in England at the end of the war and they were married in the West Undercroft of Durham Cathedral. They returned to New York in 1950, when I was two years old. So, I grew up in America and have always lived in New York. And your family?'

'My parents met during the war when father was in the Royal Navy. They honeymooned at Fort William. I think my father had fallen for Scotland when he had shore leave during the time the Malaya was at Rosyth. After the war they moved to the Black Country and we lived with our grandmother in Walsall, before settling south of Birmingham, when father began working for Cadbury's as a Factory Production Manager. It was more important to him for us to live in leafy Warwickshire than his having to catch two buses each day to and from Bourneville. In the summers my father would take our mother, Vivienne and I to the south coast at the beginning of the school holidays and leave us for a month with our grandparents.'

They were pleasantly interrupted by their waiter with the first course. They had both chosen the *Rabbit raviolo cooked and served in its' own consommé with fermented turnip*. Jasper looked at his plate and smiled at Frances.

'Bon appetite.'

'This smells yummy.'

Frances raised her glass to Jasper as a toast and he responded similarly.

They ate in silence, occasionally looking up at each other as they sipped their wine.

'Well it tasted as good as it looked,' said Jasper as he finished and took another sip of wine. 'I cannot remember the last time I ate rabbit.'

Frances drank a little more wine and smiled.

'I agree, the consommé was so full of flavour. Simply delicious.'

Once the waiter had cleared away the plates and refreshed their glasses, Frances put her hands under her chin and looked directly into his eyes.

'Tell me a little about yourself?'

'Well you know I grew up in America. We settled in White Plains north east of New York, when father joined IBM as a Systems Engineer. I was an avid reader from a young age and did well at school going on to read Classics at Cornell University.'

'When did you start to write?'

'I have always written stories since I was a small child and entered competitions. When I started teaching, I just kept it up. My first sight of success was a short story I entered in a competition winning a small cash prize. The first novel was a long time coming, but eventually it was finished and I was lucky to find an agent, who worked with me to find a publisher. I had to produce a second story before the first was published and so I stopped teaching and wrote full time.'

'Alasdair gave me a copy of *Death Comes to Albany* after I met you at Ruth's funeral. I enjoyed it so much that Alasdair has given me a copy of each of your books. I really like your main character, the rather attractive, red haired and bespectacled Detective Inspector Ahearne. I feel I know him well following his exploits in and around Albany.'

'I am in the process of getting a collection of short stories published early next year. After that my next book will be a different genre away from crime fiction and so my publisher has recommended, I use a nom de plume. I have been scratching my head trying to come up with a good one that will be easy to remember.'

'A nice problem to have.'

'More wine?' asked Jasper lifting the bottle suggesting another might need to be ordered.

'Not for me, I still have a full glass. May I have mineral water?'

Once the water was ordered the waiter returned with their main courses. Jasper had chosen *Turbot with new potatoes, cockles and celeriac mash*, whilst Frances had decided upon *Smoked aubergine risotto with feta and watercress*. They looked at their plates, smiled nervously at each other and started to taste their food. Their eating experience was interrupted by glances of shared pleasure.

'I am delighted and surprised by the quality of the food here.' Jasper announced. 'It appears English cuisine has come on leaps and bounds from a few good restaurants in London to the North of England.' Jasper paused and then apologised, 'Sorry that was a very pretentious remark. Still, it was excellent, was it not?'

'Indeed,' responded Frances, 'A real treat. Thank you so much for inviting me to join you. It has been a lovely evening getting to know you.'

'Would you like coffee?'

'I prefer to finish my water, but you go ahead. If Alasdair were here with us, he would be politely asking if he could play the piano right now.'

Jasper leaned back in the chair, put his napkin to one side and smiled.

'Thanks for your company, Frances. I have enjoyed the evening. I will have coffee back at the hotel.'

After settling the bill, he stood up and moved to the back of her chair to assist her in rising from the table. With their coats retrieved, they lightly embraced and walked to the car park to go their separate ways.

The following day Jasper arrived just after ten o'clock, as coffee was being served. Once they were comfortable, drinking their coffee, Alasdair asked, 'Did you enjoy your dinner at the Deanery?'

'Yes, it was very nice having Frances' company. We talked about Dad's time during the war and what she knew of her fathers' time on HMS Malaya. It was an interesting coincidence. I like her.'

Before Alasdair could say anything, Jasper asked, 'How are you spending your time?'

'The routine of living here takes up a good proportion of the day. The boys have visited, friends too including Frances. I rest for long periods and let my mind open to memories. I am spending time thinking deeply about theology and those Rabbis who find the Mystery through Torah.'

They each looked thoughtfully and drank their coffee.

'Tell me,' asked Jasper, 'What exactly is Torah?'

'Imagine a man in a vast desert. He is as free as the wind. He can go where he pleases and do exactly as he likes. The whole world is his. But . . . he is lost. He has no map. So he cannot orient himself and will most assuredly perish.

But now, suppose he has an invisible roadmap as straight as a die to help him, which will take him, with certainty, to a place of safety. What would such an invisible road be? Why, a compass of course!

I believe that the word Torah derives from the flight of an arrow. The meaning is, *direction*. It is precisely a compass, a flight of an arrow, which cleaves the air in the direction necessary to go to find a way to use freedom. Torah is direction, a dynamic moving creative purpose and in the end love. It is the revealed will and desire of Yahweh as written down by Moses. Like just about everything in Judaism, it derives from the experience of the Exodus, which is the key to understanding the whole experience of the Jews.'

Jasper's interest began to diminish and Alasdair picked this up and laughed out loud.

'My dear Jasper, you must forgive me for going on so.'

'You know Alasdair,' he said, 'I think I am ready to write a novel rather than crime fiction, one which is more than a theme or plot, something that cannot be summarised, something that can only be discovered and experienced by a total reading of the work.'

'Well, you are financially secure, so why not take the time to do exactly that.' He smiled at his nephew, 'A Booker Prize perhaps? You won't know unless you try.'

'You are right, I'll do some work once the short stories are published. For now, I need to concentrate on promoting my latest Inspector Ahearne murder mystery.'

Jasper's mobile phone rang and he took the call.

'The car is here to take me to London. I need to leave.'

He got up and after putting on his coat, lent over his uncle and kissed his cheek.

'Give my love to the three A's. I am so pleased to have come and spent time with you, uncle. Goodbye.'

Alasdair embraced him. He was too upset to say anything, but he thought, 'Christ! I won't see him again, ever.'

For a long time he was very still, his mind numbed and frozen like the bare earth in the grinding grip of a frost. Slowly, but with a mounting intensity of will he emptied his mind of all thought of fear.

15

COURAGE

The secret of happiness is freedom. The secret of freedom is courage

Thucydides

Alasdair decided to have lunch in his room. His appetite had diminished and he was enjoying a small serving of scrambled eggs on toast with tomatoes, when an assistant nurse knocked and entered his room.

'Just to let you know Reverend Sommersby that Frances has phoned to say she will see you later this evening. She has to attend a meeting at her son's school. She says to tell you she hopes to be with you soon after six o'clock.'

'Thank you, nurse.'

There had been no mention of this yesterday and Alasdair was worried for Frances as to what might have happened.

He spent the afternoon listening to a play on the radio, finishing the paper and listening to music. Time seemed to drag and he couldn't settle, so eventually he resumed reading *Three Men in a Boat* and it wasn't long before his mood lifted and several times he laughed out loud. Just after four o'clock the same pretty nurse came in with a cup of tea and a shortbread biscuit.

He has needed more and more help as each day passes and she helped him up and allowed him to take her arm as he walked towards the bathroom. She shut the door and waited. She plumped up the cushions in his chair, drew the curtains and turned on the lamps. The room now looked warm and cosy. She waited until Alasdair was settled before handing him his cup of tea and then she was gone.

Later, after a new morphine patch had been applied and he was in his pyjamas and dressing gown, he drifted in and out of sleep, just as he drifted in and out of pain. It was at these moments before sleep, when he felt most alive, his thoughts clutching onto the images of the day that had just passed. He considered Frances, his worries for her and took out a notepad and started to compose a poem, the words easily and lightly came into his mind.

When she eventually arrived, she seemed tense. After greeting Alasdair she moved towards the chest of drawers and turning asked, 'Shall we have a drink?'

'Good idea, whisky for me.'

As she poured the drinks, she apologised, 'Sorry I am rather late this evening, I expect you will want to be getting into bed soon.'

'Not to worry. Is everything alright?'

'I think so.' After a significant pause, she continued 'I met with Philip, his foster parents, his social worker and one of his teachers. They all think he is progressing well and are looking for a date to return home.'

'Are you pleased?'

'Worried. I cannot help think that nothing has happened to significantly change his behaviour and attitude towards me. There is no real evidence that he has changed in any way. Just that he wants to come home.'

'That's a good sign isn't it?

'You would think so. Deep down I know nothing has changed. It will be fine until the next time something triggers his violence. They represent the relevant authorities and they want to be seen as having facilitated a successful outcome. Tick in the box. Wish-fulfilment.'

'I see. Have you agreed to this?'

'Yes, I wanted to be seen as optimistic, I love Philip. I didn't want him to think I didn't. So, yes I agreed.'

She topped up her wine glass and sat down on the sofa. It was only then he noticed she had brought a large hard-back book, which he instantly recognised as being *James Herriot's Yorkshire*. Frances put the book on the coffee table, her smile widening.

'I thought you would like to have this, I know you love the photographs by Derry Brabbs.'

'Yes I do. Thank you. I will enjoy browsing through the photographs and resting my mind. Let me see.'

Frances handed the book to Alasdair and he opened it and began turning the pages looking at the stunning photographs of the Yorkshire countryside. It was just like her to think of him. To do something kind.

'How was dinner with Jasper?'

'It went well. I really like him.'

'These pictures will evoke memories. Wonderful memories. Thank you.'

'Did Jasper tell you that his Dad served on the Malaya at the same time as mine during the war?'

'Yes, he did. An interesting co-incidence.' Alasdair winked. 'A shared memory to delve into further, perhaps?'

Alasdair roused himself and sat up.

'Tomorrow all the boys will be coming to see me for lunch. The girls are meeting in Betty's for coffee and then coming on here later in the afternoon. Good for them to spend time together.' Taking her hand, he said, 'Frances, I am spending a lot of time thinking and I find it very absorbing to reflect on what I believe and what is important to me.'

She squeezed his hand and after a short silence, handed him a few sheets of typed quarto paper, faded with age.

'I like the look of this one. Would you like me to read to you?'

Looking at the pages, Alasdair handed them back to her and smiled.

'This story, *The Soldiers* had a profound effect on me when I first came across it. It is a true story, well-attested by two writers about 350 A.D. and it is about courage.'

THE SOLDIERS

A lot of Roman soldiers were Christians. They were
very hard men, the legionaries, men of leather and
iron. And I think that many of them turned to
Christianity because they were impressed by a God
who didn't sit up there and give good advice, but
lived a human life under very tough conditions in a
real world and in the process showed immense courage
and love. A God who is willing to be crucified as man
is by any standard, a pretty impressive sort of God.

Well this story concerns a regiment of Roman
soldiers. They were the 22nd Legion known as 'The
Thundering Legion' and a very crack regiment they
were. They were encamped at a place called Sebaste,
in Armenia, by the side of a frozen lake in the depth
of a very cold winter.

One morning their Commanding Officer, Marcus Junius
Sevianus paraded his men and this is what he said,
'Now I've an order here from the Emperor Caesar
Licinianus himself. It's come all the way from Rome
and it's gone out to the whole army. In plain words
the Emperor doesn't want any Christians in his
legions. He wants no more Christianity. So any Roman
solders who are Christians have to be executed.

I'm not supposed to tell you this. I'm supposed to do
it. But we've got on together in this Regiment and I
don't want to lose a single man. Some of my best
N.C.O's are Christians. I don't care what you believe.
Just keep your mouth shut. So, any Christians here?'
And forty men took one pace forward. 'All right',
said Marcus Junius, 'you've had your warning. But I
still don't want to lose you. Strip off'. So they
did. And there they stood mother-naked in the snow.

The C.O. said, 'You are going to march into the
middle of that frozen lake. And I am going to have a

118

tent pitched on the edge here with a sergeant and a
bowl of soup and a big fire outside. When you get
tired of the cold you come over and put some incense
in a brazier and bow to the Emperor's statue and
we'll have you back. Left turn. Quick march.'

And forty men marched onto the ice in the middle of
the lake. The Colonel told the Adjutant to dismiss
the regiment, but he did not go to his tent. He
stayed, with his big fur cloak, with his Adjutant
looking out to the men on the ice.

After a time one of them, the barrack room wag, started
up a doggerel song, the original Latin is not for
family listening but a polite version goes like this;

> Forty men of the Legions, God,
>   sitting on the ice.
> And let me tell you Jesus
>   it's not very nice.
> Forty men of the Legions, God,
>   very cold and chill
> Sitting on our backsides,
>   may we be forty still

And so the night passed. The Colonel didn't leave the
lake edge. He paced up and down lost in thought. Then
the dawn came and the still, humped mass of white
flesh on the ice began to move, and the thin noise of
the ridiculous song trembled on the air. But it
stopped because one piece of white flesh separated
from the rest and moved and rolled and crawled along
the ice, back to the shore and the tent and the fire
and the statue of the Emperor who thought he was a
god.

There was a long drifting silence. And then Marcus
Junius Sevianus, officer commanding the 22nd Legion,
veteran of a dozen campaigns from the forests of
Germany to the deserts of Libya, dropped his great
cloak and unfastened his body harness and his leg
greaves and his sword belt and he took off his shirt
and stood as naked as the men on the ice. And he said
to his Adjutant 'My best men are out there and if
the God who makes them the best wants forty of them,
he's going to get forty' And he walked out on to the
ice. And then there were forty.

119

Frances began to reach for her handbag. Alasdair raised his hand saying,

'Before you go, let me read this poem I wrote for you.'

'Frances, there is that about you, I know not what, that stimulates the muse of both poetry and conceptual thought in a powerful way. There are such deep resources within you. So much that is powerfully evocative. There are resonances, diffuse or discrete, which evoke like autumn skies, unimagined responses.

> *A la tres chere, a la tres belle,*
> *Qui fait ma joi et ma sante,*
> *A l'ange, a l'idol immortelle*
> *Salut en l'immortalite!*
> *Je t'aime, je t'aime, je t'aime ....*

How easily those words trip from the tongue! And never more than when I see your eyes sparkle. For then however lightly those words have been spoken by the best of men, then, held by your eyes, there are no other words to be spoken.'

He handed her the poem.

'Thank you Alasdair. I love it. A poem about me.'

She opened the door and was about to leave, but turned around and went towards him and kissed him again, this time on his forehead.

Alasdair was saddened that he could no longer do any more for Frances. He had helped her in the past. Been there. Answered her calls for help. Tried to calm things down, talked to Philip.

16

BEING INTO BEING

Aye! I am a poet and upon my tomb
Shall maidens scatter rose leaves
And men myrtles, ere the night
Slays day with her dark sword.

'Lo! This thing is not mine
Nor thine to hinder,
For the custom is full old,
And here in Nineveh have I beheld
Many a singer pass and take his place
In those dim halls where no man troubleth
His sleep or song.
And many a one hath sung his songs
More craftily, more subtle-souled than I;

And many a one now doth surpass
My wave-worn beauty with his wind of flowers
Yet am I poet, and upon my tomb
Shall all men scatter rose leaves
Ere the night slay light
With her blue sword.

'It is not, Raana, that my song rings highest
Or more sweet in tone than any, but that I
Am here a Poet, that doth drink of life
As lesser men drink wine.'

And thus in Nineveh by Ezra pound

Women are certainly very close to the centre of Alasdair's attention. When he was small, his mother allowed him to creep into her bed in the morning. She was a small woman, slim and warm. He used to lie on his right side and she would curl around him. He felt safe and loved. When she rose early, he did not feel deserted as he rolled into her space and its smell of lavender lulled him back to sleep.

It is not at all easy to say what life does centre round. Alasdair is convinced that the secret of life, the meaning of life, is not a theory, nor a set of ideas or morals or ideals. At the centre of life is a mystery of power and being which, though other than him, is not alien to him.

This is what haunts him: this otherness which is yet close to him and which he can no more deny than he can deny his own self and being. It is what gives existence and intelligibility to everything. And this is where women come in. For more than anything else, it is women who make him come alive, who make him look at what he believes and what he is capable of. In a word, they excite him. They are so real, so urgent upon his senses and imaginings. In the old medieval, Latin, it is their haecceity, their individuality, which awakens his spirit to the colour and intensity of living.

Women, other but not alien, are a kind of living parable of the greater Other which is also not alien. In them he reaches out and touches the energy which he knows is reaching out to him. In them he hears the echoes of the voice which seeks his ears. In them he meets a little of the reality which is all disclosure. In them he finds love.

And what of the Otherness which presses upon him, which becomes urgent upon him when he thinks of a woman? What of this breath, this voice, this disclosure that wants so passionately to tell him, no more to declare, to affirm to him, to proclaim to him, to certify him as to who he is. Who is he? There it is, this strange Tetragrammaton, which contains the mystery of disclosure. 'I am?' 'I will be what I will be?' 'I am the centre of personal will? I am the utterly self-conscious and therefore self-forgetful entity of desire.'

Alasdair was pondering these thoughts as he woke and didn't move until they had run their course. They were too important to put aside as these were arguments requiring answers, clarity of thought to enable him to accept death willingly and with grace.

It was later that morning, when he was dressed and sitting in his armchair with the earlier thoughts more settled and calmer in his mind that his thoughts turned to pleasure, not happiness or joy or contentment or rapture or whatever else the thesaurus offers one, but simply pleasure. Not in a conceptual way, asking abstract questions about ideas, but instead thinking of when he had actually experienced a powerful thrill of real pleasure.

It was when Alasdair was with Sylvia that he first realised what gave him most pleasure. He could not resist the undercurrent of her. Sylvia was unfortunately married to a man who no longer appreciated her and who no longer welcomed her caresses and so for some years she had been denied the pleasures of marriage. This was undeniably a minor tragedy, for never in his life had he met a woman who enjoyed every aspect of sexual activity with such immense and reverent gratitude. How men can ignore, almost nonchalantly, such perfected solicitude wrapped in a slender flame of attentive desire, he could not imagine.

For a long time they had stood beside each other, without saying a word. This had happened often before, but this time he knew that the silence would be broken, he simply asked, 'May I kiss you?'

How old-fashioned it sounds, but how persuasive it is! She consented and very soon they were standing with his arms around her. She kissed very passionately and he moved her sweater above her breasts. He simply slipped up her bra and out they came, buoyant and resilient. After a while he slipped off her skirt. She wore a pair of elastic panties tight around her bottom and thighs. He took them firmly in his fingers and rolled them down to her ankles. As he knelt to do this, his eyes came level with the sweetest triangle in creation. He was astonished. She was a redhead. A real one. He knew, of course, that she had red hair, but he was not prepared for the wonder of an orange, auburn cluster of curls that shrouded her nakedness. It was so beautiful, so undeserved, so unlooked-for, so unexpected. It was pure grace, pure gift, and pure benefaction. He was transfixed.

'How long?' he whispered, when she confessed her sad deprivation. 'You angel, you! And you of all people.'

Her attraction to him was not simply that of a woman who was glad to have an admiring man again. She had known him for many years as a parishioner and was very fond of him. When they finally came together it was a revelation indeed. Nothing would satisfy her.

'You are like a drug,' she once told him, 'The more I get the more I want you, it's like a cream bun to someone, who has been starving on a diet.'

What her words revealed was the delicious necessity of time. For time, its passing, its never-to-be-repeated, its *einmalingkeit* as the Germans say, is something to be savoured like a fine wine or a delightful caress.

To realise with profound emotion that what occurs can never be played again, like a gramophone record. That even memory can never reproduce the exact savour of event, indeed that memory can be the great illusionist of reality, that only time and nothing but time can enable us to explore who we are by allowing us to move forward from decision to decision. That is to relish time.

> *Kick off the shoes, let down the shimmering tresses*
> *Block out the horrid world and all its messes!*
> *Recline in bed at ease, wise, happy, sane;*
> *And let all ills dissolve in sweet Champagne!*

Sylvia was extraordinarily perceptive, but somehow life had persuaded her that she had a second-class mind and that her husband had a first-class one, when really it was the other way around. When Alasdair was with her and he listened to her, she blossomed. It was as if she had known all the time that she was a clever woman, but that she could only admit it when she was with someone who was sympathetic to her.

On one particular occasion Alasdair was a little under the weather and was not able to satisfy her with full conjunction and so he employed all his skill in making love to her most interesting sexual charms. With some success. When it was over she whispered, 'Darling that was as good as fucking.'

When it was over? When her orgasm was over. Sylvia simply went on and on. Cries of 'Yes! Yes!' exploded from her mouth and her whole body was seized with powerful spasms. Words simply cannot describe the power that was released by a loving manipulation of her body. He, as it were, lay back as an onlooker while this tempest of passion gripped her body which thrashed over and round and above him. A picture of Laocoon[1] and his sons in the coils of a huge serpent sprang to his mind, and the words of Bauderlaire insinuated themselves without conscious effort. 'La femme cependant de sa bouche de fraise. En se tordan ainsi qu'un serpent sur la braise . . . . . .'

But with such power, he imagined the sea, dashing against the great cliffs of northern shores in the wild days of November, taking bodily shape and swirling with arms of flesh instead of foam. She was possessed by an elemental power. So many thoughts rushed through his head: the Sybil at Delphi, the maenads, the crazy train of Bacchus in India, Judith majestic and triumphant with the head of Holofernes, the last, doomed onrush of the Minotaur before the sweet, keen blade of Theseus found the pulse deep in his bosom.

So long it lasted. And when it was over she lay for a long time, breathing softly through parted lips. Then she kissed him sweetly with her soft lips.

'Alasdair,' she sighed, 'I love you.'

He then knew what pleasure was. Pleasure was making her happy. His soul thrilled with pure pleasure. It was as if he had accomplished some knightly feat of the old romances; as if he and he alone had drawn the sword from the stone or led the dragon on a silver chain to the feet of the princess. He was lifted onto a silken bed of sweet, sweet pleasure.

And so it had been ever since. To have a woman look at him and say that he had made her happy was too wonderful for words. And the strange thing is this: that the pleasure only came when he thought

---

[1] The Trojan priest who warned them not to allow the wooden horse into the City of Troy.

125

of her and her satisfaction. Never did it come if he tried to make her happy in order to feel pleasure.

But that is so true of all emotion. Pleasure must ever be a by-product. Like happiness, like contentment, like satisfaction, it only steals over us when we are not concerned with it and when we are concentrating on something else. How significant those simple words are; look for the *something else* and the rest will follow.

So often, so very, very often has time been described as a thief, as a depriver, as a raptor, as the harbinger of death. And how ignoble this attitude is, how discourteous, how melancholy.

Time is movement, which makes decision serious. Time is the imperishable stone on which we engrave our invention of ourselves and the conquest of our fears. Time is not only the river in which we can never step twice; it is also the current, which carries along what we have constructed. Time is the mirror in which we see what we are making of ourselves.

Falling in love again is one powerful way of re-experiencing something which has already happened. And one can bring to the new experience the wealth of understanding gained in the former one. This idea can be extended: listening to a new piece of music, reading a new book or the like. Doing something again, and finding something, perhaps much, of the wonder of the *first time*.

Perhaps the secret lies in a kind of openness, a naïve kind of willingness to let whatever is going on speak to you, show you, possess you. The fatal thing is to think that it has happened before and that therefore there is nothing new in it, but the very non-repeatability of time, guarantees that it need not be the same. If we expect it to be the same, it will be. But if we are foolish and simple enough to be open to the possibility of newness, then newness can filter into the situation.

Consider the decline of Rome. Why did that decline occur? Rome had been driven by this quasi-divine urge to govern, to order things and to affiliate that order-making even with the selfish human desire for money and power. Perhaps Rome simply got tired, weary for death of the same old thing, the same old problems, the same old frontiers to protect, the same old Emperors to endure. It is not for

126

nothing that the glory of the later Empire was Marcus Aurelius and his courageous brand of stoicism. Stoicism is all that is left when the spirit has fled.

The old monks spoke truly when they spoke of *acedia, accidie.* Sloth, as it is usually translated. It is one of the worst sins. More so, because it is so hard to do anything about it.

Many sins can be resisted. But when the feeling of worthlessness, of the sheer fatigue of *having to do something about it* and not only not knowing what to do, but not bothered about knowing what to do . . . when this oppresses the spirit, it is terribly hard to know what on earth to do. It is impossible to climb out of this pit. For newness must come without. If we are open to it, it will come.

17

ALL TOGETHER

Love is an endless mystery for it has nothing else to explain.

Rabubdrabatg Tagore

The door opened, just as Alasdair heard the knock. Adam came in beaming; his smile widening, as he walked over to kiss his father.

'Hi, Dad!'

'Hello, hello. You're early? I am so pleased to see you Adam.'

'Yes, Trudy and I set off early.' He said, putting a wicker basket filled abundantly with fruit on the low table.

They embraced gently and Adam excused himself when the nurse arrived to provide Alasdair with his morning routine of pain relief. He was gone only a few minutes.

'Where's Trudy?'

'I dropped Trudy off in Harrogate and she will meet up with Susan in Betty's. They are going to have a leisurely day shopping.'

He looked out of the window. Sunshine was being reflected on the stone terrace and the early morning dew although dissipating, was still glistening on the lawn.

'It's looking to be a fine day. Shall we get some fresh air before the others arrive?'

Alasdair nodded and Adam went to find a wheelchair. Realising it was chilly, they put on their overcoats and Adam covered Alasdair's legs with a warm woollen tartan throw. Once outside Adam took a path leading through the formal lawns to the more natural setting of parkland achieved over a wooden bridge at the narrow end of the lake. They continued along rough paths through a copse into the open rough grass and on towards the summer house. It is a splendid octagonal wooden structure with a verde gris covered copper roof. A wooden veranda surrounds the building painted in cream with plenty of seating and a ramp allowing wheelchair access.

Once settled, they observed the landscape of the pastureland, which dropped away into a valley and beyond to the tree cladded hills resplendent in autumn colours. Silence is golden. Alasdair broke the silence after some minutes.

'How are Trudy and April?'

'April is enjoying her training and sends her love. She asked me to give you this.'

He handed Alasdair a small leather photo album, which he opened and smiled as he looked at the photographs of his Granddaughter.

'Trudy sends her love too. She can tell you her news later today.'

'Jolly good.'

'Let's go inside, Dad. It is getting chilly.'

They retraced their steps slowly. St Dunstan's soon came into view, an imposing three storey square house in Yorkshire stone.

'It looks rather drab and uninviting, doesn't it?' remarked Alasdair. 'Even with the burnished red covering of Virginia Creeper bathed in sunshine?'

'It certainly does. Rather daunting. A very different feel from the interior, which is elegantly furnished.'

When they were settled again, Adam thought his father looked tired.

'How about a little rest before the others get here? You close your eyes and I will read the paper. Perhaps some music?'

He went over to the bedside chest where Alasdair's CD's were stacked and browsed through them before deciding on James Galway *A Wind of Change*. They were enjoying *Always on My Mind*, when Anthony and Alex arrived together and took turns to embrace their father. As it was nearly one o'clock they agreed to have lunch. Adam helped Alasdair as they moved along the corridor and into the lift to the ground floor private dining room reserved for them.

The table was laid and decorated with a small vase of freesias. An ice bucket containing a bottle of Moët & Chandon champagne awaited them. Anthony did the honours and once settled with glasses of champagne in their hands raised his glass and invited his brothers to join him in a toast to Alasdair,

'To our wonderful father and friend, Alasdair.'

'Thank you boys. What a special occasion it is to have all three sons with me today.' Alasdair stretched his arms out as if to collect them in an embrace.

'Sit down. Please? Let's enjoy our lunch.'

Alasdair had asked St Dunstan's chef to provide a light lunch for them and to be sure to give him a small portion. They didn't have to wait very long before the *Roasted Mediterranean Lasagne* was served with a green salad. They all decide to drink mineral water during their meal.

Alasdair was happy to be in their company and listen to all the things they wanted to tell him and each other. It was noisy. All three sons talking. The conversation changing from one subject to another like darts. He was so intent trying to follow that it was a surprise when his attention was diverted to the sensuous smell of ripe strawberries as they were placed in front of him. He looked up and asked the waitress, 'Surely not English at this time of the year?'

She smiled and seemed very pleased, saying, 'From Kent, actually.'

Alex filled everyone's glass with Champagne and looking at Alasdair, raised his glass and smiling said,

'A toast to us all.'

They all responded by raising their glasses and saying in unison and without prompting, 'Amen, Amen.' A shared joke, which provoked instantaneous laughter and they clinked glasses as they hugged each other. Alasdair interrupted, raising his finger knowingly to the side of his nose and recited a poem easily from memory.

> *'When I am dead and in my grave*
> *Let all my friends rejoice;*
> *And let all sound be silent, save*
> *An angel's whispered voice;*
> *'Forego your grief, assuage your sighs!*
> *A happy man sleeps there!*

He lay between her silken thighs
And kissed her silken hair.'

Lunch concluded, Alex retrieved his banjo from its' case and began strumming. They all know he plays very badly, but no-one cared to comment and soon they all joined in with a family sing song. The years had drifted along and Alasdair couldn't remember the last time they did such things together and thought perhaps it was selfish to want to see them alone, but Anthony had explained that the girls knew they needed time together and Susan and Trudy had been looking forward to shopping together in Hoopers Department Store. He was sad for Alex that he spends so much time on his own when Rachel is abroad with the British Council.

His thoughts were abruptly interrupted, when he turned his head to see Sylvia walk into the room.

'Well I never?' thought Alasdair, 'Here IS the girl with the silken hair'. Her copper hair caught the light and her face lit up as she approached them, holding out her hand to Adam who was getting up to greet her.

'I am Sylvia.'

Adam took her hand introduced himself and then his brothers guiding her to a vacant seat. Before she sat down, she came towards Alasdair arms open and embraced him lovingly.

'Forgive me, interrupting your party,' she laughed and sat down giving no explanation as to who she was and none was needed. It didn't matter who she was, here was a beautiful woman coming to see their father. Alasdair certainly had no energy or desire to illuminate. Adam found a chair for himself and then handed her a glass of Champagne. The conversation was now directed to include Sylvia and at once the atmosphere was charged with excitement as she introduced interesting topics of conversation.

'I'll call again, soon.' She rose from her chair, gave Alasdair a hug and a kiss.

'Goodbye everyone, it has been lovely meeting you all.' She waved to them as she looked back before opening the door and then she left.

All three sons looked at him for an explanation, but Alasdair was too happy and too tired and his only thought was, 'How lucky am I?'

They decided to retire to the drawing room. It wasn't long before Susan and Trudy arrived and tea was served for everyone.

Alex was keen to talk about past memories to remind Alasdair of shared times together and he thought back to their holidays in the Lake District as young boys and opened the conversation.

'Dad, do you remember the fun we had, when you taught us all to sail?'

'Yes, I certainly do. We had been going to the Lakes a few times before I bought the boat. That was the year we camped near Buttermere and took the boat out onto Crummock Water. Ruth preferred walking and so we always spent at least one day hiking. Good times.'

Adam continued, 'Mum always made cooking out of doors so effortless. The freedom we had then. We were allowed to explore on our own for hours at a time.'

'I remember,' added Anthony, 'it was Alex who learned to sail first and was so confident that he took Adam and I out onto the water without Dad, not that there would have been room for all of us. They were great holidays. Susan and I have been back several times to The Lakes for holidays and in recent years preferring the comfort of The Waterhead Hotel in Coniston.'

Alasdair listened to them as one by one they engaged in sharing holiday memories, the girls too. He closed his eyes.

It was nearly five o'clock when Alasdair startled himself,

'Oh dear, I have drifted into my own space. What are they talking about? I want to hold onto every word but their words slip through my mind like leaves through a sluice gate, in an instant. It doesn't matter. We are here together.'

'Shall I take you back to your room, Dad?'

Alasdair rose from his chair and gave each of them a hug, before taking Adam's arm and they steadily walked back towards the lift and up to his room.

Left on his own, he realised he was exhausted and in pain. He didn't need to call for help; a nurse had followed behind them and was ready to help Alasdair change into his pyjamas, administer his morphine patch and settle him. She spoke gently to him in a light fluffy way not expecting a response, just saying,

'How nice for you to have all three sons visit. I hope you all enjoyed lunch.' Then she was gone.

On his own again, he poured himself a whisky and looked out at the huge wet stars before drawing the curtains. Feeling better, he raised himself up and reached for the crossword. No use, Sylvia's perfume lingered, demanded his attention. She always wore *Ma Griffe* by Carven, an exhilarating perfume matching her personality. He closed his eyes and thought about their intimacy. In the early days he could sustain an erection but in the last years had been unable to do so. There were clumsy attempts using Viagra. In the end they ignored attempts at penetration and found joy in other ways. There was the joy of standing naked and close as hot water sprayed over them while showering. His hands following her frame, one he knew very well. With one hand on her lower back, he gently moved the other downward until he found and gently caressed her labia and further into her vulva where his fingers sensed the honeyed moisture within. Then he gently pushed himself slightly away from her to reveal the splendour and fullness of her nipples and moved his hand upwards to stroke the stippled circles with the nail of his index finger. He crouched down and put his head between her legs, holding her buttocks in his hands while he slowly and gently sucked and licked her clitoris until she dissolved in his passion. It was sheer pleasure to arouse her and gently bring her satisfaction.

133

18

MOVING TO YORKSHIRE

Water,
running it is alive.
Take it in your hand,
it is still beautiful, but it is dead.

The following day he spent the waking hour recalling his early memories. Born in September 1921, Alasdair grew up in in Ryhope. His father, Robert Sommersby was an Accountant working for an engineering company in Sunderland. His mother, Elsie had trained as a nurse and worked at the local hospital until Richard was born in the summer of 1918 towards the end of the Great War.

The family lived on the outskirts of Ryhope in a small development of new houses, built just after Richard was born. Each house had a large front garden making it easy for the boys to play outside with their friends. The brothers grew up in a happy home with plenty of freedom to roam the lanes and fields close by. Sometimes they ventured further crossing several fields in order to reach a stream taking a pasty with them for tea and as the sun set they jumped off the rounded humps of grass onto the soft shingle and barefoot into the shallow water flowing slowly across cobbles.

When Robert Sommersby was promoted to Finance Director in 1928, he celebrated by buying his first car, an Austin 7 Swallow Saloon in two tone yellow and black. The following summer they travelled to Alnwick for their very first holiday away from home. They booked two rooms in a large rambling house paying for bed and breakfast. On the last day they drove to Craster and parked the car before setting off on a circular walk following inland tracks to the quiet village of Embleton and lunched at Greys Inn before returning along the Northumberland coastline. The sea rolled in, roaring softly on the sand and whistling up the beach in diminishing flounces of white foam. They spent the afternoon on a beach near Skaith splashing in and out of ribbed pools. After drying off, they walked to Dunstanburgh Castle perched high on a cliff and standing like a jagged tooth in the distance.

It was late afternoon when they arrived back at Craster for a well earned cup of tea and a scone. Then, a visit to Robson's to buy kippers for tomorrow's breakfast.

The boys were clever and conscientious and both were educated at Ryhope Grammar School. Their lives were very different from those living in the industrial towns like Jarrow. Richard went to Durham University to study engineering in 1936 and signed up to the Royal Navy in 1940 after graduation. Alasdair went to Cambridge in October 1938, just after his seventeenth birthday to study Ancient History and Theology. It was at the same time Hitler overran the north-west border regions of Czechoslovakia following the Munich Agreement. The Czechs and Slovaks referred to it as the *Munich Betrayal*. Everyone at home hoped Hitler had what he wanted and things would settle down.

Deep in thought, he didn't hear the tap at his bedroom door and he was pleased to see a nurse, as he wasn't in the mood to raise himself to receive a visitor.

When she left he was comfortable and refreshed. His thoughts returned to Ruth who he met in his last year at Ryhope Grammar School. She was a diminutive girl with a mischievous boyish charm. He was hooked the first time he glazed into her eyes, as blue as sparkling sapphires. Ruth was good at art and majored in the subject when she went to Sunderland Teacher Training College the same year Alasdair left for Peterhouse College. They became an item during his visits home during the long summer holidays. On his return from Cambridge in 1942 they became engaged.

When he left Cambridge, Alasdair started his career in the Church of England as a Curate assisting Reverend Harry Wormington in a village to the west of Blackhall Colliery. He was devoutly against the war and avoided conscription, something he later came to regret. He lived in a small flat above the Church Rooms.

After college Ruth found a job at the Grammar School in Hartlepool with digs nearby which she shared with another newly qualified teacher called Peggy. Alasdair drove over to see Ruth two or three times a week on his motorbike and they settled into a routine against the backcloth of war. They had tried every which way to enjoy sex while remaining virgins. Ruth had been adamant about losing her virginity after marriage. Walter and Peggy were their only witnesses when they married in secret. It was nearly four years later when their formal engagement ended with a wedding ceremony, followed a year later with the birth of Anthony and the purchase of a Watsonian sidecar for the motorbike.

In 1955 they moved to a small village near Ashington, when a vacancy arose and Alasdair became the Priest in Charge at All Saints' Church. The vicarage was a rambling stone built Edwardian house with a large garden ideal for a growing family which now included Alexander and Adam.

Then, the living was rewarded with little money and the upkeep of a draughty vicarage relied on funds from the Diocese. Getting repairs to the roof and improving the heating took ages and they spent most of those years cold and miserable. Alasdair decided to improve the family's lot and applied for and was accepted to teach Religious Education at a local boys' grammar school. It all worked out well because they were the same boys who became involved with the Youth Centre, which was another of Alasdair's self inflicted challenges. There was criticism from colleagues in the diocese and some parishioners voiced their disapproval. Alasdair was confident that the appointment would not interfere with his parochial duties.

With the increase in salary, they were able to purchase a Ford Poplar and the family began to travel farther afield and spend holidays in the Yorkshire Dales and The Lake District.

Alasdair had been taught well by Harry Wormington.

'Never, ever enter a house if a teenage girl answers the door and her parents are not at home.'

This and other advice had stood Alasdair well over the years. But in an off guarded moment he hadn't been prepared for Maggie Bellerby. She opened the door and looked straight into his eyes, cigarette in her hand. She had dyed blonde hair and wore a shiny turquoise tracksuit. Her father, had been off sick from the colliery for a while and Alasdair had been to see him a few times and today he was taking Holy Communion to him.

'Would you like a cuppa, Vicar?' she called back to him as she turned away walking towards the kitchen.

Alasdair declined. Later when he was in the hall putting on his hat and coat, Maggie came to say goodbye. Alasdair offered his hand, but instead of taking it, she grabbed his jacket with both hands, pulled him closer and her tongue went into his mouth. He tasted stale tobacco and buttery bacon.

She took her mouth away smiling. 'There!' she said. Her smile was contemptuous. Alasdair didn't panic; he didn't pull away. She let go of his coat and went back into the kitchen. Alasdair adjusted his coat, recovered his composure and turning left by the front door.

It was soon after this incident that Alasdair became restless for change. He began to look for opportunities in North Yorkshire. Ruth liked the idea too and it was she who saw the advertisement in the Church Times for the position of Chaplain and Lecturer in Theology at a college near York.

Alasdair was in his late forties, when he and Ruth moved to North Yorkshire. She had applied for and been accepted to teach art an independent preparatory school near Thirsk three days a week.

Anthony was in his first year at Durham University and Alexander and Adam were enrolled at St Peter's in York. Alex was in his first year of the Sixth Form and Adam started a two year study course for O'level exams. The timing was good for both of them as was the independence of travelling into York by bus. They bought a large Victorian red brick town house within walking distance of the college. Ruth used the family car to drive to Thirsk. There was a block of garages behind the row of houses recently built in which Alasdair kept the MG and Triumph motorbike. He also rented another garage in the same block from a neighbour to house the Mirror Dinghy, in which all three boys had learnt to sail and remained very much part of their family holidays. The family were soon settled and happy.

Alasdair had noticed Grace's attention towards him at an end of term tea party in the college grounds one summer afternoon. She was married to Ian Derbyshire, who worked in the teacher training department of the same faculty. He knew them both quite well. Grace worked in the Finance Department. In their late thirties, friends assumed that their future plans didn't involve having children. Grace was always rather nervous in her husband's company and held back. When the party was coming to an end and people were drifting away, she found Alasdair apart from the others and approached him. They chatted happily walking towards the car park slightly behind the others, when she took a pace ahead and turned around to face him and looked him straight in the eye and said without hesitation, 'Ian will be away at a conference in August, please call me?'

He stopped, moved to one side and continued to walk in silence, while he made sense of her request. He watched Grace walk on ahead, she had a slender and shapely body, and walked like a willow tree in motion. He hastened his pace and caught up with the others and after saying his goodbyes to Ian and Grace linked arms with Ruth to walk home.

At the beginning of August, Alasdair phoned Grace and they arranged to meet in York for coffee. It was such a lovely day that they went for a walk along the river afterwards. Grace was so relaxed and happy that he found himself really enjoying her company and it wasn't long before they planned their assignation.

She was in the garden when he arrived, sitting at an ornate white wrought iron table with a vase of pretty summer flowers. A bottle of chilled white wine and two glasses were also on the table. She wore a summery frock that left her shoulders bare. He had the feeling that the frock would fall from her in one movement and that underneath would be her shimmering smooth skin.

'Hello Grace, such a lovely afternoon,' observed Alasdair as he drew close and bent over to kiss her cheek. He picked up the bottle of wine, looking at it and continued, 'this looks very nice. Shall I do the honours?' And without waiting for an answer, he poured the wine into the glasses. Handing Grace a glass, he took her other hand and gently eased her to her feet. Still holding her hand he led her into the house before allowing her to lead him upstairs and into a bedroom. He placed the glasses of wine on the bedside table and still holding her hand, looked at her.

She was extraordinarily lovely. What he particularly liked was her long dark hair, rich and glorious. Her hazel coloured eyes had a light greenish tint and she looked directly into his. Her skin reflected the light. What a temptation to undress her immediately, so potent was her loveliness.

Alasdair knew instinctively Grace would prefer a lingering journey and so he kissed her bare shoulders inhaling the delicate floral scented perfume of her skin. He passed his hands along the curves of her body, before leading her to the edge of the bed and she sat down. He took off her sandals and held her feet in his hands. She smiled at him, gently and invitingly. He kissed her feet, and his hands ran under the folds of her frock, feeling her smooth legs up to the thighs before leaning over to kiss her into a reclining position. He moved his hands all over her body, as if to kindle each part of it with his touch, stroking her again from shoulders to feet. Her frock had fallen off her shoulders and partly uncovered her breasts. He pushed it further down, revealing her breasts and nipples formed as tight little dark rosebuds. Alasdair caressed her dreamily as if he were in no hurry, waiting for the flame to be kindled in her and when he began to pull her frock down, she helped him. He lifted her so that she could lie fully on the bed and his mouth began kissing every part of her body.

When he leaned over to feast his eyes on her beauty, she whispered, 'Take your clothes off.'

He undressed and kneeling at the foot of the bed gently parted her legs to reveal the sweet dark curls around her vulva, feasting his eyes on her glistening skin before gently kissing her. His mouth grew more and more ardent as he continued to fondle her flesh

139

with his tongue. She began to respond and her mouth found his. Finally, she offered herself. Even then they suspended their pleasure, and she felt him quietly, enclosed before she began to move in unison with him until joyful ecstasy rippled through their bodies, the marvellous agony of sexual release. When Alasdair slipped out of her, they lay quietly together enjoying the echoes of their orgasm in warm embrace.

'How about that wine?' He sat up and passing a glass to Grace, put his arm around her as she also sat up. She kissed him on the cheek, they clinked their glasses and sank back into the pillows sipping the wine.

'Happy?' Alasdair asked.

'Perfectly.'

Alasdair and Grace were lovers for a year, sometimes they saw each other twice in a week, other times a month or two would go by. Grace encouraged Alasdair to join the college drama group giving them the opportunity to meet and spend time together. He really enjoyed the group and was especially pleased when he was chosen to play Professor Higgins in *Pygmalion*.

When the time came Grace told him, 'Ian has been appointed Head of Department at Sheffield Hallam University, starting in September.'

'Excellent news, Grace. Are you happy about it?

'Yes, I think so. We have been making plans. We will move during the summer and get settled. I won't be looking for another job. We have decided to adopt and that will take a lot of time and energy to go through the process.'

'Darling, I shall miss you. At the same time I am very happy for you and Ian.'

'I know you are. My time with you has given me the clarity to think about the future. I gained the courage to tell Ian what I really wanted. The surprise was he felt exactly the same.'

Alasdair realised that while he had been thinking of Grace, he had become stiff and cold in his chair. It was barely four o'clock and the sun was setting. A warm crimson light glowed through the silhouette of the trees in a cloudless sky. He would need help getting up and changed for bed. He pressed the red button and waited. The small pulse of life within him seemed to be sinking.

Later when he was settled in bed, Alasdair looked through his papers and glanced *A Passing* and began reading.

A PASSING

At first it was like trumpets sounding. Like dark
skies shot through with streaming shafts of light.
There was a clattering of heavy hooves on the road
and a dim murmur that grew and grew as the air of
expectation mounted. The very statues were held in
the spell and held their heads high as if they too,
listened for the approaching glory. Rich hearts,
heavy with thankfulness, lined the road. The glossy,
green laurel hung in wreathes round the lamp-posts.
The very air was thick with the incense of
adulation.

Then down the road the sweeping tide came, an
ordered tide, disciplined and marshalled; a blaze of
music and splendour of scarlet and blue. Swords
flashed; bayonets gleamed; caparisons swung and
tossed; manes and tails danced in the sun shafts.
The music rumbled and crashed. Shining epaulettes,
braids, sword belts all of gold and silver, burned
beside the burnished steel of bits and stirrups
and spurs.

How the heart lifted. What a weight of relief rested
upon it; so heavy a relief that all was over and the
world could breathe again; heart lifted, lifted with
all its weight of thankfulness like a harvester
hoisting on his fork the full, bursting sheaf of
wheat; glad of the burden. Heavy it grew, so heavy
that the mist came before his eyes again. There was
no sense of time now, so he seemed to be looking
through the mist immediately. There was a feeling of
greenness in the air, and sweetness of meadow grass
and somewhere near, the murmur of a river. There
came a rustling of leaves and a patch of birdsong
and far over the hill...was there a hill...came
the bark of a dog. The path that led to the river was
barely distinguishable in the lush grass of the

field, save that it was freer from the yellow of the buttercup.

Now the river was in view. It sang and lilted gently over the stones of its bed, flaunting a thousand colours, of the grass, of the trees, of the sky, of the earthen banks. Chuckling in the shallows, silent in the pools, it curved and twisted under the willows, tossing here and there specks of brown foam.

'Here is the river!' said the child, 'Hurry up and we'll have a swim! There...by the Otter Pool!' How inviting the river looked. How it sparkled and flashed; how cool it flowed, cool and brown, tugging away at the leaves of the laurel bush on its banks. 'Hurry!' said the child again. 'Off with your clothes! You can't swim with all that on!'

He looked down at himself. It was little wonder that the river looked so enchanting. 'You can't swim with all that on!' And so it began. First he removed the sword belt, and the weight of medals, decorations, aiguillettes and epaulettes. Then the shining boots and spurs, and the woollen socks, and the uniform, heavy with braid and the overalls, caught up under the heels with a strap. When his clothes had all gone, he noticed without surprise that the heavy iron-grey moustache had gone too; and the grey hair and the etched lines of his face and the weight of his paunch.

The weight of years dropped from him and his body shrank into the body of a boy again. 'You can't swim with all that on!'

Somewhere, trumpets were sounding, and a glory of scarlet and blue enticed the senses of the mind; but he put it all impatiently from him and stepped with his new feet into the river.

So the old General died.

19

THE ARRANGEMENTS

Sweet quiet, gentle source
Of peaceful serenity!
Even my soul rejoices
Of futile work,
Contemplates the peace
That awaits us for eternity.

Barthold Heinrich Brockes

'Good morning. How did your weekend go?' Frances asked as she entered his room, fresh flowers in her arms.

'Perfectly well. It was perfect in every way. It is rare for all three sons to be together. The best of days.'

'Have Alex and Adam gone home yet?'

'Yes they went home on Sunday after popping in to say goodbye.'

Frances busied herself arranging the cream roses having given Alasdair the newspapers. Content in their own company they soon settled. Frances browsed through *The Sunday Times* whilst Alasdair read *The Sunday Telegraph*.

Later, Alasdair was closing his eyes to rest and Frances was stroking his hand, deep in her own thoughts, when she was startled by a nurse entering to check on Alasdair. Frances gently released herself from Alasdair and rose.

'I'll go and make tea and come back in a few minutes.'

The nurse attended to Alasdair's needs gently and reassuringly. He would not require lunch as he had no appetite. On her return Frances poured the tea and saw Alasdair was now properly awake and relaxed.

'I have wonderful news. I am going for a job interview in London.'

Alasdair patted the bed for her to sit closer.

'One of my colleagues from way back in the '80s, when I worked in The City was in Ripon on business and called me last week, so we met up.

'The City, darling. Tell me more. I am intrigued to know more.'

'Well, it seems a lifetime away when I started working in the City, having left the secretarial ranks to become a professional saleswoman. I was singled out as my performance ratings were high and a year earlier I had shown aptitude when asked to represent my manager at a meeting in Frankfurt. He couldn't attend and considered the matter too important to discuss on the telephone. He asked me if I would represent him. I didn't hesitate. I accepted and although overwhelmed by the responsibility organised my flight, accommodation and a few days later found myself in a meeting with European colleagues, who fortunately all spoke good English. It was a challenge I had accepted and which stretched me to the limits of my ability and beyond.'

'I had no idea, Frances. Unforgivably, I never thought about what you did before your divorce.'

'My manager recommended me for promotion and that is how I ended up working in The City in the early 70's and from there my career took off into marketing, education and quality management, which is what I was doing when we moved to Yorkshire. Anyhow, Toby has told me there is an opening in his company for a Customer Services Account Manager looking after distributors throughout the UK. He called his boss straight away and arranged for us to meet.'

'And? Tell me more?'

'It will change everything. A corporate role will take me back to where I left off before my divorce. I just have to believe that I can regain the confidence I had back then and embrace new challenges.'

'What will you do.'

'It sounds like I will represent the company and work with the distributors to grow the business. They are located in Ripon and as far afield as Preston, Basingstoke and Norwich.'

'Well, I'll be blowed. This is wonderful news. Well done. After all this time struggling to make ends meet and working just a few hours a week. I am so pleased for you, darling.' Kissing her hand he said, 'Imagine, I am hugging you with all my strength.'

'It has been a struggle.' She paused for a few moments. 'For most of it, you have been beside me making it bearable. You must admit we have had some wonderful funny moments together.'

Frances flung her head back and laughed, lowering her head towards him, so that she could raise her eyes in an amusing gaze.

'On one of our days out for a picnic on the moors. You will remember which one, I cannot. We left the car and walked a hundred yards across the heather to where there was a glorious, wild panoramic view of empty green miles sleeping under the late morning sunshine. Nothing stirred, there was not a sound. Closing our eyes to the sun, we let it embrace our bodies in warmth.'

'Yes I remember, it was Middlesmoor and it was spring. It was a dry, warm day. We looked across the valley to the soaring green heights, hazy in the afternoon heat.'

'That's right. We were lying on an incline so we could still see the view, when we were disturbed by the sound of an engine. You looked over your shoulder and above us on the road was a Land Rover and a man walking towards us, who could only have been the Game Keeper. You reassured him, that we knew the country code and would be careful. No matches. He was about to turn away when he looked at our picnic and asked if he could join us. So the three of us sat there in awe of the landscape drinking Prosecco out of plastic mugs and eating creamy egg and cress sandwiches. Do you remember he told us about his cousin Hamish?'

'Sorry, no.'

'Well his cousin Hamish lives on the Shetland Isles. He is a crofter and back then he was struggling. Everything seemed to be mounting up and he couldn't make ends meet. So he began praying to God. He would be up on the hills with his sheep and there he would look into the sky. "Please God, I am desperate. Let me win the Lottery!" It made no difference, but each week he continued to pray. His circumstances were worsening. One day sitting on a rock, his head between his knees, God answered him. "For goodness sake, Hamish. Meet me half way. Buy a lottery ticket." We were all laughing, when

146

the Gamekeeper got to his feet and walked back up the hill. We laughed so much that when we stopped both of us were smiling through tears. Now do you remember?'

'A good tale. Well remembered.'

Frances smiled, remembering how perfect the day had been. She straightened up, looked at her watch and collected her things.

'I'll be off to work. Hugo will be here soon. I'll pop in on my way home after work. Do you need me to get you anything?'

'Something really naughty like fudge or Turkish delight perhaps.' He paused, 'No, what I would really like are a few fresh Medjool dates.'

'Will do.' And she was gone.

When he arrived, Hugo saw how tired Alasdair looked. Once he had poured them both a whisky, he settled in the arm chair.

'Cheers, Alasdair. A good malt.'

Smiling, Hugo began to relax.

'Alasdair, I have read through your suggestions and I am honoured you should ask me to read your sermon.'

'Thanks Hugo. It really is a stunner. My friends will be in no doubt how greedy I was for life. They will be moved and uplifted. I will go as I have lived, each breath a miracle.'

'How are you feeling today?'

'Weary. Very weary, my life is slipping gently away from me. I have little pain, just an overwhelming tiredness. I discover that I am freely and without angst letting go of my dreams. I am free to accept death with grace. Soon.'

'You can leave all the arrangements to me, my friend.'

Alasdair closed his eyes. 'Thank you. Do stay a while. Shall we listen to some music?'

Hugo got up and looked through the CD's and chose Arthur Rubinstein playing Chopin's polonaises. He picked up *The Daily Telegraph* and began to read and left Alasdair to rest with his thoughts.

The world of the five senses, huge, varied and marvellous as it is, is only what our brains select for attention from the overwhelming noise and dazzle our sense organs are equipped to take in. The blind find their way by echoes and resonances we do not notice, and dogs hear frequencies our ears cannot pick up.

Our familiar world is a little manageable enclave, outside which are galaxies and pulsars, atoms and particles. We can think of atoms only by using an analogy: they are in some ways like vast spaces within which tiny things whirl round at incredible speeds. And yet this alien world of atoms is not only around us, not only inside us, not only infused with us, but as two metals blend to form a stronger metal.

Just as a space with things buzzing round in it can be used as some sort of crude analogy of the realities of physics, so the half glimpsed world of physics can be used as some sort of crude analogy of the world of spirit.

The world is made of flesh and stones and it is made of quarks and neutrons and it is made of spirit, and all three do not merely occupy the same space in different ways, nor do they merely interfuse like an emulsion, they are all one, and we separate them only in order to try to perceive. We can go back to the simplicity of saying Jesus manifested himself and then stopped doing so and in that way, he showed himself and then stopped showing himself.

The music stopped and Alasdair raised himself from his thoughts.

'Hugo, I have enjoyed many visitors in the last few weeks as word circulated about my condition. Family, friends, lovers and even those with whom cross words have been spoken have each said their goodbyes.'

He looked for a response from Hugo. He saw none. No reproaching look.

'Thank you for agreeing to make the arrangements when the time comes for my funeral. I should like Brian, my dear friend and old colleague from the Territorial Army to play *The Rowan Tree* on his bagpipes during the Procession. Charlotte has already arranged for the choirboys from Ripon Cathedral School to sing the anthem *Gaudete!* from *Piae Cantiones of 1582* and she will sing *At the end of the day* followed by *Wish me luck as you wave me goodbye*.'

148

'One last item, Hugo I should like *The Dark Island* to be piped during the Recession.'

So, it is done. Alasdair sank back into his pillow and closed his eyes, raising his hand to his dear friend.

'Now I am ready. So tired, so very tired. Pervixi, neque idem fortuna malignior un quam. Eripet notis quod prior hora dedit.'[2]

Taking Alasdair's hand, Hugo bent down and kissed him on the cheek. He then left quietly saying nothing. There was nothing more to say.

After a while Alasdair's thoughts drifted to when he was at Cambridge. He was studying Theology while his brother Richard was serving in the Royal Navy. Listening to the war time broadcasts of Winston Churchill and how things could have been so different if in 1940 Neville Chamberlain hadn't resigned and advised the King to send for Winston.

It was just after four o'clock as the nurse was leaving that Frances came in and after smiling at the nurse, greeted him. She handed him a small brown paper bag.

'I managed to find the dates.'

He opened the bag.

'Lovely to see you.'

He took out a date and popped it into his mouth. He was savouring the plump sweetness and unable to answer when Frances asked, 'Shall I go and put the kettle on? Tea or coffee?' She waited.

'I think coffee would be good with the dates.'

It was clear Alasdair was very tired, because when she returned he was lying on top of his bed. They drank their coffees and nibbled at the moist sweetly flavoured dates in silence. When they had finished, she sat on the chair next to his bed.

'I wish I wasn't so tired.'

---

[2] Yes, I have lived life to the full, nor shall a fate unkind take away what the golden hours have bestowed.

Propertius, Roman Poet.

Frances held his hand and spoke softly to him.

'Let me read *The Princess* to you.'

Of all her attributes, Frances' voice is the most commented on, softer than BBC newsreaders and combining clarity with warmth.

The Princess

A long time ago, there lived a Princess. Her father
spoilt her and so she grew up having everything she
wanted. Non-one refused her, because her father had
the power of life and death over them.

In time she grew to be a beautiful young woman and
she fell in love with a handsome young man, who did
not return her advances. As she always got what she
wanted, she challenged the young man, as to why he
shied away. 'In truth, your Highness, my heart is
already spoken for. I love Whispering Dove your hand
servant.' The Princess was so angry that she wept for
hours and then in a pique decided to punish him.
People were always being punished in the arena. So,
she made the guards arrest the young man and keep
him imprisoned until the next games.

The day came and she sat on a dais with her father
high above. The young man was brought into the arena,
looking scared and wretched. As the noise of the
crowd died, the King stood up and challenged the
young man to exit from the arena. He had two
choices; one door led to a caged tiger waiting to
pounce into the arena and kill him. The other door
led to freedom.

The crowd was silent for a few seconds and then
people began shouting and pointing. Amidst the
noise, he lifted his face to see the Princess. Her
remorseful eyes drew his glance to one of the doors.
He took a deep breath and raised himself and walked
slowly, but boldly towards the door.

Once through the door he found his love trembling
behind it. He had trusted the Princess and now he
knew that she was beginning to understand love.

151

Alasdair showed Frances the draft order of service and asked her to pray with him. He held her hand and began.

'The Lord is my shepherd; therefore can I lack nothing.'

Frances picked up the order of service and joined him.

'He shall feed me in a green pasture; and lead me forth beside the waters of comfort.'

Alasdair closed his eyes and stopped. Frances continued, her sweet voice calming him towards a restful sleep. When she got up to go, Alasdair mustered the words, 'Bye, bye . . . . . .' but was too tired to open his eyes. Frances gently kissed his cheek and left.

20

DENOUEMENT

The petals fall in the fountain,
the orange-coloured rose-leaves,
their ochre clings to the stone.

Ts'ai Chi'h from '*Lustra*' by **Ezra Pound**

It was four o'clock in the morning, when Anthony received the call from St Dunstan's telling him that his father was slipping in and out of consciousness. He was at his father's side in less than an hour. The nurse stayed with him and reassured him.

She said, 'Hearing is the last sense to fail, so he may well be able to hear you.'

Alasdair opened his eyes, startled. He looked at Anthony. He smiled and closed his eyes.

Anthony understood. 'You're doing fine, Dad. You're almost there.'

He chose *Memory of Trees* by Enya to play before settling in the chair beside his father's bed. He took Alasdair's hand and recited from memory . . .

Tyger, Tyger, burning bright,
In the forests of the night:
What immortal hand or eye
Could frame thy fearful symmetry?

In what distant deeps or skies,
Burnt the fire of thine eyes?

153

On what wings dare he aspire?
What the hand dare seize the fire?

And what shoulder, and what art,
Could twist the sinews of thy heart?
And when thy heart began to beat,
What dread hand? and what dread feet?

What the hammer? what the chain?
In what furnace was thy brain?
What the anvil? what dread grasp?
Dare its deadly terrors clasp?

When the stars threw down their spears,
And watered Heaven with their tears,
Did he smile his work to see?
Did he who made the lamb make thee?

Tyger, Tyger, burning bright,
In the forests of the night:
What immortal hand or eye
Dare frame by fearful symmetry?

Songs of Experience by **William Blake**

He was aware of the music. He didn't open his eyes. He was aware of Anthony's voice. He breathed deeply. A kind of joy came over him. He had been thinking of Ruth. He had loved her, but had been unfaithful. He knew what he had been. He had no regrets. What do any of us really know about love? A diffuse and glowing relief passed over his mind, as when one is suddenly brought in from the cold to the unexpected and lively companionship of a warm fire. He heard the rasping sounds of his breathing and was aware of his body taking a long deep breath.

The nurse was near at hand and just after eight o'clock she placed her hand on Anthony's shoulder and declared Alasdair gone. He kissed his father and left the room to call Alex and Adam. Later, much later he remembered to call Frances.

'Yes, I will be at the funeral. Alasdair asked me quite some time ago to read the passage from Revelation, ending *I am the Alpha and the Omega, the beginning and the end.*'

After the funeral, many of the congregation joined the family at The Boar's Head. The invitation at the bottom of the Order of Service clearly stated Alasdair's wish for everyone *to make merry and raise a glass!* Frances was enjoying meeting old acquaintances she knew in Moreton but had seen little of since her divorce, when Anthony caught her eye and approached with a stunning bouquet including white roses and chrysanthemums. He kissed her cheek and handed her an envelope and said,

'The letter is from my father. Thank you for being his friend.'

She touched his arm, kissed his cheek before, turning to say her goodbyes.

She drove to Harrogate. By now it was raining and she had to walk uphill with the wind against her trying to shield herself under her umbrella as she walked towards Parliament Street. Finding a seat by the window at Betty's, she sat down looking out over Montpellier Hill and the pretty gardens beyond drenched by the rain. The trees in the park were swaying in the wind. She ordered a glass of Gewürztraminer. She sipped the deliciously cool wine turning her thoughts to the day's events. Finally she opened the envelope and read the note.

Dearest Frances, I thought I would put something down on paper so that you could, if you wished, refer to it from time to time. No-one ... no-one ... could have done more for Philip than you have. We are peculiarly helpless in troubles like this. On the one hand, we want to keep on fighting, we don't want to give up. On the other hand, not to accept that the matter is largely out of our control can put an intolerable strain on the psyche.

I do really believe that if it were a matter of how he was treated when tiny, then things would have improved greatly by now. No-one could have done more than you to give him a real chance to find his true self. So I think that the trouble goes deeper, back into his actual make-up.

Now the other thing is this; I know people who believe that they cannot sing ... simply because they were laughed at when they were little. It is very easy unconsciously to absorb the opinions of other people about oneself.

So ... you are not clumsy. You may like to imagine that you are, but you can show great sensitively in handling things. You are also, and of course you know this yourself, very clued-up indeed, and very capable.

You are nearly always right. I have relied on your judgement many times, and never found it at fault. You are also good at intuiting ... dreadful word ... and easily get to the heart of the matter.

In the course of a long and happy life I have come across many, many very capable people. None more than yourself. And that is the simple truth. And your capacity for giving is wonderful.

You have every reason to be thankful for being who you are. We are by no means in control of our own success. The world is not plastic in our hands. We can only do so much. Whatever our equipment and talents, we have always the surge of circumstances and the good will or otherwise of other people to deal with. Success in life is not to be gauged by how we "get on", but by how we have managed to deal with often powerful extraneous forces ... and, believe me ... you have had some pretty powerful ones to face. Just imagine, if you had had different forces to cope with; if the understanding and support had been there earlier and a thousand other things ... imagine how your own powers would have made something very different out of experience.

You must know how very, very much I rely on you, your judgements and your attitude towards me. How very, very much I let myself be enfolded by the deep warmth and comfort that you breathe. You are so precious. And I want so much, so very much, for you to be happy... all the time... so never stop believing in yourself ... I believe in you ... absolutely. Love, love, love Alasdair

She sobbed quietly. It was a while before she re-read the note and absorbed what Alasdair was saying to her.

Frances thought about her friendship with Alasdair and at six o'clock the pianist arrived and began playing a repertoire of classic songs; they were very comforting and she decided to stay and have supper. A waitress took her order for another glass of wine together with fish and chips. She was feeling relaxed when she picked up *The Times* from the rail holding newspapers, each neatly folded over and secured on a long rod. Her meal soon arrived and didn't disappoint. The chips were chunky and golden brown. The cod was piping hot. She opened up the crispy batter to release the steam before squeezing lemon all over the fish. She paused momentarily breathing in the pungent aroma before dipping a chip into the tartare sauce, and biting through the crisp exterior to enjoy the soft, fluffy texture of the potato. It was delicious and she closed her eyes to savour the taste. She ate slowly and when finished, she turned the pages of the newspaper at a steady pace as she read the gist of yesterday's news. She thought about Philip.

She was very tired when she arrived home and went to bed early. Frances had the strange sensation that for a moment everything was in balance.

For I am persuaded, that neither death, nor life, nor angels, nor principalities, nor powers, nor things present, nor things to come, nor height, nor depth, nor any other creature, shall be able to separate us from the love of God which is in Christ Jesus our Lord.

Romans 8. 38–39

Part Two

Walking on eggshells

1981
FALLING IN LOVE

5th January. My life is as interesting or as uninteresting as anyone else's. Today is the first time I have written in a diary. I am typing each entry as I find writing even with a fountain pen tiring. The thumb on my right hand was severed years ago attempting to catch a serrated cake slice. I cannot bend it, but it is capable of tapping the space bar on my IBM correcting golfball typewriter, which was acquired recently when the firm changed to word processing and staff were given the opportunity to purchase old equipment. I chose the blue one.

Wouldn't it be nice to write daily? An impossible thought. However, the first entry will recall how I fell in love with Edward.

It happened at some point after about a year. There was a subtle unspoken polarity of feeling. We weren't consciously flirting, but we laughed a lot and both knew it would happen and we both knew the other knew. That is happiness, the certainty and inevitability of an attraction. Eventually, we plucked up the courage and took that first step, the first physical contact beyond which there is no going back. And when we kissed my senses exploded with desire.

That was a few months ago. I met Edward at a customer meeting in The City, when my company presented a new financial system to the senior partner in his practice. As Managing Partner, he was involved in endorsing and ultimately implementing the new accounting system.

He is extraordinarily handsome with aquiline features. His hair has an auburn tint and recedes above his forehead, kept short to balance already thinning hair. When he smiles his hazel eyes shine brightly and hold your attention. His physique is muscular reflecting that in his early thirties, he continues to play football regularly. I sometimes watch him on a Saturday morning. At six foot three inches Edward is much taller than me and we fit together nicely when we walk arm in arm. We do a lot of walking.

On Boxing Day we went to Kempton Park and the highlight was the King George VI Stakes. We saw the Queen Mother in the winner's enclosure looking radiant. A very special day. So, I am in love with Edward and feel like a lotus flower opening its' petals.

31st January. A luxury, sleeping in this morning. Last night I attended my first opera at the Royal Opera House. At lunchtime my manager asked me and a colleague if we would like to attend because two customers had dropped out from the party. We saw Verdi's *Un ballo in maschera* with Luciano Pavarotti as Gustavus and Montserrat Caballé as Amelia. It is set in Stockholm in the year 1792. Gustavus, King of Sweden loves Amelia, the wife of his closest friend and has been told by a fortune teller that he will be killed by a friend. Like most Italian operas, it leads to tragedy. I was capativated by the music and the opulence of the set and costumes while listening to Luciano Pavarotti's powerful and thrilling tenor voice. Goosebumps, just remembering the sound and brilliance of the performance.

Sunday, 22nd February. A wet cold day as it has been all week. Tonight, I cooked supper at home for Edward for the first time. He was less than impressed with my basement flat in Charlwood Place, but in the evening with the curtains drawn and candles lit, one is not aware of the lack of light entering the sitting room. It is cosy and, most importantly, it is close to The City and near St James's Park where I love to walk at the weekend and have grown to love the routines of city dwelling, including shopping in Tachbrook Street Market nearby. Never more than thirty minutes from anywhere I want to be. Some mornings the air is refreshingly still and when I walk along the Embankment to the office, the misty sun envelops me in a warm glow. The house has been newly converted into three flats and mine is the basement. It wasn't long before damp was evident. It took two attempts to re-line the concrete floor and walls with an improved damp proof membrane to get rid of it. Perhaps after all, the house was built over Tach Brook, a tributary feeding into the Thames. That aside, we had a lovely evening together and ate *Fettuccine Alfredo* followed by *Scaloppine di vitello al Marsala* both from Marcella Hazan's *The Classic Italian Cookbook*. He hadn't eaten real Italian food before and liked it a lot. We drank a sparkling Italian wine. Edward gave me a lovely hug and said, 'I love you.' Well there is no doubt that I love him.

3rd April. Early this morning, I picked up my post to open and read on my way to the office. My mother's weekly letter was included. That sense of excitement and love never leaves me. Then there it is, on the last line *All my love, Mum xxx*.

There has been an attempted assassination of President Ronald Reagan. He is recovering from a bullet wound, but the report doesn't say how serious is his injury. Inevitably, old arguments are being brought up calling for stricter control of guns. It had raged over John Kennedy's death then waned, raged again after the deaths of Martin Luther King, Bobby Kennedy and recently of John Lennon.

26th April. Edward and I have returned from Geneva. He was there for a conference at The Ramada and I took an early flight so that we could meet at the hotel late Friday morning for coffee before taking a taxi to the Hotel Pax. It was just as I imagined, offering us a comfortable bedroom and en-suite shower without any frills. Light through the tall windows flooded into the room and at night we could close the wooden shutters. Located to the east of the city with views over Lake Geneva, it was only a short walk from The Museum of Art & History and as soon as we had registered and unpacked we set off to explore arm in arm, Edward being very pleased with me for having booked such a pleasant hotel.

We decided to climb the steps up to the Cathedral of St Pierre, which rewarded us with a panoramic view of the old town and lake. By the time we returned to the old town we were hungry and went into Café du Centre for lunch where we shared a bowl of *Marmite du Pêcheur* before rummaging in antique shops and taking lots of photos.

Edward had reserved a table at the Hotel d'Angleterre for the evening. The hotel dominates the Quai du Mont-Blanc and its whole facade glistened in gentle lighting as we approached in the early evening. Everything about it was luxurious. I was allowed to keep the menu from which we chose the *Carpaccio of scallops with green apple jelly* followed by *Fillet of char with sorrel sauce and baby root vegetables*. Afterwards we walked through the city streets and had coffee in a café before returning to Hotel Pax.

In the early morning we opened the shutters and window and stood together looking out across the lake. The sky was clear blue and we felt the cool air on our faces. After breakfast we wrapped up and headed for the dock to take the steamer to Lausanne looking out and beyond to the Alps and passing Chillon Castle. Vineyards cover many of the slopes leading down to the edges of the lake. We had a lovely afternoon looking around the historic streets of Lausanne and found a small café for lunch in Escaliers du Marché. It was warm enough to sit outside and we drank cool Gewürztraminer, whilst tucking into a bowl of steaming *Moules mariniére* and dipping torn pieces of baguette into the delicious sauce. We caught the train back to Geneva and arrived back just before dark and stopped off at Café Papon for a beef burger served with melted Swiss cheese and accompanied by a cool light lager.

The flight back today went smoothly. I am happier now than I can ever remember being.

3rd June. Edward phoned to tell me that Shergar, a three year old colt owned by the Aga Khan won the Epsom Derby by ten lengths ridden by Walter Swinburn. At odds of 10/11, it wasn't a big financial reward, but Edward was very pleased with himself.

We have decided it would be nice to take a holiday together somewhere warm and agreed Corfu would be a good choice. I have often thought of holidaying there ever since reading Lawrence Durrell's *Prospero's Cell*. My sister, Vivienne and her husband David went there a few years ago and I am sure they will have good ideas about where to stay.

4th July. Getting up early this morning, the sunlight streaked through the sitting room window, deliciously soft and subdued. I prepared a picnic and took the train from Waterloo to Ascot where Edward met me at the station. He had taken the roof off his Porsche and we drove to Cliveden in Buckinghamshire, a National Trust property and garden gifted by the Astor family. The house and grounds are set high above the River Thames with panoramic views over the countryside. We were keen to see the Italian style Long Garden with its topiary and the pagoda in the Japanese garden. Afterwards, we meandered through the beech woodland and along the riverbank until we found an area set back from the river and surrounded by an abundance of rhododendrons long since flowered. It was just the right place for our picnic. Edward poured the Lambrusco and we sat on the warm grass with our faces upwards to allow the sun to warm us. We ate our prawn sandwiches and fell about laughing as we took handfuls of cherries and popped them into each other's mouths. I picked out those attached to stalks and placed them around my ears like earrings and posed for Edward to take my photo. Afterwards we stretched out looking up at the sky. We closed our eyes and let the sun warm our faces. As we were about to leave, I got up and pulled him to his feet and started to dance, singing *It's so important to make someone happy. Make just one someone happy . . .* We stopped dancing and he pulled me to him and whispered, *One girl you're everything . . . . .*

29th July. This evening I watched the highlights of the wedding on television of Lady Diana Spencer and Prince Charles after walking home along the Embankment. I had spent the previous night in an office doorway outside the entrance to St Paul's Cathedral to see the arrival of guests and Diana. It was a very friendly night in the crowd.

4th October. Home listening to *Bridge over Troubled Water* and reflecting on a wonderful holiday with Edward in Corfu. Dassia is on the east coast framed by deep pine woods with secluded sandy beaches with dazzling views across an aquamarine sea to the mainland. We stayed at The Dassia Beach Hotel, which was simple yet comfortable. Our room was on the ground floor and when we opened the french doors there was a stretch of grass outside leading to the edge of the beach. We hired a scooter for a couple of days to explore the interior of the island along white dusty scented roads stopping to walk in the olive and lemon groves and lunching at open-air tavernas set back from the roadside in the shade of grape arbours. Riding back we took the coastal roads and looked out at the white limestone cliffs with small white painted buildings with their terracotta roofs, nestling below against the backdrop of a pale blue sea.

Once we were accustomed to the heat, we settled into a routine of relaxing at the beach, swimming and then lunch in a local taverna. We really liked *Bordétto*, a dish of cod cooked in a peppery sauce, accompanied by tzitzbira a local ginger beer, which was very refreshing and less acidic than the local wine. In the cooler evenings we walked into Dassia or through the pine forest before supper at the hotel.

There were several tours available during the week and we chose to travel to Gastouri south of Corfu Town to see The Archilleion, a summer palace built by Empress Elizabeth of Austria. The gardens on the hill look over the surrounding green hills and valleys and out to sea. The centrepiece of the gardens is a marble statue on a huge pedestal of the mortally wounded Achilles. His face is depicted full of pain gazing skywards. On the return journey we stopped at a local taverna for supper and were entertained by a troupe of musicians and dancers. The women formed a circle in their multi-coloured head-dresses and full pleated skirts with black boleros stitched with gold thread. They formed a circle and began a slow rhythmic dance surrounding the young men, each with a hand on his hip and head thrown back as they too danced in circles.

On my birthday we took a taxi to Vinieri Bistro and ate *Barbouni*, grilled red mullet served with a green salad. It was such a beautiful

166

evening we decided to walk back to the hotel. The night was silent, except for the sea grinding and crushing against the rocky outcrop of the shoreline.

10th October. Very nervous. Today the Chelsea Barracks were bombed by the Provisional IRA killing two people. The nail bomb was targetted at a bus carrying soldiers, many of whom were injured.

I remember my walks along Sloane Avenue to the King's Road and along to Markham Square to see Penny, my vivacious confidant friend from work. She always has a strong opinion on whatever subject we may be discussing. King's Road literally was a private royal road leading westward to Hampton Court Palace. We often used to meet at Peter Jones Department Store to purchase china from the Medallion dinner service by Thomas. We would also walk up Sloane Street and once we treated ourselves to expensive shoes and handbags from Charles Jourdan. Our favourite shopping was in Casa Pupo where we loved buying the Portugese ceramic dishes and ornaments. Penny loved buying pieces decorated with frogs. We both have a pair of doves. Sometimes after work, we would take a taxi from The City back to Chelsea just for the thrill of being driven down The Mall. Penny now lives in Paris with Ian, her new husband.

30th December. We spent Christmas apart but happy. Edward was keen to spend time with his brother and together with their father enjoyed playing snooker. He called me each evening. I stayed with Mum and Dad and we went to Vivienne and David's for Christmas Day and I joined them again on Boxing Day. We drove to the Nags Head in Great Malvern for a ploughman's lunch and then set out for a walk in the Malvern Hills starting from St Anne's Well. When we returned to the car, the sky was littered with soft puffballs of lilac cloud merging into a dark purple blanket above a rising moon. It was quite dark when we arrived at Mum and Dad's for a warming pot roast supper followed by mincemeat pies and Christmas cake.

1982

PRIX DE L'ARC DE
TRIOMPHE

2nd April. After reports that Argentina has invaded the Falkland Islands, a BBC journalist, Laurie Margolis managed to speak to an islander at Goose Green, who confirmed that Argentine forces have taken control of the island.

15th May. The possibility of being together more permanently became a reality when Edward's divorce was finally formalised. He has been separated from Sarah since she moved to Cumbria two years ago. Now she wants to re-marry and started divorce proceedings last year. It seems the most natural thing to do, to leave my flat and move in with Edward. It is a four bed-roomed modern detached house in Ascot with a double garage and small tidy garden. Built for aspiring middle management, one looks very much like another. It is in a quiet cul de sac of six similar houses set well back from the road. The surrounding area is very attractive with mature trees.

14th June. Argentina has surrendered.

I have moved in with Edward. It was wonderful sleeping in the same bed. Waking up this morning, I put my arm over him and planted my hand flat against his chest; Edward took my fingers and squeezed them lightly.

168

5th July. My two-year secondment for a charity based in London started today. It involves a lot of evenings with the flexibility of working from home.

We were invited to lunch with Edward's senior partner on Sunday. We took a change of clothes in order to play tennis in the late afternoon. Patrick and Melanie live in a large 1920's house on the Wentworth Estate near Virginia Water. There were twelve of us for Sunday lunch including their son and daughter. I cannot imagine cooking for so many, but Melanie was very organised and several guests including me helped her tidy up in between courses. It was a warm afternoon, so we spread out into the garden to relax. Around five o'clock Patrick began organising those who wished to play tennis into a tournament. A few preferred to swim and take a sauna. We left just as the sun was setting. Melanie is a lovely hostess and did everything to make me feel comfortable and at home. It is clearly a lifestyle towards which Edward has aspirations.

7th October. We have just returned from Paris and saw *Ardross* run in Prix de l'Arc de Triomphe at Longchamps. Edward was aghast and really upset at Lester Piggott's use of the whip. He was narrowly beaten by *Akiyda* ridden by Yves Saint Martin. We stayed a couple of nights at Hôtel Scribe in the opera district. The hotel wraps around the corner of rue Scribe and its spirit of elegance prevails from the vast lobby throughout. The wood work in our bedroom was painted pale grey and I noted how elegant it looked against the cream walls and stylish furnishings. We looked out onto the River Seine and when we opened the full length windows, protecting us was a tiny balcony with a decorative wrought iron screen and trough overflowing with bright red hardy fuchsias. We dined at Restaurant le Lumière on the first night, named in reverence to the Lumière brothers. It was Louis Lumière who showed his first films at Hôtel Scribe in December 1885. We chose two courses from the table d'hôte menu and were delighted with the *Creamy Celeriac Soup infused with Truffles* followed by *Duck Breast roasted with Junipers in a Rich Sauce* and were pleased that coffee was also included. When we returned from Longchamps, we were too tired to dine out and had a salad served in our room. Everything about the trip has been perfect. Edward is happy. I am happy.

18th December. We had our first dinner party on Saturday. It went really well. We invited Patrick and Melanie together with Edward's neighbours. Edward chose a wine for each course. To begin I served a *Turban of Sole and Salmon Filets* filled with a mousseline and then steamed. The centre was decorated with watercress and served with melba toast triangles. This was followed by *Coq au Vin* served with Dauphinoise potatoes and Savoy cabbage. The *Chocolate Marquise* was very rich, decadent and a delicious crowning glory to the meal. Edward chose Recioto Valpolicella, a dessert wine, which countered the sweetness of the chocolate. Melanie helped me make the coffee. She is a very energetic, bubbly person encased in a small frame with an explosion of tightly curled black hair around her face.

I was elated when everyone had left and amazed when Edward complained that I hadn't contributed to the conversation. He asked me, 'Are you up to it?'

We sat at the bottom of the stairs and he pondered aloud whether it would be better if I returned to Pimlico. I couldn't understand and cried; eventually he allowed me to stay.

This morning Melanie phoned to say how much she had enjoyed the evening. A pity Edward didn't take the call.

1983
THE BBQ

9th February. Yesterday evening Shergar was stolen from the Ballymanay Stud in County Kildare. The shocking news has been met with dismay far wider than the racing community. It is believed a £2 million ransom was demanded by the gunmen during the raid.

13th March. The World Ice Skating Championships in Helsinki are over. The pure theatre and most original performance of *Barnum* pervades. Christopher Dean wore a formal white suit and Jayne Torvill a short white dress with an aquamarine satin cumberband and bow at the back. They had been helped in their performance by Michael Crawford, the stage show's star.

24th April. This evening, I have been listening to David Bowie's *Let's Dance* album over and over. My favourite is *China Girl* with Bowie singing over the sounds of a bluesy rock guitar.

16th July. Yesterday was ghastly. I slept in the spare room and am upset, confused and weary. This is the history of my day yesterday.

A friend of Edward's from university invited us to a barbecue in Beckenham. I prepared a selection of salads to take with us and forgot to check the road atlas for a route. The journey was a disaster, getting lost in and around Kingston upon Thames and then couldn't find the right road out of Croydon. Without warning, Edward drove to Croydon rail station and ordered me to get out. He told me that he had had enough. He would go onto the party alone. He also said what I thought was very strange, that I was a passenger on his train.

Stunned and upset, I caught a train to Clapham Common and there waited for a train to Ascot and walked the three miles along dark country roads, passing large opulent residences with no street lighting. It was after eleven o'clock, when I got back to spend the night in the spare bedroom. He is cooking breakfast. I'm not hungry. Joyless, I feel cold.

21st August. I woke full of energy and fresh. The last month has gone so quickly and Edward has been kind and attentive doing everything he can to make me happy; the Clapham Common incident is behind us. We made love for the first time since that evening and his touching me was like a dance. Once the marvellous agony of sexual release was over I lay in his arms a long while before turning on my side and he snuggled up behind me warm and sleepy.

5th September. We spent the weekend with Vivienne and David. It was our parents' fortieth wedding anniversary on Sunday. Vivienne and I had planned a surprise party to include our relatives. They travelled from Southampton, St Asaph and Dudley all to be with them on a very special day. I had made and iced the cake earlier in the week and just needed fresh roses from Vivienne's garden as a finishing touch. Vivienne and I spent Saturday preparing a buffet lunch and David worked on getting the house and garden ready. Edward spent the whole day either reading a book in the garden or watching horse racing on the television.

It wasn't easy facing uncle Charles after so many years and making light conversation with him. It was best to be polite and not to spoil an otherwise lovely day.

14th October. Cecil Parkinson has resigned after it was revealed that Sara Keays is pregnant with his child. Evidently they have been lovers for years. She writes with bitterness in *The Times* that he derided her for wanting to keep the baby. He is married with three children and was widely tipped as Margaret Thatcher's successor.

We are planning a skiing trip to the Austrian ski resort in Kitzbühel next spring with Patrick and Melanie. Edward is keen for us to ski together beforehand and so he has booked a week in St Anton. It has been a busy few days getting ready for the holiday. Thank goodness for C&A where we were able to buy our ski jackets and accessories. An early start tomorrow.

17th December. Home from a fabulous week in St Anton to find the Harrods' bombing is all over the Evening Standard. It is frightening.

We had good snow in St Anton and skied every day. Most days after lunch in a mountain restaurant, I relaxed for an hour taking in the sun outside, while Edward took the drag lift higher and enjoyed skiing on a red run. One day he skied to St Christoph and it was very relaxing being on my own in the town. Our guest house didn't serve dinner and so we were free to eat out each evening in the après ski bars and cafés. There were always English skiers to meet in the bars and to share our experiences on the slopes. We kept bumping into them at different times on the slopes or in the on-piste eateries and several times skied together as a group.

We got up very early this morning just as the sun was rising and took the chair and drag lifts to the start of a gentle run before leaving. The sun was up and we looked down to the dark outline of St Anton and across to the west to the irregular humps and horns of the Alps. Edward put his arm around me and we savoured the stillness. I kissed Edward and he hugged me before he turned his skis downwards. He skied the slope ahead executing perfect turns carving the snow, his long shadow ahead of him. He sped through the trees to the right of the slope and disappeared over the next rise. I breathed in the cold air before letting go and skied down taking care over the moguls and staying on piste. He was smiling when I eventually reached the end of the run and skied into his arms.

27th December. Edward is keen for us to move, somewhere new for us both. I am going to see an estate agent tomorrow and put my flat in Charlwood Place on the market. We will start looking for a new home in the spring.

1984

PIPPINS

12th February. Yesterday we returned from a week skiing in Austria with Patrick and Melanie. We took a Lufthansa flight to Munich and then by shuttle bus to Kitzbühel. It is a charming traditional medieval town much bigger than St Anton. On arrival, we hired our skis and bought the lift passes. The cobbled streets in the centre of town are traffic free with the snow piled high on both sides keeping the pavements clear. As we walked through town, the snow crunching under our feet, we breathed in the sharp tingling air. Huge sloping roofs each spanned several buildings, which are a mixture of yellow, blue and pink, many with windows framed by dark wooden shutters. Beyond the buildings and overseeing the town is the high gothic tower of St Catherine's Church. We stayed in a fairly large chalet style guesthouse within walking distance of the cable car. On our first evening, we had a good look around and everywhere we looked the bars and cafés were full of people in groups laughing and hugging each other. We soon found somewhere to eat and realised we were all exhausted after the travelling and settling into this lively town of Kitzbühel. Walking back the snow fell lightly on our faces.

Neither Patrick nor Melanie have skied before, so we began on the nursery slopes. After a few days they began to really enjoy the skiing and we took the lifts to higher slopes. Most afternoons we sunbathed after lunch at one of the mountain restaurants. It was surreal sunbathing, whilst drinking hot chocolate high above the tree line surrounded by snowy peaks. The sunlight was dazzling on the pristine snow against a crystal blue sky. Edward usually left us for an hour to take a drag lift higher to a more difficult run and then caught up with us towards the end of the afternoon so we could all ski down the mountain together. Being tall, slim and athletic, Patrick soon began to look competent and graceful as he skied tackling moguls effortlessly.

It is the best feeling coming in from the cold snow; your fingers and toes are aching from the chill of it and then sitting near the fire, your cheeks start to flame followed by the pleasure of thawing out whilst drinking glüwein.

On our last day, Melanie and I took a break from skiing and took the train to Salzburg to visit the birthplace of Mozart. It was the most extraordinary feeling walking through the rooms on the third floor of Hagenauer House and seeing Mozart's childhood violin, his clavichord and family portraits. We found a café for lunch and then headed towards the Cathedral Square. As we approached the cathedral, we looked up at the statues of the apostles Peter and Paul bearing a key and sword. Inside the cathedral we walked towards the bronze baptismal font with lions at its base where Mozart was christened. We arrived back in plenty of time to catch up with Patrick and Edward to enjoy our last evening in Kitzbühel.

14th February. What an enjoyable evening! We watched the ice dancing at the Winter Olympics in Sarajevo. We were travelling and missed Torvill and Dean's short programme but today we sat glued to the television to see them dance *The Bolero.* It was mesmerising. Perfection. They received perfect scores and won the gold medal.

15th February. The news is full of admiration of Torvill and Dean's performances at the Olympics. They have stunned the world. We also got to see a reprise of their *Paso Doble* short dance with Jayne as the bull fighters' cape. I could watch it over and over again.

28th March. Last night Edward hosted a client together with his wife at the opening night of Starlight Express at the Apollo in Victoria. The set featured several race tracks that extended into and around the auditorium and up to the balcony. A huge steel bridge lifted and tilted to connect the various levels of the set.

We were told that rehearsals hadn't been going well, so Trevor Nunn changed the setting only weeks before opening night. He was in Central Park in New York where he saw young men on roller skates showing off with dance moves and jumps. Arlene Philips had to change the choreography and the cast had to learn to dance and act on skates. It was exhilarating.

Afterwards Edward drove me to Richmond, to pick up my car. We agreed that I would follow him home; it seemed a very natural and friendly thing to do. So off down the M3 motorway we went, but I couldn't keep up. Edward indicated and pulled up on the hard shoulder. He jumped out and came over to my car. He was angry and told me to keep up.

I don't enjoy night driving and was now extremely nervous and somehow began to follow the wrong car and slipped behind. Again, Edward pulled over onto the hard shoulder, but this time when he came to speak to me, he leaned into the car and removed the keys from the ignition and drove off. It seemed like forever before he returned. When he did he simply threw the keys into the darkness and drove off.

I was scared out of my wits, being alone on the motorway and even with the help of the headlights, couldn't find the keys. I put on the hazard lights, but no one stopped. So, I waited for sunrise before finding the keys and then driving home and tip-toeing into the spare bedroom.

Edward left for work early this morning. Thank goodness I don't have any appointments today, so can work from home. Lots to do, but all I really want to do is cry.

5th May. We have moved in. Well I moved in; Edward was away in Dublin meeting clients. It couldn't be helped.

Pippins is converted from two estate cottages on the Devil's Highway in Hampshire. It is an irregularly built house of two storeys standing among gardens and shrubberies. The front has been painted white and is half covered by a clematis. Not in flower now, but looked good in the sale particulars. It has a red tiled roof. The previous owners have added a single storey kitchen extension and double garage both with pitched roofs. The front garden is defined by a rustic fence and sweeping drive up to the garages. The sitting room has been enlarged without finesse and Edward has already costed-in plans to re-vamp the downstairs to create a more homogenous living space. First we will settle in. Our mortgage interest is fourteen percent.

20th May. When I looked out this morning the sheep were bleating after the rain, the hedges were dripping and the birds were singing. Later I met Myra. She lives with her elderly father in a cottage at the end of the lane. She asked if she could help with housework and I was delighted to accept.

We have worked so hard this weekend decorating one of the guest bedrooms. I chose a Laura Ashley design of tiny pink clover flowers for the wallpaper and bed linen and have already started work on making matching curtains. Edward has bought a sit-on Westwood mower to cope with the orchard and gardens and mowed the lawns on Friday evening, when he returned home from the office. He has become more contented and happy. Moving from his old house and past seems to be working. We have made friends with Victor and Daphne our near neighbours, just a hundred yards down the lane. They have encouraged us to get involved in the horticultural society and Edward has plans to make beer for the summer show.

19th June. The sale of my Pimlico flat has gone through. We can now get on with some of the changes needed to Pippins. Summer has arrived and we can see more clearly how the garden is laid out as the herbaceous plants begin to emerge. There is a bower at the further end with honeysuckle and jasmine climbing through. To one side is a stream with Cotswold limestones arranged at different levels to create the idea of a natural stream running through the garden with pools at different levels. The water lilies in one of the pools are beginning to flower in profusion, swanlike and elegant. Edward is keen to put Koi in the large pool, but first needs to research their care.

14th July. The sun blazed and we had a lovely day with Victor and Daphne at the horticultural show. Victor won prizes for his vegetables, but Edward's beer and my strawberry tarts were not elevated to any form of recognition. We ended the afternoon having tea in their garden.

1st September. Waking early, the grass was still heavy with dew and the sun was rising the colour of melted butter. It was a perfect day to be in the garden and I planted five hundred daffodils in the orchard. Over dinner, I announced I was pregnant. Edward was delighted, he hugged and kissed me and said, 'How wonderful. Shall we marry?'

22nd September. We spent the day in London to buy an engagement ring at Richard Ogden's in Burlington Arcade, Piccadilly. Edward convinced me that the one I chose was rather too expensive, so we settled on an Edwardian ring with a square sapphire set with a diamond either side. Afterwards we had lunch at Fortnum's and then took a cab to Brompton Road to browse in Harrods. Edward noticed a large shed in the middle of the road, could be a cricket pavillion, but it was painted green with a black pitched roof. There were a few cabs parked by. Edward asked the cab driver, who was delighted to tell us that it is a shelter providing rest and refreshment for those with *The Knowledge.*

25th October. Edward and I were married on 20th October. Once Edward's family were settled into Pippins, we left them after supper and drove to Richmond Gate Hotel so that we could enjoy an evening together, just the two of us followed by a leisurely morning before our big day. Vivienne and David drove down with Mum and Dad to The King's Road and we met them inside Chelsea Registry Office in the Old Town Hall. Dad looked smart in his dark grey suit, tall with a straight back and elegant air. Both were tanned from their recent holiday in Greece and Mum must have been feeling the cold as she wore a fur stole over her pale pink suit.

Me, well I wore a bright blue moiré silk suit with a long, full skirt by Caroline Charles. Frederick Fox obtained matching fabric and made me a lovely pillbox hat with long curving feathers and a short veil to just below my eyes. I chose a posy of coral pink roses from Moyses Stephens in Marylebone and matching button holes for Edward and those attending the ceremony.

It was all over so quickly. David took lots of photos on the steps outside the Old Town Hall and when two Chelsea pensioners walked by they were happy to be included.

We had decided on family and witnesses at the registry office and to meet our friends afterwards at Lichfield's Restaurant in Richmond. It was a very happy occasion with our family and friends enjoying a buffet lunch, served with Quincy a white wine from the Loire Valley with a hint of citrus and fresh finish.

It was quite late in the afternoon when we returned to Pippins for Champagne and wedding cake. Vivienne and David took Mum and Dad home once we had all relaxed and Edward and I had opened our presents. The following day once Edward's family left, we set off for The Sign at the Angel in Lacock. We chose the right weekend to see Stourhead in all its' glorious autumnal colours. The garden was created by Henry Hoare who began work on the garden in 1744 with the aid of the architect Henry Flitcroft using the natural valley of the River Stour to create a spectacular landscape setting classical sculptures around the lake. The garden is designed to delight and surprise visitors by revealing its views and buildings gradually as you encounter them during your walk. We lunched at the pub on the estate which is run by National Trust volunteers.

30th November. There are streaks of burnt orange across the sky this evening, highlighted by the trails of aeroplances long since gone. It was my last day in the garden for a while. The late autumn leaves are lying on the ground, which Edward will collect another day. I concentrated on a final check around the garden, soft pruning of the roses and shrubs and cutting back the dying herbaceous leaves. It wasn't long when a robin arrived to keep me company, trusting me. Cartoon cute, it followed my every move and flew down close to my feet to peck the soil revealing a tasty morsel. He stayed a while before flying off to another garden to confide with a neighbour. By noon the sun was really warm.

The result from the amniocentesis arrived; there is a blue ribbon under Edward's pillow. I was sure I felt tiny flutterings.

1985

B IS FOR BEAR

10th January. A perfect January morning, and a feeling that spring has already come. There is no wind, the sky is cloudless. I cannot believe that it is still winter and that the snow will probably fall soon and whiten the earth. The hour is of spring and I feel so happy. I have a whole free day, nothing unpleasant to do and feel like a schoolgirl, who has overstayed her holidays.

22nd February. This was the last day of my secondment and I spent the day in London talking through the work with my replacement. Arriving home, Edward was already there and had booked a table at Chez Nico, owned by the charismatic Nico Ladenis. We have been a few times and he is charming, unless, of course, one asks for salt. We never have. We were both relaxed and Edward was so reassuring about everything. A new beginning full of expectations.

30th March. What surprised me was how nature called on me to spring clean the house today, so close to my labour. I just did it. My bag is packed.

10th April. Now, settled at home, I never dreamed how much I could love my son. Philip is asleep. Mum has gone home and I have made a cup of tea and need to catch up.

Our beautiful son arrived in the early hours of 1st April, much to the annoyance of Edward to have a son born on April Fool's Day.

We spent the morning gardening and at lunchtime I noticed a plug of mucous. In the evening, we watched *Apocalypse Now*, while I ironed and monitored my contractions. When I called the Royal Berkshire Hospital, it was late evening and I told the nurse that the contractions were every five minutes. To her question, I answered, 'Yes I am coping with the pain.'

She told me, 'Call back in the morning.'

They knew best and so we went to bed. Sometime in the early hours of the morning, I woke Edward with the most primeval scream.

As Edward helped me downstairs, he warned, 'No time to call for an ambulance, we need to get to the hospital.'

He didn't pick up the packed suitcase with the hospital notes, nor did he know exactly where the hospital was as he hadn't been with me to hospital visits.

When we arrived, Edward rushed to find help. I staggered out from the back seat of the BMW and got down on my knees. When a porter came with a wheelchair, I asked him to put the blanket on the ground. Philip was born just underneath the canopy of the hospital entrance.

After the birth Edward went home to freshen up and then came to visit me the next day on his way to Manchester to discuss his brother's new business venture. He returned on the Wednesday to collect me and Philip as we were allowed to leave the Royal Berkshire Hospital and drive to the Wokingham maternity unit. En route we called in at Pippins to freshen up and call Victor and Daphne so they could walk over to see Philip and share in our happiness.

While at Wokingham, Philip was experiencing problems feeding and he also had an infection. It was decided we should return to the Royal Berkshire, where we had a room off the ward which gave us privacy and space. I experienced an overwhelming feeling of despair and fear. Once Philip was feeling better, I cheered up and we went home after a few days. Edward took three days paternity leave. He spent most of his time looking through the Thames Valley Trader and driving out to look for a car for his brother Simon's new enterprise, which Edward is helping to finance. In three days, he brought me one cup of tea. He told me that cleaning and looking after him wasn't to come second to the baby. So while trying to relax and enjoy the beginnings of motherhood, he was making lists of chores for me to do. The mid-wives arrived one morning to find me vacuuming. This was while Edward was on leave to help me.

Fortunately, my parents came to stay and Mum stayed behind for a few more days to help. The list of jobs got longer. And one morning Edward instructed me to clean the Westwood and tidy the garage. It never occurred to me to say NO. Mum was horrified. This may have contributed to the difficulties I am experiencing breast-feeding. I feel too tired to be joyful. I just feel anxious.

15th April. Philip is unwell. We went to see Patrick and Melanie at the weekend to introduce Philip and it was clear after lunch that Philip couldn't settle and was in discomfort. Today, Dr Fraser has diagnosed tonsillitis and prescribed Amoxicillan. He recommended a change to bottle feeding. I can't hold back my tears.

1st June. Philip is two months old today. This evening, looking at Philip in his cot, I felt an overwhelming sense of love and purpose. There he lay looking up at me with his legs in the air with such a lovely mischievous grin, surrounded by his Teddy, Snowman and Tigger.

Mum has given me a lovely illustrated book to chart Philip's progress with first impressions and photos. With the arrival of summer, we are all spending more time in the garden. While Philip sleeps in his pram, we are keeping the garden tidy and planting to improve the look and colour.

I have taken Philip into Reading several times for afternoon tea at Heelas Department Store. When I hold him, he clasps my hair and gold chain, so it won't be long before he can hold a rattle.

Philip is amused by a mobile of butterflies hanging above his cot, which allows me to get on with chores. There is also a duck mobile hanging above the chest of drawers where I dress him while singing nursery rhymes. He smiles and has started to laugh and make noises. There is a Dick Bruna alphabet frieze attached to the beam that runs around the bedroom.

It seems a long time ago when he was three weeks old and was very poorly with tonsillitis and couldn't suck. He has taken to SMA. One advantage is that Edward can now give Philip his feed and he is really enjoying doing so.

18th June. After lunch today, I laid out a picnic blanket in the garden and a softer cotton quilt over it and placed Philip on his tummy. Within reach there was a large plastic brightly coloured ring with different shapes attached and I lay down by his side, turning my face towards him talking to him about all sorts. I then rolled over onto my tummy and opened Dick Bruna's *B is for Bear* upright in front of him and turned the pages making up a story for each picture.

At tea time today, Philip had his first real food, just two teaspoons of rice cereal. He has moved from his wicker cot into a larger pine cot, which will convert to a bed later. He is surrounded by Teddy and friends and activity centres attached to the end and side of the cot. I photographed him today lying on his tummy raising his head and shoulders absorbed with the bright colours. Later, I watched Edward in the bath with Philip and afterwards I took a photo of Edward holding him looking really at ease and happy being a Dad.

27th June. It is time to contact employment agencies to find a nanny for when I go back to work in October.

Mum and Dad are staying for a few days. I am enjoying their company. We had our first evening out since Philip was born. I drove to Richmond and got the train to Waterloo and met Edward and his clients at the National Theatre. We saw Anthony Hopkins in Pravda. He plays a white South African media mogul. Our seats were so close to the stage he loomed over us and was quite mesmerising. Of course, it is satire on the newspaper industry and in particular the press baron Rupert Murdoch.

The house was quiet when we got back and after a night cap, Edward went to bed. I wanted a quiet space to reflect on how happy we were this evening.

Edward's clients are staying at The Petersham Hotel in Richmond and we will meet up with them tomorrow at Wimbledon. We don't need to leave until eleven o'clock, so I will have a chance to spend time with Philip before leaving him with Mum and Dad. We shouldn't be home too late.

10th July. Philip has grown so fast, no longer fragile to hold; he is robust and dressed in a blue check romper suit today with white socks and I have put him in his baby bouncer on the kitchen table to be near me. His face is smooth and oval and framed in fine blonde hair. He is looking at me and smiling. Another photo for the album.

13th July. It has been a splendid day and with time on my hands, I made pear puree and poured it into an ice-cube tray to freeze along with the apples I did a few days ago. There is now a really good selection in the freezer including purées of chicken, carrots and mashed potato. It is just so easy to take a selection and heat in the new microwave.

I watched *Live Aid* for a couple of hours this afternoon, while Philip was napping. Leading up to the event, there was a lot of publicity and Bob Geldof with sheer determination and tenacity persuaded many artists to perform. He was passionate about doing something to help the starving in Ethiopia. Edward and I watched this evening, but we missed Queen's performance and are looking forward to seeing highlights from both Wembley and Philadelphia tomorrow.

30th July. Today was our annual visit to Glorious Goodwood with friends. I usually prepare a picnic as we like to watch from Trundle

Hill. It has become a tradition. It was disappointing that no-one offered to prepare the picnic this year, particularly with me being a new Mum.

I was up very early and under pressure to finish preparing the picnic in time for us to leave and I asked Edward to keep an eye on Philip. Later when Philip was crying in his cot, Edward point blank refused to take him out and console him. When I picked him up, it was obvious he needed his nappy changed. I asked Edward to help and he refused. I pleaded with him. Jumping out of his chair, he grabbed me and shook me and then taking hold of my hair pushed me along and banged my head against the kitchen wall. I could feel the roots of my hair being torn from my scalp. Tears burned my cheeks. It took a while for me to calm down and to compose myself. We arrived late for the rendezvous at the Spread Eagle Hotel in Midhurst and put on a show of togetherness. Patrick put a bet on for Philip, *Time Machine* ridden by Lester Piggott. It didn't win.

10th August. Philip can now be put into a baby bungee, which is like a sling attached to a very thick length of rubber and a sprung metal hook which fits onto the beam in the sitting room and the architrave to the en suite bathroom. It means I can get dressed in the morning, chatting to him and laughing. Philip loves it.

30th September. Geraldine started at the beginning of the month. She is twenty one and has just completed a two year course at the nursery nurses' training college near Reading. Her parents live abroad and so living with us will suit her nicely. She and Philip are getting on well. We have decided Geraldine will join us once a week for supper.

Philip's first bottom centre tooth is through and the next one is on its' way. I love him so much, I can feel my hearbeat.

It has been a long day. I drove to London to meet my manager to discuss my options and have been offered and accepted a job in the Education Department, which is only a twenty minute drive from home. It sounds perfect and I start on 5th October. Everything is falling into place.

29th October. Now back at work, I try to be home by six o'clock in time to bath and put Philip to bed and read him a story, my favourites at the moment are *Mog the Forgetful Cat* and *Peace at Last.* Geraldine has a boyfriend, so most evenings she drives to Reading to spend time with him and his family.

Edward has been promoted and moved to the office in Radlett. It is a long journey down the M3 and then onto the M25 and he leaves early and arrives home late.

3rd November. Yesterday Edward's brother Simon, his wife Erin together with their daughter Claire, drove down with Edward's parents. I spent the evening preparing the buffet for today's christening. Edward and his family went out to the pub after supper. On their return Simon helped me before retiring. Edward didn't lift a finger to help. I was so exhausted, I could have cried.

Philip was Christened today at All Saints' Church, Swallowfield at eleven o'clock during the family communion service. He looked charming in a cream silk romper suit and behaved perfectly. When we got home we drank champagne and gave a toast to Philip. The buffet lunch seemed OK and everyone enjoyed themselves. Vivienne and David left with Mum and Dad just after three, not wanting to be too late back as they both have to work tomorrow. Patrick and Melanie were in good form. Patrick looked different, more relaxed and casually dressed with designer labels clearly visible. His hair was different too.

28th November. Yesterday, Edward arrived home at eight o'clock, while I was still putting Philip to bed. Geraldine was out. Philip was fretful and crying and I didn't want to leave him crying. Edward insisted that he was hungry and wanted to eat supper. I stayed where I was with Philip.

Minutes later, Edward stormed into the bedroom and started hitting me and dragging me out of the room. Philip screamed. I tried to get passed Edward back into the room and he continued to hit me and picked up my handbag and swung it at my head several times. It has a very large heavy buckle. I managed to free myself and flew out of the door and ran outside along the lane, losing my shoes in the dark; too scared to stop to find them, I hardly knew where I was going or what to do next. I was conscious of nothing but the confusion of my own thoughts. Knocking on the door of Broom Cottage I asked Victor to come home with me. He was very kind and gently persuaded us both to calm down, but he agreed with Edward, taking the view that children should be in bed by six o'clock in the evening. When I rose wearily this morning, my eye was very bruised and I have lumps all over my head. I called the office to excuse myself and spent a quiet and reflective day. Not for the first time, I let my thoughts ramble around as to how I should do something. What?

28th December. Our first Christmas with Philip has gone well. We spent the day with Philip quietly. On Boxing Day we drove to Solihull to stay with Vivienne and David. We were late because we drove around in circles looking for a garage to buy petrol. Mum and Dad joined us for lunch.

Philip received a wonderful Christmas present from Penny in the form of a large push-a-long *Thomas the Tank Engine* with a handle to help him walk. In no time at all he got the hang of it and amused everyone by his efforts to walk. I took lots of photos. Penny has always been a generous friend and has a discerning choice in gifts. We occasionally catch up for lunch in Richmond, where she and her husband now live. I haven't told her about Edward's behaviour.

1986

PHILIP'S FIRST BIRTHDAY

12th February. Geraldine told me Philip took his first steps today unaided.

22nd March. Back from skiing with Patrick and Melanie. Patrick and Edward shared the drive through France to Avoriaz. We stayed en route in L'Amançon. On arrival, and having left the car in the covered car park we took a horse drawn sleigh to our apartment in Les Residence Fountain Blanches in the centre of Avoriaz. It was snowing gently and delicate large flakes were landing on our anoraks and eyelashes when we looked up. Once settled in the apartment we walked into the centre to hire skis and purchase our lift passes. After we had stopped for coffee, Melanie and I went off to explore the shops and buy groceries. We skied every morning as a group and in the afternoons after lunch, usually at Le Chalet du Verard, we split up. Sometimes Patrick and Edward would ski together and Melanie and I would ski down to to the apartment and enjoy a leisurely walk around the centre. We each cooked a couple of evenings, so there were always a few items to buy. There were a great number of restaurants to choose from and after a couple of evenings we were inclined to return to La Chapka a bar with good pub food and a pool table. Edward and Patrick shopped for wine, olives and cured meats, which we enjoyed at six o'clock once everyone was showered and refreshed for the evening. Melanie had packed cards and most evenings we played contract bridge until late, so we went to bed exhausted and slept well.

23rd March. Glad to be home to see Philip. Mum and Dad have just left for home and it seems they enjoyed their stay spending time with Philip, which allowed Geraldine to keep to her regular hours and routine.

Edward's parents will be coming down for Easter and he has a list of jobs for them to do. I need to concentrate on the arrangements for a one day course next week, which is being hosted by City of London University and will cover an introduction to the finance sector. This is the first course I have managed alongside an educational establishment rather than using internal speakers at our training school. It has proved to be popular and is oversubscribed.

29th March. The post arrived with a lovely letter from Mum enclosing photographs of their time with Philip taken in Wellington Country Park, by the lake, on the miniature train and Philip running down the hill.

A dullish day, though fine enough to be in the garden. Edward spent the morning cutting the lawns with Philip on his lap driving the Westwood. They both looked like they were having a lot of fun.

1st April. Philip's first birthday. We had a tea party for his friends each accompanied by their nannies. The sitting room was covered with balls, building bricks, a telephone, a shape sorter and a red plastic wheelbarrow with a yellow ball at the front for steering. An interesting and most useful present is the solid yellow plastic Teddy seat currently being used by a large soft toy clown. Earlier I took a photo of Philip sitting in the Teddy seat with *Peace at Last* open in his hands. Now everything is back in the playroom. Philip was already in bed fast asleep when Edward arrived home.

12th April. We have had a really good week with Erin and Simon. Claire is older than Philip and he enjoyed following her around. We stayed at Cockbury Court near Winchcombe and although it was fairly cold we wrapped up warm. We spent one day at the Cotswold

Wild Life Park and Philip just kept saying 'Ooooooooh'. He became particularly animated looking into the penguin enclosure. We took a ride on *Bella* the miniature railway around the gardens and then Philip and Claire played on the swings and slides in the adventure playground.

28th April. News is beginning to appear that two days ago a Soviet nuclear reactor in Chernobyl exploded and released radioactive material across much of Europe. Will it reach England? It is very worrying.

25th May. We spent the weekend at my sister's celebrating Dad's seventieth birthday. However, it started so badly. We were due to leave after lunch on Saturday via Reading to collect a few items of shopping for Edward. Just as we were about to leave, he noticed a button missing on his shirt and asked me to sew another back on. I suggested there wasn't time and he could change his shirt. He did so.

When we were in Reading, he took ages shopping and then when we were about to drive on to Solihull, he diverted back home and told me that we wouldn't be going. Eventually he gave way and we set off. We were late. I didn't know what to say to Vivienne.

9th June. At home this afternoon with Philip. I made us a picnic, found a large cardboard box and began to read *Whatever Next* by Jill Murphy. Philip helped me find the colander and then together with Teddy he sat in the cardboard box with the colander on his head ready to go to the Moon. We had tea soon after we arrived and then packed everything up for the return journey. I read it to him again this evening when I put him to bed.

I am packed ready to fly to Edinburgh for a three day course arranged with Stirling University. We will be staying on campus and with the help of staff at the university have a varied and interesting agenda planned with noteworthy speakers. This will be the first course away from home and am nervous with excitement.

7th July. This evening Geraldine and I ate supper together and she gave me a selection of photos of Philip playing with his friends. One in particular is charming of Philip in his dungarees, open sandals and white sunhat, watching the older children blow bubbles. Another is with Amelia and Thomas in the paddling pool with nothing on except his white hat. In the background, Geraldine is on a sun lounger relaxing.

My favourite is Philip with Pippa playing with a cookery set and he is laughing and looking cute in his white Osh Gosh dungarees decorated with images of coloured hand prints.

8th September. My manager will accompany me tomorrow when we fly to Manchester for an advanced finance course being run in conjunction with Manchester Business School. There will be several high profile speakers from banking and insurance and our most senior salesmen will be attending.

30th October. This evening Ester Rantzen presented a programme *Childwatch* aiming to detect those children at risk before their lives are in danger. A helpline is available now for children to call if they need to talk to someone.

HOLIDAY IN IBIZA

17th January. I am tense whenever Edward is home. His tone today was not untypical; he lambasted me with a list of chores needed to be done. He tries hard to conceal his behaviour when Geraldine is around. I try hard to do what pleases him, but it is never enough. Each day I wake hoping that this day will be different, today will be different and he will love me. He did love me, but that was before Philip arrived. This evening he deliberately manipulated a situation by arguing in front of Philip while he was having tea in his high chair. He walked over to the fridge, took out two milk bottles and dropped them on the floor in front of me. Then he walked out.

There is a deadweight in my heart. It's been there awhile in the background and I can't quite throw it off.

4th March. Last night we went to see '*Swan Lake*' at the Royal Opera House. Edward was hosting clients. During the interval, we were ushered upstairs to the bar where an area had been reserved and a waiter served us champagne and canapés. Afterwards we walked to Rules in Maiden Lane for a late, very late supper. It was an extraordinary experience walking into the Edwardian styled restaurant with creamy gold walls covered in mirrors, busts, old play bills, drawings and caricatures. We all chose the same light meal of *Dorset Crab Salad* followed by *Blueberry and Almond Tart* together with a reasonably priced Sauvignon Blanc. It is where Edward VII entertained Lillie Langtry. It was a delightful evening. Edward was loving.

14th March. We are all tired this evening after our journey back from Chamonix. It hadn't been an easy journey driving back to Geneva airport with swirling snowflakes caught in the car's headlights slowing us down. Our apartment at La Riviere was close to the town centre overlooking the River Arve. The first afternoon was taken up in the ski hire shop being fitted for boots and skis. We hired skis for Philip too, just so he could ski along with us holding him. He wasn't old enough to be left in the ski crèche, so we met Geraldine and Philip at the restaurant next to the top of the cable car for lunch most days and a couple of times I went back down with them to give Geraldine a break and once I took Philip swimming. We had one serious altercation during lunch when Edward told Geraldine very firmly that she wasn't to interfere when he was around. He would decide how to deal with Philip, was how he put it. Yesterday, Edward wanted to ski a red run, so I returned to the apartment and sat by myself on the balcony in the sun. It was very still with no breath of wind and the great silence of snow was interrupted gently by the river flowing by. In that silence my thoughts turned to Edward and his behaviour. Geraldine had stood up to him.

1st April. Geraldine organised everything. I just ordered the Thomas the Tank Engine Cake and bought all the tableware, swag bags and balloons to match. The Memorial Hall was a perfect venue as all the toys are there for the mother and toddler group including a trampoline and climbing frame. When we sang Happy Birthday, Philip blew out the candles. He didn't notice Geraldine with her face just behind his head blowing gently too. Edward and I have just watched the video together. He looks awkward and ill at ease.

5th April. Vivienne and David came for the weekend bringing a wonderful Big John tractor for Philip. As yet he cannot pedal for himself and so David spent a lot of the weekend pushing him along the lane. Smiles all round.

15th April. Geraldine has given in her notice. She argued with Edward during our skiing holiday in Chamonix. I have just discovered I am pregnant.

19th April. Today, Princess Diana visited the London Middlesex Hospital to open the first unit dedicated to treating people with HIV and AIDS. She is shown talking to patients and then she did something remarkable; she shook hands with one of the patients wearing no gloves. It was a heartwarming moment; one that will linger on in my mind always.

2nd May. Tony Blair moved into Downing Street today. I voted Conservative, but am impressed with him as a person and am hopeful he will do well.

Not so happy a day for me. I cannot remember why Edward was angry. I was so frightened, that I locked myself together with Philip in the bathroom. Once Edward had calmed down and I could hear him outside mowing the lawns, I ventured into the bedroom, only to find a pile of torn clothes on the floor. Looking out of the window, I saw below more strewn on the path below. Something is brewing. Last night he kicked me out of bed. I seem to be walking on eggshells.

10th June. The agency have found me a temporary nanny until Polly can start in September. Philip has lost Geraldine and is becoming very clingy. This has only made Edward more annoyed and he has made it clear that he is going to break the 'Mummy, mummy!' whining habit and how he does is is up to him. I am not to interfere.

15th July. We went to Reading to book a holiday and when we arrived in the multi-storey car park Philip started to cry as we unloaded the buggy. Edward gave Philip a sharp slap to his head and when I showed my annoyance, Edward glared at me.

'I have changed my mind; we won't be going on holiday. Let's go home!' 'Come on,' I said, 'we have other things to do.'

His response was to kick me on the back of my legs, as I began to walk away from the car with Philip in the buggy. Edward got back in the car and drove off. After shopping, Philip and I went home in a taxi.

20th July. We spent Sunday working in the garden with Philip, which pleased Edward and so today we were in good spirits and drove into London and did some shopping in the sales and booked a week's holiday in Ibiza, departing Wednesday.

30th July. We returned from our holiday in Ibiza yesterday. It had been a long outward flight and we had started very early. Philip had been tired and fretful the whole time and as usual Edward had shouted at him rather than soothed him. On arrival at our hotel we found our way to a beach restaurant and had lunch. Philip was still fractious and I gave him his dummy. Edward told me to take his dummy away from him and shouted, 'He is too old for a dummy, I am going to break this dummy habit. Give it to me.'

He grabbed it and threw it away onto the scalding white sand. I picked up Philip and returned to our hotel room to try and settle Philip down for a nap.

Within minutes, Edward stormed into the room and slapped me very hard across the face and then got on the bed with Philip and shouted at him to stop crying. He held him tightly until Philip at last went to sleep.

Every day was tense, each day carried its own ordeal, whether it was in the dining room or wherever we were. Whenever Philip was naughty, he got slapped and then he was slapped again when he cried. When I interfered, the worse it was. The tension just hung there like a thick cloud.

On the last day of the holiday we were sightseeing in a hired open jeep and stopped at a restaurant for lunch. In helping Philip out of the jeep, I dropped Teddy. When I picked Teddy up to give him to Philip, Edward told me to leave Teddy behind. I shouldn't have tried to persuade him to change his mind, because Edward immediately changed his mood and cancelled lunch. We drove away everyone upset.

'Where are we going?'

'We're just driving.'

It wasn't long before he started hitting me and when we stopped at a junction, I hopped out with Philip in my arms and ran. Edward followed me, shouting and throwing stones. I went into the garden of a house, ready to knock on the door for help. Edward coaxed me to return, telling me he would stop if I apologised. I assured him that I would if he didn't hit me. So we agreed and I got back in the jeep.

We continued our journey, my not knowing if there was a plan to find another restaurant or just return to the hotel. After a few minutes Edward's anger returned and he announced that he was going to find somewhere quiet and teach me a lesson. We were already driving through a remote wooded scrubland. Philip was in my arms and drowsy by now. When he stopped the jeep abruptly, I began to get out with Philip in my arms, but he pulled at my dress and jumped after me and pulled me down to the ground, punching me. I started screaming and calling for help, which startled him and he let go. Edward turned in disgust and drove off, leaving Philip and me stranded.

When I had recovered my composure, I walked carrying Philip a little way and found a café. In my purse, I only had two hundred pesetas. I bought cold drinks and then walked a little further to wait at a bus stop. It was hot, while we waited. After half an hour a bus turned up and somehow I found the way back to town and walked into a smart hotel and asked permission to rest in the lounge. I stayed there with Philip until he had slept for a couple of hours. While waiting, I desperately tried to think how we could leave this island without returning to the hotel, but I had left my credit cards back at the hotel and in the end had no choice but to return to Edward.

The return flight was just as awful with Edward slapping Philip on his legs and bottom and telling him to behave. On arriving home, I put Philip to bed for a sleep and Myra jollied me up. Everything seemed to be calmer now we were home. Even Edward seemed happier. I bathed and looked in the mirror at my pregnant belly and the bruises blooming around my hips, arms and thighs. I went to bed and curled into a ball drawing the duvet close over me; sad thoughts rattled around my mind. Edward joined me soon afterwards. I didn't want to, but I didn't resist. He was on top of me rythmically pounding me. I held his shoulders. He didn't see my screwed up face, my lips trembling and the tears in my eyes. When it was over, he turned to face me and like so many times before, I greeted his gaze with a smile.

1st August. A day with Philip on my own. We walked through the thicket into the Wellington Country Park. Philip climbed on the dinosaurs before we had a ride on the miniature railway. After lunch, he had a snooze, while I prepared tomorrow's dinner for Edward and myself. This evening, he soon succumbed to sleep and I watched him resting soundly and hoping, but not quite believing that recent events were far from his thoughts.

2nd August. The candles were lit and dinner was served. I had taken extra care keeping it simple, choosing *Boeuf Bourguignon* a firm favourite of Edward's. It is the most used and messy page in my copy of Elizabeth David's *French Provincial Cooking*. We drank an inexpensive Claret. I told him that I was anxious all the time as to how he would react to any situation. He was reassuring and accepted that he had behaved badly. He agreed to control his temper with the caveat that I mustn't interfere. He is concerned that I am letting jobs pile up and I have agreed to sort out a few things.

15th August. It's late and I am so tired. My parents came this weekend and Patrick and Melanie joined us for lunch today.

Edward, as usual spent the morning in bed reading the papers. I took him breakfast in bed. My Mother worked with me in the kitchen preparing lunch and when Philip got bored, she and Dad took him to the Country Park for a ride on the steam train and a walk around the park, so that he could climb on the large dinosaurs dotted around the park. Philip was happy and relaxed with Mum and Dad.

Lunch was the classic *Salmon en croute* using a recipe by Prue Leith that I liked and trusted. The salmon was laid on pre-cooked flaky pastry in the shape of the fish. Fresh pastry was wrapped over the salmon fillets seasoned with lemon juice, butter and dill and then decorated to look like the fish itself. When finished, it looked superb.

At eleven o'clock Edward called me from upstairs, asking for coffee and I replied I was too busy. He came downstairs, looked at the dish on the kitchen table, took out a large knife and proceeded to slash the salmon while threatening me, 'I have told you before not to take so much trouble over a meal!'

By the time Mum and Dad returned with Philip, things were patched up and somehow Edward and I got through lunch. He was a perfectly charming host.

Philip hasn't settled after our holiday and has become very aggressive towards me and his soft toys. Tonight, when I put him to bed, he started kicking me and pulling my hair. I am still shaky after the holiday and have decided to make enquiries about legal advice regarding divorce. My diary is undoubtedly a comfort. I feel better for having written it down, however hard the experience.

I nearly forgot! Sad, sad news. Patrick and Melanie are to separate. He met Isabel skiing with his golfing pals. Patrick has moved out and he and Isabel are buying a thatched cottage in Long Crendon, Buckinghamshire. Last year, there were subtle changes in the way Patrick dressed. Now I know why. I feel so sorry for Melanie. Twenty three years of love and marriage thrown away. Both their children are furious with him.

21st August. Last night we were at Wembley to see Madonna in her *Who's That Girl* concert. Edward loves her music and I was pleased to go with him, even though I am still troubled after our disastrous holiday. The music was electrifying and is still buzzing around inside my head.

1st September. Summer is fading. This morning I went into Philip's room and as he woke he said, 'Daddy not hit Mummy anymore.'

9th September. Polly arrived today and has settled in. She is a very confident young lady and I already feel comfortable in her company.

16th October. I saw a solicitor last week. He will prepare a draft affidavit should I decide to petition for divorce. Mum and Dad don't need to know until I am absolutely sure.

When I looked out of the window this morning, it was dark and stormy and just as I was getting ready to leave for the office, Edward called me from downstairs to say that he couldn't drive out of Devil's Highway, that there was a tree blocking the lane. He was on his way to the sitting room to turn on the television. Shortly after he came running upstairs to say that a powerful storm had caused devastation across the south and south west with winds gusting up to one hundred miles an hour. We watched in horror as reports came in of falling trees, deaths due to chimney pots falling and at sea. Later, we ventured out and walked along the lane. We called in to see Daphne and Victor to check they were okay. Victor had already telephoned the Highways Agency to report the tree blockage, but as all the emergency services were very busy we understood our obstruction was a low priority. Edward went back for his chain saw and he and Victor removed some of the branches cutting them up for logs. After lunch Philip had a nap and Polly went for a walk. Edward watched horse racing on television and intermittently kept up with the news. We both remembered Michael Fish saying that there wouldn't be a hurricane before we went to bed last night.

1st December. Why Edward was annoyed with me? I was giving Philip his supper in his high chair and he came storming in, grabbed Philip's plate and threw it on the floor. Then he went to the fridge and took out a couple of bottles of milk and dropped them on the floor.

I was too tired, too upset and too pregnant to care. Walking calmly to the phone, I dialled 999 and logged a call with the police. Shocked, Edward immediately rushed around clearing everything up, which was faintly amusing and so when the policeman arrived, there was no evidence. After taking statements, the policeman declared I was emotionally unstable and smiling at me said, 'Not surprising really, dear.' He bade us good night.

15th December. The divorce papers arrived today. It was the last day in the office before my maternity leave and I had a lovely day with my office colleagues. My manager gave a short speech before handing me a glorious bouquet of cerise roses and oriental lilies together with a Teddy bear and a John Lewis voucher.

I haven't dared tell Edward, that I have seen a solicitor, and am worried that I now have a secret.

28th December. Christmas is a haze. Vivienne was recovering from a hysterectomy and I was heavily pregnant. Somehow we all survived. Mum and Dad bought me a CD with Freddie Mercury and Montserrat Caballé singing *Barcelona.* I saw her perform with Luciano Pavarotti in Verdi's *Un ballo in maschera* all those years ago. It was at the time when I was falling in love with Edward.

I spoke to Edward today of my intention to petition for divorce. We talked all afternoon. He has persuaded me not to go ahead, he says he will try harder. He has even agreed to seek professional help if his behaviour escalates. He seems to understand that he has been unreasonable. We are for now reconciled. Our second child is due in a few days time. This is not the time to petition for divorce. I feel trapped. I hope to see a change in Edward. I need to see a change.

As my due date approaches I am resting and enjoying listening to music and particularly *Barcelona*, which inspires a feeling of euphoria.

1988

OLIVER ARRIVES

10th January. Oliver was born on 4th January. It touches my heart how beautiful he is. This morning, when I lifted him out of his cot and distractedly kissed his forehead, it came like a flush of warmth, that intense feeling of love and a promise to do everything in my power to protect him.

Polly took care of Philip during my short stay in the maternity unit at Wokingham, she brought him in a couple of times to see his new brother. Edward came each evening on his way home from the office.

I am so pleased to be home. The sitting room has several vases full of flowers. Edward is attentive and seems delighted with Oliver. Breastfeeding is going well.

Waiting for me on my return were two presents from Edward. Not wrapped, but none the less very thoughtful of him. A bottle of perfume, *Victorian Posy* by Penhaligon's was accompanied by a book of poems, sweetly scented inside and reflecting the floral theme. I read the introduction to discover that the perfume was created as a result of a request from Dr Roy Strong, for an exhibition entitled '*The Garden*' for the Victoria and Albert Museum in 1979.

6th April. It's been a dry spring with sharp winds until now. Can it be true? Easter in Wiltshire with no incidents. Edward was relaxed and happy. The converted dairy near Marlborough was on an estate and we had access to the garden and woods. One charming photo is of Philip sitting with his arm around a bronze garden statue of a kneeling cherub.

Oliver is thriving. This evening, when I bathed him and dressed him for bed, I looked at his dense, pearly limbs and drew in the milky smell of him. Now, he looks serenely peaceful sleeping in his cot with his Teddy for company.

23rd April. The sun is shining on my last day of maternity leave with the inevitable return to work tomorrow. Now Philip is three years old, he will start nursery school, just mornings. I will drop him off at Freshfields on my way to work unless work takes me out of town. This gives Polly the morning to herself with Oliver.

7th May. It has been wet for so long. So much so, that the greenery is lush, bursting everywhere in the garden. It is Polly's day off, so naturally I took the day off. Once Philip had been dropped off at nursery school, I continued driving south to Yately Common. It is lovely holding Oliver in the Snugli around my front with the top of his head peeping out under my chin. I needed a good walk and the fresh air was good for us both. We walked through the scented wood, the pine needles soft under my feet. As we reached the field, the sun came out with the sunlight streaming through the canopy onto a dazzling carpet of bluebells, like scattered sapphires.

15th May. Having just finished reading *The Times* before retiring, it is worth noting that the Soviet union have begun withdrawing their military forces from Afganistan, following the Geneva Accord signed last month by Pakistan and Afganistan. Since 1979, the Soviets have been bogged down in a conflict alongside the Afghan communist government against muslim guerrillas, known as mujahideen, who in turn were supported by the USA.

After three weeks back at work, the pain in my breasts continues. It was so bad today, that I had to retreat to the bathroom and express milk. To make matters worse, I fell asleep at my desk this afternoon. Perhaps I have returned to work too soon? Silly question, obviously too soon!

19th June. We have just had a week in Devon with Vivienne and David. We stayed in a white painted long house not too far from Dartmouth. We did lots together and Philip loved being with Vivienne and David who took him on a large wheeled tractor from Bigbury Beach over to Burgh Island Hotel, the infamous art deco hotel where Agatha Christie wrote her novel *Evil under the Sun*. Philip enjoyed looking in the rock pools and running all over the beach, in and out of the water. He was laughing and happy. On our last day we all caught a steam train from Dartmouth to Kingswear and returned on the ferry. Great fun.

3rd July. Mum phoned this evening to tell me about their holiday in Cyprus. She told me that Dad had returned with an attractive tan compared with her rather sunburnt look. They had stayed in Protaras in the Larnaca region, on the south west of the island. Mum swam nearly every morning in the shallow waters while Dad soaked up the sun in a deckchair. They visited the Tombs of the Kings in Pathos to the east and took several trips including one inland to Tamassos passing Mount Olympus, which I had always assumed was in Greece.

17th July. Last night, Princess Diana and Prince Charles were at the *Bad* concert at Wembley. We took Polly and one of her friends looked after the boys. Home late, but what a fabulous concert. It was simply incredible from start to finish with Michael Jackson exuding energy.

18th August. An absolutely perfect August morning, beginning with a light dew on the ground. Polly had the day off in order to spend a long weekend with her parents. I decided to take the boys to The Vyne at Sherborne St John. It isn't far down the A33 and we were there in no time at all. The children are too young to visit the Tudor palace, but there was lots to do outside. We took a stroll around the walled garden before heading off along the Lime Tree avenue. Philip runing ahead, in and out of the trees and when he saw the bridge over the lake he ran across and shouted back for us to hurry. While he waited he waved his arms about and did star jumps. The path took us into ancient shaded woodlands with dappled light streaming through warming our faces. Eventually we retraced our steps back to the Summer House where according to the handbook, the oak is over six hundred years old. Close by was a play area and as soon as Oliver was out of his buggy, he enjoyed crawling around on the soft lush grass. Soon it was one o'clock and we went to the The Brewhouse tearoom for lunch. Walking back to the car park, beyond the wall lay the wide golden sweep of a cornfield; the breeze stirred the ripe ears into motion. *England, this sceptred isle.*

When we returned home, Edward was already mowing the grass in the orchard. After greeting us, he took Philip with him to ride on the Westwood, while I put Oliver in his cot for a nap. Sitting quietly in the kitchen and enjoying a few minutes to myself, reading the paper with a refreshing cup of tea was a pleasant end to the day.

10th September. It is six months since I returned to work and I am managing to enjoy the active lifestyle that being a working mother of two children and running a home entails. Polly gave me a lovely picture of Philip taken at his nursery school. He is sitting at a desk with a picture puzzle book open looking straight into the camera and smiling, such a handsome little boy with deep blue eyes.

18th November. It was cool and showery driving towards Ascot racecourse. It wasn't long before we drove out of the rain into a perfect autumn day, windy and cold with the sky swept clean of clouds. We arrived in good time for an early lunch and then settled into the afternoon's racing. I like to choose horses ridden and trained by people I have heard of and so chose *Sharp Song* in the Handicap Chase ridden by Peter Scudamore and trained by Jonjo O'Neill. He was doing so well until he was pulled up after the ninth hurdle. In the same race Edward chose *Prize Asset* and won a lot of money.

12th December. News this morning of a terrible rail crash at Clapham Junction.

15th December. It is now known that thirty five people have lost their lives at the Clapham rail crash. Many more are seriously injured. It appears that a crowded passenger train from Basingstoke crashed into the rear of another train that had stopped at a signal just south of Clapham Junction and then sideswiped an empty train travelling in the opposite direction.

24th December. Both our parents are here until Tuesday. Vivienne and David are visiting friends in Oslo. I drew up a list of duties for each day, so that they don't fall over each other trying to help. It has worked so far. It has been mild, so we have all enjoyed a walk in Wellington Country Park, which is at the bottom of our garden and just a squeeze through the bushes. No gate. We assume right of access until told otherwise.

26th December. Edward is unwell. I went to Kempton on my own today as host to his clients, who were invited to attend the meeting in one of the corporate boxes. Patrick and Isabel were there. She is a beauty, pale skinned, tall with cropped blonde hair. Patrick organised a sweepstake and over an indulgent lunch and afternoon tea, I enjoyed every single minute. When I arrived home Edward hugged me and said, 'Patrick phoned to say you were marvellous! I am so proud of you.' Our parents enjoyed their day looking after Philip and Oliver.

31st December. As I look back through this years' diary, it seems to me that despite all the odds it has been a happier year.

1989

MOVING TO YORKSHIRE

4th January. I took the day off to enjoy Oliver's first birthday. Polly excelled herself with the *Hickery Dickery Dock* cake and it was nice to spend the day with her. The usual nanny crowd and their charges arrived for tea and I enjoyed catching up with Geraldine. She plans to marry next year. Oliver is such a lovely little boy. Philip's friends were there too, so he enjoyed running about with them when we went through into the country park. No-one noticed the cold.

9th January. Edward has been appointed Senior Partner at the Leeds office. He has found a flat to rent, while we sort things out. We talked a lot over the weekend. The past year has flown by, most of the time in harmony, so I have decided to go with him to Yorkshire. My manager will discuss options with me, once he has had time to circulate my CV to departments in the North of England. We will start to look for houses in the spring.

10th March. Polly has agreed to move with us to Yorkshire at least until Christmas to help us settle.

16th March. Desert Orchid has won the Cheltenham Gold Cup. Edward went on his own. He told me that Dessie had run from the front and his bravery and obvious enjoyment of racing was something he would never forget. He came home happy, slightly drunk and shared his winnings with me.

The other day Philip went to a party dressed as *Paddington Bear*, so it was rather nice to look at the photographs that Polly took while we ate supper.

3rd April. Today, the children at Philip's fourth birthday party sat watching Coco the clown, while he did tricks with Philip and his magic wand; Oliver was always just a step away. I made the cake which was decorated with sugar paste cut-outs of Tom in grey and Jerry in a rather brightly coloured orange, onto which were highlighted their features using black edible ink. Philip's friends with their nannies were here and as they all know each other very well enjoyed the afternoon. Afterwards, while Polly took Philip for a walk, I bathed Oliver. There was lots of foam and he lay on his back with just his face peeping through happy and smiling. Once dressed for bed, he sat on my lap and I sang a few nursey rhymes before laying him down to sleep contented.

15th April. News is still coming in following a fatal crush of people at the Hillsborough Stadium in Sheffield, during the FA Cup match between Liverpool and Nottingham Forest.

20th April. It is now known that the crush at Hillsborough occurred in a standing area allocated to Liverpool supporters and that as many as ninety six people were killed.

23rd April. We have just returned from a house-hunting trip in Yorkshire. One stands out and we have expressed an interest subject to the sale of Pippins.

Vivienne and David came down to look after the children on Friday and have just left. They enjoyed themselves and Polly was on hand if she was needed. One thing struck a chord, when Vivienne told me that when she put Philip to bed on Saturday evening, he asked, 'Have I been a good boy today?' She reassured him but was saddened by his question.

27th May. We have completed on the Dower House in Moreton, a lovely quiet hamlet to the south west of Pateley Bridge. It is a six bedroomed Victorian stone built residence with an acre of garden and a paddock. Edward will be moving out of his flat in Leeds and be there while necessary work is done to heating, electrics and internal refurbishment. We are due to exchange on Pippins next month and then Polly, the children and I will join Edward. I am driving to Leeds on Sunday to stay with Edward for a few days and see the manager responsible for Total Quality Management as there is an opening in the York office.

4th June. The Chinese authorities response to protest demonstrations has escalated to a massacre in Beijing's Tiananmen Square. The BBC film footage shows a young man dressed in a white shirt and dark trousers holding a bag in each hand walking towards a tank. As the tank moves to avoid him, the young man moves to challenge. The tank stops and he climbs aboard and attempts to talk to the men inside. He descends and the action is repeated until protesters encourage the young man to move away. The tanks arrive into an almost empty square. Most of the protesters have left. The previous days have resulted in hundreds of deaths in Bejing.

10th June. We are settled in. We now live in Yorkshire. I start my new job in York in a couple of weeks. Most of the building work is completed but there is still a lot to do in order to make the house comfortable. The kitchen is very old fashioned and dingy, but too big a project for now. I caught my breath as I drove through the gates into the circular drive at the front of the house and thought, 'This is really ours.'

The Dower House is a large imposing Victorian double fronted stone built house with a tall gabled porch and a sun-bleached oak door over which is a decorated stained glass arch. The floor of the porch is decorated with ceramic tiles and there is a small window on each side, before entering the hall through a half-glazed door. The hall is long and wide with the sitting room and dining room doors to the left and before reaching the stairs, there is a smaller hall leading to another room and a side entrance. At the end of the hall is the kitchen and beyond to an enormous store room and secondary stairs. Upstairs the windows are so large that it is light and airy. Polly has the bedroom with the en-suite bathroom tiled in royal blue. The decorator has already papered her bedroom with the same wallpaper from Pippins so her soft furnishings match and I have ordered festoon blinds from Laura Ashley, which will arrive in a few days.

Our bedroom together with a bathroom and two bedrooms one for each of the boys' is at the other end of the landing with a door between and at a the end of the corridor are the back stairs down to the kitchen. The bathroom is shabby but serviceable, although not having a shower is a nuisance. There is a large window on the half landing and beyond are walled pastures below a huge sky. Ewes with lambs are in a nearby field, white as snow. There is a sense of peace and a nearness to the wild.

18th June. We are beginning to explore our new surroundings. To the northwest, and closest to the Yorkshire Dales National Park is an area that becomes increasingly rugged and remote the further back along the valley you go. It pulls you like a magnet, drawing you further into its midst, tempting you with an ever-changing panorama at every turn, rise and fall.

Yesterday, we took the boys to Brimham Rocks. Perched nearly 1,000 feet above sea level on the heather cloaked Brimham Moor with views across Nidderdale. It is a Yorkshire dale in a classic sense with sweeping contours and a fierce beauty on a grand scale. Secret paths dart this way and that, the bracken and rowan trees fighting for space amongst the lichen covered rocky giants. Philip loved being able to run free, jumping over the bilberry bushes and rocks, while Oliver was happy watching from his buggy as Edward and I walked on the paths leading in and around giant stacks of stone carved by erosion.

Today, we attended our first morning service at St Lawrence's Church. We walked through the lychgate up an incline bordered on one side by a copperbeech hedge towards the square west tower in Gothic style. The inside is plain with a simple nave and chapel. The fluency, charm and ease with which Reverend Sommersby spoke held his congregation spellbound. He is a charming man endowed with an excellent humour, graceful in movement.

23rd June. Just when we are happy and settled, Edward arrived home in the early hours of this morning. He was caught speeding on his way home from Leeds after meeting colleagues for a drink. He has been breathalysed and charged and will await a court summons. They kept him in a cell until he was sober enough to drive home.

1st July. Earlier today I met Alasdair Sommersby. Philip came running into the house to tell me. I picked up Oliver and we went outside just as he was dismounting. He looked at me fully in the eyes and smiled as he greeted me, but as he did so, he loosened the tension on the reins and his horse stepped to one side onto my foot. It hurt, but I thought nothing of it, as I was interested to meet him and so were the children who had already been acquainted. He is an attractive looking man, aged I suppose about seventy with a youthful manner, compact in stature and was dressed in cream jodhpurs, and black riding boots with a dark blue polo neck sweater. His face is thin, worn and transparently pale, but not wrinkled. He handed me the *Moreton News* and informed me that the summer garden party would be next Saturday and hoped to see us there. Later he rode by again, this time being more careful to keep his horse under control and handed me a large chocolate heart wrapped in red foil as an apology from Milo. Edward joined us and made a joke and we assured him that we would all be at the garden party.

8th July. This afternoon, the summer garden party was held at Thorngarth Lodge, the home of Florence and Sebastian Sawyer. It was only a short walk along the main road and together with Polly and Edward's parents, we arrived in good time. Polly already knows several people along with their children. Philip was soon running

213

around with Daniel, one of his friends from the mothers and toddlers group. I watched him with Oliver in the buggy while he threw giant darts into the grass. Alasdair escorted us around the garden introducing us to several neighbours and then to his wife Ruth. She is a small well rounded woman with long silver hair swept off her face and drawn back tightly into a French pleat, revealing a classic bone structure emphasised by long pendant silver and turquoise earrings. When she smiled her face became radiant and her eyes, which are stunningly blue, sparkled. Tea was served from the Sawyer's kitchen together with scones and cream and we settled at a table in the garden enjoying the surroundings in the sunshine. It was all over by four o'clock. Florence Sawyer has invited us to supper and will confirm dates soon.

12th July. I went with Edward to Leeds Magistrate Court today. Our solicitor represented him, but to no avail he has a twelve month driving ban. We sat down this evening working out how we are going to cope. He is going to have to base himself more in the Leeds office and rely on colleagues for longer trips. We have decided that for now I will take Edward to Harrogate station in the morning on my way to York and collect him in the evenings once the children are in bed. When Polly can't babysit, he will have to get a taxi home.

6th August. Last night we had supper with Sebastian and Florence Sawyer together with Alasdair and Ruth Sommersby and two other friends we hadn't met until tonight. Charlotte Crampton is an operatic singer and her husband, Henry is an architect. The kitchen is enormous with a long oak refectory table that would easily seat twelve people. I gave Florence flowers and she cut the long stems of the roses and arranged them in a small vase together with the delicate bright green stems of euphorbia and placed them on the table. Sebastian accepted the bottle of Sancerre from Edward, smiling approvingly as he looked at the label before announcing that he had prepared the beetroot soup himself. He served the soup in thick earthenware bowls on large dinner plates, each with a hearty crust of wholemeal bread. The soup had an earthy sweetness with an accent of horseradish. We all had seconds. Edward sat opposite Henry and they were engaged in very pleasant conversation together. When the chicken dish came out of the oven, the kitchen was filled with a gentle anise and citrus scent. The chicken pieces had been marinated in a fennel and orange vinaigrette and then roasted together. Sebastian served a light sparkling rosé wine with the chicken and we helped ourselves to sugar snap peas and new potatoes. Edward's Sancerre was served with the summer pudding. Appetites satiated, the silence was engagingly interrupted by Alasdair telling us a story about his appearance as Professor Higgins in an amateur production of *Pygmalion*. He is one of those stimulating people who excite you like sparkling wine. I was happy listening to everyone talking and Edward was too engaged to notice that I said very little.

Shyness often overwhelms me and the more people I am with, the more alone I feel. It was late when we walked home holding hands and Edward put his arm around my waist as we crossed the road and then he stopped and turning towards me put his other arm around me, drawing me in, he kissed me.

19th August. It was such a nice day, we decided to drive to Whitby after breakfast. I loaded the car with a hastily put together picnic and plenty of bottles of water together with changes of clothes, towels for the boys and even remembered the bucket and spades and a rug. We set off up the east cliff towards the ruins of Whitby Abbey which dominate the headland. The day was cloudless blue, sharpened by a salty wind coming from the sea. We took our time walking up the steps leading to the abbey. I gave Oliver to Edward and carried the buggy whilst holding Philip's hand. We had our picnic on the grass and relaxed in the sunshine. Edward chased Philip in and around the ruins. Afterwards, we just had time to walk along the cobbles in Henrietta Street to Fortune's smokehouse where we bought kippers for the freezer. Edward often enjoys kippers for breakfast at the weekend.

Later we walked slowly down the steps towards the town, where we discovered The Magpie Café and decided to have tea there. At four o'clock it was fairly quiet and we went upstairs so that we could sit by a window and look out at the harbour. We ordered fish and chips along with a pot of tea and milk for the boys. They slept in the car on the way home and were happy to go straight to bed as soon as we arrived home just after seven o'clock. Edward had planned ahead and rented the video of *Rain Man* for the weekend and so we crashed out on the sofa and drank wine while we watched Tom Cruise and Dustin Hoffman as brothers unknown to each other until their father left a fortune to one of them. The one, who had been institutionalised since a small boy. What followed was a poignant journey of personal discovery for the other shallow and greedy younger brother. Afterwards, leaving Edward to watch *Match of the Day*, I tidied up and got ready for bed.

7th September. Mum's letter arrived in the post telling me that she and Dad will be joining Vivienne and David for a holiday in Majorca next month. Vivienne and David regularly take a villa holiday in Puerto Pollensa on the north east coast of the island during the autumn.

It was Philip's first day at Ripon Cathedral Choir School. He looked so smart in his maroon blazer and short grey trousers. We were introduced to his teacher and she was happy for us to stay awhile. I then drove to the office and Polly took Oliver home for what I hope will be a pleasant routine. When I got home this evening, Philip was so animated and talkative. We had a lovely time together before bedtime. Once he was nearly asleep and tucked in with Teddy, I turned to leave and looked up to see through overcast skies, the sun tinged with pink had cast a mellow light through his window. There is so much sky in Yorkshire.

Tina starts helping me tomorrow, she was recommended by Florence Sawyer and is going to help with the housework and ironing.

24th September. This evening we attended the Harvest Festival and supper afterwards in the assembly rooms at Moreton Park, the guests of Lord and Lady Rossiter. We both felt that we had spent the evening as if strangers from another world looking on at something that was charming and beyond reality. The boys were tired when we got home and happy to go straight to bed.

8th October. A few weeks ago it dawned on me that Oliver hadn't been christened. Godparents agreed and diaries checked, we chose this weekend. Alasdair preferred for Oliver to be christened during a regular family service and so that's what happened today. Vivienne and David came for the weekend with Mum and Dad and Edwards' brother drove across the Pennines bringing his family and parents. Tina helped me prepare a buffet and several neighbours from the congregation joined us for lunch back at home. Polly helped too.

18th October. Edwards' parents are here again, so that his Dad can help with driving Edward to appointments.

Yesterday, we were having supper all together with Polly when after a remark I made, he shouted at me in front of everyone.
'Either do as I say or GET OUT.'
Before leaving the dining room, I turned to Edward and said,
'I can't get it right for you, can I? I won't ever get it right.'

This morning over something very trivial, he smacked Philip and locked him in his room. Philip was getting hysterical. Edward's mother muttered something forlorn and went out into the garden because she couldn't stand it. Eventually Edward was persuaded to let him out. He drove off without his Dad.

10th December. Last night, we were out with one of Edward's clients at their company dinner dance in Harrogate.

It was close to midnight when I suggested to Edward we leave. He was irritated but reluctantly suggested he phone Lucy to see if she could stay on until two in the morning. I had only booked Lucy until midnight to babysit as Polly had gone home for the weekend. He returned to the table and announced so all could hear.

'Everything is OK.' As he sat down, he added, 'I just offered her another ten pounds.'

I smiled and thought, 'Hmm, I wonder if it IS alright?'

One of the other guests leaned back on his chair, smiling thoughtfully looked at me and said, 'Don't worry one can always throw money at it.' He looked pleased with himself and continued, 'Cmm Cmm . . . . . . of course there was the wealthy business man and the vicar's daughter. He asked her to sleep with him; she was aghast and replied "No". He then offered her twenty thousand pounds. She hesitated for a moment or two and then replied "Yes, alright, then". "Young lady" said the business man, "we have established what you are; now we just have to haggle over the price. How about fifty quid?"

The men laughed out loud. The disdained looks on most of the women's faces were clear to those who wanted to see. If there was an awkward moment, it passed.

I had been sitting at this table with people I didn't know. They were the directors of a company Edward worked with. It was nice of the Managing Director to invite us. After the first hour of getting to know them and eating a fine dinner followed by a couple of dances, Midnight had passed. Quietly excusing myself I went to the lobby to phone Lucy at home.

'How is everything Lucy?'

'Fine, Mrs Campbell.'

'Edward says you are OK to stay on later. Is that right?'

'Not really, I have to be up at six to feed the horses and muck out the stables. I didn't know how to say No, he was insistent.'

'OK, Lucy, I will do my best to get home as soon as possible.'

Having checked my appearance in the Ladies Room before returning to the table, I remained standing and said in a voice pitched rather high.

'Thank you all for a lovely evening, but Edward and I should really be getting home now.'

Placing my hands on the back of the chair and clenching my fingers, I waited nervously.

'Frances, please sit down, I am not ready to leave.'

Edward looked away. I did not sit down. I steadied myself, raising my voice a notch or two.

'Edward, we really must go.'

Edward turned to face me, looking resigned and smiled at the other guests.

'OK.'

He turned to his host and beamed.

'Thanks for a great evening.'

He raised himself out of his chair and walked around the table either shaking hands or patting shoulders and saying, 'Enjoy the rest of the evening.'

It was well after midnight when we left the foyer of the hotel. We were only just outside the door, when Edward pulled me around and pinned me to the wall. He grabbed my hair and shook my head against the wall.

'Frances!' He exploded. 'Don't you ever, ever embarrass me in front of my friends?'

I knew better than to scream. When he finished, we walked towards the car. He handed me the keys. We got in and I started to drive home. He barked at me, 'You know how important they are to my firm.'

A few moments later, he clenched his fist and banged it hard on his thigh. 'You bitch!'

He then looked sideways at me and swung his arm around my neck and pushed my head downwards. I braked. The car stopped. He forced my head down hard hitting the gear stick again and again as I struggled to raise myself, screaming in agony.

He composed himself. 'Go on Frances! Drive home.'

We remained silent for the rest of the journey. I pulled into the drive and parked the car before walking into the house and went straight up the stairs. I was in tears and frightened; my left eye was throbbing. Edward went into the sitting room to pay Lucy and drive her home.

Today my face is bruised and sore; Edward has ordered me to stay at home and not go to work. I will need to see Dr Muir in order to take several days off work and allow for the bruising to fade. I have taken a photograph of my bruised face. What is dreadful, is knowing that it will happen again. The only time I really feel safe is when Edward is absent from the home. Polly has made me a cup of tea and told me she was sorry that Oliver hit me. So that's what Edward told her. Bloody coward. For a time last year, there was the possibility that we could be happy together.

12th December. Dr Muir has given me a note allowing me to take a week off work and it refers to a head injury. Lucy had an accident, she was thrown from her horse and has broken her arm. It was the morning after the Christmas dinner dance.

16th December. This evening was the Moreton Christmas Party. I did my best to cover up the bruise around my eye. When asked, I told Evelyn Bainbridge that I had slipped and fallen over the Hoover. She looked at me, pulling a face. 'That's what they all say.'

She showed no sign of empathy, just a flat statement of the truth. Lord Rossiter spoke with Edward about playing for the cricket team next summer. Edward is delighted. Polly enjoyed herself too. I am going to miss her.

20th December. Good fortune. Sally is here to spend a couple of days with Polly before she joins us after Christmas. Polly will be heading home and has plans to travel.

24th December. It is late. We have just got back from Midnight Mass at St Lawrence's. Lord and Lady Rossiter together with their guests arrived in formal dinner dress and sat in the front pews. Edward loves being part of this community and because he loves it, he wants us to be a part of it. He promised me he will try to make things better. I want it too, but need to dig deep in my resolve to make our marriage sound. Even as I think about it, I know deep down I will fail, if not now sometime later. Did I just slide into marrying Edward, not knowing how to extricate myself? No. I loved him.

1990

BLONDE AMBITION

1st February. Looking out this morning from the morning room window, the lawns at the front of the house are covered in snowdrops.

Edward and I had a really amusing evening at a murder mystery party hosted by our neighbours, Nicholas and Bridget. It was a 1930's scenario with Edward dressed as a golf professional and me as a news reporter. Such a lovely coincidence that there was a thirties style dress in Laura Ashley and matching cloche hat. We were in tune. He was attentive and loving towards me.

3rd April. A full house for Philip's fifth birthday on Sunday. Vivienne and David came with Mum and Dad. Edward's parents came with Simon and Erin together with Claire. We had an entertainer called *Uncle Dennis*, who seemed to know most of the children and just in case he didn't each child was given a named label. Philip and Oliver were given feathered indian head dresses and there were lots of other hats for the children to choose and wear. Every child was involved in a trick and then there was disco dancing before the the Teddy Bears' Picnic I arranged for them in the dining room. Vivienne videoed the proceedings and later we watched the video all together before the family left. There was only one sour note. When we were tidying up Mum asked Philip, 'Shall I ask Daddy to put you to bed?' Philip responded by saying, 'No, he's mean.'

17th April. Having read the spring edition of *Moreton News*, I rang Alasdair and offered the Dower House as a venue for the summer garden party. He was delighted. Nowhere is regional pride so jealously upheld as in North Yorkshire and several people have told me, 'This is God's own country!'.

As a family we had a quiet Easter going to church on Sunday. Lord and Lady Rossiter were there with friends. Alasdair greeted everyone as they left in the sunshine.

On Easter Monday, we drove to Embsay to ride on the Thomas the Tank steam engine. While I settled Oliver and his buggy onto the train, Edward took Philip to meet the *Fat Controller* and then to the front of the train to step up into the cab to talk to the driver and fireman. Philip was allowed to blow the whistle. It is only a thirty minute ride to Bolton Abbey and we were soon walking towards the ruins from the village green. The path took us past the Priory to the banks of the River Wharfe. Oliver and I crossed on the bridge and Edward picked up Philip and jumped across the Stepping Stones. The path led us up an incline covered with clumps of white and yellow daffodils and then into woodland and down to the ford at Pickles Beck where we came to a small wooden bridge, which we crossed and walked to the pavilion for lunch before returning to Embsay on the train. Tired and happy the boys were soon asleep this evening.

1st May. The house is quiet. Philip is at school and nanny has taken Oliver to Mothers and Toddlers for the morning. Patrick and Isabel left this morning after breakfast.

They arrived in time for dinner on Saturday. Edward was keen to invite our new Yorkshire friends including Alasdair and Ruth. Charlotte and Henry Crampton completed the party, which was lively with conversation and stories. Alasdair helped me clear away the plates in between courses. We started with *Chilled cucumber and mint soup* served with slices of toasted Ciabatta. This was followed by *Lemon sole Véronique* with Jersey Royal potatoes and asparagus. It was served from a large platter surrounded by the sauce and decorated with chervil. It was the dry Vermouth in the sauce that packed a flavour punch. The highlight was a *Charlotte Russe* dessert with a raspberry sauce. There was a selection of cheeses as an alternative.

Coffee was served in the drawing room giving everyone a chance to realign themselves in conversation.

Sally worked on Saturday so I could concentrate on preparing the meal and Edward went to see as Manchester City at home against Derby County with his Dad. This enabled me to enjoyed a leisurely approach to preparing the evening meal. Sally and the boys were in and out of the kitchen and chattering away and I joined them for lunch, which Sally prepared.

On Sunday we visited Ripley Castle. Patrick drove as his Range Rover accommodated everyone. Ripley Castle has been the home of the Ingilby family for over seven hundred years, taking centre place within the small estate-owned village. The boys enjoyed running around the parkland. Isabel preferred the walled gardens with their wide herbaceous borders where the Wisterias were in bloom. However, lovely Isabel is, it is difficult to relax and enjoy her company, knowing how upset Melanie is following her divorce from Patrick.

Yesterday Edward and Patrick had a business meeting in Leeds, so Isabel and I went to York and looked at the shops in the Shambles, a narrow fourteenth century street with overhanging timber framed houses, originally populated by butchers. We then had lunch at Betty's Café Tea Rooms in St Helen's Square. We went early to avoid queuing and found a table by the window. We both ordered *Rarebit with Worcestershire sauce & Yorkshire ale*. While we waited we drank mineral water and relaxed watching passers by. When it came, the rarebit was piping hot and delicious. We declined coffee and set off towards The Castle Museum. The museum stands on the site of York Castle and was once a debtors' prison. We enjoyed strolling down the re-constructed street, Kirkgate. We were inspired by the collection of patchwork quilts and were much moved by the collection of Christmas cards sent home during the First World War, some embroidered by local women and sold to the soldiers.

13th June. It's official. The Berlin wall is being demolished and the reunification of East and West Germany is happening.

7th July. What a glorious day! Edward enjoyed being host to the Summer Garden Party. Having mowed the grass in the paddock for car parking, Edward was in charge of the music.

My family arrived mid morning. Vivienne and David were tasked with helping on the book stall, while Mum and Dad took care of the boys and made lunch for us.

Lord Rossiter opened the party with a short speech and then the games began. Some were new to me, like *Splat the Rat*. Later, Lady Rossiter came into the kitchen and thanked me and the other ladies who had worked all afternoon preparing tea and scones with cream and jam. What a bargain, just fifty pence to attend, including afternoon tea. The marquee was a good decision as initially there had been light rain, but as the afternoon wore on, clouds gave way to blue sky. Alasdair and Ruth circulated and were seen to tuck into the scones. Before they left they came over to thank me for a lovely afternoon. It took ages for Harry Bainbridge to count the money, but when he announced the grand total raised, I was delighted. We had previously agreed half for St Lawrence's and the other half for Yorkshire Cancer Research. It took some time to clear away, particularly the books which were loaded into a van to be taken to the local Oxfam bookshop. Mum and Dad left with Vivienne and David just after six o'clock. We then sat in the sitting room and watched *The Little Mermaid*, while we ate sandwiches before the boys went to bed. As I walked downstairs, I stopped at the half landing and looked out at the vale and the grey and silver sky with splashes of sunlight giving way to the evening. A perfect day.

22nd July. We stayed in London after Madonna's *Blond Ambition* concert at Wembley on Saturday.

It was elaborately choreographed and a sexually explosive performance with a few uneasy moments, particularly when she sang her song *Like a Virgin* during which she simulated masturbation.

It was a lovely morning of flashing sunshine between clouds as we drove home on the M40. Where the motorway cuts through the

Chiltern Hills, we saw Red Kites circling overhead then soaring away across the fields. We stopped off at Vivienne and David's for lunch and to pick up the boys before driving back to Moreton. After bathtime, I snuggled up with the boys and read a chapter from *Wind in the Willows* before their bedtime. Philip knows the story from the audio cassette recorded by Alan Bennett, which I play on long journeys. Philip can mimic his words; he said ryhthmically, *There is nothing, absolutely nothing, half so much doing, than messing about in boats.* This amused Oliver. We all laughed out loud.

2nd August. Iraq has invaded Kuwait. Iraq has claimed Kuwait as Iraqi territory as it had been part of the Ottoman Empire's province of Basra. Britain became responsible for Iraq's foreign affairs in 1899 and drew up the border between the two countries in 1922, making Iraq virtually landlocked. There had been disputes arising from oil pricing. Iraq accused Kuwait of over producing and the price of oil had slumped resulting in huge losses to their economy.

5th August. At last a project to get my teeth into; it is a new initiative for the company to comply with a British quality standard and achieve company wide accreditation. I am responsible for the Marketing & Sales Division in the north, which includes the Warwick office. This means I will see a lot more of Mum and Dad. There will also be meetings at our Head Office in London, so it will mean quite a lot of travel.

22nd August. We went to York races today with Nicholas and Bridget, who always go for the Ebor Handicap. It is a very pleasant racecourse and we all came home with winnings. Nicholas and Edward are becoming good friends and are planning to do more together. Cycling was talked about a lot today.

6th September. I had my first project meeting in London today. The house was quiet when I arrived home, the boys long since in bed.

Sally very kindly cooked supper. I was tired and didn't really want to listen to her concerns about the boys behaviour. Edward became animated and looked at me and said, 'I will sort this out.' A feeling of foreboding overwhelmed me, but I was too tired to respond.

23rd September. All day I went about with a sense of autumn's richness. I breathed in the air, smoky and damp. Earlier the boys and I ran around the garden collecting beech nuts and taking them in handfuls to feed the horses in the paddock.

Sally came with us to the service of Harvest Thanksgiving at St Lawrence's which was followed by supper at Moreton Park in the attic room above the garages. The boys behaved well and enjoyed the games. We arrived home happy and tired.

28th September. It is my birthday. Before Edward left for his office he gave me a big hug and a nice card. Later, Philip came into my bedroom with Oliver following behind and gave me a card, which he had decorated himself together with a big kiss. Alone now and looking forward to a day to myself. Edward is taking me out for dinner this evening at The Sportsman's Arms.

29th September. Harrogate was my destination yesterday, beginning in the cosmetics department of Hoopers, where I bought a new Christian Dior nail polish. Then on to Jaeger with a generous gift voucher from Edward in my purse. It was a rather exhilarating feeling knowing that there would certainly be something lovely to choose from and be able to treat myself. I wasn't disappointed and bought a charming two piece in linen. Both the top and skirt are buttoned at the back with the top in a slightly lighter tone from the deeper taupe skirt. Lunch at Betty's concluded my outing, arriving home in plenty of time to have a leisurely bath and get ready for the evening. Our table at The Sportsman's Arms was booked for eight o'clock and we set off in good time and on arrival relaxed in the lounge, whilst browsing the menu. It was too warm for a fire to be lit, but the room was still very cosy with soft lighting and comfy chairs around a Victorian tiled fireplace. Too early in the season for pheasant, we both decided on *Fillets of Turbot with leeks and a cream sauce*. We finished with *Pears baked in Marsala wine*. Edward chose Sancerre to accompany the meal. He was attentive all evening.

15th October. Oliver has a happy disposition and Edward does appear to be more gentle towards him, although he doesn't always get away lightly. Oliver is a very slow eater and lacks concentration. Meal times with Edward are increasingly curtailed by his threat to Oliver, 'Eat it up or go to bed.' This just makes Oliver tense and he more than likely cries. This is immediately followed by, 'Stop crying or go to bed.' And he goes with Edward chasing him. It hasn't taken Oliver long to realise that he prefers to go hungry and to go to bed rather than the hassle of eating lunch with Daddy.

29th October. Oliver is in bed asleep. Philip has had another tantrum. Recently Edward has used the slipper on his hands. He has to hold them out. He told Philip, that the next smack was because Mummy tried to interfere. Philip tried to fight back. It is very distressing and I am at a loss what to do.

6th November. We allowed the village to use the paddock for the bonfire. Everyone contributed to the fireworks and a couple of young guys, who I don't know, were responsible for letting them off. Several of us brought flasks of mulled wine and toffee apples to share. We stood as close to the fire to keep warm as we could without being covered in ask sparks being thrown off from the dying embers. The air smelled of autumn. It was a good turn out. Edward made sure the bonfire was out before we came home.

I woke up in the early hours hearing the patter of feet. I got up to find Philip hovering outside our bedroom door half undressed and quickly took him back to his room and changed him and his sheets, staying with him until he slept.

12th November. An early morning start for me on Monday in Manchester and so I decided to drive over Sunday evening and stay in an hotel. On arrival home tonight, Edward informed me that Philip had got him up three times in the night. When I saw Philip, he told me that Daddy had smacked him. No wonder he is an unhappy little boy. It is a sad fact that I have done a lousy job of protecting him from an insensitive, overbearing bully. Where does his graceless and meanness of spirit come from?

18th November. Last night Nicholas and Bridget came for supper together with Alasdair and Ruth. Edward was enjoying telling everyone about JK Galbraith, the American Economist valued by Margaret Thatcher, who had visited his university. Smiling, he turned to me.
'Frances, do you know anyone famous?'
I could only say, 'No.'
There was a long pause before the conversation picked up again with Alasdair entertaining us with one of his stories and soon everyone was smiling and laughing, the incident forgotten.

Getting ready for bed and thinking about what happened, I realised that no-one would think badly of me for not knowing anyone famous. This is what he does, this is what he always does. He is a master at it, making me feel worthless. Despite this, the evening was really enjoyable and the pheasant casserole was delicious.

28th November. The Dower House was calm today. I was alone for most of the day and was busy in the garden planting Graham Thomas shrub roses in the flower beds either side of the front door. Graham Thomas is my favourite in colour and fragrance, repeat flowering even into winter time with its' faithful companionship. It was my favourite rose when we lived at Pippins.

In the late afternoon, the rain fell in a peaceful soft way and later, I turned on the radio to find out that Margaret Thatcher has left Downing Street. This evening watching BBC News, she looked tearful. Such a betrayal.

8th December. What a lovely evening. The snow had fallen heavily yesterday and was still in drifts around the lane, so we drove slowly and carefully to Moreton Park. Santa made every child feel special. Lord Rossiter was in good spirits and together with Alasdair engaged with everyone to join in and perform a party piece. He encouraged Charlotte's daughter to sing *Who Will Buy My Pretty Flowers?* As the evening wore on, the room became warm from the heat of the fire at the end of the room. Alasdair sat at the piano and started to play well known tunes and everyone who could, got up and began to dance. Sally took Philip by the hand and I picked up Oliver as we attempted to do the *Oki Koki*. Philip loved it and we all laughed loudly. Edward joined in when the *Gay Gordon's* was announced and then we left as by then Oliver was tired.

27th December. Once the family left yesterday, Edward and I took the boys for an invigorating walk around Brimham Rocks. Arm in arm, with Oliver in the buggy, we watched Philip run and jump about. We felt in tune.

We were at ease and happy, so we decided to take the boys to *The Jorvic Viking Centre*. We set off early this morning to avoid queuing. It was quite amazing to see life pretty accurately as it would have been in the Viking-Age city nearly one thousand years ago. The reality of the houses, and workshops together with the sounds and smells was very impressive. I was so pleased to see Philip enjoying himself and really engaging with the story and pulling faces at the nauseous smells that wafted around as we walked through the streets. We stopped at MacDonald's for lunch on the way home. Edward lit a fire in the morning room and the boys and I watched *The Snowman*, while he read the papers. Once Oliver was in bed, Philip watched *Mutant Ninja Turtles*, a video he had been given for Christmas. It was much later after supper that Edward and I finally settled and watched a video of the film, *Silence of the Lambs*, about a young FBI cadet who confides in an incarcerated and manipulative killer in order to receive help in catching another serial killer. We were impressed by the acting of Anthony Hopkins and Jodie Foster, although emotionally exhausted by the end.

As a new year beckons, I have come to realise over the past twelve months that however shaky and unpredictable life is with Edward, it is a life I have chosen.

1991
THE LAKE DISTRICT

17th January. Since the invasion last year, the United States has been moving forces into Saudi Arabia concerned that the Iraq army in Kuwait is in easy striking distance of Saudi oil fields. In response to Iraq's invasion of Kuwait and the defence of Saudi Arabia, coalition forces started air attacks on Iraq.

7th February. We woke to a deep covering of powdery snow outside. Beyond, the fields on the hills were freckled with snow. We decided to stay home. Edward built a snowman with Philip; Oliver and I watched in between running around and looking at our footprints in the snow. When Sally took charge of the boys, we went around the garden shaking low branches heavy with snow as best we could. During the day an easterly wind brought heavy snowfalls and tonight the temperature has dropped significantly.

28th February. Ceasefire. The Iraqi army is in retreat from Kuwait.

13th April. The Friends of John McCarthy campaign to release him has been organised by his girlfriend Jill Morrell and been politically active since 1988. Thousands attended a rally today in Trafalgar Square on the fifth anniversary of his capture; many were wearing yellow ribbons. Brian Keenan, who was released a year earlier also attended.

1st May. I spent a few days in the Lake District, leaving Sally in charge; having decided a while ago that I needed some time alone. It must have been after one of Edward's episodes. My best, it seems, isn't good enough. Edward and I have discussed our situation many times over and I am always swayed by his arguments. In the past few weeks all has been calm and pleasant, but I am still worried about the future. The truth is I am frightened of Edward. That's why I went to the Lakes, to spend time alone and to get my thoughts together. I can't just hope that things will be different. There was only one question. Do I stay?

I arrived in Ambleside on Monday in time for lunch and had a good look around the shops. From there, it was a short journey to Coniston and The Waterhead Hotel, where I stayed for two nights, recommended by Alasdair and Ruth, who know the area well. It is a very comfortable hotel built in grey stone with large gables at each end framing three smaller gables in the top roof space. The history is interesting, as John Ruskin, the illustrious Victorian artist and social critic was a frequent visitor. He lived just across the water and many of his visitors stayed at the hotel, including Charles Darwin. During the Second World War the hotel became a school for evacuees. The village of Coniston has a long association with notables. Tennyson spent his honeymoon here, Turner painted the mountain scenery and Arthur Ransome used Coniston Water as the setting for *Swallows and Amazons*.

The following day was glorious. I drew my curtains and took in the view across Coniston Water to the wooded hills. The sky was a pale powder blue dotted with small puffball clouds circulating. The restaurant was flooded with light and I sat by the large windows with the same view across the water. It was just after nine o'clock, when I took the launch along Coniston Water and stopped off at Sunny Bank for a picnic lunch provided by the hotel. Finding a secluded spot on the beach inlet I stretched out soaking up the sunshine on my face and legs. Eventually, I did begin to feel hungry and delved into the paper carrier containing a tuna and cucumber sandwich, orange juice and grapes. Happy to gaze across the water my mind wandered and for a time it was idyllic. My appetite satisfied, I set off northwards along the lake shore towards Torver Jetty. The path was rather narrow and crossed with numerous small becks. I stopped at Moor Gill Foot resting on a grassy bank enjoying the solitude. What happiness it was to sit and clear my mind of all thoughts. What a renewal of heart and mind!

Approaching Torver Jetty, I passed through a little gate into a stand of amazingly tall trees, some must have been over one hundred feet tall. The water was choppy on the return journey and really quite cold. I was pleased not to have to go out again. While staying there, I read *Three Men in a Boat* by Jerome K Jerome. It had been on my reading list for ever. It is a rather silly lighthearted story and just what was needed. It is the sort of book which can be picked up and put down without any worries about losing the plot as there is none.

On my last day, I enjoyed a leisurely walk in the gardens and along the lakeside before packing up and setting off for home. Driving towards Ambleside, I turned off to the right and meandered along to The Drunken Duck Inn for lunch. It wasn't too busy and was certainly worth the detour as my ploughman's lunch was very good value and came served in a picnic basket wrapped in a gingham cloth. The circular walk at Tarn Hows through beautiful countryside with majestic views of the mountains didn't disappoint.

Once I started to drive across the Pennines, I couldn't wait to get home and see Philip and Oliver. I arrived home in time to join Sally and the boys for supper. I bathed Oliver while Sally and Philip watched the *Jungle Book* video and then it was time for Philip to get ready for bed. After his bath, he hugged me very tightly, the scent of the soap lingered on his skin.

Edward was pleased to see me when he arrived home. The question which needed answering was, 'Do I stay?' It is too big a decision right now, although an innate sense that I shouldn't stay still permeates my thoughts.

28th May. Philip is spending a few days away with Vivienne and David. They have taken him to Portsmouth and are staying in a Holiday Inn just by Clarence Pier and the fun-fare. Vivienne telephoned this evening to say that they had been to see HMS Victory and a Naval Rating took them around, telling Philip about the *monkeys* who were small children and helped with the loading of the gun barrels. Afterwards they took a ferry to Gosport on the other side of the estuary and walked along the marina full of sailing boats and then went on the submarine HMS Alliance. They plan to go to the fun fare tomorrow. Vivienne passed the phone to Philip and he was very excited about his day.

3rd June. Philip seems very settled on his return and told me about going onto HMS Victory. He thought it was cool. Vivienne did mention that one evening Philip had a tantrum and got into a terrible temper and cried himself to sleep. She was helpless and frustrated that she couldn't calm him down.

13th July. Yesterday Edward and I attended the school sports day and watched Philip in the sack race. We were both relaxed and when we got home, we decided to have afternoon tea in the garden. We watched the boys playing Hide and Seek in and out of the copse at the bottom of the garden. The heat of the afternoon sun eventually gave way to a balmy and serene evening. 'May we stay little longer?' Philip asked, as he ran up to me and climbed onto my lap. All we could hear was birdsong.

8th August. After five years as a hostage to an Islamic Jihad organisation, John McCarthy has been released. There are pictures on the BBC News of him arriving at RAF Lyneham. Terry Waite remains a hostage.

Philip has been attending Nippon Dai Budo Kai for quite some time now and today he was awarded a junior orange belt.

18th August. We have returned from Puerto Pollensa on the North East coast of Majorca. We stayed in a villa within walking distance of both the beach and the pretty town. Being away for a whole fortnight has done Edward and me a power of good. He relaxed and enjoyed being with the boys. The villa had a small swimming pool and the boys had fun jumping in and swimming. They had bright red inflatable vests, which are so much nicer than the rubber rings of yesteryear. We hired a car and explored the island.

17th September. An innocent remark by Sally about Philip's behaviour has sparked renewed action by Edward to provide swift and sharp punishments to stop his bad behaviour. More slapping. Edward recently took him to a football training session one Saturday and is concerned that Philip seemed very timid and introvert. At the same time the school has become concerned about his behaviour bullying other boys. Edward now uses the slipper on Philip and if he cries he is slippered again.

24th September. A Health Visitor came to see me today after school, so that she could meet me and the boys. We had a long chat and she recommended we seek help from the Family Therapy Team.

14th October. Taking the day off, Edward and I attended the Children & Families Service clinic. Dr Connor explained how she and her team would work with us to help. Edward kept referring to my having no control over the children. He was sceptical about involving Dr Connor and as we had self-referred, he couldn't see the point of it all.

24th November. Freddie Mercury has died, just days after announcing he has AIDS.

1992

HELP!

4th January. Oliver is four years old. He is a happy little chap. Being a Saturday, we decided to spend it as a family with no party. We had really good seats in the stalls at Harrogate Theatre for the afternoon matinee of Dick Whittington. The sound effects were really loud, but it didn't seem to worry Oliver who looked happy and mesmerised by the flamboyance of the actors, their costumes and scenery. Philip was captivated and several times jumped out of his seat laughing and clapping as he responded to the actors. He sat next to Edward and they laughed a lot together. I noticed just once, Philip sitting on Edward's lap. Afterwards we made our way from the theatre to Betty's Café Tea Rooms for supper. We prefer to dine downstairs, when the children are with us, in the Spindler Room as the shaped banquette seating is more enclosed and private. Looking at John Spindler's marquetry is rather soothing and it seems a lot quieter.

15th January. Help! I need Edward to stop bullying Philip. We need to go back to the family clinic and seek their help. He has refused.

22nd January. Philip and I saw Dr Connor today. As we got out of the car, Philip decided he didn't want to go and had a tantrum, which continued while we waited to see Dr Connor. Her interest was mainly with Philip and his behaviour. She came out straight away and asked me if Philip was being abused. She believed his pale complexion and very tense demeanour were symptoms of abuse. In Edward's absence and due to his absence, she phoned Social Services and informed me that in due course we are to be interviewed separately by a Social Officer and a Police Woman.

5th February. Edward has agreed to a big project in London and will be away quite a lot during the next few months. He told me last night that he has already been looking at rental properties in Surrey. He will fly back to Yorkshire alternate weekends unless work prevents him from doing so. It is decided. My immediate response was that of relief.

7th February. John Major has signed the Maastricht Treaty in the Netherlands founding the European Union. Silly man!

21st February. We have been informed that following our interviews, no action will be taken. We have also received a letter from Dr Connor inviting us to continue working with her team. Edward again refused.

6th March. Sally is leaving us. She confided to me that the home environment is too stressful and she is anxious whenever Edward is home. She spent her last day with Libby who will be taking over from her next week and as she lives locally will not live-in. She is going out with a rather nice young man, who teaches domestic science at the local comprehensive school.

1st April. After Philip opened his presents, we took the children to MacDonald's for lunch and then drove to Brimham Rocks. It was a sunny afternoon, if a little chilly. In the distance we could see the green valleys of the dales, with their stone walls snaking down from the higher fells. The boys were well wrapped up and Oliver was running everywhere trying to keep up with Philip.

Later in the early evening, I snuggled up on the sofa with the boys and read *Old Bear*. It is one of my favourite books to read to the boys and tells the story of Bramwell Brown, Little Bear, Duck and Rabbit as they attempt to rescue Old Bear from the attic.

17th May. We have just returned from a few days in Virginia Water. The boys really enjoyed seeing Edward. The flat is fairly tiny but we managed. It was a nice sunny day on Saturday, so we went for a walk around the lake and were surprised at the size of the Totem Pole and how it was so dominant in the landscape. We saw Melanie after our walk and stayed for lunch.

It was a long drive back today. The boys were very tired and quickly fell asleep this evening. I peeped in before I retired. Philip was lying on his back arms stretched above his head, so I gently moved them and pulled the duvet over his shoulders. Oliver was curled around his teddy. I left the light on in the bathroom, something I would never do if Edward was home. In the early hours Oliver appeared at my bedside, damp and tearful. I swept him up in my arms and once he was changed into dry clothes popped him back into his bed with clean sheets. He was asleep as his head touched the pillow.

17th June. Libby took the boys to the circus this afternoon. Oliver stroked a snake.

25th July. We all needed a holiday and Edward was keen to camp in France and decided on Eurocamp on the south west coast of France. We went by ferry and drove to Bourgneuf en Retz to stay over night before driving the rest of the way to the campsite at les Sables d'Olonne on the Atlantic coast of the Vendée. The weather was glorious and we settled and relaxed the moment we arrived. Everything was so easy for the children, who soon found playmates. Each morning we enjoyed fresh baguettes from the camp shop and the boys swam in the pool or messed about on a nearby cove with its rocky outcrop. On one occasion we drove inland to La Roche-sur-Yon and stopped en-route at Les Jardins du Loriot for a stroll around the botanical gardens, where we found several greenswards for the boys to run about. The best day out was our trip to La Rochelle wandering around the Old Port guarded by its' medieval towers where French migrants embarked for their new lives in Quebec. We had an early supper at a small seafood restaurant close to the picturesque harbour. The drive back to the campsite as the sun set in the west was reassuringly a very happy one.

While we were away we discussed a voluntary redundancy plan that my firm was offering staff and whether with less travel and business commitments I would have more time to focus on the family and that would have a positive effect in providing a less stressful environment for everyone.

I signed the paperwork this evening.

9th August. This evening looking out at the vale, the sky is grey with silver splashes of sunlight and I can't help worrying if I have chosen the right course. It has been on my mind since I signed the redundancy paperwork last month. Is it too late to change my mind?

Meantime, the world has been enjoying the coverage of the Olympic Games in Barcelona. Me too, though I didn't stay up for the closing ceremony this evening as I had to prepare for work tomorrow. Linford Christie won the men's 100 metres.

10th August. Edward left early this morning for a symposium he is organising in Chicago, which is a repeat of the one he delivered in Miami last month. He is very excited.

21st September. Yesterday a referendum was held in France as to whether to ratify the Maastricht Treaty. It was narrowly approved. Why weren't we given the option. Maastricht is a step too far.

28th September. Tidying up this evening, I found a new wallet in Edward's chest of drawers. He already has a smart leather wallet I

240

bought from Harrod's last Christmas. Edward doesn't spend money on expensive accessories.

9th October. My last day at the office. If I had discovered the wallet earlier, would I have tried to cancel my redundancy package? Not an easy question to answer as working part time might be a good answer in the long run. Except that now I have to deal with the enormous bombshell that Edward is serious about Lois, who he met at the symposiums in Chicago, where she was part of the production team. She lives in Fort Lauderdale.

20th November. Windsor Castle is ablaze.

12th December. We have decided to have Christmas lunch at the Four Seasons Hotel. Edward will be returning to London afterwards and will collect Lois from Heathrow on Boxing Day. Leading up to this decision, there was one conversation when Edward told me.
'Lois says that I shouldn't stay with you, if you don't love me.'
'Of course I don't love you, I am afraid of you!' The words rambled around in my mind, but I didn't reply. There was a time when I was convinced I loved my husband more than anyone. Now all I feel is sorrow and emptiness.

Tidying up my desk, I looked at my 1981 diary and read my thoughts when I first met Edward and fell in love. Even then there were gnawing feelings of misgiving, here it is in black and white! Why didn't I listen to my heart? Perhaps, the joy of being wanted, confused with love. Did he love me? Yes, I think he did in the beginning.

25th December. Lunch was a very civilised affair. Both Philip and Oliver behaved very well. After the Queen's speech, I took the children to the hotel spa for a swim. By the time we walked home it was nearly five o'clock. It was very foggy and the dampness in the air dripped onto our shoulders. Edward gave each of us a hug and left. I am taking the boys to stay with Vivienne and David tomorrow for a few days. There is a sense of foreboding and yet at the same time I feel a huge sense of relief that it is over, like the passing of a great black cloud. The house will be sold. This lovely old house in this charming hamlet will be sold. Will any of this make sense to the children?

1993

DOWER HOUSE FOR SALE

20th January. Today, was Bill Clinton's inaugural ceremony and I was moved by the poem *On the Pulse of Morning*, written and read by Maya Angelou. I watched it again on replay and chose a few lines to keep:

> *Here, on the pulse of this new day,*
> *You may have the grace to look up and out*
> *And into your sister's eyes,*
> *And into your brother's face,*
> *Your country,*
> *And say simply*
> *Very simply*
> *With hope —*
> *Good morning.*

She has written several autobiographies on her life growing up in Stamps, Arkansas in a racist world. At the presidential gala the night before a cast including Michael Jackson performed. Fleetwood Mac also took to the stage to perform *Don't Stop* which had been Bill Clinton's campaign song.

4th April. The Dower House is now on the market. Edward and Lois are visiting his parents this weekend and he wanted to drive over and show Lois our home today. I didn't want to meet her in my home, so I set off early and took the boys to Whitby. It is a wonderful drive across the moor, but I was hesitant to drive up Sutton Bank as usually Edward would drive and it isn't easy, but I needn't have worried, in a low gear I managed very well. There is something wonderful about approaching the coast. The light changes and there is a sense of excitement. Philip and Oliver are no different from how Vivienne and I used to strive to be the first to see the sea, when Dad drove us to the south coast for our annual holiday. The boys like Whitby and were happy to amble around. We had a picnic lunch on the west cliff looking out to sea. Afterwards, we walked down to the beach and the boys had a kick a bout. It was sunny and quite warm in the sunshine. By four o'clock it was cooler and they were ready to climb back up to the top and have tea at The Magpie. By now it was reasonably quiet and we were able to find a table by the window upstairs. The Magpie never disappoints, the boys behaved really well. The cod was cooked in a crispy batter with soft flaky fish underneath, served with chunky chips. We all had ice cream to finish. Looking out across the harbour, it was low tide and beyond there was a red haze in the sky. Sea birds were flying, screeching; some on the shore line were feeding. We were a happy trio walking back up the hill to where the car was parked and we seemed to be home in no time. By eight o'clock Philip and Oliver were bathed and in their beds succumbed to sleep. Leaning over them for another kiss, they smelled clean and sweet.

20th April. I have finished reading Maya Angelou's first published memoirs, *I Know Why the Caged Bird Sings*. The title draws you in and reminds you that it is possible to both lose control of one's life and to have one's freedom taken from you. Angelou's description of being raped as an eight-year-old girl overwhelms the autobiography, although it is presented only briefly in the text. She bravely raises issues of trust, love and the naturalness of a child's craving for human contact and the confusion engendered by the power disparities between children and adults. She is quoted as saying, 'There is no greater agony than bearing an untold story inside you'. I offered no resistance, as the memories pushed deep down in my own subconsciousness, began to emerge. I couldn't hold back my tears. Not then. Not now.

27th April. My solicitor has advised keeping the application low key to avoid any aggravation. I reluctantly agreed. There is to be no mention of any abuse or even naming Lois just a bland statement that Edward and I are estranged, that he is living in London. She will send me a draft petition together with possible hearing dates. It is the end of something. Something that didn't live up to my heart's desire. It failed before it began. What a mess!

28th May. The divorce petition has now been served on Edward care of his solicitor in Manchester.

4th June. We arrived home rather late after the long journey, so it was a quick sandwich and a glass of milk for the boys, while they watched the cartoon film *Dumbo* before bedtime. They were so excited, telling me about their stay in London with Edward and Lois. How they had been given roller skates and had been to Kensington Gardens to try them out. They couldn't remember where they had eaten but had been to a couple of nice restaurants for lunch with Lois when Edward had been working. The thing that really breaks my heart is that they now do these things with Lois. Edward was polite to me when he arrived at my parents to drop the boys off earlier today. I didn't invite him in, my parents are too upset. Mum made a lovely cold salmon salad for lunch, followed by her favourite raspberry trifle. Afterwards, we all went for a short walk to the playground, where the boys let off some energy before the drive back to Yorkshire. It is only nine o'clock, but I am exhausted and emotionally drained. The boys will now spend time during school holidays with Edward and Lois. Edward takes it for granted that I will drive up and down the motorway to achieve this. He emphasises that I am not working or at least not much and so he presumes that I can be at his beck and call. No mention at all of the cost of petrol. Philip and Oliver' happiness is most important and I now have to share them with Lois. It doesn't seem real.

9th July. It was a truly bizarre afternoon today. Edward and Lois drove up from London and arrived for the school sports day. I didn't know they were coming and only spoke with them when they asked if they could take the boys somewhere for tea afterwards. It was unsettling, but I agreed. The boys were brought back at seven o'clock and after a polite exchange when we agreed a date during the summer holidays for the boys to visit, Edward and Lois left to drive over to Manchester to spend the weekend with Edwards' parents. It is good for Edward to see the children, but the thought of another woman playing mummy fills me with dismay.

23rd July. It is so nice to be home with Mum and Dad. I drove down early this morning with the boys to meet Edward at Corley Services north of Coventry on the M6. Philip and Oliver were so pleased to see him and looking forward to their weekend together. Edward is planning to take them to both the Natural History Museum and Science Museum. I am happy to be here and relax for a few days before returning to Yorkshire with the boys on Sunday evening. Vivienne and David are away on holiday, so I won't be able to visit them during my stay. Tomorrow, Mum and I plan to have a good look around the shops in Solihull and have lunch at Beatties. She and Dad are planning their fiftieth wedding anniversary in September at Woolley Grange, Bradford upon Avon. It is an easy driving distance for Vivienne and David. The boys and I will stay the night before to break up the journey from Yorkshire. It has lots of activities for children including complimentary childcare. Just what we all need. It has been a difficult year so far.

24th August. I read through Edward's affidavit this evening. Absolute poppycock! I cannot believe what he has written and can only assume it is written in this way to influence Lois. Most disturbingly, he is currently contemplating commencing proceedings for a residence order for Philip and Oliver because he is extremely worried by the deterioration in the behaviour of the children since he has left the matrimonial home.

25th August. A letter has arrived from the Children & Families Service Unit following Edward's meeting with a social worker inviting me to attend an observation session at the clinic with the boys.

26th August. After appearing before the Judge with my solicitor and sitting opposite Edward, I arrived home this evening exhausted. The decree nisi was granted. You can never really wipe away a marriage. A piece of paper cannot expunge the memories. Edward was already there when I arrived home. Tina and her husband were looking after the children. Tina refused to leave until my return. Edward was asserting himself and had been rude to Tina, so she had already rung Alasdair, who came around just after I arrived home and stayed until he had smoothed the ruffled feathers, which certainly needed smoothing. He left once Edward was calm. Edward then went upstairs to say goodbye to Philip and Oliver, before driving over the Pennines to stay the night with his parents. He was gone. And later I walked around the house, wrapping my arms around myself asking, 'Is this it? Is this what I really want? A single mother? No, of course not. What I knew in my heart was the magic of days that will come no more and that time can never restore. To be free of Edward? Yes.'

I looked into the boys' bedrooms. First, Philip the child conceived when we were in love, sleeping soundly. Then Oliver, snug as a bug with teddy. I kissed each of them. On the verge of tears, seeing them gave me hope.

The Order for Maintenance of forty pounds per child per week seems fair, as long as I can find a job soon. It has already proved difficult, however confident I am of my business skills particularly in Quality Management. It is too early to worry about money as I still have some redundancy money remaining.

1st September. Dr Connor called me at home this afternoon after our appointment at the clinic. It was surreal being videoed during my interactions with Philip and Oliver. Dr Connor raised her concerns regarding the children's visit to Edward following comments made by the children. In particular, one incident, which I knew to be true because Edward had told me of it and had been proud to say that Lois had backed him up on the disciplinary action. During the children's last visit, Philip was rude to Edward, he refused to apologise and was then made to stand with his back to them until he apologised. Two hours later he did so. Dr Connor recommended that I block visits in the short term until a welfare assessment has been made.

21st September. Both boys are now swimming well. Philip has achieved both Water Skills bronze and silver awards and swam eight hundred metres. Oliver has achieved Water Skills levels three and four awards.

I haven't received any maintenance for the boys.

15th October. Nelson Mandela and F.W. de Klerk have been awarded the Nobel Peace Prize.

16th December. We exchange contracts on The Dower House tomorrow. Edward called me this evening to say the estate agent had advised him the buyers were insisting on a £10,000 reduction in the price before signing. Edward told me that he would only agree to the reduced sale price if I take the financial hit as part of the divorce settlement. Stunned and immobile in a world that was spinning around me and out of control, I agreed.

1994
ANNUS HORRIBILIS

10th January. Libby has gone. With the sale of The Dower House, the children and I have moved to a converted barn at Hampsthwaite, which we are renting until our new house is completed in April. Our furniture and most of our belongings are in store. The couple who own the barn have been very pleasant in settling us in and have invited us to a Cèilidh being held in the village hall at the end of January.

Philip still wants to continue his Karate and I have found a class in Knaresborough starting next week.

7th February. Winter doldrums heightend by the receipt of the report written by Mrs Harrow, our social worker, following five sessions at the clinic with the children. They saw Philip and Oliver together three times and then individually on one occasion each. She writes that both boys were well behaved and when they began playing with various toys in the room they relaxed and felt more able to talk. Her recommendations are more or less l'aise faire. The boys are to continue to have regular contact with Edward and he is advised to 'consider other ways of disciplining the boys, perhaps a system of rewarding rather than punishing.' And, of course, but impossible that Edward and I discuss beforehand any issues relating to the boys that may undermine the other parent's authority.' The example she gives is Edward suggesting to Philip that he buys him a puppy during his stay in London.

I cannot get to sleep at nights now. My thoughts clatter about in my brain and will not let me rest.

21st February. It is raining. The clouds are banked up against the hills. I miss the views from the Dower House.

During the Winter Olympics in Lillehammer, the golden couple of British ice dancing Torvill and Dean made a big comeback ten years on from Bolero. Their free dance routine *Let's Face the Music and Dance* was a pure light hearted dance in the Astaire and Rogers tradition and the audience loved it. They are still the best of the best and it is very disappointing for them to be awarded a bronze medal.

22nd February. The Decree Absolute is pronounced. I have also received a letter from Dr Connor asking me to make an appointment following a letter she has received from Edward, reminding her of his concerns and claiming that I am an unfit mother. It seems to me that he needs to prove to Lois that everything is my fault and that he is the good guy in all this.

8th April. A marvellous warm day and all the plum and cherry blossom out, so I drove to Ripon to see our new home, which is nearing completion.

Patrick and Melanie's son was married last Friday. He has converted to Judaism in order to marry his sweetheart and first love. It has taken him several years of study and cultural changes alongside his medical studies. I hired a fabulous evening dress in black lace, with a velvet Alice band in my hair, which had a short lace veil just covering my eyes. It was a chilly evening, so took my cashmere camel coat for the wedding ceremony at the Manchester Reform Synagogue. The ceremony was performed under a white canopy decorated with flowers. Patrick and Melanie were represented by two members of the Jewish community. The reception was held at The Midland Hotel in St Peter's Square. Edward and Lois were there. He had the gaul to phone me a few days ago and tell me that it would be a sophisticated affair with evening dress and hoped I would dress appropriately. The photos prove I looked fabulous, unlike Lois who seemed dazed and would have looked better if she had put a comb through her hair. Even her dress was drab. Melanie looked stunning in a petrol green evening gown encrusted with stones around the neckline. It can't have been easy for her: surrounded by friends isn't the same as being with your husband together as mother and father of the groom. Patrick's new wife, Isabel was also at the top table, looking glamorous. Patrick is demonstrably happy.

10th April. At last we have moved into our new town house in Ripon. It is a three-storey town house in a development near the River Skell. The front of the house overlooks a paved square with newly planted trees. The boys have the top floor with a bedroom each, a sitting room and shower room. On the first floor is the master bedroom with en-suite shower and two further bedrooms and a family bath-room. Downstairs is an open plan kitchen and dining room with an adjacent sitting room with French windows leading out onto a small patio garden. The narrow front garden is bordered with wrought iron railings. There is plenty of space for everyone. The hall is roomy and I chose black and white chequered ceramic tiles for the floor and a fitted pine corner cloaks cupboard.

15th April. The boys had such a great time at Newby Hall adventure playground today, so I have bought a seasonal pass until September. It is closer than Brimham Rocks and means Colette, our new au pair can take them after school and with me at weekends. Several of their friends like to go too, so they can meet up. It has been thoughtfully designed for children of all ages. It is set amidst undulating lawns bordered with mature trees and there is a beautiful willow which drapes itself beside the waters' edge of the shallow canal over which there is a rope bridge. A wooden platformed ferry is pulled by ropes across the water. There are plenty of climbing frames and swings built mainly with natural wood. Riding on the miniature railway brings back some of the happy memories at Pippins.

17th April. In the post another letter from Edward, copying his solicitor, criticising me and stating his concerns over the children's

251

clothing, lack of visits taking the boys to see his parents and expecting to see the boys in London on alternate weekends. I had to put the letter down and read it again this evening. He also criticised me for allowing Philip to spend a few days with Vivienne and David without his permission, referring to them as *people*. He also suggested he reduce my maintenance and buy the children's clothes himself, by reducing my maintenance to two hundred and forty seven pounds a month.

22nd April. Mrs Harrow visited today with a colleague, who looked after Oliver, whilst she and I talked with Philip. I was able to tell her that there has been a marked difference in Philip's behaviour, far fewer tantrums. He is exploring his new independence outside the home, making new friends and making arrangements himself in the communal play area. The River Skell is only fifty yards away and he seems very happy wading and fishing for trout, crayfish and bullhead fish. Oliver isn't old enough to join him just yet. One thing she did say was that Philip, just like anyone else, is able to choose how he behaves. The session ended when her colleague came downstairs to apologise that Oliver had spilt red nail varnish over the cream sofa in the boys sitting room upstairs. How on earth did she allow him to even open the bottle and where did he get it, he must have gone into my bedroom. She was with him. That this had happened in her presence, when she was in charge. She was in my home, a member of a team that is telling me how to be a better parent and Oliver got the better of her. Practically, my lovely Laura Ashley sofa bed is now a ruined mess.

I have just written a reply to Edward's letter explaining why the boys didn't have a good selection of clothes with them for their visit at Easter. We had only just moved into our new home two days before the visit and I hadn't finished unpacking. I also informed him that I had invited his parents to stay this coming summer but they have declined.

4th May. Waking early, the dawn was lovely and the birds' song beautiful. Now, life is so different. Since we separated, the boys have been to see Edward and Lois several times during the school holidays and they seem to enjoy their visits to London. Edward has now bought a flat in South Kensington. I usually meet Edward at Corley Services on the M6. It is such a long way from Ripon to London just for a weekend. Too tiring for the boys. That is what I told Edward when he wanted Philip to stay with him when Lois planned a weekend away. I told Edward it wasn't OK and followed it up in a letter, but when he spoke with Philip on the telephone, he told him that he would be coming to collect him.

10th May. My solicitor suggested I inform social services and the police. On my return home I contacted Mrs Harrow's manager and he did not think my action was unreasonable. I also spoke to the Headmaster and he suggested that in the best interests of Philip and Oliver, they be collected early from school tomorrow to avoid any potential confrontation in front of them.

13th May. Edward arrived at school to collect Philip on Friday and was told that I had already collected the boys. When he arrived at my house at four o'clock, both boys were out with Colette at Newby Hall. He was furious and started shouting. He went away and came back armed with a can of black spray paint. He sprayed the front door and my Volvo and used the word *ZIGGI* in large letters right across the garage door. When he came around into the back garden and started banging on the French windows, I called the police.

Later in the evening the police rang to say they had caught up with him on the M62 on the way to see his parents. He had been charged with criminal damage and released.

Frightened that he would come back the next day, I booked a couple of nights at the North Lakes Hotel in Penrith. We set off after tea, north on the A1 and then onto the A66 westwards to Penrith. We arrived in time for supper at the hotel and soon the boys were bathed and asleep in bed. After breakfast on Saturday, we visited the charming market town of Keswick and we ambled along its cobbled streets looking into interesting shops. We lunched in a small cafe and then drove south of the town towards Derwent Water and hired a rowing boat. Out on the water, it seemed my cares where miles away and I began to relax. We laughed a lot and, for that day, we were happy. When we got back to Ripon this afternoon, Edward's father phoned offering me money to pay for the damage if I withdrew from court proceedings. I told him that it was up to the police.

1st June. Philip spent the weekend camping with his friends in the Cub Pack. They camped near Bishop Monkton and were very lucky with the weather for their first camping experience. He is growing up fast.

17th June. Yesterday, Wendy Wilby was ordained as the first priest in our diocese. My next door neighbour invited me for coffee this morning and was keen to tell me that her husband, who is a Canon at Ripon Cathedral has decided to resign from the Church of England as he doesn't approve of the ordination of women. She thinks it might be in the newspapers and has asked me to be aware that journalists might come knocking. They came this afternoon and introduced themselves as from *The News of the World*. I politely closed the door.

23rd June. On arriving home this evening, there were two Ansafone messages from Edward. He had been in court to answer the charge of criminal damage to my car and property in May.

First message:

'You're rude, you're arrogant and it ain't over. I am afraid you are impossible to deal with and therefore I am going to take whatever steps . . . I am fed up with dealing with this and by the way I am pleased to say we had a very good result on Wednesday and that most people, in fact everybody recognised

254

that you are a bad influence. Tough on you. So, I am sorry. I hope you hear about the decision and how I am paying you back. It is impossible dealing with you. You are dreadful and I tell you what, I will have access to these children one way or the other. You will not get away with this.'

Second message:

'One other thing, you may need to get your cheque book out because you are going to be in court soon and you are going to have a lot of costs ahead and Yeah. Ha ha ha ha.'

I feel sick to the bottom of my stomach. I am afraid. I am afraid of everything.

25th June. Another letter from Edward, this time two pages in length criticising my care of the boys and my inability to budget. Edward signed the letter, *Ziggi.* It was posted the day before the court hearing.

Alasdair came to see me and I made us a quick lunch of poached eggs on toast. He read the letter. He shook his head slowly looking at me and leaned forward, taking my hand. 'This aggression will ease with time. He is lashing out at you to conceal his own guilt'. Already, I begin to feel the quiet influence of Alasdair.

2nd July. Lois phoned and spoke to Philip this evening. Later Philip lost playing Chinese marbles with Colette and he started being provocative. Eventually, I put him in his bedroom and held the door closed. I insisted he agree to calm down and stop kicking the door. When he finally agreed, he had thrown his clothes on the floor, thrown a drawer from his chest of drawers at the door and written *mummy fuks* on the wall. When he came out he was very uptight and wouldn't talk to me and went downstairs and shut himself in the cupboard under the stairs. How should I have handled this situation? I have started to doubt myself, do I give in too often? Am I confusing the children with a lack of boundaries, to which Edward alludes? I am consistent in my love and warmth to both children.

Lois sent the boys a card saying she was looking forward to seeing them on 15th July. This visit was arranged with me and I have agreed to meet Edward at Corley Services on the M6. I will then spend the weekend with my parents.

5th July. The boys ganged up on me, they were so naughty that I broke down and sobbed for a long time. Between them they threw a jug of water on my bed, emptied shampoo on my bedroom carpet and threw my possessions around. Oliver smashed a beautiful Royal Doulton figure *My Lady*, given to me by my Mother and which I love. Philip's behaviour is being mirrored by Oliver. I feel an underlying dread of something inevitable and beyond my control, always under the surface, but not knowing what it will be. Joyless, I feel isolated.

10th July. Earlier today, I wrote to Edward and Lois providing them with information on the personal needs and current behaviour of the boys prior to their week's visit. For Oliver, I wrote that his bedwetting continues and that he cannot help it as he either has a small bladder or is feeling insecure and that it is best to wake him around ten o'clock in the evening and take him to the toilet. I also pointed out that Oliver cannot get to sleep in the dark. For Philip, I wrote that his recent tantrums are very disappointing and believed they were directly connected to secret arrangements with Edward and coming to terms with his father losing his self control and damaging my property.

22nd July. We were all tired after our journey home yesterday. Mum and Dad were pleased to see the boys and we enjoyed our tea of prawns with salad followed by Marks & Spencer's lemon cheesecake before walking to the playground so that Philip and Oliver could run about and play before the long journey back to Yorkshire.

30th July. It rained all day and still it rains. I saw Dr Connor at the clinic yesterday and she confirmed that the deterioration in behaviour of the children is linked to the pressure being put on David as his father tries to arrange clandestine meetings. The tantrum on 5th July was only two days after a long telephone conversation with Edward when arrangements were made for a rendevouz and visit to London. The meeting was especially important for me as Dr Connor was supportive of my parenting against a background of complaints received from Edward recently. I now truly believe that his anger is merely a ploy, rather than genuine concern regarding the children.

On an impulse, I suggested to the boys that we take a picnic to Brimham Rocks today. They were delighted. I had enjoyed time to myself each day while they were at Summer Camp Kick and now it was the weekend. Oliver did Minor Soccer and received a prize for best goal save and Philip was a member of the winning team. Now Oliver is six years old, he can run around almost as fast as Philip and climb too. The rock formation is the result of natural erosion by wind, frost and rain creating amazing shapes. The Druid's Idol is an extraordinary feat of natural balance standing improbably on a small pyramid shaped stone below a tier of several vast stones. It turned into a wonderfully, happy day.

This evening, I wrote my reply to the Manager of the Children & Families Service Unit following Mrs Harrow's report and commenting on all aspects of the report and particularly to the conclusion which alludes to Edward and I bringing up the children harmoniously. I wrote, 'Regrettably the assessment has failed to identify a major character trait in Mr Campbell, namely his need to exercise absolute control and dominate all those close to him. Such a character trait is hardly conducive to settling matters in a normal, reasoned way'. My letter ended with the words, 'Knowing that Mr Campbell has abused Philip and myself physically, and all three of us mentally, consistently over a number of years, I am disappointed at the passive and weak recommendations contained in the Social Services assessment.'

5th August. An absolutely glorious day. Not a cloud in an iridescent sky this morning, so I went for a walk across the fields, gold with buttercups, towards Fountains Abbey and got as far as Studley Royal where several red deer were grazing. I presume it was hot enough to tempt them to the stream. I rested in the shade, staying a while to observe them and listened to the birds coming from every direction. Walking back through the lime tree avenue my eye was led down through the deer park to the stone arched entrance to the estate and beyond to Ripon Cathedral in the distance. The walk did me good.

The boys have enjoyed another week of sport, this time in Ripon at the new Tennis Centre. Philip achieved his Lawn Tennis Association Yoplait Tennis Award 3.

17th August. What a terrible day! The court hearing went badly. My application for an increase in maintenance was denied. Edward informed the judge under oath that his current employment had been terminated. When we were walking away from Court my solicitor turned to her junior and remarked, 'You win some, you lose some'. So that's it, that's how she feels about my predicament. Just another client and another invoice to be prepared and sent. What did Charles Dickens say in *Bleak House* about the law being the servant of a long purse? It will be with a heavy heart that I call the Headmaster tomorrow to inform him that the boys will not be attending next term. I now have to enrol them in one of the local state schools. Colette will be going back to Paris to study at École Polytechnique at the end of the month and I won't be recruiting another au pair.

20th August. At last! I received confirmation of a six-month contract with a manufacturing company near Northallerton, who have decided to implement Total Quality Management. I will be defining their major processes, running workshops in all departments and working with their Administration Manager to document the management system. This is my first real consultancy project and I have negotiated hours to fit in with school and start mid September.

25th August. The boys were excited on the journey home, telling me about their short holiday in London. They had flown as unaccompanied minors from Leeds/Bradford Airport. They told me that Edward and Lois were married on Saturday. No-one told me.

1st September. Philip has been spitting at the slightest provocation. He has also reverted to urinating on the carpet. Today, when I was speaking with a friend on the telephone, he came back from fishing and made it clear he wanted my attention and some minutes later, he dropped maggots on the kitchen floor and started kicking me. Why was he upset? Nothing and everything. He seems to be out of reach from me. Where has the sweetness gone?

8th September. It is a fine evening and I can hear abundant birdsong and swallows are gathering in the sky. Is it too soon for them to be leaving? The boys started at their new school today. I enjoyed walking with them to school rather than driving. Dr Muir has suggested I see a psychologist to help with my depression. She has also prescribed Prozac.

24th September. Edward called this evening, announcing in a pompous and conceited tone that he and Lois were now living in America. They flew out last week and are looking for a house to live near Fort Lauderdale. All that fuss and then he just ups and goes. It also makes sense about his telling the judge he had no employment. Of course, he had already settled his affairs here in England.

I received a reminder from my solicitor that my account is overdue.

4th October. St Lawrence's Church was full this morning for Ruth's funeral service. Alasdair found the strength to deliver the eulogy, although by the end he was visibly upset and several times he had to stop and wipe away his tears. Each of his sons read a passage from the Bible and Charlotte Crampton sang Psalm 23 beautifully. Afterwards, Alasdair and his family went to the crematorium for a short ceremony, while the congregation moved on to The Old Deanery in Ripon for coffee and were joined later for a buffet lunch by the family.

259

1st November. Out of the blue Toby telephoned. I haven't seen him since I left The City. He is organising a Christmas reunion at Brokers Wine Bar in Leadenhall Market.

30th November. The boys will be visiting Edward and Lois in Fort Lauderdale for Christmas. He has sent the tickets without the unaccompanied minor excess, which I will have to arrange and pay for. They leave on 19th December returning on 5th January, so I will need to let the school know they will miss the first two days of the spring term.

14th December. Oliver and I watched Philip in the nativity play in the cathedral this afternoon. The setting was wonderful and when Philip delivered his lines from the pulpit, as the Arch Angel Gabriel, we could hear every word. We met up afterwards and Philip showed us the carvings in the choir stalls. He has been learning about Lewis Carroll at school. Carroll's father was a Canon at Ripon Cathedral and when we looked at the carvings, in particular the one showing a griffin catching a rabbit, it is only a hop, skip and a jump to see how the young Carroll could have created *Alice's Adventures in Wonderland*. There is a complex system of gypsum caves beneath Ripon which may have inspired Alice's fall into the Earth.

19th December. My sadness was diffused by the boys excitement at getting on a plane to fly to America. I put a copy of their school reports in one of the cases for Edward to read. It is clear Philip is thriving in the new school and that Oliver is struggling.

21st December. The A1 was running so slowly yesterday on my journey to stay with Mum and Dad, made worse by poor visibility caused by pelting rain.

An early start this morning. I decided to catch the train from Birmingham International and Dad very kindly drove me. From Euston it was an easy journey on the underground to Bank and walking along Lombard Street I felt the emotion of happier times. The market has an ornate arched glass roof structure over cobbled floors and it was bustling with City workers, probably from Lloyds of London. Six of us made the lunch at Brokers Wine Bar. From our table we had a good view down onto the market. There was such merriment in being back with friends. Toby is now working as finance manager of a company based in Berkshire. The rest have stayed on and in various stages of marital bliss or not so blissful divorce. So, not just me. I am home for Christmas and happy to be with my family.

1995

HOLIDAYS IN AMERICA

21st January. The boys received a letter from Edward and Lois with photos of their holiday in Fort Lauderdale. One shows Edward and Oliver sitting in a racing car ready to drive off with Oliver at the wheel on a children's version of a Formula One track.

7th February. My first appointment with Jane Beecham, a psycologist with a practice in York went well. She got to the root of my angst pretty quickly realising that I have never felt good about myself. She was quite direct and asked if there was an incident in my childhood which was painful to remember.

It wasn't easy and it took me some time to decide whether I should tell her, but she was there to help me. So, I told her that when I was eight years old, my uncle put his hand inside by bathing costume and his fingers fumbled around and between my legs. I adored uncle Charles and this felt strange and wrong and wasn't reassured by his explanation that this was our secret. I remember, he told me, 'One day you will be mine'.

Uncle Charles was everyone's favourite; he was charismatic and as busy as he was, he was attentive to grandma and grandpa, which with Mum living so far away meant she was grateful. He was a successful business man with a beautiful wife and lifestyle to match. He always drove big expensive cars and dressed immaculately and when he came close, you were aware of a warm and inviting aroma. He had thick wispy eyebrows framing deep blue eyes.

In the summer holidays Vivienne and I used to spend lazy Wednesday afternoons with auntie Hilary and our cousins at Mudeford Sandbank, near Christchurch, where they had a beach hut. Wednesday was nanny's day off. Auntie Hilary was everything I wanted to be. She was pretty with the palest blonde hair framing her face. Her life with uncle Charles was dreamlike to me as a young child. We were sometimes invited to spend time with the family on their yacht messing about in the waters around Cowes.

Jane believed I had grown up in a family which didn't communicate well and that this was the reason I couldn't tell my mother what had happened. I am not sure I agree, as a lot of little girls keep quiet. Uncle Charles knew full well that I would struggle to make sense of what happened and also be fearful of the consequences. I carried this secret and never having discussed it had not determined or even considered how it would play out when I approached my teenage years or how to protect myself, uncle Charles on the other hand knew exactly how it would play out.

It was the summer before my sixteenth birthday when I was spending a few days on my own with his family on their boat that he devised a reason for just the two of us to return to the mainland. I have no idea whether auntie Hilary assumed he would return me to my grandparent's house, but it is unlikely she would have checked as they didn't have a telephone. We spent the night at their home.

After that night, and when I was back home it wasn't long before his business interests brought him north and he regularly stayed overnight. My mother encouraged me to join him for nice suppers at smart restaurants, my father always looked rather gruff and I could see his disdain, but he never said a word. Neither did I. Each time the evening ended in a deserted track or lay-by and the generous rear seat of his large Jaguar provided the spacious interior for intercourse. Then home. He was the persecuter and me the victim, but at the same time I felt guilty and compromised because he gave me presents. He manipulated me and I learned very quickly to manipulate others by not telling the truth. I was too frightened to tell my parents because I believed it must be my fault. He abused me and he abused my mother's love. I still feel a dark shame after all these years. Jane assured me that I was too young, too small, too inexperienced to directly confront him.

With so much divulged and shared for the first time, I began to relax and told her that my overwhelming desire is to please and to be liked and cannot bear the idea that I might upset someone. At the end of the session, I was exhausted. Jane put on music and talked me through breathing and relaxation exercises. Coming home, it was like walking on air.

6th April. The boys were so excited this evening and spent ages packing their suitcases. It has come around so quickly that it doesn't feel real that they are travelling to Florida to see Edward again. Tomorrow, I will drive them to Manchester Airport for their flight to Miami and lots to do before spending Easter with Vivienne and David.

25th April. Philip and Oliver were exhausted after their long journey home from Miami and slept soundly waking around noon on both Saturday and Sunday. They both enjoyed their visit to the USA and are a little disoriented settling back with me looking after them. Philip certainly misses Edward and had a good cry on Wednesday night. It can't be easy for him or Oliver. Nothing prepared me for Philip's awkward behaviour on Monday morning, when he refused to go to school unless he wore long grey trousers. I had shortened every pair because they had holes at the knees. I offered him blue cords, black jeans or grey tracksuit bottoms. In the end I took Oliver to school and came back to deal with Philip. Fortunately, I had arranged to help Alasdair muck out the stables at South View and when he arrived he sat with Philip and I allowed him to take control of the situation. It wasn't long before they came downstairs and within a few minutes they were walking hand in hand across the square and on to school. Philip was probably testing me after coming back from his father's.

5th May. When I collected Oliver after school today, his teacher told me that Oliver seemed happy this week and hadn't put a foot wrong all day. Philip played in a school football match yesterday against Holy Trinity and won.

I have decided to offer B&B accommodation in August when the boys are in America. I will move upstairs to sleep on the top floor leaving the three bedrooms on the first floor available for guests. The Ripon tourist information centre will take bookings.

I rang uncle Sidney and asked if we could come and stay for a few days at half term. I broached the idea of his teaching Philip fly-fishing on the River Conwy and uncle Sidney was really pleased to be asked. So, that is good news.

We are currently enjoying a hot spell and it is pleasant to be out and about in short sleeves.

2nd June. A warm rain is falling gently and we are back home, happy and exhausted from a few days in Denbigh. Growing up, I didn't think to ask my father about his childhood. So I was delighted when uncle Sidney gave me an insight into how it was when he and Dad grew up in Walsall. One evening when the boys were settled in bed, uncle Sidney poured Joan and I glass of wine each before helping himself to whisky. A large good humoured man with a fat face and receding silver grey hair, he sat back in his armchair and began to tell us of his childhood. He told us his story with jovial pride when he and my father lived at Number 2 Rabies Street. At the back of the house looking left and right were small iron work furnaces with their chimneys belching out smoke. Sidney had a paper round starting at six thirty in the morning earning him three pence each week. School started at nine o'clock and at twelve noon the boys went home to deliver and collect washing for Grandma's customers. At two thirty, they were back at school until they left at four thirty in the afternoon.

He was at pains to tell me that they walked everywhere because there was no money for a bus. There was always dripping and bread to eat. Grandma would often ask one of them to take a jug to the grocers for a chunk of meat and gravy.

Their father was a toolmaker and foreman. My father followed him into apprenticeship at the age of fifteen, working for Lucas Industries. Sidney started working for the railway at sixteen but left to work at an asylum against the wishes of my grandfather.

My father signed up at the beginning of the war, choosing the Navy. He wrote to Sidney encouraging him to join the Navy before being conscripted and then being unable to choose which service. Sidney travelled to Singapore and Ceylon with the Navy before being recruited to look after navy personnel with mental illness at a hospital in Fareham, where he lodged with Joan's aunt in her house in Flint. After the war Sidney trained as a nurse, working in a private hospital in Graylingwell. This was pre-1948 and before the National Health Service, when doctors wore black jackets and striped trousers. Joan was a nurse and told me how nurses lined up for the Ward Sister to check cleanliness of uniform and finger nails.

19th June. Mum and Dad came for the weekend. It helped talking things over and my outburst of tears did me good. Every day I feel more positive about the future and am keeping confrontation with the children down to a minimum. However, I am at a loss why Oliver has chosen dental care as a battle ground. I remind Oliver every morning to clean his teeth, but if he doesn't, I don't force him. He seems more relaxed after his bath in the evenings and it isn't an issue. It must be to do with getting ready for school. Maybe he is anxious.

My advertisement is now in the Ripon Angling Centre, asking if anyone would be willing to teach a young eleven year old to fly-fish.

Dr Muir has reduced the dosage on my Prozac prescription. I had my last session with Jane Beecham today. She took me through a series of coping strategies on how to set limits and not be imposed upon as she believed if I were more assertive the children would respond and their behaviour improve. Afterwards, just like every other session, we listened to music for a few minutes, whilst she took me through simple relaxation exercises. I hope to be off anti-depressants before Christmas. Writing in my journal is undoubtedly cathartic.

A retired major telephoned this evening and has offered to teach Philip to fly-fish. Philip is very excited to meet him and I have arranged for him to visit us after school next Wednesday.

1st July. Good news. The interview with Harrison Wallis went well and they have offered me the job, starting 1st August. It will be the most menial of office work comprising filing, making the coffee and general office duties. But, it comes with the flexibility to work part time and fit in with the children. Poverty clearly awaits now my redundancy money has been exhausted. But for now, it is the only offer on the table.

The boys are both well. Oliver has started taking riding lessons on Saturday mornings. It is a tight fit as we have to be back in time for Philip's football. Alasdair has given him a riding crop and he hasn't put it down all week, even sleeps with it, for now until he loses interest or has shown it to everyone he knows so they can truly be sure that he is learning to ride.

The longer evenings mean that the boys are playing out until quite late and are really tired and ready for bed. They are making friends.

Philip has spent a few evenings with the major close by fishing in the River Skell and today caught a brown trout, which I gutted and stuffed with sliced lemon, butter and thyme before grilling it for his tea serving it with brown bread and butter. He was very pleased with himself. Oliver and I had pizza.

25th July. The boys are participating in a week of sport just like last year and the person organising it is Oliver's teacher. Oliver is playing cricket and Philip is playing football. My boys are so different in character. Oliver is easy going and smiles all the time. Philip is serious and reticent. I try to do all I can to engage with them and make them feel safe and happy. I know that Philip has already found life difficult.

I can't leave Oliver alone with Philip. Too many times Oliver has been crying because Philip has hurt him. Next week the boys will travel to Fort Lauderdale to spend a month with Edward and Lois.

30th July. Alasdair will soon be leaving Moreton and returning home to York once his tenants move. It was his last service as Priest in Charge this morning and St Lawrence's was full. Afterwards, he came for lunch together with a few of our mutual friends. We enjoyed a simple cold salmon salad sitting in the sunshine on the patio in the back garden whilst drinking Prosecco. Alasdair was in good form and before he left recited a poem he had doodled during lunch. When he left, he handed me the scrap of card he had written it down on. It was difficult reading his scrawling hand . . . .

At a Luncheon Party

The tides of love swing gently too and fro
And loves meet and kiss and part and sigh,
Soft whispered vows, like gently melting snow,
Dissolve to silence as they fade and die.
The surge of passion crashes on the shore
And waves of glory leap to shake the sun
Then, reft of all this treasure in their store
They sink to rest again, their power undone.
But sweetest, steadfast friendship constant flows
And never fails or falters or forsakes,
But o'er its winding bed it onward goes
And all around a fertile Eden makes.

10th August. The past few days have been hard work. Once the boys left I cleaned the house from top to bottom in readiness for my two guests who arrived from Germany on Saturday. I have moved up to the top floor and they have my bedroom with its' en-suite bathroom.

Fritz was a prisoner of war at the Ure Bank POW camp in Ripon. Alasdair invited himself for supper last night. Fritz told his story of how he spent two years as a prisoner of war and had wanted to come to Yorkshire to show Marlies where he had been imprisoned and where he had done engineering work repairing bridges on local roads. He has also traced a young girl called Carole, who befriended him and is now a woman in her mid fifties. Alasdair has kindly offered to drive them to Keighley on Saturday, where they will stay for another week and meet up with Carole and her family.

21st August. It was so lovely having my parents to stay this weekend. On Saturday we drove over to Whitby and had lunch at The Magpie Cafe. Alasdair joined us for supper in the evening, staying long enough to be courteous before heading off home. I phoned Philip and Oliver in USA and we all got a chance to speak with both of them. They are really enjoying swimming every day and have been out on Edward's yacht fishing for Atlantic sailfish.

The house is let for the last week in August and I am going to spend a week with Bridget and Nicholas.

30th August. Edward called to tell me what a great time everyone has had. I spoke with Philip and when Oliver came on the phone he blurted out that he was having so much fun he wanted to stay with Edward and Lois and didn't want to come home. When he handed the phone back to Edward, he was suffocatingly smug asking me what did I think? I put the phone down and sobbed. There was nothing Bridget or Nicholas could say.

10th September. Lots of photos of the boys arrived in the post from Lois with a nice covering note. They both look lovely and brown with their short haircuts bleached in the sun wearing tee shirts with the USA flag and their denims cut off at the knees.

15th September. Oliver hasn't settled back at school and ran home today. We went back together and I spoke with his teacher, who is very concerned about his behaviour. I too am concerned because he

269

is constantly being hurt when he plays with Philip. It is serious enough for me to do all I can to avoid their playing together on their own. Philip is keen to join Ripon City Panthers under eleven's Football and so that will keep him occupied on Saturdays and get rid of some of his angst. His teacher at school is the coach and believes Philip will do well. Just last week someone I considered a friend told me that Oliver would not be invited to play with her son anymore as he had misbehaved using bad language.

20th September. Edward has written another scathing letter about Philip's behaviour and his surliness during the holiday. Should I let Oliver go to America? Philip hasn't been invited. Edward has certainly always been happier with Oliver and less controlling. I called Alasdair this evening and he is going to call in tomorrow to discuss the situation. Then I will call Mum and Dad.

2nd November. Edward and Lois have signed an agreement that Oliver will reside with them on a temporary basis until the end of June next year and then reviewed taking into account Oliver's wishes and with the agreement that Edward will cover the expense of Oliver's travel to the UK in order to have contact with me during the school holidays.

13th November. We spent the weekend with Mum and Dad and saw a lot of Vivienne and David. No-one is sure about Oliver going to America, but no-one has advised me by saying 'Don't.'

Before lunch on Sunday, we watched the BBC's coverage of the Service of Remembrance at the Cenotaph in Whitehall. When will the Germans feel free from the stigma of the swastika? An unanswerable question.

22nd December. I have packed two cases for Oliver and one for Philip. It was hard saying goodbye to Oliver at the airport, but he seemed so genuinely happy that I felt pleased for him.

1996

OLIVER LEAVES
FOR AMERICA

21st January. Edward rang today, explaining that in order for Oliver to stay in America, he will need a Green Card and for that he needs me to sign a sworn statement witnessed by a Notary that I am willing to relinquish physical custody of Oliver to Edward and Lois. It makes sense but is quite scary. It is too final. If I don't agree, Oliver will have to return to the UK at the end of March. Why didn't I look into this more thoroughly before he went. Would I have let him go?

4th February. Tonight, with a full moon shining, the cold was irresistible, so I went into the garden and looked into the enormity of the sky. It feels strange without Oliver. Philip and I are getting on OK. He seems relaxed. We went to the West Yorkshire Playhouse to see Peter Pan and the actor who played Captain Hook signed Philip's programme.

16th March. A note from Lois with several photos of Oliver. There is one of him ice skating taken in January on his birthday. Another with a friend in their blue and yellow cub uniforms and one of Oliver holding a live lobster, looking astonished.

My thoughts however, are drawn to the distressing tragedy today when a man entered a school in Dunblane and gunned down sixteen children and their teacher. The television coverage confirms that the gunman killed himself afterwards.

30th March. Philip has been playing rugby this week at Harrogate RUFC. Alasdair called around today and we drove to Studley Park, walking into the wild side where the deer are to be seen. He is a good friend and companion. Afterwards, he stayed for lunch, just a quick sandwich and coffee.

He took me by surprise, when he left. Not in a good way. Without warning, instead of kissing me on the cheek, he put his arms around me and pulled me towards him and kissed me full on the mouth. He saw the expression on my face and immediately apologised. We have known each other a long time. I have known Ruth. We are friends. I enjoy his companionship, his support and especially his advice. What was he thinking?

31st March. Oliver was unable to visit this Easter as he only has one week off school. Philip and I have made a carrot cake for his birthday tomorrow. He has invited friends for tea after school. We have put up balloons and went to Blockbuster's to choose a video and hired *Dragon Heart* about the last dragon who must co-operate with a dragon slayer to stop an evil king starring Sean Connery and Dennis Quaid.

5th May. More photos from Lois, including one of Oliver in San Francisco by the docks with seals basking in the background. It breaks my heart that Oliver now calls her *Mom*. It feels odd that we share the same surname.

10th June. Edward has written that Oliver won't be able to visit England this summer as his Green Card hasn't come through, but hopes that Philip will visit him and Lois for a month in July. He will send the air ticket. With the letter came a lovely third grade school photo of Oliver looking very happy with lots of freckles over his nose. He looked very smart in a jacket and tie. There were a couple more showing Oliver with his baseball team and running in an egg and spoon race at his school sports day.

The cricket season is underway and I took Philip to his first away match today and found I knew some of the parents. I relaxed for the first time in a long while.

13th June. Philip came home after his activity week at Bewerley Park playing football with a certificate entitled: *Hitting your head and not the ball award.* Next week he will be attending a Cycling Awareness programme.

2nd July. I am learning to fly fish this summer, so that I can accompany Philip. The major gave me my first lesson today and Alasdair has loaned me a fly-fishing rod and reel. Philip and I have been to the angling shop in Ripon to buy flies and bait together. With a common interest, I am hoping our relationship will improve. He is thinking about taking up fencing, as there is a class locally on a Tuesday evening, so that will be another interest for him.

25th July. Philip left for USA this morning, very happy. Edward phoned to say he had arrived safely and I spoke briefly to both Philip and Oliver. Both sounded very excited. Back from the airport, Alasdair popped in to see me and stayed for lunch.

2nd August. It was lovely to pick up the phone and hear Philip at the other end. He was excited to tell me that Edward and Lois have bought a gorgeous, black Scottie puppy.

1st September. Two young seventeen year olds are coming to stay with me for twelve months while they train to become Gamekeepers. Freddie is travelling down from Hexham with his parents tomorrow and Christopher will arrive tomorrow. He is driving from Hull. It has been arranged through Harrogate College where they will attend one day a week for environmental studies. Philip has moved into one of the bedrooms on the first floor, which used to be Colette's leaving the smaller one for Oliver when he visits. He didn't like moving, he wanted his old room back. He wanted what was familiar to him as children do. Don't we all.

4th September. Philip started at Upper Nidderdale High School in Pateley Bridge today. It is set in the most glorious of settings with a back drop of the Yorkshire Dales. Surely he will be happy.

21st October. Vivienne came to see me on Sunday evening after her Soroptimist International Conference in Harrogate. I joined her on Saturday evening and met a few of her friends for drinks before we settled into our seats. The theme *Highway to the Millennium* focussed on women making a difference. Delegates were from Europe, the Americas and Africa. The delegate from the Cameroons, who gave one of the vote of thanks looked stunning in her colourful traditional dress and it surprised me that she had been able to travel so far to attend.

After supper on Sunday we were reminiscing and our conversation drifted to when we were smaller and to uncle Charles. Vivienne told me that he had come on to her when she was a young pre-teen girl. Looking at Vivienne with some alarm, I asked her what happened and she told me that she had told Mum and it went no further. I said nothing.

15th November. Post today from USA. It was a lovely note from Oliver with a couple of pictures of him dressed up as Dracula for his Halloween. He is wearing a collared long cloak lined in red and his face has been covered in white face paint with a touch of red indicating blood drooling from his fangs. The second shows him sitting at a table with a mountain of chocolate and sweets, his hoard from the evenings' activities.

1st December. Surely Oliver can't still be waiting for his Green Card, which is the excuse Edward has given me today for his not being able to travel to England for Christmas. It is a year since Oliver went to live with Edward and Lois.

Mum and Dad are here and were a distraction. We had a lovely walk around Fountains Abbey. It is the remains of a Cistercian foundation and there is a certain charm about the willowy grasses growing out of the roof and every crevice stuffed with wild scabious waving in the wind. We could see the row of toilets extending out over the River Skell, which served as the abbey's drainage system; fresh drinking water came from the springs on the hillsides.

1997
THE RUSSIANS COME
TO STAY

17th January. A rather upbeat note came today from Lois with more pictures of Oliver. Dressed in black with sunglasses, he and a friend are awarded first prize in a school costume competition. Other photos show Oliver with friends in a forested area at a picnic celebrating his ninth birthday and a cute one of him with a chameleon and another on his father's boat fishing with Lois. Her photos feel like crumbs from their table. I expect she thinks I should be grateful. She means well, but it just hurts so much. It is now a year since I last saw Oliver. I drift from day to day with no earnest desire other than to get through the next day.

7th February. Philip came home today with his Certificates of Achievement, showing clearly that he is doing well in sport, mathematics and German.

25th March. A clear sky tonight. Philip and I looked out of his bedroom window and we saw Haley's comet with its' sixty million mile train. I put my arm around him and he looked up at me smiling, his beautiful blue eyes were full and clear.

29th March. Oliver is home for Easter. This is his first visit since he moved to Florida. It has seemed so unreal that he wasn't able to visit before now. Edward and Lois agreed to regular visits and I have been separated from Oliver for fifteen months. He has brought good reports from school and lots of photos. We will be going to Vivienne and David's for Easter and I can't wait for us all to be together again.

9th April. Last night there was a marvellous moon and a clear sky as we drove back home and I feel emotionally well having had my family around me. Mum came shopping with me and the boys and very kindly bought them roller blades and wrist guards. So of course, today they were excited and up early. I took them to Wakefield skate park, which is a huge industrial interior, busy and noisy and they loved it. Philip is very keen to go again and take his BMX bike. Tomorrow, we will take Oliver to the airport. The holiday has gone so quickly and has been a very happy time for us all.

12th April. Another late evening reflecting on Philip's behaviour and what I can do. There are days when I believe he is dealing with his anger, but under stress he has violent outbursts and now he is older this can be very frightening, especially when wielding a knife. Whatever upset Philip today, there is no excuse for punching me in the face.

15th April. During a routine doctor's appointment, Rosemary asked me about the bruising around my eye and cheek. Although she hasn't been involved in any of the formal meetings, she has received notes from the Children & Families Service. Last year Philip had refused to co-operate with Mrs Harrow and so Rosemary suggested contacting Dr Michael Powell, Clinical Psychologist specialising in paediatrics.

2nd May. A long and exhausting day. Philip and I have been to see Dr Powell and it has been agreed that Philip will see him on a weekly basis.

Tony Blair arrived at Number 10 Downing Street. A new era. Education. Education. Education.

15th May. Philip received a letter from Edward and Lois saying that it won't be possible for him to visit this summer. I phoned and spoke with Lois, who appears to have joined the offensive, by berating Philip's behaviour and insisting that he should live with her and Edward. She painted an extreme picture of how Philip will be stealing cars, using drugs and generally be in trouble if he remains in my care. Throwing caution to the wind, I challenged by telling her that Edward's past wasn't so great. I went on, telling her that he had driven for nine months without a driving licence having been banned for drink–driving in July 1989, that he had kept two unlicensed guns at The Dower House in an insecure place, took LSD to get through his finals and just to be sure she got the message that Edward had encouraged Philip, aged four, to drink whisky and ginger ale for fun on several occasions. She put the phone down. It occurred to me that Edward's life is constructed of lies, falsehoods and half–truths told to make him look better, stronger, more interesting than he was. He lied even when he didn't need to, when there was no point.

11th June. Having collected Oliver from the airport today, I just cannot contain my happiness at seeing my little boy. Philip was pleased to see him when he arrived home from school and after tea, they went out to find friends to play with in the square. Oliver was tired and went to bed early, while Philip and I watched another Ninja Turtle movie. All seems well.

20th June. I have agreed with Ripon College to have foreign students to stay this summer. They are trained ex soviet soldiers due to join NATO and will be here to improve their English before travelling to the USA for further military training. Each student will stay with me for two weeks. They will be coming from Armenia, Uzbekistan and Azerbajan. To make room, Freddie and Christopher will double up and share a bedroom until they leave at the end of July.

27th June. The information I requested from Ripon College arrived today about Armenia, Azerbajan and Uzbekistan. Firstly, I read about

278

their religions, which I considered would be important. Armenia is predominantly Christian and Islam is the main religion in both Uzbekistan and Azerbajan. Over ninety percent of the population are Sunni in Uzbekistan and around eighty five percent are Shia in Azerbajan. I hadn't realised that there were different factions of Islam.

29th June. Alasdair came for lunch today and he very kindly explained how Islam began and how after Mohammed's death disagreements led to schisms in Islam resulting in Muslims deciding either to follow Sunni or Shia. It didn't happened because of religious differences, rather the issue of who should succeed the Prophet and on what principle should the appointment be made. Abu Bakr who was Muhammed's friend and loyal colleague was elected as the first *caliph*. Trouble started when Muhammed's son in law was appointed as the fourth *caliph*. Not everyone was in favour and it caused a split in Islam that continues to this day. Philip and Oliver listened attentively. Philip surprised me by telling us that at school he had learned about Muhammad and that Muslims believe that the Qur'an is a continuous stream of revelations by God to one man during his lifetime unlike the Bible which is a library not a single book. Well done Philip!

18th July. It has been a busy two weeks having Gevorg living with us. He is from Armenia and speaks very good English. He is dark haired, tall and well built. He is good company and has been helpful in trying to engage with Philip and Oliver by playing football with them before supper when he gets back from college. He left this morning and I have been busy getting the house ready for Zarif. He arrived this evening. He is from Uzbekistan and looks very smart in his national uniform.

25th July. Zarif cooked Dimlama this evening, an Uzbek harvest stew. He first fried the cumin seeds, which sizzled, darkened and crackled and only then added the onions, handfuls of them together with rather a lot of garlic cloves before adding the lamb. When it was browned on all sides, he layered thinly sliced potatoes, carrots, red peppers and tomatoes with a final layer of cabbage leaves. He put the casserole in the oven for an hour and then cooked the rice while I laid the table. We were an interesting collection of human beings sitting around the dining table: Christopher and Freddie our game keepers, the children, me and Zarif an ex Soviet Union solider from Uzbekistan, who was proudly looking forward to a new life for himself, his family and his country.

1st August. Knowing Tahir was from Azerbajan and likely to be a Christian, I asked if he would like to accompany us to Ripon Cathedral for evensong during his stay. Oliver was very keen. Philip wasn't bothered, but agreed to tag along and we have decided to go next week. Over supper Tahir told us about Azerbajan and how the name translates to Land of Fire because of the natural gas fires at Yannar Dag on a hillside outside Baku, where the earth burns perpetually and has done for thousands of years. In 1920 Azerbajan was annexed by the Soviet Union greedy for the oil.

9th August. Philip and I took Oliver to Manchester Airport and then onto see Edward's parents on the way home. Tahir was in charge of supper. Tahir explained how with the break up of the Soviet Union in 1991, smouldering Armenian–Azeri frictions escalated into violence and that a truce was agreed rather than peace in 1994. He was injured when his helicopter was shot down. None of his patriots from Azerbajan had met the Armenians during training in England and he told us that it will be difficult to work with soldiers from Armenia when he goes to the United States. Of the three ex Soviet Union soldiers who have stayed with me, Tahir has been the most relaxed and enjoyable as a house guest. Just like Gevorg and Zarif he enjoyed cooking for the family once each week, but in addition he was happy to help with mundane tasks without being asked.

Oliver is back in America.

The gamekeepers have gone home after their year with me. Tahir goes to America next weekend. So then, it will be just me and Philip.

31st August. One of the lowest moments of the year. It was announced today that Princess Diana has died in hospital after a car crash in Paris. I have spent the day in shock watching the news coverage. With HRH status Diana would have been looked after by the very best British security officers. I am cross, upset and like many others in denial that this beautiful woman is dead.

9th September. Philip had his first fencing lesson at Ripon School this evening. I stayed to watch and could see he was getting to grips with the technique very quickly. After we got home, we saw Mum on the nine o'clock news with her friends from the West Midlands Gas Board. UNISON have won their case in the European Court of Human Rights in Strasbourg against West Midlands Gas Board for insisting women retire at sixty years old. Mum will now receive compensation eighteen years after she retired.

20th September. I received a Clinical Summary Report regarding Philip from Dr Powell following their sessions, which Philip now wishes to end. He confirms that Philip has had to contend with a series of adversities in his background which have been risk factors in the development of his behaviour. He writes:

> 'Philip witnessed domestic violence, seeing his father verbally and physically abusing his mother, and experienced emotionally damaging rejection and physical abuse in his own relationship with his father. Philip's father appeared to develop a somewhat better and preferential relationship with Oliver, Philip's brother, and there has always tended to be conflict between the brothers with Philip largely bullying and acting out angrily towards Oliver. Mrs Campbell described herself as becoming significantly depressed after the divorce, carrying the legacy of her own abuse, damaged relationships with her children and guilt feelings about failing to get it right/protect Philip. . . . . Philip's anger has a number of legitimate sources given his past early experiences and damaged family relationships.'

There is more, but it is hard to read and digest. I am aware of the roots of Philip's troubles and understand boundary setting, but putting into practice the right approach has been immensely difficult, often in the face of very demanding circumstances.

2nd November. After lunch I walked along the River Skell to the parkland at Studley Royal. I crossed the dam on the wooden bridge where the river leaves the lake and followed the path along the steep-sided valley crossing one side of the Skell to another by a series of delightful little arched stone bridges. In the distance I could see several red deer; one was at the water's edge drinking. He gave me a long cool stare. Walking back a bird was singing close by, defending his territory and letting everyone know he's going to be around for a time. Probably, it was a winter thrush or blackbird. I stood still and listened in the cold, crisp fragrance of winter.

Later I collected Philip from school and when we arrived home, there was a letter from Edward, inviting Philip to stay with him and Lois this Christmas. Philip is very excited.

28th December. It has been an interesting few days having a Japanese student staying during the Christmas holidays and I wasn't sure how Dad would react. How any of us would react. Masaji was so charming, he soon won Dad over and we spent Christmas in harmony. That is until Edward called to tell me to collect Philip from Manchester Airport tomorrow morning. He told me that Philip has misbehaved and is being sent home in disgrace. Mum and Dad are still here and will stay on a few more days so they can see Philip. An early start tomorrow.

1998

ALL HELL IS LET LOOSE

12th January. Another batch of photos from Lois showing a happy, Oliver. One shows him with an enormous collection of key rings mounted on a pin-board on his bedroom wall with many more hanging between the fingers of both his hands. Another shows him with the little Scottie puppy. Oliver is dressed in black with a red Walkman around his neck. They are pictured outside their home against a background of tropical palms in bright sunshine. With the photos is a letter from Oliver telling me he now plays in central midfield position in his local soccer team.

1st March. I have no idea what kicked off Philip's tantrum, but I couldn't calm him down. He was throwing things around in the kitchen started squirting Fairy Liquid on the dining room carpet. I chased him upstairs and he slammed the door. I left him to calm down.

10th May. Alasdair and I spent the day together. We decided to drive to Middlesmoor for a picnic. We stopped at The Yorke Arms for coffee and then drove a few more miles beyond Ramsgill and stepped out into the splendour of a leafy lane before walking for a spell through a coppice where we were met by drifts of bluebells. They grew in such a crowd that they filled the hollow places and deep shadows with a sweet azure mist among the bright young fern. Further on we found a stream and walked along the water's edge watching the little fish darting and flitting in the cool depths. Afterwards, we continued our journey and it wasn't long before we were alone on wild moorland where nothing stirred and the spreading miles of bracken and green fields reached away until it met the hazy blue of the sky. We walked a little way looking across the Nidderdale Valley towards Scar House Reservoir before spreading out a rug over the bracken. I had prepared egg sandwiches and brought a selection of fruit. First, out came the wine glasses and the chilled Prosecco. It was a cloudless day and there was silence, except when the wind sighed over the hill top. The view matches anything in the world. A happy day.

26th June. I collected Oliver earlier today from Manchester Airport. When we got home, he asked to play with Philip's Nintendo and I stupidly agreed. I asked Oliver if he was enjoying using his Nintendo at home in America. He reluctantly told me that the money he received for Christmas and his birthday had been taken from him to purchase a new brace for his teeth after he had broken not one but two of the braces he had fitted. That's why he never wrote thank-you notes to my parents, Vivienne and David. When Philip came home from school to find Oliver playing with his Nintendo, he went berserk. He started shouting and kicking me. Oliver screamed and ran outside. It is late and all is calm again. The boys are asleep. I could do with a drink, but I do not have alcohol in the house. I can't afford it.

7th July. Having endured so much criticism from Edward and Lois, I couldn't resist writing to them after our visit to the dentist today. He very kindly gave me a written opinion of his observations of Oliver's dentition and that in his opinion his teeth should be left until his remaining permanent teeth have erupted before a more accurate assessment of orthodontic needs be made. I added for good measure, 'It was spiteful and cruel of you to take the money my family and I sent to Oliver for Christmas and his birthday, especially as we see so little of Oliver. Our feelings of anger were amplified by the fact that your presents were not confiscated and that on his birthday, the full works were spent on a limousine outing for Oliver and his friends.'

15th July. Oliver's presence has set off Philip this summer and all hell is let loose. Doesn't Philip understand that as I haven't seen Oliver since last summer that, I want to be generous with both my time and love. Philip just keeps losing his temper. The slightest comment or action escalates into violent uncontrollable anger.

I have felt guilty for a long time, that if I had found the courage to divorce Edward when we were living at Pippins, there is a strong possibility that Philip would be a very different young boy today and fear this feeling of guilt gets in the way of being a good mother. Oliver is scared. I am scared. Scared of my inability to make things right, to set and maintain boundaries.

He has attacked me several times and last night he got into a terrible rage and started hitting me, pulling my hair and kicking me. My neighbour heard the rumpus and called the police. Not only has he hurt me but has kicked the hall cupboard until it has caved in and is now broken in bits. He seems out of reach. Away from me.

22nd August. In my letter to Edward earlier in the month I told him that it will be best for Philip to attend a boarding school and that I will take my pension early in order to fund his education. I received his reply today and am re-reading his letter tonight. It is another tirade of criticism saying that Philip needs clear boundaries, something I am incapable of providing and that sending him to a boarding school will be seen as a reward rather than a route to developing his character or solving the problems. He and Lois are recommending a tough love boot camp in the USA for a twelve month period, which they will fund and then will expect him to re-enter family life with them in Fort Lauderdale.

He concludes, that Oliver will no longer visit me in England unless on the rare occasion he is in Europe, when he may visit for brief periods. Otherwise, I must travel to the USA and spend supervised and limited time with Oliver. The letter ended with the notification that he will no longer be paying maintenance for Philip.

31st August. In my reply to Edward, I made it clear that Philip will attend boarding school in York. He wants to go. He wants to be good. He also wants to do well and get good exam results so that he can do his A level course in Ripon with his friends.

9th September. Philip started at his new school today. It was exciting packing my grandpa's old chest with all the things he needed, the list seemed endless. He shares a dormitory with four other boys and although rather drab, I don't think boys mind too much. It won't be until 28th September that I receive my retirement lump sum from Standard Life, which will fund the school fees. I know financially it is a very stupid thing to do, taking my pension at fifty years old, but I am pleased to do so if Philip thrives.

Later in the evening, I opened *A Victorian Posy*; I closed my eyes rubbing the marbled endpapers and inhaled the sweet fragrance of a still midsummer afternoon. Curling up on the sofa with a glass of Shiraz, I began reading and skipping through the anthology of poems. Poems of apple blossom, violets and forget-me-nots. Poetry needs to be recited aloud and the more I spoke, the calmer I felt. Not joyous, but not fearful.

28th September. Pension day. Pay the school fees. Pay back debts to Vivienne and David, Mum and Dad.

1999

ALASDAIR'S FUNERAL

5th February. This evening, Philip arrived home unannounced. I called the school to tell them he was home and safe. He misses his friends. He wants to come home at weekends. He can't. I don't feel safe.

4th June. It is ten years since the massacre in Beijing's Tiananmen Square. Kate Aidie was the BBC correspondent in the square during the three days of killing, the only foreign journalist to witness the atrocities and who managed to get the footage out of China. Today the Chinese are flourishing, however they are still ruled by bullies.

6th June. Philip was reluctant to return to school after half term. He didn't want to leave his friends and didn't want to board. What he wanted was to change schools and go to the same school as his best friend in Ripon. It was also clear that Philip and his friends were beginning to experiment with drugs and therefore his ability to think clearly left him and he flatly refused to go back to school after half term. We had an argument. Philip took hold of something hard and long and thick, maybe a broom handle and he hit me. He hit me very hard over and over again. All I could do was go into a defensive foetal position and try to protect my head. When he stopped, I dashed out and ran to a neighbour's house. They called the police. Within minutes they arrived, calmed Philip down, handcuffed him and took him away.

It is almost a year since the last awful attack which had resulted in his going to boarding school. Was it a soft option? This time I am not going to be soft. For Philip, for his future relationships, if I can't control him, he has to go somewhere else, where he can be encouraged to accept the boundaries for behaviour. I am so disappointed that boarding school hasn't been the answer. Philip is fourteen years old and is being held overnight in a police cell.

7th June. My solicitor telephoned the police and social services to ensure that they were responsible for the next steps. Of course, there wasn't anywhere for him to go straight away. And here is the *rub*, the mother of one of Philip's friends – most likely the friend who has encouraged him to leave his school in York and experiment with drugs – works for Social Services and has very kindly offered to have Philip until a foster care placement is found.

Surely Philip understood that there were consequences. The look in his eyes can only be described as hatred when he was getting ready to leave and I knew at that moment that a child's ability for reprisal is infinite. With Philip having collected clothes and personal belongings, I somehow found the energy to pack for my trip.

I haven't seen Oliver for twelve months. At the same time I am desperately anxious for Philip and how he will cope. God Damme it! Does Philip have any idea how much I have paid for boarding school?

My heart is pulling in several different directions. It would have been so easy not to get on the plane and stay and try and sort things out with Philip. Trying to sort things out with Philip seems to have been the focus of my life for so long it clouds every thought and action. They have Vivienne's contact details.

14th June. I am on the plane, not in a dream. It is real. I really am going to visit Oliver. I am on the flight from Manchester to Atlanta, the first leg of the journey to Fort Lauderdale and am savouring a glass of wine and browsing through magazines Gardens Illustrated, House & Garden and The Lady, which I bought as an indulgence.

I cannot settle. My mind is in turmoil. I should be happy because I am going to visit Oliver. But it isn't that simple. Now that I am on my way, I am looking ahead at how I will be greeted by Edward and Lois.

As yet, I have no idea whether Edward will agree to my having Oliver for the whole of the ten days or whether I will have to return him home each evening. They even mentioned in a recent letter that they are considering whether I should be supervised whilst with Oliver.

For now, I can do nothing about it. Breathe deeply. Try and relax. I am on the plane travelling in a time warp.

15th June. It was dark on arrival at Miami Airport yesterday evening. Years ago, I would have and did jump into a left-hand drive car and just drive off. But I am older, with less confidence and the idea was quite frightening. How on earth did I imagine that I was going to find Lighthouse Point? And in the dark.

The man on the Hertz desk sold me insurance, which bumped up the cost, but eventually I was on my way with a little complimentary map and details from Lois, scrawled in her recent letter. It was a while before realising that I was on Route 95 going south in the wrong direction. If I didn't do something I would eventually arrive at The Keys. I froze and kept driving for ages before I found the courage to turn off and go back northwards.

It was a while later and in the suburbs near to where Oliver lives, when I became so stressed and upset, I started screaming. Edward had informed me that it should only take thirty minutes from the airport. I took another wrong turning and stopped. My head in my hands, I was distraught. Just then a car stopped and a tall all-American jumped out of his car and walked towards my car. He saw how upset and desperate I looked. He looked at the address and offered to lead me to the house. He duly did and I arrived just before ten o'clock in the evening, much later than expected.

By now I was not only nervous about meeting Edward and Lois, I was completely exhausted. They welcomed me into their home, well into the reception area, which is like a large hall with seating. I drank a glass of water. They sat opposite me and began to set out the conditions upon which I may have Oliver. In my heart I was so angry. They have no right to treat me like this. It hurts so much, but I sit there and agree to their terms, because if I don't I may not be allowed my holiday with Oliver. He was excited and getting his things ready. He is now eleven years old.

With good grace we leave and it is late and now I have to find the The Floranada condo apartments. It is dark and it takes me a long time to find it, even though it is only supposed to be ten minutes away from their home. On arrival we have to raise someone to let us into our apartment.

It is a small apartment in a two-storey complex adjacent to a swimming pool. It is home for the next ten days. The beach is close by. Tomorrow is another day. It is so good to see Oliver. I have never doubted his love.

20th June. We have packed a lot into our first few days. Oliver has been showing me local attractions and restaurants he likes. We have been to the beach a couple of times and enjoyed swimming in the Atlantic Ocean. It wasn't too cold or choppy. Yesterday, we went to Kmart in Boca Raton and kitted him out with new roller blades, helmet and wrist guards. He is looking forward to going to the skatepark tomorrow to try out. He is hoping to meet up with friends too.

25th June. I took Oliver home this morning and we waited for Edward and Lois to return from wherever they had been on holiday. We waited a long time. Everything went smoothly on the return journey to the airport and I am now looking ahead to dealing with Philip's situation. At the same time I also have to think about what Oliver told me last night.

He said, 'I am not supposed to tell you this, but I think Dad is abusing me. He hits me with a heavy plastic rod on my hand when I am naughty and several times he has thrown me into the canal at night.' I asked whether Lois knew, he replied 'Lois makes herself scarce when Dad takes me into the garage to hit me and although she has been there once or twice when Dad has thrown me into the canal it usually happens when she isn't there.'

If I tell Edward, he will punish Oliver for telling me. For a long while on the flight home, I was very still, my mind numbed, but slowly and with a mounting intensity of will, I emptied my mind of all thought, striving to expose my feelings in their simplicity as to what course of action I must take.

26th June. Back home, I have made contact with Philip and he seems fine. The handwritten notes I made on the plane are now typed and in my diary.

27th June. I took a deep breath and rang Edward asking to speak with Oliver. Edward told me that I couldn't. He told me that Oliver had behaved badly following his holiday with me and had told Lois that she wasn't his mother during an argument. He told me that Oliver would not be allowed to phone or write to me. I collapsed in quiet sobs.

7th July. I met with the Mrs Harrow, our social worker in her office in Ripon today. We are visiting the foster carers with Philip tomorrow and she wanted to agree with me a routine for Philip. He will start his new school in September, decided in my absence and located near to his foster carers' home from where I will collect him once a week after school and spend time with him. He is also allowed to visit his friends in Ripon one evening also during the week, when I will collect him and give him supper. He will also be returned home for the weekend and collected. So, I will be seeing quite a lot of Philip, but now have a team backing me and protecting me should things get out of hand as these privileges are earned and taken away if Philip steps out of line. The pace of change is up to Philip.

8th July. After meeting Philip and his foster carers at their home, Philip and I drove to Studley Royal. It was a lovely sunny evening and we both enjoyed walking by the side of the lake. All was calm. Except, of course, I am worried about James. Earlier today I contacted the Child Protection Unit in Florida and was told that corporal punishment is approved of unless the child is injured, but agreed that throwing Oliver into the canal was bizarre.

25th July. I received a letter from Edward concerning Philip together with various USA offshore adolescent programs for teens to help them replace inappropriate attitudes, behaviours and habits. Tranquility Bay in Jamaica is described as a *behaviour modification school*. Also enclosed was blurb on Adolescent International Transport for defiant youths and reference in his letter that all we need to do is make the decision and have Philip collected at a date and time that is not divulged. The escorts provide safe, secure, therapeutic transport of the teenager, which I understand to mean if they resist, they are drugged or handcuffed.

I called Alasdair and he came round this evening with a full bodied Rioja and over time I was able to tell him all the good news about seeing Oliver followed by all the upsetting news. What to do? I listened to his counsel and calmed myself. A diffuse relief passed over my mind, as when one is suddenly brought in from the cold to an unexpected pleasure. He told me that I am no longer a prisoner of the past and that the goodness in my heart will determine the present and future for me, Philip and Oliver. I am to trust myself.

1st August. Dr Powell has written to me following a referral from Social Services informing me that with his consent, Philip will be attending more counselling sessions. The weekly appointments will be arranged after school with his foster carers.

22nd August. Earlier this evening, the phone rang. It was Edward informing me that he will stop the seizure and secondment of Philip. Philip has not wished to speak or write to Edward since the day he returned Christmas 1997 and there have been no further invitations from Edward for Philip to visit since, just letter after letter criticising me and how I cannot control him. Enough time has passed since 1993 to reflect and it is a truth, that Edward has always talked about *control* rather than *love*. How did it all begin? Why did Edward turn on me?

12th September. Philip spent a lot of time with his friend Tom on Saturday and he stayed for supper and afterwards they watched a movie. We went for a drive on Sunday morning after breakfast and took time out to walk around Studley Park across the stepping stones and taking the path to the left following the stream, where we saw a roebuck drinking. Startled, it jumped up the bank and out of sight. Philip didn't say too much about his new school. He has only been there just over a week, so early days for him to settle. I drove Philip back in time for tea.

17th September. Alasdair called me this evening from St Dunstan's. He has been there a few days and is settled. He seemed cheery even though the diagnosis isn't good after his last blood transfusion *curdled*. His word. He will tell me more when I see him.

20th September. It was a pleasure taking Alasdair out today. We were lucky that it was sunny, albeit chilly and the drive along the River Nidd was as charming as ever. We were welcomed by a blazing fire on arrival at The Yorke Arms. Alasdair enjoyed the outing and was in good form, although he was extremely tired when we returned to St Dunstan's. His joy outweighed any regrets he might have had in the effort it took him to do so. Always a wonderful story teller, he has found a collection of his scribblings and I read to him a delightful story of *Diodoros* before I left.

21st September. On my way home from work, I popped in to see Alasdair for a cup of tea and a chat. I didn't stay long as Anthony had been to see him earlier in the day and he seemed rather in need of a nap. It is easy for me to pop in on my way to work for twenty minutes. We laughed when I suggested this as it is his *twenty minute* rule. I did, however, take up his time to tell him about the letter from Oliver saying that he doesn't want me to contact him. The language was adult and must have been dictated by either Edward or Lois. Oliver is eleven years old, he wouldn't use the word *appropriate*. Alasdair read the letter and was sympathetic, but saddened by my despair at being estranged from both my sons.

23rd September. My journal acts as a sort of midwife, bringing me back to my proper self after the unhappy days of senseless arguments with Edward.

I popped in to see Alasdair briefly this morning on my way to work. He was very much looking forward to Alex coming for lunch. After work, I drove to Philip's school for a formal review meeting. As well as Mrs Harrow and his foster carers, there were representatives from the school and an Educational Social Worker. Philip has made some progress and the hope is that he will return home in six months.

24th September. My birthday was an ordinary day and I went to work as usual. When I got home there were lots of cards from family and friends, but they all seem so far away. There was no card from Oliver. My melancholy lifted when my neighbour knocked on my door with a beautiful bouquet of roses and lilies from Alasdair. When I arrived at St Dunstan's later in the afternoon, he had arranged afternoon tea with champagne. Philip rang this evening to say he was looking forward to the weekend. Happy, happy day? Perhaps?

30th September. I met Alasdair's nephew, Jasper today. He is a very engaging, vibrant man. I spent this evening having dinner with him at The Old Deanery. It was Alasdair's suggestion and Jasper liked the idea. I cannot remember the last time I enjoyed myself so much. The years have flown by since my divorce and I seem to have been in a social desert. I have only just managed financially, so no spare cash to go anywhere unless with the children. If I had met someone, their inclusion into our lives would have made a difference, would have benefited us all, but I have never felt confident to include anyone into my chaotic life. Jasper and I got on very well. I felt at ease and he was very attentive. When we parted and shook hands, his fingers were long and cool and he held my hand momentarily longer than I expected. I can hardly believe that this tall, handsome man has just spent an evening with me.

1st October. This morning, I told Alasdair all about dinner with Jasper and he gave me one of those looks, tapping his nose as if to say, 'I knew you two would get on.' Alasdair was looking forward to seeing Jasper later.

Philip will be home for good before Christmas. He wants to come home and my meeting with his foster parents, social services and Headmaster together with Philip went well. I am not sure how he can have changed his attitude and behaviour so soon, but at least he has agreed to continue to see Dr Powell on a regular basis. Their optimism outweighed my inner feelings of concern and I had no choice but to agree. Inwardly I felt scared.

5th October. Anthony phoned today. Alasdair was so very brave, right to the end. Anthony informed me that he died with a smile on his face, which is comforting to know. To die well. This is something we all want.

15th October. St Lawrence's was packed for Alasdair's funeral. I wasn't at all nervous standing in the pulpit watched by everyone as I read the passage Revelation 21 verses 1–7. Those I met at The Boar's Head once were friends. Strangers now. Several clearly looked surprised when Anthony greeted me with a beautiful bouquet of scented white roses and hugged me. I will cherish the letter written by Alasdair and will refer to it when I am apprehensive and doubt myself.

20th October. Philip was on good form this evening. He really seemed to be making an effort to engage with me. We decided to walk to the village pub and have supper. Philip was upset to learn of Alasdair's death and we reminisced about the times we had both helped out at the stables. We ordered our food and when the sausages were brought to our table, they had a good well-cooked colour and were served with caramelised onions and a creamy butter mash, piping hot. Philip said, 'Yummy!' I said, 'I love you very much.'

31st October. Tomorrow, I need to get up early and drive to Oxford for my interview. I can hardly contain my happiness and excitement at the idea of a corporate salary after years of making do on a pittance of child maintenance from Edward until he stopped paying me anything last year.

1st November. The job is mine. Soon, I will be able to buy two British Airways tickets to Florida for me and Philip. We will visit Oliver at Easter even if I have to stand outside their house with a placard and walk up and down the street. I am tired of being bullied by Edward and Lois. My God, I will assert myself and see Oliver.

26th November. I will be working from home. I have returned from my induction training with a laptop and printer. I now need BT to install the modem. The small bedroom on the first floor overlooking the square will be ideal as a study. My next trip to London will be for the start of year meeting mid January. I will discuss with Philip plans for when I am away. In future he will have a say. This is now obvious to me. Somehow it wasn't before. His behaviour excluded his involvement in decision making and resulted in more and more escalations. I was too pre-occupied. We have a new chance. I need to talk to Philip.

13th December. Philip was up early this morning, anxious to get to school on time. I noticed the hills were bathed in a rich tawny light, rather sad. Leaving me to get on the bus, he was cautiously polite. No hugs. Before I knew it I was crying and all I could think of was how beautiful he was as a baby and how I cannot remember when he last hugged me and kissed my cheek. I have lost them in different ways. But I have lost them both.

17th December. Philip has settled back into a routine at home with me. We talked today about going to visit Oliver in Florida in the spring. He likes the idea as we would be staying in an apartment and he wouldn't need to stay with Edward and Lois. For his sake and possibly for Oliver too, I am comforted that I have kept a diary during the past difficult years as I should wish them to know what I faced and allow them to judge for themselves, when they are grown up. Remember me. I held your hands.

20th December. This morning, I received a Christmas card from Jasper. He will be coming to England next year to promote his new book. He has written a quotation in the card from *The Unbearable Lightness of Being* by Milan Kundera.

> *We can never know what to want*
> *because, living only one life, we can neither*
> *compare it with our previous lives*
> *nor perfect it in our lives to come.*

29th December. It was dark when we got home, the moon almost full and then snow began to fall. I turned up the heating and we had cheese on toast.

I am happy to be back home having spent Christmas with Vivienne and David, and seeing Mum and Dad every day. Philip was relaxed and happy. For me it has been a healing process. Being with the people who most cared about me.

On Christmas Day in the late afternoon, I took courage and rang Edward asking to speak with Oliver. He allowed me one minute and listened to our conversation on the phone extension. Still, it was wonderful to hear his voice. He sounded delighted to speak to me. As I knew he would be.

Once I started reading *Bridget Jones's Diary*, I couldn't put it down and read into the small hours. Bridget is instantly engaging as a single, slightly overweight, boozy, smoking Graduate living in London. Inspired by her, I shall summarise my year as follows, omitting the alcohol:

★ Philip hated boarding school
★ Philip went into foster care
★ I went to see Oliver in America
★ Alasdair died
★ I started a new job
★ Philip is back home

A new millenium is on the horizon. I remain hopeful for the future, but there is something deep down, I am trying to repair. I tell myself to keep going. Keep smiling.

Author's Note

In writing *Smiling Through Tears*, it has been an enjoyable experience choosing poems and musings and researching events in history, only known to me previously as a sentence in a conversation or a newspaper article. Space precludes my including biographical notes, but with the help of the internet, I hope you are inspired to find out more about the individuals detailed below.

Maya Angelou 1928–2014

William Blake 1757–1827

Dietrich Bonhoeffer 1906–1945

Charles Pierre Bauderlaine 1821–1867

Barthold Heinrich Brockes 1680–1747

Robert Browning 1812–1899

Winston Churchill 1874–1965

Charles Darwin 1809–1882

John Donne 1572–1631

Ralph Waldo Emerson 1803–1882

John K Galbraith 1908–2006

John Keats 1795–1821

Paul Klee 1879–1940

Abraham Lincoln 1809–1865

Maimonides 1138–1204

Talwin Morris 1865–1911

Ezra Pound 1885–1972

Philo of Alexandra 20 BC–50 AD

Arthur Ransome 1884–1967

Christina Georgina Rossetti 1830–1894

John Ruskin 1819–1900

Bertrand Russell 1872–1970

Jean-Paul Sartre 1905–1980

Sir Roy Strong 1935–

Rabindranath Tagore 1861–1941

Lord Alfred Tennyson 1809–1892

Thucydides 460–404 BC

Count Leo Tolstoy 1828–1910

Oscar Wilde 1854–1900